A
HALF-BUILT
GARDEN

RUTHANNA
EMRYS

A TOM DOHERTY ASSOCIATES BOOK · NEW YORK

A HALF-BUILT GARDEN

Edited by Carl Engle-Laird

A Tordotcom Book
Published by Tom Doherty Associates
120 Broadway
New York, NY 10271

www.tor.com

Tor® is a registered trademark of Macmillan Publishing Group, LLC.

Library of Congress Cataloging-in-Publication Data

Names: Emrys, Ruthanna, author. | Engle-Laird, Carl, editor.
Title: A half-built garden / Ruthanna Emrys ; [Edited by Carl Engle-Laird].
Description: First edition. | New York, NY : Tordotcom,
a Tom Doherty Associates Book, 2022.
Identifiers: LCCN 2022008327 (print) | LCCN 2022008328 (ebook) |
ISBN 9781250210982 (hardcover) | ISBN 9781250210975 (ebook)
Classification: LCC PS3605.M886 H35 2022 (print) |
LCC PS3605.M886 (ebook) | DDC 813/.6—dc23
LC record available at https://lccn.loc.gov/2022008327
LC ebook record available at https://lccn.loc.gov/2022008328

Our books may be purchased in bulk for promotional, educational, or business use.
Please contact your local bookseller or the Macmillan Corporate and Premium
Sales Department at 1-800-221-7945, extension 5442, or by email at
MacmillanSpecialMarkets@macmillan.com.

First Edition: 2022

Printed in the United States of America

0 9 8 7 6 5 4 3 2 1

For Linda Weisenfeld Gordon and Samantha Lynn,
with hope for the future beyond us

A
HALF-BUILT
GARDEN

CHAPTER 1

The first power was nature. In humanity's infancy, power was not yet ours to hold. Laws and forces beyond human comprehension shaped our lives, and everything we did was aimed at survival.

The second power was spirit. Incomprehensible forces took on form and personality. We struggled to comprehend their whims, and power was born from divine approval.

The third power was law. We decided what we thought right, and set principles above any king. Power became at last a human thing.

The fourth power was money. The forms we built took on life of their own, and the power we created escaped from our grasp and devoured us.

The fifth power is nature. We understand the wisdom in the forces that first shaped us, but now we adapt to them, learn from their patterns, and dance with them. Power is ours, but not ours alone, and we can create harmony with the world.

—from *The Dandelion Manifesto*, v.2.3,
released December 2043

In the bad old days (the commentary said later), nation-states had plans laid in for this sort of thing. They'd have caught the ship on satellite surveillance. They'd have gotten in the ground with sterile tents and tricorders and machine learning translators, taking charge. In a crisis, we still look for the big ape. But the view from below has long since supplanted the view from above, so there were no satellite pictures committed indelibly to collective memory. Instead, the embedded water sensors near Bear Island suddenly sent out alerts for skyrocketing phosphate levels. And instead of a big ape shouting orders, the world got me.

It was 3:22 a.m. on Monday, March 2, 2083, and I was on call for sensor events along with eleven other volunteers for the Chesapeake Bay Watershed Network. I was first in the ground, even though our consensus judgment of the reading was malware noise, because I was already up with Dori. She'd been awake and crying for well over an hour, and I almost cried myself at the excuse for a handoff. I woke Carol with truly sincere apologies—but I had to go check out a Watershed emergency, see if you can get this baby back to bed.

If it'd been ten degrees colder, she wouldn't have bundled Dori into a sling and come out with me, and this would've been a different story. But the kid quieted down as soon as we stepped out onto our walk, and I admitted that there probably weren't *really* dangerous pollutants on site, and if there were my wife and kid could stay back. The night was balmy and smelled of lilacs. The illumination curfew had kicked in, and stardust stretched across the old Maryland suburbs like a parade scarf. My mesh asked me if I wanted night vision, and I told it quietly to fuck off.

"In a couple of months it'll be too hot to take her outside most nights," said Carol, and we held her up to the moon, and snuggled her against our chests, and she fell asleep in the car seat of the Watershed-sponsored ride as soon as it started moving.

"You will reach your destination in twenty-eight minutes," the ride told us, and we looked at each other and at the baby, and then slept happily in each other's arms the whole way.

At the drop-off Carol took the sling and managed to shift Dori without waking her. Then we walked across the bridge and picked our way along the path—I didn't turn on night vision, but I did up the tactile gain in my soles—all the way to the north-side cliffs. And there we found a palace, where before had been only root-cracked stone.

Silver, I thought at first, gleaming in the moonlight. But I blinked and saw black metal with the iridescent sheen of a grackle. Human eyes weren't made for it. When I toggled my lenses to night vision, the palace shed a rainbow of heat across the budding clover.

I messaged the network: **Not a false alarm. Not a spill. Need more sensors.** I wasn't sure what else to say, or if sending a picture would get me accused of snooping. Hell, I wasn't entirely convinced the thing would show up on-screen.

"You see that?" I asked Carol, nervous until she nodded. She wrapped her arms around Dori.

"Palace" was the closest word I could find, and it wasn't very close. It was a quarter-acre spread of spires and domes, fractal at the tips, narrow peaks spiraling in intricate patterns. It sloped down from three larger promontories, swooping at the edges as though it wasn't quite ready to meet the ground. It ticked softly, like a cooling pan. As I watched, part of it seemed to fold in on itself, and then out again showing a different design. Then another, and after that another, and I realized that it was constantly renewing itself one section at a time, a shifting landscape mesmerizing as a sunset.

Dori shifted and murmured against Carol's chest. I scanned for radiation, let out a breath when I found nothing worse than background.

"What are they dumping in the water?" Carol whispered. "And why?"

I queried the sensors again. "It's tapered off, but we're still getting weird organics." *Whatever's in there, they make waste. And dump it.* "It's not just a bot probe."

I thought of old movies: people approaching spaceships with their arms wide in welcome, incinerated by lasers. *I should go home. I should send them home.* But my breath came fast and short, like the moment the midwife had placed Dori in my arms, like the first time Carol's lips brushed my ear. I wondered if a thousand of these things were dropping across the world, or if this was the only one. I imagined telling Dori, years from now, that we could've met people from another planet, only we were trying to protect her. Or we could stay—and tell her that *she* met them.

I gripped Carol's hand. We shared a look, a nod, and I leaned briefly against her, grateful for unspoken agreement. Some things are more important than keeping your kid *safe.*

Screw being too nervous to tell anyone, though. Whatever risk we took for ourselves, we owed something to the rest of the world. I started my lenses recording, fed the livestream into the network. I flicked from ordinary vision to heat to electromagnetism, sending all the data I could gather. On that last setting I caught a darker patch near the palace's center. I tried heat again, increasing the sensitivity. The same section showed cooler, spring green where the rest burned orange and yellow.

"Something's broken there," I told Carol. Confidence faltering, I added, "I think. There's a cool patch, sort of jagged, and not in a symmetrical way."

"It doesn't look like it crashed. Are they sending out, I don't know, some sort of distress beacon?" She stopped. "Maybe the organics *are* a distress beacon?"

I started giggling. "Help! Poop!" I'm sorry, I know this isn't the sort of quotability people look for in historical events. But Carol started laughing too, and neither of us could stop, and then Dori woke up and started crying and we *froze*. There are *humans* who get vicious when they hear a baby wail. But no lasers burned out to shut us up. I tapped my mesh to view the diaper monitor. "Guess what?"

"Distress beacon?"

What was I supposed to do? Carol unhooked the sling, and I laid it down on the chilly grass, and I changed Dori's diaper right there in front of an alien artifact of unknown origin. I hoped Carol was wrong about the organics, because I wasn't quite willing to try a urine-soaked pad of smarthemp as our first communication attempt.

"Are you still recording?" asked Carol.

"Yep. This is for posterity." We switch off after diaper changes, so I pulled on the sling, adjusting it for my thinner shoulders, and cuddled Dori. "Hope you're appreciating this, posterity."

Carol isn't obsessed with sensory extension the way I am, but she knows every type of communication technology there is and she's always happy to help brainstorm. "Okay, assuming they don't talk to each other through effluent streams, they obviously know enough about *our* signals to find an uninhabited spot close to a big city. Are they sending anything that looks like a phone signal? Dandelion network encryption? God help us, wifi?"

"I'll look." I started scanning, frequency by frequency and format by format. Meanwhile our own network was starting to wake up. When I checked messages—automatic reflex even now—I found the anticipated accusations of snooping, but also suggestions for signal searches, and full files of every message humanity had ever posted out to the silent stars. I added a tick to the ongoing vote over whether to share with other watershed networks. People needed to know, and we needed the support.

No phone signals. No local network—at least not on any familiar frequency. I worked all the way down to radio before I found it.

It wasn't only radio, but sound, transmitted the same way we do it, the same way we've *been* doing it for almost two hundred years. They'd picked an empty bit of spectrum just below the NPR legacy transmission. I gave up on the limited bandwidth of lenses and earrings, and passed the signal to my palette. The speaker blared.

"It's music," said Carol.

"Human music." Drums and trumpets finished with a grand flare.

A simpler melody began, a series of electronic tones that ran in a loop, dah-dee-dah-*bum-bum*.

Are you getting this? I sent to the network. **We need to identify it.**

Could be a stand-in for an equation, suggested someone, and within a minute the board had branched into three teams: music folks, math folks, and everyone else speculating wildly about other possible meanings. The tone series faded, replaced by singing, high and fast and soaring.

The third group burst into excited activity. **Gujarati, that's Gujarati, someone connect with the Ghats-Narmada network now!**

Then the music group: **It's Bollywood. Sounds like something from a couple decades ago—hold on, I know a database for that, if my old log-in works.**

Dori yawned, blinked, and swiveled toward the music. "Bop!" she announced.

"Bop," I agreed. "Carol, what are they playing this stuff for? Why a movie soundtrack?"

"Showing off their good taste?"

The Chesapeake network exchanged handshakes with Ghats-Narmada (where everyone was awake and in work shifts, but no longer working), and hurriedly navigated the protocols to affirm that yes, this was worth the contagion risk. The antivirus icon flickered in the corner of my lens as our network filtered out a dozen minor infections, well within its immune response. A minute later, the answer came through.

It's an obscure science fiction movie from the 60s. *Beyond the Clouds of Dust*—this is the theme when the spaceship arrives.

Carol and I stared at each other, and about thirty people posted in unison: **IS IT FRIENDLY?**

Yes, they share this weird healing potion, and there's a really cool three-way interspecies love story.

Dug up a match for the first one, said someone else. **It's from a radio play about alien refugees in Brazil.**

The music changed again. "I know that one," exclaimed Carol. "That's one of Dinar's old anime series—and it's another one where aliens are friendly—I mean, the ones who have that song as their theme are friendly, there are about five others—"

I found that second one! It's an American film from over a century ago, and it's what the aliens play to introduce themselves. And yes, they're friendly.

"We come in peace," I said. My voice sounded too loud, or maybe too quiet. "They're saying they come in peace. And they want to talk."

That would have been a good time for cynicism—for someone to ask if we believed them, or if their definition of peace looked anything like ours. But no one wanted to spoil the moment of joy. We didn't want to play nation-style realpolitik, or be properly mature and suspicious. We wanted to *talk*.

However complicated things got afterward, I still can't regret that.

CHAPTER 2

"Carol," I said. "Weren't you working on a radio transmitter for your sweater swarm? Could we mod that to send a response?"

"Yes, but I didn't bring my sewing kit, I brought the diaper bag. Maybe Athëo and Dinar could drag it over? Or we could ask the network if someone nearby has one."

Already in it, came a network response, while Carol was still trying to work out a plan with our co-parents.

"They don't want to wake up Raven," she said. "It's one thing to come out here with Dori and find—" She waved at the palace.

"But another to wake up a toddler with a runny nose and bring them someplace you know might be dangerous, yeah." Even if Raven, at almost two, was more likely to appreciate the experience. But Athëo and Dinar had only moved in a month before Dori was born, and Raven was just learning to call us Mom and Eema; it wasn't our decision to make.

I bounced on my toes, jiggling Dori and shaking out my nervous excitement. I watched the network traffic as people arranged to bring in a radio transmitter, more sensors, a better sample kit than the one I'd packed for basic nutrient protocols. I tried to think of something to do in the meantime.

"Do you think they can see us?" I asked. I tried to imagine how we'd look to an observer who'd never met humans before. Two hairless primates standing side by side, one carrying an infant. Would they notice that Carol was taller and broader across the shoulders, or that my eyes were brown where hers were hazel? Would they even be able to separate us from our tools: understand that my denim and Carol's cotton dress were clothes rather than skin, that Dori's infant curls were part of her while the smartmail mesh helmeting our adult scalps came off at night?

"We don't even know if they have eyes," said Carol. She hugged me, and I realized that I was shivering in the clear winter night. Her touch brought the world beyond the palace back into focus: the bare-limbed maples and pawpaws, the dry whispering grass, the splash of the Potomac against the cliffs. Dori, head resting heavy and warm against my chest. I breathed the moment of miraculous stillness, about to break against the unknown.

Amid the shimmer of the alien construct, near the base of the closest peak, something moved. I flicked back to night vision, added a standoff chemical scan. We clung more closely.

"What are we doing here?" I whispered. "We're not qualified for this. I've repped the Chesapeake in carbon negotiations *one time*."

She shrugged against me. I marveled at the familiarity of human anatomy, that I could read her thoughts in that little shift of muscle. "More than I've got, unless you count dickering over yarn and circuits. But we're here, and no one else is. We'd better not fuck it up."

Against the spill of warmth—eighty-seven degrees Fahrenheit, a spectrum of steam and oxygen and nitrogen and remnant volatiles—a warmer figure scrabbled. I held my breath, squinted irrationally, and upped the light gain on my vision. The creature—alien—person, that had to be the right word, stepped lightly down the side of the palace and into the rock and scrub of our world.

They were long where we were tall: a dozen narrow limbs supported a body scaled like a pangolin's. More limbs, flared or pointed at the ends, spread from the sides of their torso back toward a broad, flat tail. There wasn't enough light to tell color, but the shade of their scales varied, mottled dark and pale. Two large eyestalks bulged from the sides of what I decided to assume was a head; smaller sensory organs dotted the head in complex patterns and diffused down their back.

I swallowed. The realization that I was still recording, that my next sentence would be remembered for as long as humans kept records, froze my thoughts and my tongue.

The alien tucked their tail under themselves and rolled back so that they lay rocking on the curve of their own body—limbs scrabbled to sweep pebbles from beneath—and they tapped their dark belly. Small antennae or cilia covered the glistening skin there revealed. I caught my breath: clinging to those cilia were two miniature versions of the alien. One bent its head back, twisting sideways to point an eye at me. It let out a whistling warble, which the other echoed at lower pitch.

Dori twisted her own head around, lips parted in delight. "Bah!"

"That's for history," I told her. I knelt down to match the alien's new height, and Carol joined me. "Welcome to Earth. What's *your* name?"

The alien brought two pairs of limbs together, drawing one across the other like a bow. Pitched oddly, but clearly comprehensible, I heard: "These are Diamond and Chlorophyll. I am Cytosine. What's your name?"

Kids first, apparently. "This is Dori. I'm Judy Wallach-Stevens, and this is my wife, Carol."

Music spilled from Cytosine's limbs, that same five-note series from the initial transmission. "We understand each other!"

"Yes. You've been listening to us?" But of course they had: watching our movies, picking up our broadcasts, well over a century's worth of stories and school videos and documentaries and news. What were they like, to follow all that and still want to meet us?

"Yes. That's how we learn. You haven't heard our songs yet, but you are far advanced and we didn't dare wait. It's reassuring to know you're civilized like us."

Wait, what? Beside me, Carol stiffened. But whatever cue had made them call us civilized, I didn't want to admit confusion. If they were anything like humans, the other side of that line could be unpleasant—maybe even fatal.

I heard a ride door slam, and someone walking down the path. This discussion was about to get a lot less controllable.

"We're glad to have you here," I said at last. I hesitated, not wanting to claim unfounded authority. "I'm present for the Chesapeake Bay Watershed Network. May I ask who you're present for?"

Simulated human laughter, drawn from Cytosine's bowstring limbs, somehow eerier than words produced the same way. "Yes, of course. I'm first mother of the *Solar Flare*"—limbs pointed at the palace behind them—"here on behalf of all the families of the Rings. We can help you escape this world."

I pulled Dori close. "Escape it? Why?" Scenarios tumbled through my mind: an incoming comet missed by our scant satellites, methane reservoirs breaching their tenuous tissue of permafrost and geoengineered shields—or Cytosine's people teleporting nine billion people to "safety" before appropriating Earth for their own purposes.

"Hallo," called a voice behind me. "Radio Free Terra is in the—oh, shit." The newcomer, bearded and thickly built and wearing a they/them badge, set down a box of equipment and gaped.

"You're late," Carol told them. "We're past exchanging radio signals, and on to . . ." She trailed off, and I wasn't sure how she should finish that sentence either. "Cytosine, this is Redbug. They build old-style radios, like you used to send those songs."

Probably the *Solar Flare* had simulated the radio electronics with some sort of advanced computer—then again, maybe they had a geek in the depths of their ship who enjoyed tinkering with circuits as much as Carol did. I pictured a beaver-pangolin hunched over a workbench, swearing at uncooperative pliers. Whether Cytosine intended threat or apocalyptic warning, their people must be as weird and varied as us. The thought kept me from spinning off into flights of panicked speculation.

But the distraction served another purpose: I posted the question to the network. If there was a comet someone could redirect telescopes; high methane readings would trigger a cobweb of dispersed sensors.

Query sent, I steadied myself. "Why do you think we need to escape?"

Cytosine curled more tightly, stroking Diamond and Chlorophyll—mirroring my embrace of Dori? "All species must leave their birth worlds, or give up their technological development, or die. You are very close."

"Is that a philosophical statement, or are we facing a specific danger?"

Redbug glanced between us, obviously fascinated but also obviously even more nervous than I was. "I'm just gonna be over here, setting up a base station, okay?" Carol waved them toward an open patch of moss-covered rock.

Cytosine had been rocking a little—thinking? "Philosophy. And empirical observation. Species breed out into vacuum, or die amid their own poisons at the level of technology you have now."

"*All* of them?" Carol had that tone in her voice, the one that caused sensible people to back up and scurry for citations.

"This is the fourth world we've visited after picking up signals, and the first where we've arrived in time."

"Maybe because we're doing something right?" I suggested, more sharply than I'd meant to. *We've never done this before. Don't fuck it up.*

"Because you're closer. Your planet is a hundred and sixty light-years from the Rings; we could build the tunnel as soon as we found your signal and arrive within the survival window. Why won't you believe me?" That rocking again—frustration, maybe, or anger.

"Your world is pushing the edge of your species' temperature range. Your seas are scarred by barren patches. Your atmosphere is out of balance. Have you not noticed?"

"Of course we've noticed," I said. "We've been doing something about it!"

"Worlds aren't meant to support technological species. They're birthing burrows, not warrens." Their voice rose in exasperation—how closely had they studied us, to catch the melody of our language as well as the words? And what should we make of that effort?

Chlorophyll let out a high, keening cry. They didn't sound much like a human baby—more like a miserable cricket—but the distress was unmistakable. Diamond joined in at lower pitch.

Then Dori, of course. I busied myself trying to comfort her, grateful for the respite. Perhaps that was why Cytosine had brought their own kids out? The children had diffused a tense diplomatic parlay. A few arguments at those carbon negotiations would've benefited from the interruption.

"I think she's hungry," suggested Carol. "Them too." I saw what she meant: Cytosine's belly glistened more brightly, and two long triple-forked tongues licked out across it. Shrugging, I pulled down the side of my shirt and let Dori suckle as well. I shivered and pulled the wrap close. Aching warmth pulsed between us, pulling me back to practicalities.

"Look," I said to Cytosine. "Leaving aside the, the philosophy, what are you actually asking us to do?"

Limbs scraped out speech. "Leave, and join us."

"The hell!" said Carol. I put a hand on her.

"We will share everything we've learned," continued Cytosine. "We will show you how to build tractable environments, make space around your star to grow and thrive. We will show you the secrets of tunneling. We'll make new symbioses together amid the great cloud of worlds. We will be sisters."

My sisters don't usually come to my house and demand I move out. "That sounds pretty exciting. What are you going to do with the Earth after we move out?"

Cytosine rocked back, eliciting squeaks of complaint. "I told you. We're a technological species too; we aren't meant for life on worlds."

I took a deep breath, held Dori tighter. "And what are you going to do if we say no?"

More rocking. "I don't know. We thought you were like us."

At this point, I want it in the record, I pinged the network telling them that this was beyond my skill set, that we needed to identify the most experienced negotiators from every network, and that I'd try to wind things down until we could get a proper team in the ground. And the network agreed. I tried not to get too distracted by the thread traffic, which hadn't yet surfaced any useful suggestions about what I should say, but was neck-deep in critique of what I *had* said.

A few more people had joined us on the island, all tech experts— they'd tracked my feed, and joined Redbug in setting up an impromptu base camp. They were swearing in urgent whispers over tent pegs and screens, arguing over equipment requirements. It looked gloriously restful and easy. Coral light etched the river, and I'd gotten about two hours of sleep. Exhaustion muffled my reactions. Once I'd had a chance to nap, surreality would give way to awe, or terror, or the paralysis of fully understanding what I'd done. But by then, I hoped, it would be someone else's job.

CHAPTER 3

Carol and I made our excuses to Cytosine. I don't remember exactly what we said—that we needed to confer with unspecified committees, that we'd explain later how humans were keeping our planet livable, maybe even that Dori was cold and needed to go inside. But whatever we said, they went along with it and scurried back into their palace-ship. They seemed at least as flustered as we were—not the best foundation for whatever real negotiations would follow. I was just glad to get away. I didn't sleep on the ride home.

We trudged through our yard, where the promissory glow of dawn had given way to crisply bounded colors. Carol stopped to fuss with the winter-mulched garden. She restacked tomato stakes scattered by the last windstorm, and tested the soil where we'd just planted peas. Inside I plucked a sprig of apple mint from the foyer wall and relished the sharp, solid taste. I kicked my boots off in the general direction of the mud mat.

"You're awake early," said Athëo dryly as we entered the dining room. "Long night up with alien polluters?" He spoke quietly, mindful of Dori conked out against my chest. Exhausted, I swayed for her. No other mammals stirred—the dog and Raven must've still been upstairs with Dinar.

"How's the spread?" I asked.

"No one on the Chesapeake network is talking about anything else, except for the dedicated monks at the treatment plant. They're reporting the latest energy production figures with great determination. Other watersheds are starting to pick up our news." He waved at screens for the household's secondary networks, projected on the table in between hard-boiled eggs and goat cheese and pu-erh pot. Reassuring, solid things: I turned up the input on my lenses and saw supply chains leading to a neighbor's flock, the herd of goats that kept our invasives in check, and a summary icon that, if I followed it, would show me every step of carbon-balanced tea importation from the Mekong watershed. The networks were familiar, too. Carol's textile exchange and Dinar's corporate gig-work watercooler and Athëo's linguistic melting pot and the neighborhood's hyperfirewalled energy grid scrolled over polished pine. Only the content was strange. The last time they'd all dovetailed on one topic had been when Maria Zhao died and every network devolved into *Rain of Grace* quotes.

Athëo went on, hesitating: "Are they . . . what are they like? Did you really *talk* with them? How could they be speaking *English*?" This last not with disbelief, but half-exaggerated disgust. When he wasn't actively on call for public safety mediation, Athëo put hours into everything linguistic, from translating academic papers to making up a conlang with no verbs for a Calgary playwright. If we'd had to translate Ringer from scratch, he'd have been thrilled.

"They're like giant pillbugs with tiny pillbug babies," said Carol, yawning. "They learned English by listening to old radio shows and watching movies, and the subtle effects on their vocabulary will probably keep you busy for years. They'd be adorable if they just wanted to share the secret of starry wisdom or something."

"They want us to leave Earth," I said.

Athëo rose from the table to look out the window: early-rising chickadees and finches clung to the feeder, dropping sunflower husks among the lilac bushes. The sky was clearing, powder-blue, into a perfect morning. He pressed his hand to the pane. Through the glass, the faintest edge of chill would seep against his fingers. "Are they going to *make* us? We're just starting to get things right."

It was the refrain of our generation, particularly personal for Athëo. And what would my parents think, who'd helped place the first illicit sensors in the Potomac and barricaded factories to enforce the first crowd-sourced decisions of the nascent Dandelion Revolution?

"Maybe they can make *your* parents leave the planet," I suggested to Athëo. I cautiously wrapped my arm around his waist, still unused to touching him, and stretched my fingers beside his on the glass. "I have no idea what they'll do. I don't think *they* have any idea. They thought we'd be excited."

"*Why?*"

"'Technological species aren't meant for life on worlds,'" quoted Carol.

"So we should give up our technology," said Athëo, "or give up our world."

"They never suggested that first one," I said. Dori stirred and murmured. I kissed the top of her head. "How bad are the critiques? I must have earned them. I'm not qualified for any of this."

"Who is?" asked Carol. "And I was there too."

"Yeah, but Judy was recording." Athëo returned to his cooling tea and the primary network screen. His touch sent text skittering upward. "The whole thing is under her ID, so ninety percent of the feedback is for her. Most people are focused on the actual aliens and their signals, but you *have* come in for your share of flames. The worst are from other watersheds—we're just starting to get those messages passed through. You shouldn't take it personally." He grimaced sympathetically; he knew exactly how hard that was. I still flinched. "By most of our treaties this counts as a local issue, and no one's happy with that."

"I'm sure not." It would be ours, though, until someone could show an environmental impact outside the Chesapeake watershed boundary. Even then, people would be reluctant to travel; the bulk of the problem-solving would be ours by virtue of being *here*. Only the critique would be unbounded. I sighed. "Just tell me we're putting together a real ground team?" I sat, spread cheese on a slice of pumpernickel, and considered whether it was worth draining my inbox now to avoid the flood later.

"Of course they are." Athëo flashed a smile. "They've put out calls for people who've been in at least three successful internetwork negotiations, plus at least one international or corporate. Working with nation-states is as close as we come to aliens, right? No one knows what *they're* going to do about this either. Oh, and we're pulling in biologists—everyone who's worked with multiple biomes, plus one person just visiting from the Tongala-Baaka network."

"The where?" asked Carol. She poured a cup of pu-erh and sipped it steaming.

"Australia—drains near Melbourne."

"Oh, good," I said. "This *should* be a biology issue. Or psychology. Anthropology. Physics, maybe. Anything but water chemistry and textile engineering and . . ."

"Network management?" suggested Carol. "You grew up drowned in it."

"Listening to my parents' stories about negotiating dandelion structural philosophy—or to Aunt Priya monologuing about operationalizing it in code—does not make a good profile for interplanetary negotiations. Especially since my few actual contributions have been on the sensory weighting algorithm." My lenses highlighted my spiking pulse rate and raised volume—I was going to wake Dori. I took a deep breath. "Sorry. I'm just terrified the network will decide to put me in the team after all, because I was there first. And I'm a little scared of the critiques. If I lose rep over this, I won't have weight on the things I'm good at."

"The algorithms would have to get pretty buggy to cut your weight over this," said Carol. "No one really knows how to make it work. The whole team'll be terrified—if they aren't, we should disqualify them."

"Do you want to go to bed?" asked Athëo. "I don't mind dealing with other people's critiques. If you shunt me your inbox I can sort the messages, and you won't be flooded when you get up. You can cover the afternoon shift with Dinar."

It was tempting. I was exhausted. But the idea of someone else looking at those messages made me shudder, even more than the thought of going through them myself. It was bad enough that Athëo could see the public flames. "I'll go to bed in a minute, and take you up on the shift exchange. But I'll deal with the messages myself after I wake up."

"I can take Dori," said Carol.

"I'll take Dori," countered Athëo. "You've both been up all night."

"I should bring her up to our room," I said doubtfully. "She'll need to nurse again in an hour."

"They've got babies with them, did we say?" Carol waggled her hands against her chest. "Cytosine was nursing, or close enough. She oozed milk all over her belly."

My breasts let down just from the reminder. I hadn't put on pads before we left, and if I soaked through my shirt I'd definitely wake Dori. "Do you think 'she' is right? I forgot to ask, and Ring people may be just as complicated as human people."

Carol glanced at Athëo, who looked worried again. She grinned. "You got some nice peach fuzz coming in there. Higher testosterone doing the trick?"

"Yeah." He rubbed his chin self-consciously. "Thanks for talking to Dr. Parekh. I never know what to say."

Carol, who'd had her pituitary implant since she was twelve, shrugged. "You say 'puberty is hard and I didn't get any help with my first one, please keep experimenting until we get it right.'"

Athëo rubbed his eyes. "Jesus, I hope these people *don't* play the same stupid gender tricks as humans."

"I'll ask," I said. "I mean, I'll suggest on the network that the team should ask about their pronouns. Cytosine said they'd be our sisters. Do you think that means anything? Most of the old shows they learned from would've said 'brothers.'"

"Maybe they think women are a different species," suggested Carol. "Some of those old shows sure act like it."

Athëo began undoing my wrap. "Baby. Here. I'll feed her freezer milk and I swear neither of you will dry out or get mastitis if you skip one feeding. The watershed network will take care of the Ringers. The world won't fall apart because you took a nap; that's what networks are *for*."

Carol fell asleep instantly, still wearing socks. Her melatonin and dopamine and basically everything but estrogen and testosterone all do exactly what they're supposed to naturally; I'm not so lucky. I spooned, nose buried against the curve of her neck. I thought of everything I should've said to Cytosine, and the commentary I should add to our recording, and what Redbug would do if anyone came out of the ship to look at their radio rig. Then I got up and retrieved my mesh from its stand, settled the cool smartmail back over my bare scalp, and let the Network flow back into my lenses. I paced while I caught the flow of the threads, avoiding the squeaky board next to the closet and the bassinet awkwardly wedged beside it. I got a fatigue alert, EEG waves passing on my mental state along with more deliberate signals, and dismissed it.

I eased in, catching up on half-deserted policy decisions. Streambed restoration for the Paint Branch, a proposal for using a new algae species in water treatment, the carbon budget for importing tea and coffee. There were still a few people working on those threads, refining options and adding weight to their favorites; I wasn't the only one who found this stuff soothing. A network in flow is like a walk in the woods for the mind. If I weren't exhausted I'd have done that too: gone down to the Anacostia, or out to Rock Creek Park with the soft pine underfoot and the spray of mossy water beside the path and the creak of crows, everything connected in a system that I could contribute to but never control. That's truth, tangible as a planet.

Reluctantly, I turned my attention back to the main discussion. While I moaned at Athëo, the crowd had been breaking down the issues.

Problem: Alien ship in Bear Island. Apparently no other ships—Chesapeake issue only? Options: *Redefine potential harm to give other networks access. *Argue for local authority and keep negotiations focused.

Problem: Profiles needed for diplomatic team.

Lots of detail there about desired expertises, none of which I had, and abundant profiles in response. Some people had worked in dozens of internetwork and international projects; one had written a series of papers about speculative xenobiology, projecting possible adaptations for fifty known exoplanets. *They'll take care of this.*

Problem: Ringers think humans should abandon Earth.

Refined Problem: Ringers may try to force humans off planet. Options: *Fight back (with/without state support, with/without corporate support). *Just say no (there ain't room for 10 billion in that tiny ship). *Find out what they really want—this makes no sense as an end goal. *Hand over all the corporate shills and leave Earth for the rest of us.

I shuddered and flagged that last option. Dinar often picked up corporate gigs to help make our household contribution goals, and she was hardly the only person in the network, or even the neighborhood. We all shared the benefit and responsibility for the harms done. Even the corporations themselves, billionaire lords and serf-employees huddled behind their fencelines on their artificial islands, deserved agency as long as they avoided hurting anyone.

Problem: Seven corporate requests for Bear Island access—they all want to negotiate for whatever tech the Ringers brought with them. And then they'll sue us over the "intellectual property" rights, of course. Options: *Keep 'em out. *Let them in, but *after* we know what's on offer. *Offer a spot for everyone who's met their carbon budget, and watch them scramble for proper documentation. *Set commons requirements for whatever they learn. *Tell them to send a *small* embassy, and hope they take a while to work out the details.

I watched the votes tick up, raw and then filtered through the algorithms that brought in the weight of individual voter expertise, riparian representation, and our community's long-term ethical preferences. Tempting as it was to use the Ringers as a carrot for the corporations' always-sparse carbon documentation, people seemed to prefer predictability with our old enemies; the request for a limited embassy was pulling ahead. The suggestion to set commons requirements had already hit threshold, and was being refined into an open task.

Problem: US gov has to notice this eventually—predictions about what they'll do? Other fossil states, too, if they've got the means.

Problem: Anyone notice the Ringers have stopped broadcasting? What are they doing in there?

Freaking out that we hadn't followed their script. But *why* did they have that script? Why assume that ten billion people would be thrilled to leave home? Then again, I didn't always understand why humans made the assumptions they did, or why it had taken a century and a half of industrial pollution to figure out that we wanted to stay on this planet and had better bust ass to make that possible. Maybe it'd taken them a few years too long, on their own abandoned world.

They said they've been to other planets, and found everyone dead, I submitted. They've never talked to anyone but themselves. I curled on the bed again, my back against Carol's living warmth and my fingers trailing on the palette. I tried to imagine it—a galaxy of dead worlds and fallen civilizations, Cytosine's people always arriving a few years too late. It could give anyone strange ideas. Let's try them tomorrow when we have a team, and they've had time to process. I fell asleep, still watching the responses scroll.

When I woke up, the problems had been refined further. My swollen inbox forced itself into my mesh, blighted fruit of refusing Athëo's offer. A flagged message flashed red at the top of the queue:

Problem: The Ringers came back outside, and they won't talk to anyone but Judy Wallach-Stevens.

CHAPTER 4

Carol followed me downstairs, carrying Dori. Dinar stood at the kitchen counter making bread, a shoulder-length glove over her left arm to keep from gunking up the prosthetic as she folded and slapped dough. Kyo leaned against her knee with his nose twitching, eternally hopeful for shed scraps. Raven sat on the floor. They stared, fascinated, at the recording of our night's adventures. "Eema, bug!"

"Kind of," I said. I spread my arms wide. "*Big* bug!" The toddler laughed, and Dori eeked. I recognized Dinar's corporate feed scrolling beside the floured board. "Dinar, have you seen this morning's threads? They want *me* back out there!"

"What for? Not that you aren't terrific, but Athëo said we were putting together a diplomatic team." She poked the glove to roll the fabric back, and with her still-clean hand stuck a slice of the previous day's bread in to toast.

"Thanks—I'm going to have to nurse and run, and I'm starving. Apparently the Ringers don't care if I'm qualified. I have no idea what they want me for."

"Maybe they've got a water quality problem." She got out the jar of goat cheese, and smoked salmon from the aquaculture share. "Or aren't satisfied with their current sensory organs?"

"I shouldn't take all that, I had some yesterday."

"You're nursing. Eat your protein."

"Yes, ma'am." I took a slice, and Carol helped me arrange Dori. "Maybe they do. Have a water quality problem, I mean. I think I caught a damaged spot on their ship. But that doesn't explain *only* wanting me."

"Could be they liked something you said?" suggested Carol.

"They didn't last night. Dinar, what do you know about the companies trying to push in? We started with seven asking, but they all got quiet once we asked for a limited embassy. How are they going to work that?"

Dinar shrugged, returning to the dough. "They aren't telling gig-pickers this stuff, and I've pushed as hard as I can without getting dropped. But there are a bunch of new admin support requests today."

"Are you going to take any?"

"I'd better. Gotta cover my share of the neighborhood resource goals. And I won't learn anything by staying away."

"We can do without corporate resources," said Carol. "And we'll have to, eventually."

"They're not going to disappear any time soon—someone has to keep talking to them, or they'll never change enough to join the rest of the world."

I let them argue the old controversy, and nursed Dori while I gobbled my toast. She'd already earned her place in history, so I was glad to leave her safe with the household this morning. I would've liked Carol along for moral support—but it was me the Ringers had asked for. I had a horrible suspicion that they weren't asking because they *liked* me. I didn't want to spread the blame.

I mulled it over on the train out past Bethesda, and then along the half-mile bike trail to the river. Humans I understood. But the constant background hum of my brain modeling social interactions, all my immersion in watershed and neighborhood politics, told me nothing about Ringer motivations.

At least chemistry was still chemistry. This time I linked my mesh with standoff sensors to pick up fine gradations of organics and pollutants, and set my shirt to give detailed tactile feedback for their input. I might not know what the Ringers were thinking, but I'd know everything they exhaled and excreted. Along the riverbank, forsythia and speedwell rippled oxygen.

I rolled the bike up the path toward the Ringers' cliff. A few hours' worth of visitors had packed the gravel flat. Around the palace, Redbug's hodgepodge equipment had blossomed into a village of tents, screens, sensors, and electronics. A tiny network of Things pinged my mesh, all keyed to the Chesapeake's security protocols. I shunted the requests aside for later; I wanted their input desperately, but didn't want to crash all my channels because some yutz hadn't set their firewall right.

The diplomatic team were obsessing over signals. Maybe the right song, speech, or Shakespeare quote would draw the Ringers back out of their palace. On the network feed, a dozen problems focused on what we should share; a playlist queued waiting for the diplomatic team's go-ahead. For now, the big screens facing the palace-ship stood blank.

"They've seen that stuff," I said to the tech on duty. "Every signal we've spilled into space; they know it well enough to play *us* deep cuts."

She shrugged. "A deliberate message is different. They don't know what *we* think makes a good introduction to humanity." Of course, looking at the problem threads, neither did we.

It was easier talking to the tech expert; I wasn't about to take over her electronics for no good reason. But I could read Eliza Mendez's profile as easily as anyone. She was a cetacean specialist who'd spoken for Atlantic ecosystems at dozens of intercontinental summits. One of her essays, on whalesong as a metaphor for carbon negotiation, had been part of the context packet for my own first diplomatic effort: something I'd read for inspiration late at night when the whole thing seemed overwhelming. She had every qualification to represent the Chesapeake Network to another species, and I didn't blame her for looking at me like, I don't know, an eel trying to pass as a dolphin.

"Find out what they want from the rest of us," she told me. "They're asking the whole species to up and leave our homes; they can't expect to work through one person."

"Unless they're a hive mind," suggested Abi Diawara. They'd written the speculative xenobiology series. "You only talked with one of them, right? Maybe they think you're the queen."

I sat through another half hour of circular speculation. At the end, though, streaming the highest-fidelity recording I could support, I stood alone in front of the *Solar Flare*. Strange volatiles wafted from its surface. The dark spot had grown. I waited.

The ship's skin split, just as it had the night before. Warmth spilled down from the open door. But no one came out.

I scanned again, nervously, and found nothing toxic. Against my spine, fine patterns pantomimed something close to ordinary terrestrial atmosphere. I hoisted myself over the lip of the structure, and stood on something not terrestrial at all. I let the texture through my soles: stippled like plaster, an easy grip for a Ringer's dozen legs but little traction for human feet. It shifted under me, extruding amoebic knobs like a climbing wall. I hauled myself up the slope with no particular dignity, and pulled myself through the aperture.

The first thing I noticed was the air. It might be terrestrial—but kin to the thriving swamp DC had replaced rather than the cool afternoon outside. I'd expected sterility; instead I found something more like Dinar's greenhouse or the aquaculture dome. I tasted humidity, wet leaves, orchids, and something like shed snakeskin. I breathed abundance.

And then held my breath, too late, as I thought of dangers. Bacteria. Windblown seeds. Insects, or their equivalents, and scuttling scavengers carrying the remains of meals out spaceship doors and into the wide new world beyond. Maybe they couldn't survive here, most of them. But maybe I'd already scuffed my shoe through the spore of some alien kudzu, or coated my lungs with their native *E. coli*.

I told myself that, logically, I'd already been exposed last night, and Cytosine had tracked everything onto the rocks of Bear Island. Not to mention their latrines dumping into the Potomac. Here I was, and I didn't have much choice about inhaling.

A forest of vines and machinery spread around me. Greenery sprouted flashes of metal. Consoles poked from bright flowers. Something flitted in the shadows of the ceiling, and the floor grew soft moss. Sterility would've been safer, but I couldn't blame them for wanting wilderness.

Movement among the twists of wood, and a Ringer came into the little clearing around the door. I thought it was Cytosine again, but I'd never met another Ringer for comparison. Maybe they all carried twins everywhere they went.

Nothing ventured, nothing gained. "Cytosine?" And she'd only ever met a couple of humans. "It's Judy. You wanted to see me."

She rolled back, hooking a limb around a convenient twig. Shock filled her violin voice. "Where is Dori?"

I put out a hand to steady myself, only afterward realizing that I'd dug my nails into whorls of green-brown alien bark. Cool as any earthly root, its dew mixed with my sweat. "She's at home. With Carol. We don't—Do you—" I swallowed questions I wouldn't be able to unsay. Suspicion bloomed. Why they'd asked for *me*. "You *do* bring your children everywhere."

"Certainly to something this important. Why didn't you bring them? Are they ill? Or did we misunderstand?" Cytosine rocked harder. One of her kids squeaked, long and piercing, and she stopped to stroke them delicately. "Carol, who was with you. You called her your wife, but you held the child. Which of you is their mother?"

Some things I couldn't be diplomatic about. "We're both her mothers," I said shortly.

"But which of you birthed the child?"

"Where I come from, that's a rude question. Why does it matter?"

The second kid, the one who hadn't squeaked, dropped suddenly from Cytosine's belly and ran out toward me. They stopped, raised limbs, and belted out, "Mother mother MOTHER."

"Your kid speaks good English," I said.

"Diamond lives up to their name." She—given Cytosine's obsession with motherhood I decided to keep going with "she" until told otherwise—scooped the kid back to safety. "This is one reason we bring children to difficult discussions. They interrupt slides into frustration. They make us stop and think."

"That makes sense." It probably would've prevented a few wars on Earth, if everyone had to pause their insults to change diapers on a regular basis. "We don't have the same tradition, but I can bring her if you promise not to—oh. It's for that too, isn't it? Everyone has their kids along, so no one is going to start anything dangerous."

"Yes, exactly. And it shows strength. We've both persuaded mates to sire children for us, and we both have the fortitude and determination to carry." She rotated one of her eyes, unexpectedly. "Unless you don't."

"Carol and I are both mothers," I said, trying to sound determined and fortitudinous. "And we're both recognized as mothers by our society." I remembered her kids licking her belly. "We both *nurse*." Now was not the time to explain genetic recasing, or any of the other mechanics involved in combining my DNA with Carol's.

Cytosine shifted on a dozen limbs. "You'll bring Dori next time?"

"Yes." And wouldn't that be a fun household discussion? My co-parents were probably watching the live feed now, but that wouldn't forestall arguments later.

"All right." She wrapped limbs around Diamond and Chlorophyll. I wondered how untrustworthy I'd made myself seem, doing something so gauche as leaving my kid at home. Sort of the equivalent of putting your hands behind your back when someone offered to shake. "Maybe you'll make more sense to the tree-folk."

I'd gotten used to her angular limbs mimicking human speech—had scarcely noticed this morning the strangeness of how she talked. But now she pressed her legs together and sang out in what had to be her own form of speech. Clicks and chitters, squeals and long notes like singers warming up for choir, alto and baritone and countertenor weaving in and out of harmony while someone angrily rummaged a closet.

I was glad they'd learned *our* language.

Something dropped from among the vines. I'm sorry to admit that I screamed. I clapped my hands over my mouth, and a good thing too, because more somethings dropped even as a couple of Cytosine's people poked round-eyed heads through the forest at ground level. I wasn't paying attention to them; they were just weird. It was the things—people, damn it—who'd been in the trees who set my every primate instinct to red alert.

They were bundles of giant hairy legs, half again as tall as a human. They were green and brown as the vines, except where they glowed neon and ultraviolet and jewel-toned at random angles. They had too many eyes. They looked like giant bioluminescent tarantulas, and everyone on Earth with a phobia of invertebrates was now hiding behind a couch. My mesh helpfully informed me, based on scans of density variation and basic knowledge of the square-cube law, that they probably *weren't* invertebrates. To make up for that, they sported paired pincers at intervals among their multitudinous knees, and small mouths at other intervals. There were, when I checked the record later, only five of them, but you couldn't have convinced me at the time.

One of them set up screech-singing from those mouths, and a box strapped to one leg translated: "I told you! I said we looked like their obligate aversion triggers for venom! And you said no, you're too big, you have ten limbs, you look completely different!" They dropped their . . . center bit, there wasn't much body other than the legs . . . to below my eye level, and crept toward me slowly. I made a great effort of common sense and didn't step back. "See, I do look very different from a spider. Even the giant ones in your practice-fear entertainments. I have a skeleton, and soft fur, and I eat bugs and leaves and fruit. Also all those spider-monsters look completely neuter, and I'm male."

Another spider-thing keened, and their box laughed and said, "She may not be used to us, Rhamnetin, but she can tell *that*."

"Bet you couldn't," said Rhamnetin.

"Your gender signaling, if any, is entirely opaque to me," I said in as serious a tone as I could manage under the circumstances.

"Would you like to touch me?" he asked. "I promise I'm not venomous or aggressive. It might help."

"It might." Cautiously I reached out and stroked his leg, keeping well away from pincers and mouths. It was actually easier to overcome my nerves up close. I had, as Rhamnetin suggested, seen and been alarmed by giant spiders in movies. I'd never touched one. I dug my fingers into wool-dense fur. He smelled green and musty, a little like someone who'd just finished running. His limbs were fractal at the ends, I saw: tipped by spider-like fingers or toes gripping tight to the moss.

"Rhamnetin is my cross-brother," said Cytosine. "His job is . . . difficult to translate." She choired a word, notes rising and falling.

"Jester. Red team," suggested Rhamnetin. "Asker of awkward questions."

"Didn't you say you've always been too late to contact other species?" I asked Cytosine. Unless, it occurred to me belatedly, they *were* in fact the same species, and their gender signals were no-shit that obvious.

"Outside of our home system, yes," said Cytosine. "But the second ring were born one orbit out from our own. We watched their newborn civilization through our telescopes, and built ships to meet them."

"Our sisters landed beside our first farms," said Rhamnetin. "They taught us their tools—and we figured out how to make them better." Was it my imagination, or was there a sardonic edge to his explanation? But I could see the appeal—if Mars had been the canal-strewn ecology we once believed, we'd have been eager to talk, even knowing the dangers.

CHAPTER 5

Cytosine introduced me to the rest of the crew-slash-family. I wasn't quite clear on whether they ran a ship together because they were related, or whether the relationships existed because they ran a ship together, or a mix of both. The three other pillbugs were Cytosine's mates. I thought I'd be able to tell them apart with practice, even if at the moment their varied patterns blurred to Rorschach blobs in my overburdened memory. I put in a request for someone to adapt a prosthetic facial recognition algorithm across species, and tried to focus.

The spiders—"tree-folk"—were three brothers counting Rhamnetin plus two "cross-sisters," and a "cross-niece" that startled me all over again by flinging herself out of the vines onto her mother's vine-like limbs. The niece was about my height, but I was quickly setting new standards for appropriate leg-monster size. A lizard-like animal, multilegged enough in its own right to look like a scaly centipede, clung atop the childless sister. Humans joke enough about pets as kid-substitutes; my general attitude was that I'd believe it when I had to change Kyo's diaper at 3 a.m. Here I suspected the substitution meant serious politics.

Cytosine ushered me toward the rest of the ship. Rhamnetin, who seemed happy to offer helpful commentary along with awkward questions, trailed along. I started a twine-ball app, building the map from the door as I went. The two things I wanted to know—aside from *everything*—were what was going on with that damaged spot, and what they were dumping into the river. Those points glowed on my blank map-space, here-there-be-dragons filling the area between. At least the ship's interior seemed to match the external topography. No "bigger on the inside" nonsense to mess up my measurements, or add worries about spatial distortion to the obvious hazards of pollutants and invasives. Though the network was rife with speculation on why no one had spotted the thing landing.

I kept my network window small, and tried to balance input with focus. The golden rule of "in the ground" is that you decide yourself when you're up for channeling the world, and when you need flow. Mendez had violated that rule by asking me to play puppet, and I'd been seriously tempted. The killer was that if the Ringers caught her signal, they'd realize they hadn't really gotten the person they demanded. But my lenses streamed excited speculation about how interplanetary symbiosis might work, and whether Rhamnetin distributed neurons among his legs like an octopus.

This is beautiful, I posted, and terrifying. Problem: They have a full freaking ecosystem in here. There are plant-things that seem happy to grow in a plastic substrate—or possibly, so help me, grow plastic for convenient harvest. There are insectoids in every color including see-through. That skittery orange thing just gobbled what looked like a fast, angry feather. Depending on their biochemistry, we could be dealing with dozens of invasives at once.

"Are all these organisms from your homeworld?" I asked. Watching Rhamnetin pick his way carefully around what appeared to be a large nest of sand and sticks, I added, "Or both your homeworlds?"

"Some of them," said Xenon. He was one of Cytosine's mates, and seemed to be the ship's bio specialist. "There are two thousand nine hundred and sixty basic niches required to keep a habitat stable, and about a tenth of those on an open-system ship like the *Solar Flare*. Where an original species isn't optimal, we design our own. Pollinators, for example—the natural ones are fragile, so the—"

They drew out a word in the Ringer language, and Rhamnetin offered, "Stone bees?"

"The stone bees combine genetics from both rings, are more durable, and can pollinate all our core crops."

"Huh." Pollinator preservation wasn't the crisis it had been a generation back, but new apiarine plagues appeared all too often. I was torn between thinking about how easily "fragile" species could be outcompeted, and wondering if Ringer genetic engineering techniques would work on earthly bees without forcing us into a monoculture. I couldn't imagine boiling down the whole Chesapeake to a couple thousand interlocked species for portable convenience. "What happens if they get out?"

"They'll probably pollinate your crops," said Cytosine.

"Don't you try to keep them on the ship?"

"In the aggregate." Limbs waved on both sides. "A habitat population needs to be resilient to some loss."

I swallowed. "Our pollinator niche is full. We'd rather not have *our* bees competing with yours."

Another ripple of limbs. "System competition is impossible to avoid entirely. We'll find a balance of cooperation soon enough."

"They won't carry illness, if that's what you're worried about," said Rhamnetin. "Everything on the ship has universal inoculants."

At which point every expert in deep healing and first aid and medical programming in the Chesapeake simultaneously posted **FIND OUT MORE ABOUT THAT!!!** and an explanation of why invasive species suck got pushed to the back of the queue.

"Look," I said to Cytosine after ten minutes and forty-three seconds of channeling biobabble. "I *can't* stream this whole thing verbally—eventually, you have to talk directly with people who aren't me. If you come outside, you can talk with the medical crowd directly. Dr. Mendez and Mx. Diawara could dive deeper than me all on their own."

Cytosine made a sawblade noise. "How many children have they mothered—and left at home, I suppose?"

I winced, and checked the personal section of their profiles. Nothing about kids in either case.

Mendez: **I've known several dolphins since they were calves, does that count? Plus my five niblings. That should be enough for anyone.**

They'll want to talk to your sibs, then. Or the dolphin moms.

Diawara: **How are we going to explain nonbinary parenting to these ignorant colonizers?**

Me: **I don't want to tell them anyone's gender other than "mother" until we know who else gets rights in Ringer society. I'm also getting a weird vibe from the way Cytosine talks about parenting. I think we're missing something—can someone with more bandwidth set up a problem thread?**

I minimized the network window again and focused on Cytosine. "Are you seriously only going to talk with people who've got kids living with them right this moment? Even leaving aside grandparents and parents with children in their Transit Year, plenty of people make the world better without breeding. We value them, too."

Cytosine failed to respond. Rhamnetin hesitantly brushed her side with a hairy leg. "They've got one small world, and nine billion to feed. It's adaptive."

She made a dubious skirl. "Show her the hammocks."

The hammocks—large nets spiraling up one of ship's towers,

around a central core of hydroponic food crops in rainbow colors and with twice the oxygen output of the forsythia—were fascinating. Everything was fascinating, and frustrating. I couldn't get any nearer the dark spot than I could the topics Cytosine avoided. Every time I made to wander in that direction, I got steered away. So it was real, and she didn't want to talk about it. I considered bringing it up directly, but I'd probably run out Cytosine's patience with blunders for the day.

I found the source of the runoff without a problem. Their waste disposal wasn't that far off from our own methods except that they hadn't bothered with a couple of key filter stages. When I expressed that perhaps the river didn't need their excess nutrients, I got another reassurance about the absence of alien plagues—which was great, way better than the alternative, but not sufficient to the river's needs. Even Rhamnetin, who I'd rapidly and maybe unfairly judged as more flexible than Cytosine, obviously didn't get it.

"You can't control every variable on a planetary surface," he told me. "That's why we left."

I tried to picture it. Human spaceflight had been largely the business of corporations for decades: proprietary satellites streaming encrypted images to their owners, mining probes chasing asteroids they could split without paying carbon fees, and the occasional NASA launch every few years when their congress got in the mood to fund research. Corporate oligarchs had once paid billions to spend a few hours in orbit. If the Ringers spotted the tiny habitat of mummified corpses on Mars, would they see seeds of our future? But they'd had neighbors right next door, and a welcoming place to land. More incentive to head up and out, and an easier path when they tried. By the time their glaciers started melting, they must have known pretty well how to keep themselves alive amid the vacuum and radiation.

I could understand wanting to stretch like that—especially with people waiting. Get the view from above, and below, and all around. But I couldn't understand giving up Earth to do it. Three-thousand species preserved to make a predictable and controllable ecology, and how many left behind? Somewhere on those sacrificial pyres they must have left equivalents of periwinkle and firefly and otter and iguana, intricate curves of coastline and river and half-melted glacier, the Marianas Trench and Mauna Kea.

And hard as it was to imagine leaving the planet behind forever, it was even harder to imagine leaving the Chesapeake. Except for my

Transit Year and six months of exchange apprenticeship in Chicago, I'd lived *here*. I could fill Cytosine's ecological slots from the banks of the Anacostia alone.

"Where are you from?" I asked. I wanted that to be a deep question for them, too.

Cytosine scraped limbs. "I'm not sure what you call our sun." Which made sense, if they'd been getting their data about humans from broadcasts and not big astronomical catalogues. She went on. "The Rings are a little under a hundred and sixty light-years from here. We came as soon as we heard you."

"You've been traveling for a hundred and sixty years?" But it would have to be more, wouldn't it? Unless they'd found a way around one of nature's stricter limits. Was that the "tunneling" she'd promised to share?

Before Cytosine or Rhamnetin could reply, another pillbug skittered in. One of her mates—no kid, and I thought I recognized the subtle pattern of ripples along his back—though I couldn't remember his name. Someone in the network helpfully scrolled back my recording and identified him as Phenylalanine.

A screen flashed open amid the plants, floating in the air where three beams intersected. It showed the island outside, where new humans stood in front of the ship. Mendez was talking with them urgently. Both newcomers wore formal suits with sashes, the sort you might still see on Constitution Avenue when Congress was in session, and the sort of over-the-top smart eyeliner that's supposed to let folks read your expressions from across the room.

"They just got here," said Phenylalanine. Their mimicry wasn't nearly as good as Cytosine's, and odd notes wrapped their vowels.

"Humans really do hide their kids most of the time," said Cytosine. "I thought it was only a taboo in your movies."

"We could never figure out why so much of your fiction doesn't show children," added Rhamnetin.

I shrugged uncomfortably. I wanted them over this hang-up, but I wasn't eager to let the old governments start posturing at the Ringers, either. "Are you going to ignore them too?"

The Ringers, both kinds, reeled into a torrent of flutes and broken violins, which ended when Cytosine said, "All right, Rhamnetin, take your brothers and find out what they want. But don't let them in until we have a good reason to trust them."

Rhamnetin went rigid for a moment—anger or excitement or something else. "Judy, come with us? You can check my translations."

"I'll do my best." I didn't point out that Mendez would do it better; he wouldn't believe me and I wanted to see this for myself anyway. I messaged Mendez on an open channel: Who are these people?

Mendez: NASA, they say. They've got IDs, but not the whole set of authorization records you usually see when feds get around to authorizing something. I think they might be rogue.

That was interesting—maybe less dangerous than if all the agencies were acting in concert, but also less predictable. Some agencies tried regularly to undermine the watershed, perceiving us as rivals for authority. Others considered us a tool to get things done; our Bear Island sensors had been placed in "partnership" with the Park Service for decades, forestalling any other agency trying to zap them. NASA . . . we didn't deal with often, not since they'd lost funding for their environmental satellites. Congress approved the occasional space probe, and telescopes pointed at the stars, but didn't think it their business to look back down. Our spheres rarely overlapped.

Back at the hatch, the two other male spiders waited, fidgeting, for Rhamnetin to join them. If I'd shown up childless the first time, would I have gotten a squad of low-ranked spider-brothers instead of Cytosine herself?

Me: Mendez, can you show the NASA reps some of my records before these folks come outside? If any of them are arachnophobic . . . Stories cycled through my head, shows where some minor misunderstanding or moment of fear led to war. They're not armed, are they?

Mendez: No way to tell, but I'll give them a heads-up.

Rhamnetin's brothers gripped the shifting palace surface easily, while I eased myself down with a bit less confidence. The NASA reps didn't look phobic. More awestruck, lips parted in delighted smiles. One of them was older, whiter, and dark-haired, and looked like it'd been a while since they'd last pulled on a suit. The other was younger and shorter and better-tailored. Her lapel was festooned with pins for the agency, the larger U.S. government, and her pronouns, along with a couple that I suspected of being unfamiliar skill badges.

"Hello," she said, stepping forward. "On behalf of the United States of America and the National Aeronautics and Space Administration, welcome to Earth. I'm Dr. Nyri Bakkalian, and this is Connor Goldsmith. I hope we'll be able to work together closely and peacefully." The silvery lines around her eyes moved to emphasize friendliness and confidence, though I could see in her widened pupils the effort it took to get through that speech without stumbling. I sympathized.

Rhamnetin offered a long limb, toes—fingers—manipulative appendages flared. "I'm Rhamnetin, and these are my brothers Astatine and Ytterbium—on behalf of the Rings and the crew of the *Solar Flare,* we're glad to be here."

Bakkalian took Rhamnetin's foot and shook it solemnly. Rhamnetin offered another to Goldsmith, who accepted after a bare moment's hesitation.

"And I'm Eliza Mendez, with Ambassador Wallach-Stevens's diplomatic team, for the Chesapeake Bay Watershed Network." I blinked at the promotion, but it made sense. If Cytosine could have childless people on her team, then I could too. Mendez took Rhamnetin's third proffered limb, and in the next few minutes that screenshot would be scanned for viruses and shared with every major feed in the world.

Then Rhamnetin's brothers had to shake limbs, and I introduced the remainder of the Network team, and it was all very convivial and content-free for a few minutes. My lenses scrolled analyses and suggestions. One thread warned that other watersheds, determined to have hands in the ground, were already negotiating air travel for their own representatives. Given that there were hundreds of watershed networks worldwide, that would overrun the old gathering constraints, not to mention everyone's carbon budgets, in about two minutes. Nor would it be fair to the more cautious watersheds, the ones still holding back from committing resources. I upvoted the suggestion to insist on single representatives from larger consortia, and added detail to the estimate of how many visitors the Bear Island ecology could actually handle. We'd need to loop those reps into the Chesapeake network, too, or else spin up a whole new network focused on extraterrestrial relations. The first option would be much faster, the second more equitable long-term. We might have to go for speed; this situation had considerably less inertia than any climate shift.

Eventually we settled on the broad rocks around the palace. Mendez brought out camp stools for the humans, while the Ringers draped over rocks in trailing spirals: three fuzzy galaxies arrayed on the cliff. A few yards away, the Potomac swirled between its banks. Patterns against my spine whispered healthy oxygen levels, nitrogen a little too high, the ongoing trace of outflow from the ship. My mesh told me to expect rain in about two hours. The river would rise, racing toward the Atlantic.

"So how does the United States of America relate to the Chesapeake Bay Watershed Network?" Rhamnetin asked. Right. Awkward questions.

Bakkalian smiled sweetly and said, "Technically, this is U.S. territory. A national park. We're sorry we didn't get here earlier to welcome you properly."

"The Chesapeake doesn't claim specific territory," I said. "We claim our actions. We take care of everything in the watershed, every place where the river acts." What happened next would depend on how the Ringers themselves defined power. Were they more likely to recognize a government built on laws, on paper-and-pixel boundaries? Or a network defined by measurable flows of matter and energy and obligation? At least corporate reps hadn't yet stuck their noses in to confuse the issue further.

The newcomers broke out a projection set apparently designed as an introduction to Earth, with convenient opportunities to compare points of reference. The set was thorough but old-fashioned, with distortions from translation through three or four generations of format. NASA must have birthed it in some ancient era of blue sky budgets, stored against the day when it'd be needed. Rhamnetin and his brothers jostled to answer questions about thermodynamics and how they represented the periodic table.

It was fascinating, but I kept thinking about Cytosine and her mates, refusing to deal directly with NASA because they'd come childless. Clearly the Rings had a place for people who couldn't nurse an infant. The spider boys were educated, and trusted to handle negotiations. And the Ringers *had* landed near what the U.S. was still pleased to call their capital city. A century and a half of broadcasts would have told them that mattered; only the last fifty would even mention the watershed networks. The gradual fading of real federal power was rarely reflected in entertainment, where agencies still provided a good excuse to convene an ensemble cast. What would Cytosine do if she found the old powers more amenable to her offer of rescue?

The NASA folks certainly considered this a chance at *something*. They talked up their government as a preeminent human power, mentioned other nation-states briefly, watersheds and corporations not at all. Bakkalian did everything but beat her chest to assert dominance over the other humans, even asking Mendez questions in a way that seemed to imply rank between them. If spiders looked for big apes (big bugs?) as instinctively as we did, they'd see one here.

I didn't want to push my way into that crest-waving contest, promotion or no promotion, but I drew Goldsmith aside. "What's NASA doing here? Even I know your bailiwick's space, not treaties. Are you here repping your whole government, or just Goddard?"

"Haven't you ever heard of science diplomacy? And it's your government too." He cocked his head ironically. "Or aren't you a U.S. citizen?"

There was only one right answer to that question. "Of course. I pay my taxes, the years the IRS is allowed to collect. But I pay for roads through the neighborhood network and transit through Amtrak and healers through the watershed."

"The U.S. founded Amtrak."

"And built the roads. But you don't do much with them these days. So all I want to know is, how'd NASA get picked to do *this*?" I was being harsh, but I could imagine what would happen if Cytosine's plans got caught in the internecine struggles of nation-states. Half their factions would support dragging humanity offworld just because the other half *didn't*. I needed to know how small and fractious a group this pair represented. And—maybe just a bit Machiavellian—I hoped the Ringers would overhear us, and get the idea that the NASA folks weren't all they claimed.

He shrugged easily. "Threats and opportunities from space are part of our mission statement."

"So you came on your own—without authority from Congress."

"Representing the United States government." His tone stayed even, but there was an edge to it. Agencies played constant games with conflicting laws and directives, often hoping for forgiveness when permissions stalled out. It had to be stressful. Weird as my current status was, I was glad the Chesapeake could give me authority simply by being *there* with me, immanent, backing and advising my actions.

"Our way works better," I said.

"We'll see." He nodded at Bakkalian, or at Rhamnetin.

Bakkalian waved at us, dignity broken by a childlike grin. "They have a *Dyson sphere*!"

"What?" demanded Goldsmith. The tension of our argument dropped like someone had cut off the power; he hurried to her side. "You're shitting me!"

The network threads burst into explanation before I could even ask. My first thought had been a geodesic dome, like Dinar used for winter tomatoes.

It's a structure, or a bunch of them, built around a star to capture all its energy. Hundreds of millions of times the surface area of a planet.

How many problem threads can we start at once? You'd have to deconstruct your whole solar system for the material to build one! The first humans who came up with the idea proposed breaking down Jupiter for parts.

I'd been hurrying after Goldsmith to see what the fuss was about. Now I stopped, breathed against nausea and the mental image of girders blotting out the stars.

They left their planets behind—and then did what with them?

Mendez looked queasy too; Diawara seemed as fascinated as the NASA pair.

"It's not *finished,* of course," Astatine said. "We've been working on it for almost—" He paused, shuffled legs. "Close to a thousand years. It'll probably take another three or four thousand to fill the orbit."

"Have you figured out how to make a shell stable?" asked Goldsmith. "Or is it more of a swarm?"

"It's thousands of separate structures," said Astatine. "Some of them are clustered, but we can boost or shift gravity when we need to reposition." Goldsmith nodded, an engineering expert's grimace of satisfaction.

"They're beautiful," added Rhamnetin. "You should see how they glitter in the sun. The habitats shine like jewels."

"What . . . what did you make them from?" Queasiness roughened my voice. I'd wanted the details that made them ache when they were away from home, and here they were.

Three-pupiled eyes blinked in my direction. "Right now we're mining our outermost planet for material. Our current outermost planet, I mean."

"Haven't worked your way down to your old homeworlds, then," I said, and Mendez glared at me.

Not that the gravitational eff▥▥◖†◉Ω◿◠◯❂⌗╗ ▼♥◙ ░░░
╬╠■│⅃≠━█▌◊∩←–△△△△≡

I flinched, tried a different thread and then databases, sensor feeds, and found more of the same—half-sentences trailing into incomprehensibility, even on older posts. My inbox wouldn't load, though the "Please try again in a few minutes" error message was readable. Mendez's glare devolved into an unfocused frown.

"Not just me?" I asked quietly, and she shook her head.

"Are you two losing threads?" asked Diawara. The NASA folks were looking at us oddly.

"My academic network is still up," said Mendez. "But people from other watersheds and some of the interest groups are reporting trouble too."

"Shit," I said. The worst of the malware epidemics had been decades ago, and the risk of open channels always seemed a bit abstract. But we'd been passing more information than usual these past few hours—and rich data too, not just text. "What about you lot?"

"The federal network is fine," said Goldsmith.

"It should also be pointed out," said Bakkalian, "that the federal network uses a completely different protocol, and has the bandwidth of a clogged pneumatic tube."

"Fine, like I said. Same slow and glitchy as always."

"Are you having trouble with your communications?" asked Rhamnetin. "We're not picking up any change."

"If you're still focused on the radio and television broadcasts, you're missing ninety percent of what we say," said Goldsmith. Of course the encrypted dandelion network signals weren't made to be picked up by anyone outside their specific protocols. If you didn't know they were there, you wouldn't find them.

I started to ask if the Ringers had anything we could use, realized that any comms system we didn't already have would be useless. I sent a text home instead, hoping the private messaging system was still up and that Carol might know more than we did. I tried the common board—found it still functional, but overloaded and slow. The plaintext messages were running minutes behind; nothing was getting through without a dozen layers of scans and metadata stripping.

Maybe the crash shouldn't have changed anything. The Ringers were right here; I still wanted to know what the hell they'd done with their solar system and what the hell they planned to do with ours. But with the network drained from my mesh, I felt naked and brainless. And even less qualified than before to represent the watershed, let alone the planet. *Shit. How many watersheds have their reps in the air right now?* But air travel, like rail, had its own hyperfirewalled network, and wouldn't casually open channels even today. Any reps en route would get here safely, but cut off from the threads that gave them authority, the webs of knowledge that let them ask the right questions and make the right decisions. And with the Chesapeake down, we wouldn't be able to integrate them into our own decisions.

No. We'd have everything back up and running by the time they got here. Wouldn't we? I was catastrophizing based on a few minutes of corrupted messages. I checked the network again, like scratching a mosquito bite, managed a few readable half sentences before everything devolved to nonsense again.

Redbug poked their head out of the tent. "Are you folks seeing this?"

"Everyone's seeing this," said Mendez. "Any word on a fix? Or a cause?"

"I'm on call this week for debugging malware." They ducked their head. "I'm supposed to organize—but there hasn't been an event this extreme in decades. I can't work from here. And I can't work from home—my household has text, but the whole neighborhood's out of power."

"Wait," said Rhamnetin. "Your communications are out so you *lost power*? Do you need us to send shuttles?"

Ytterbium shoved him, knee against knee. "It's a planet, you moron. Their life support's fine."

"But how did you lose power?" demanded Diawara.

"My neighborhood's full of programming experts, and some asshole was being clever with the firewall settings. I don't wanna hear how stupid that was, I want to know where I can get multiple screens and a functional grid so I can coordinate with the rest of the on-call team."

I texted home again. **Dinar, we still have power, right?**

This time I got a response right away. **Of course we have power. When's the last time you saw our windmill kites posting to a decision thread?**

Great. How many people can you feed on short notice? And how many species?

CHAPTER 6

The common house for the neighborhood was reserved for the aquaculture committee all afternoon. That was my excuse for inviting everyone to our place—even though they'd have cleared out in a minute if we asked. But at the common house the entire neighborhood would've dropped by to gawk. Redbug would probably have bitten someone, and I might have too.

Also, I was pretty sure Dinar had been waiting her entire life to host the first interspecies dinner party and hackathon on an hour's notice. After a few mediated texts between her and Rhamnetin and Xenon, we determined that the Ringers' augmented immune systems could handle most of what we might feed them—and once it was explained that we had kids, Cytosine actually agreed to join us.

That left the awkward question of transport. I didn't want to bring our guests through the gauntlet of the Metro system, not without being able to warn riders they were coming. And with the network in its current state, I couldn't arrange a private ride.

"How many people would your shuttles carry?" I asked Rhamnetin. Which is how I ended up squashed into a moss-lined oval pod with Redbug, two slightly rumpled NASA emissaries, and half the crew of the *Solar Flare*. Along with Cytosine and Rhamnetin, there were pillbug mates Glycine and Xenon and Rhamnetin's sisters Carnitine and Luciferin. And of course Cytosine's kids and Manganese, the spider cross-niece I'd met earlier. The thing was about half the size of a bus, with the same iridescent skin as the ship, and it *hovered*.

"You have *antigravity*!" exclaimed Goldsmith, and the Ringers spent the trip trying to explain the tech while I gave directions to Glycine, who'd never flown over a planetary surface before.

Dinar cooks extraordinarily well, and can pull together anything from a kid's birthday party to an end-of-harvest drink-and-screw shindig with perfect propriety. Which I supposed was why, despite my recommendation to keep our genders from the Ringers, she'd set a basket of pronoun badges on a table in the foyer, nestled prominently below the apple mint. They were the fancy set her parents had given us for housewarming, and as formal as you could get: the words calligraphed below the standard symbols just in case you didn't have all the icons memorized. Say, because you were from another planet. I glared at the pile and considered dropping a jacket on top, but knowing Dinar she'd simply pass them around later. I surrendered and slapped a She/Her on my chest to supplement the standard version pinned to my collar. Redbug and the others followed my lead.

Cytosine twisted one round eye at the basket. I wondered if I needed to explain the custom, but she plucked another She/Her for herself—I got it right!—and They/Thems for Diamond and Chlorophyll. Xenon took a He/Him. Glycine hesitated, then swiftly fixed a They/Them badge to their carapace.

"What are you doing?" demanded Xenon. "The kids we sired are still clinging to their mom. That's 'he' in English." He added something in their own language, presumably the equivalent pronoun.

"It doesn't have to be," I said. "Around here, pronouns aren't just about the role you play in breeding. Like I said before, not everyone even has kids."

Cytosine ignored me. "You're my mate."

"I am," agreed Glycine. "But I've carried before, too. I'm taking this one." They skittered out of the foyer, forestalling further argument.

Being on an alien ship had been weird. Having aliens in my dining room was weirder. They squeezed between table and sideboard, examining the yellow walls and hurricane lamp and watercolor landscape of the Anacostia with all the wonder such exotica deserved. Rhamnetin, excited, kept maybe four legs on the ground, the other six raised in as many directions toward whatever attracted his interest. I took Dori from a slightly frazzled Carol and introduced my household. Raven wiggled out of Athëo's lap to exclaim, "Baby play!" to Diamond and Chlorophyll, who wriggled in response until Cytosine released them to go have a cultural exchange over the duck train.

"Where should we set up?" asked Redbug.

Dinar grinned. "We've got a bunch of screens ready for you in the living room, and crickets and dip—your team can go right in when they get here. Let me know if you need anything else to get the world running again." She turned to Cytosine. "Thank you so much for coming. We're honored to have you and your family here. I hope you'll let me know if we're missing anything that makes for better hospitality in your culture."

I could see how much she'd done already. For starters, we normally had the screens set up in the dining room, and toyboxes in the living room. But this way Redbug could concentrate, and anyone hanging out at the table would have a great view of kids playing. The chairs were mostly in the living room too—obviously the Ringers couldn't sit in them, so we'd all stand around with our food potluck style—but a couple remained so that kids could have laps when they wanted them, and so I could nurse. She hadn't missed a beat with the parenting politics. That meant the badges were deliberate.

The bread Dinar had been kneading when I got up was baked now, sliced and steaming. She'd broken out a jar of caramel peach jam and the strawberry with real vanilla, along with the open mulberry and pawpaw. There were rounds of injera too, along with the European-style loaf, ready to wrap around chestnut salad and sweet potato stew. I smelled cinnamon and nutmeg and the sweet sting of ancho peppers.

A hairy leg dropped over my shoulder. I eeked, and Dori squawked in response.

"I'm sorry," said Rhamnetin. "I shouldn't have startled you."

I swayed, patting Dori's back. "It's okay. Dori, look, fuzzy fuzzy." Then I blushed, because that's probably not how you're supposed to describe an alien emissary, even one who's got your co-parent's jam all over his mouth-pincers. But Dori said, "Oooh" and patted him and then tried to grab a fistful of fur.

"Sorry," I said. "Dori, don't pull!"

"It's okay," said Rhamnetin. "She's so little. Do you all start out so small?"

"Smaller," I told him. "When she was born, she was about—" I stretched my hands to cradle an imagined newborn. "How big do your people start out?"

He lifted his foot about half a meter off the ground. "Manganese is growing fast." His foot swooped up. "But Diamond and Chlorophyll were almost as small as Dori. Plains-folk don't lay eggs—their babies stay inside them until they're ready to hatch."

"Eggs sound awfully convenient," I said, before wondering if that was too much of a giveaway that I was the one who'd borne Dori.

"The hatcheries take good care of them," he said. "But sisters have to visit frequently. Manganese left a bunch of pheromone samples in storage for her brother-eggs because we weren't sure how long we'd be here. But we'd never have done that if our mission weren't so important—it makes a difference when they come in person."

"That does sound less convenient," I said vaguely, overcome by the urgent desire for a Ringer reproductive biology text. "Speaking of convenience, what should we call your two species? I've heard you say first ring and second ring, and sisters and brothers, and plains-folk and tree-folk, but . . ."

"We call each other a lot of things. Mostly it's poetry, or early pidgin, when we were explaining ourselves with pictures and elemental tables. Hydrogen and oxygen, or tree and plain . . ." He offered the names in his own language, not so convenient for immediate conversation but I recorded them for reference.

"Tree-folk and plains-folk make sense. Humans are a little of both, really."

"That works. When you're meeting someone new, you have to build a commons." He fidgeted, then asked abruptly: "Do you have a bower?"

I tried to parse that. "I'm sorry, what?"

"A high, quiet place where we can talk."

"Oh." Some of what I saw on the ship slotted together: the tree-folk were arboreal, coming down to the dirt to work with the plains-folk. They were certainly built for it. "Our bedroom's upstairs, if you don't mind that it's messy." Athëo and Carol had probably made it worse while getting the common space into emergency guest-shape.

Rhamnetin handled stairs easily, leg over leg up the banister. I caught Carol's eye as I left; she nodded and returned to a conversation with Glycine and the NASA folks. I almost handed her Dori, like I would've if I wanted a quiet conversation with a human. But Rhamnetin would probably take it as an insult. Besides, she was getting wriggly and I suspected she could use a break from the crowd.

In our converted attic bedroom, I detangled her from the sling and laid her on a blanket. Carol had hashed together a crossbar with dangling baby toys: a stuffed bear, a little mirror, a striped ball. Dori batted them happily. I settled on the couch, and felt vaguely guilty for not having a giant cat tree. At least the tilted attic walls were painted with the silhouettes of branches and birds; "bower" wasn't a completely unreasonable description.

"Humans can see wavelengths from about 400 to 700 nanometers, right?" he asked. "Your signals cohere into images at those lengths; everything else just looks like noise."

I blinked; that wasn't one of the awkward questions I'd expected. "Yes, that's about right. There's some variation, of course. Why, what wavelengths do you see?" I was already thinking how to simulate their perceptions: shifting frequencies in or out of visibility, maybe translating the input from extra cameras into stimulation patterns on my back, like I had with the chemical readouts. "Do you see the same way with *all* your eyes?"

"Down to about 300, and up to 1,000. We spliced the high end into our genome a long time ago, when we needed to work in darker environments with the plains-folk. Only I've got one bad eye with a narrower range that won't take genemods." He bobbed a knee at me. On Earth, low-wavelength vision like Rhamnetin's natural range was an adaptation to better distinguish plants in daylight; infrared was for night hunting. He went on: "But *you* react to higher wavelengths."

"Oh. Yes, we have our own technology for seeing in ways that don't come naturally." I tapped the fine wirework mesh draped over my skull. "This can translate infrared or ultraviolet for my lenses, or create tactile representations of chemical structures. It's useful, but it's also something I do for fun." I managed to resist going into a geeky rant on the subject; Rhamnetin was obviously trying to get at something.

"So you could see the damage to the ship."

"I didn't imagine it, then!" I bit my lip. Admitting what I'd seen might not be the best idea—I was alone with a member of Cytosine's crew, and she clearly hadn't wanted me to know. I didn't think he'd try to hurt me, not when everyone knew we were up here, but that was human logic. And he might still threaten me, or use some unguessed technique to make me forget what I'd seen. But since I'd already admitted it—"Why didn't you want us to know? Maybe we can help."

"After the way you reacted that first conversation, we thought you might like our ship better broken. But I hope"—he swirled a leg to gesture at the room around us—"you at least understand wanting to go home. Even if you don't understand why our home is a good one."

"I've got no objection to your home. Unless—before the network started acting up, you were talking about your Dyson sphere. If you want to break down *our* solar system for parts, that *will* be a problem."

One that would be neatly solved, if they couldn't get back in touch with their homeworld. Maybe Cytosine had been right to worry.

"There's still plenty of room in ours. But *couldn't* you use more room here? And you can't be attached to your gas giants the way you are to this world's ungovernable ecology. They're completely uninhabited."

"First of all, there are bacteria on Io. That counts as an ecology. And second, beauty is worth preserving whether it's alive or not. You ought to take a closer look before deciding that a bunch of—of space stations—are a good replacement for mountains and canyons and rivers. Or Saturn's rings, or Jupiter's thousand-year storms. We can manage with the room we've got. We fucked things up for a few centuries, but we're finally starting to get it right, and all that work is worth preserving too. We've done things *you* said were impossible, while you've been busy caging your sun." I was breathing too hard, and Dori whimpered anxiously. I picked her up, tried to pull myself back to some semblance of diplomacy. "Won't your people come looking for you, if you disappear?"

"Yes, of course." Rhamnetin brushed the ceiling with two legs. After a moment I realized that he was reaching for something to grab—a branch, a bar, whatever "up" a tree-dwelling species would go for when they were nervous. "No, they won't. If we never tunnel back, the protocol is to assume some unknown danger. After all the species we've found that destroyed themselves, we've speculated about falls spectacular enough to make the whole system deadly, or even contagious. One of our attempted contacts came close. They found a way to pull in comets—we think with the goal of mining resources, or replacing the water they'd spoiled. But they pulled too hard, and one smashed into their biggest continent. Primitive gravity manipulation is a terrible idea planetside; their whole orbit was full of debris and miniature singularities. The ship barely got out." He pulled his legs back down, bracing one against the wall. "This is the first time I've heard of a tunnel engine breaking down on its own without warning. Astatine swears it's not anything about this system— everything breaks *sometimes,* no matter how well engineered—but that's not what they'll bet on at home. We need to set up the ansible antenna and tell them what happened. Otherwise they'll mark Earth as a hazard, mourn, and move on." He crouched low. "Which sounds like what you want. But I beg you. We have family at home, sibs and cousins and friends and colleagues who'll miss us. If Manganese can't go home, her brothers will never hatch. My sisters will never be able to lay more clutches. And your species *has* survived. People should know, and celebrate. The loss of those dead worlds is a blow every time—we grieve for everything they could have been, what we and they would have gained from our symbiosis. Would you put our five trillion in mourning, rather than meet them?"

I shivered. "I don't want to, no. But you're threatening everything *we've* done to survive. You were horrified that we might not want what you're offering. When we keep saying no, what will you do? If it's a choice between keeping you from your home and meeting your people, we'd be glad to *meet* them. If it's a choice between us keeping you from your home, and you forcing us from ours, then I'm sorry. We're not that selfless."

So many things I didn't say. It wouldn't only be up to the watersheds, especially with our networks crashing. NASA might think the best course for humanity *was* to leave Earth, or that it was a chance to regain their lost power. Any corporation could offer the Ringers space to build an antenna on one of their sovereign aislands, and probably would in exchange for first crack at mining the outer planets—and at using the Ringers to regain *their* former power. If the watersheds refused to help at all, we could lose the very progress I was trying to preserve.

And the antenna—why did they even need our approval? It had to be big, impossible to hide from sensors. And it had to be fragile, something humans could break even with a thousand years of tech separating us.

"It's not only for our sake," said Rhamnetin. "We're . . ." He paused. "Joyous. That you've survived to meet us is a wonder, and the most important thing that's happened since the Rings met. But it doesn't mean you're doing everything right. You're the closest world we've visited, and your signals were younger when we found them, and we got to you faster. You still *need* us. We have the map for how to survive not only the pollutants you struggle with now, but the dangers that come with every next step for a thousand years. Carbon dioxide and methane release aren't the last or worst threats you'll encounter. Let us help you."

"Let you help, gladly," I said. "But we can't let you decide alone what form that help takes." I sighed, remembering lessons before the carbon negotiations: always make sure you *know* what people are asking for. "Tell me what you need for your antenna, and then we can talk about terms." Better to have them work with us than have NASA or the corporations take over the contact—though the cost of missing some key point in a treaty was terrifying. Assuming the Ringers, unlike all too many humans historically, were inclined to keep treaties.

Rhamnetin rose at the opening. "Setting up the antenna will take about two weeks. It has a lot of delicate parts, and much of it is built from local carbon—we'd actually draw it out of your atmosphere, if that helps."

Footsteps echoed up the stairs. Redbug poked their head around the corner of the well. "Sorry to bother you, but all the Network folks we can get need to check in *now*."

CHAPTER 7

Back in the dining room, Athëo and Luciferin curled around a tablet; Athëo was playing back a recording of Ringer speech. "Right, and the difference between those two cases means what exactly?" He sounded cheerfully frustrated, like he always did in the thick of a new language. Cytosine was talking with Dinar while the toddlers arranged blocks. The NASA reps huddled around the pawpaw jam. Rhamnetin broke off in their direction, and I fretted as I followed Redbug into the living room.

"I don't care what's going on," I said. "My input's against leaving the Ringers alone with the NASA reps. At least let Dinar keep Cytosine distracted, and we can catch her up later." I'd have preferred someone on Rhamnetin as well—whatever his official rank, he seemed to get stuck with all the most awkward and important conversations.

I tried again to access the Chesapeake feed. Just like the previous fifty times, text came through briefly before dissolving into gibberish. No hint of anything higher-bandwidth, no video or graphics or sensor readings. No sign that the weighting and aggregation algorithms were doing anything with that text or the sensor readings embedded across the watershed, let alone their usual seamless job of integrating human and ecosystem input to guide our decisions. Surrounded by people, the missing connection made me feel isolated and helpless. Goldsmith and Bakkalian might be hamstrung by the limits of their permissions and authorities, but within those bounds they could operate alone. Dandelion networks, though, were living things, as dependent on the flow of information as I was on breath and pulse. Cut off that flow and we devolved into sputtering, isolated neurons.

Normally, this type of collapse was next to impossible. Backups and firewalls stood fast, filtering hazards when we relaxed our cautious constraints on cross-network interaction. Even with the last day's promiscuous connections, this should never have happened.

"No, it shouldn't," said Redbug when I said as much. Their team spread around the living room, nine out of the dozen who'd been on call, and an assortment of equipment ranging from tablets to a standalone simulation engine modded out of all hope of network compatibility. Screens shone on every clear patch of floor and wall: three showed the garbage currently infesting the networks, three more showed source code, and one showed the still-readable text chat in the shared board. "This isn't random opportunistic malware. It has to be deliberate sabotage."

"Of the negotiations?" I felt queasy.

"As a starting point," said one of the tech experts. "We haven't been able to trace everything yet, but it looks like it targets the core aggregation and preference algorithms used by every dandelion protocol network, and by basically no one else. Nation-states use older protocols, and the corporate networks evolved in completely different directions."

"I still think it goes after the threading code," argued another team member. They scrolled through one of the programming screens, and pointed at something I could barely recognize as a few lines of SEED. "The algorithm corruption is just a side effect."

Redbug quelled the incipient argument. "Either way, the point is that someone looked at an alien spaceship landing, and saw a great opportunity to undermine the watersheds."

"Or a reason to attack us," Diawara said.

The conversation from that point divided into an argument over who might have created the virus (a nation-state trying to take over the negotiations, corporations trying to break the limits on their powers, one of the radical anti-algorithm groups that demand "pure democracy") and an argument over how to respond (restart and pray, hard shutdown while we sorted out the code, and five possible fixes way beyond my technical understanding). I hoped quietly that it *wasn't* NASA, so far ahead of the other non-network groups in both guts and response time. I liked them in spite of everything—would they consider this necessary? What options would I have upvoted, if some state military had scooped us at Bear Island?

And who would feel backed into this kind of desperation already? Not NASA—they had better and cleaner options. It had to be someone who'd hated us already. Someone who'd had resources in waiting, and needed only this push to use them.

I tried to ignore the persistent sense that arguing this stuff out in our living room, with a handful of co-present colleagues, was *wrong*. Even taking into account the people we could reach through the shared board, and the slightly dubious feedback from the patchwork simulation engine, it didn't seem right to make decisions of this magnitude in analog. It wasn't even just that we were leaving out millions—billions if we stretched to other watersheds—of people with a stake in our decisions. Trying to keep all our ideas organized without real threading, without the algorithms constantly picking out key ideas and sorting possible approaches and marking the valence and weight of our responses, felt like analyzing river chemistry by drinking a glass of water.

On the practical side, the Chesapeake tech team settled on a graded restart, where they'd bring an earlier version of the network (much earlier, given the uncertainty about how long ago this thing had been planted) online, and gradually iterate from the hopefully-still-functional backups, combing each one until they were sure it was safe. The other watersheds we could reach on the shared board were doing the same. We'd almost certainly lose the first day's threads on how to handle the Ringers, not to mention a huge batch of air and water quality data—but at least we'd be back on track. Assuming it worked.

On the culprit-identification side, we didn't get anywhere beyond educated guesses. Hopefully the team would find fingerprints while combing the code. Then we'd have to ID whoever left them, and stop them from doing it again.

The non-tech-experts drifted back into the dining room and kitchen, both more crowded than they'd been earlier. Neighbors had caught word either that the Ringers were here, or that we were a hub for Network repair. Most watersheds had apparently rethought in-person travel in the face of the network instability, but emissaries had arrived from the Ghats-Narmada and the Mississippi. Dinar had welcomed them all, and now Mendez gathered the watershed reps to negotiate policy. Options were scribbled on paper, pebbles stood in for upvotes, eyeball intuition replaced algorithms as we counted votes and drew charts to integrate expert input. One newcomer caught my attention: alone of all those who'd arrived so far, they'd brought a kid.

I made my way around the table. Bakkalian and Goldsmith were introducing the pale, dark-haired visitor to Rhamnetin, and Cytosine had come over as well.

"Viola St. Julien," she said, shaking my hand around the tight-snugged infant. She'd taken a badge, placed high on her shoulder away from the wrap. She stifled a yawn. "And this is Brice. I'm with

NASA's science diplomacy corps, heading up our embassy to the Rings. My apologies for not coming earlier—I was on leave." She smiled ironically, acknowledgment that her leadership probably followed the same logic mine did. Brice wasn't much past cat-sized, and St. Julien's makeup didn't quite disguise the shadows under her eyes. I was impressed anew by how quickly the agency had changed up their plan. Nation-states had a reputation as slow, ponderous creatures, kaiju as likely to trample you from inertia as malice. The watershed networks had grown like dandelions through the cracks in their actions. The truth, at least here, seemed more complicated.

Raven and the two Ringer toddlers joined us, diverted by the promise of someone even smaller than them. (Could I call them *toddlers*? They seemed about Raven's level mentally, but with a dozen legs walking couldn't be much of a challenge.)

"Baby!" announced Raven, and Diamond and Chlorophyll climbed on Cytosine to get a better look. She wrapped a limb around each and held them up for a better look. "Baby!" they screaked in unison before chittering at their mom.

"They want to know if Brice can come down and play," said Cytosine. "But I think they may be too young?"

"Definitely." St. Julien rubbed Brice's back, producing a burp and a startled look. "They're a month old tomorrow."

"Congratulations," said Cytosine. "May you have many mates."

St. Julien opened her mouth, closed it, and after a moment her eyes crinkled with amusement. "Thank you. I'll tell my family you said so. And congratulations on yours, if that's appropriate at this late date."

"I'll grant it," said Cytosine. "You didn't have an opportunity when they were born."

"We have a great deal to make up for," St. Julien agreed. "I think the crowd is making them fussy—why don't we go out on the porch, and you can tell me all about your mission here while I walk her. Do yours keep you moving constantly when they're little, the way ours do?"

Cytosine returned her kids to their usual spot on her belly, and curled around them. She made a full circle this time, tail tucked over head and limbs flattened against her carapace, and rolled across the rug. "Like that, for about half a cycle."

"Now I know how you got everyone into space so quickly." St. Julien laughed, shaking her head. "No vertigo." The two of them—five of them—went outside chatting, while I marveled at how easily she'd used the kids to get Cytosine to herself.

Eventually it got late, and most of the humans drifted off to their homes or to the neighborhood common-house bunks. The Ringers, similarly diurnal or picking up on the social cues, returned to their ship. The tech team seemed to be planning an all-nighter, and no one complained. Dinar drew a curtain across the living room, muting their stream of conversation, swearing, and general coding-related mutters. Somehow—I suspected the food had something to do with it—we all agreed to keep meeting here, rather than at Bear Island or the common house, until connectivity was restored.

The whole household was on the same shift now, which was going to suck for the next 2 a.m. feeding. We gathered up plates and bowls and offered them to Kyo for his enthusiastic prewash. I stayed to help Dinar with the dishes; I wanted to talk.

But I felt anxious. It was barely a year since Carol and I first met Dinar and Athëo, assured by our mutual shadchan that we had compatible parenting and negotiation styles, and complementary skills and interests, and that we'd like each other well enough to run a household together. All that was true. But it was also true that we'd been in a rush, that we still didn't know each other as well as if we'd courted before the constant scrambling fatigue of childcare—and that outside of child-rearing, sometimes even within it, I didn't have a sense of which way they'd jump on judgment calls. It was easier by far to trust the network, where everyone's mistakes would cancel each other out, than to negotiate decisions in my own household.

"You did an amazing job," I told her first. "Sorry to dump everything on you last minute, but . . ."

"You thought I'd be into it." She grinned. "I was. And they seem like nice people. A little squirmy, but they like kids. And peanut stew." She considered this while she pushed bowls through the sonic. "And not in the same way."

The sonic hummed, dislodging food particles from the stoneware and dropping them into the compost collector. I rinsed and scrubbed to get the last bits off, then stacked everything in the sterilizer. "They're kind of weird about gender, though."

She stopped feeding the flow of dishes, and looked at me square on. "You want to know why I put out the badges."

"I know why you put them out," I said. "I know how much Athëo cares about being recognized as a man. I just think that under these circumstances, being a little vague about our genders could've avoided some serious risks. The Ringers are already paternalistic—totally the wrong etymology, fuck English—toward humanity. We know that to the degree that their genders are anything like ours, they're matriarchal. Cytosine made a huge deal about asking who'd actually been pregnant with Dori, and I made a huge deal about not telling her, and I have no idea how she'd react to learning that Athëo gestated Raven. From what she said to Glycine it's probably a serious social breach." I stopped, took a deep breath. "How we handle the next few days may literally decide the fate of the planet, and I didn't want to give the Ringers more reason to doubt human judgment than they already have."

Dinar began working the sonic again, setting down plates harder than strictly necessary. "First, you don't know, not really. Carol had a normal childhood, and normal parents who had a back-up name ready when she told them she was a girl and handled it like sensible people. She's barely had more trouble being female than you or me. You *can't* get how different it was for Athëo; Carol barely does. His parents might as well be time travelers. That damn technophobic cult." Her voice filled with quiet fury, as it always did when she discussed Athëo's family. I didn't blame her. Athëo's suspicion of any sort of religion was entirely understandable, which didn't stop it from being a major source of tension for the household. "He had to *fight* to be seen. And when he isn't, when people get it wrong—it mostly hasn't happened in front of you because most people aren't assholes, but sometimes he can barely talk afterward." She paused. "I'm telling you this because he hates to talk about it, and he shouldn't have to. Don't bring it up with him."

"Okay," I said, shaken by her anger, and the fact that I *hadn't* realized how badly my recommendation would hit Athëo. It was the sort of thing I'd worried about from the first: his scars from not being able to take civilization for granted, and whether he'd be able to share with his kids the things his own childhood lacked.

Dinar went on. "After Raven was born, in the hospital. He hadn't started testosterone yet, of course. Most trans men never go through the wrong puberty these days, and they weren't used to dealing with it in the maternity ward. We wrote up directives, a big sign, everything, but the doctors kept misgendering him. And he tried to kill himself when Raven was two days old."

I hadn't had a clue. "I'm sorry, I didn't mean to—"

"I know you didn't. But you need to know how much these things matter for him, and he's not the only one. Frankly, you grew up in a good area, with good parents, and I think prejudice is maybe a bit abstract to you."

"Dinar, I may not have grown up with Purists, but there were kids who drew swastikas on my palette to get a rise out of me. People cornered me on the playground to tell me I was going to hell." And my parents, bless them, had always had strong opinions about how I ought to handle that. None of which had ever involved *avoiding* conflict. It would be nice, sometimes. "Maybe someday humans will grow out of that stuff entirely, but it hasn't happened yet."

She slapped the counter, fabric-muffled metal thumping against marble. "Then why are you so ready to bow to someone else's prejudices? Isn't it bad enough that *human* bigotry still shapes what we can do safely? These people aren't our overlords, they haven't conquered us—why should we twist ourselves to make them comfortable? They aren't hiding the things that make *us* uncomfortable! If we want to be their equals, we have to act like it. Make them take us on *our* terms, and do our best to take them on theirs. That's the only way it's going to work, and that's why I put out badges and made sure they saw all of us holding the kids, and didn't apologize for it." A handful of silverware clanged into the sonic.

"I—maybe you're right," I said. "I don't want to just conform to their beliefs. But there have to be priorities. For me, the most important place to hold fast is convincing them that *Earth* is worth keeping. I had a big argument with Rhamnetin upstairs. He's the most open-minded of the lot, but even he thinks we should leave our planet behind. And they probably have the power to make us do it. We have too many examples of human cultures pushing others from their homes by force. The fact that they'd be exiling us with supposed charity instead of genocidal malice—I don't think that would make much difference to the outcome."

"And the Native Americans and First Nations and Australian aboriginals, did any of them get to keep their land by acting white? They converted, changed how they dressed, even changed how they treated gender. Did *we* ever get anywhere by acting more Christian, or by trying to fit into the boxes they built for us? We survive by being stubborn about who we are, whatever else happens."

I sighed. "I wasn't suggesting we hold off for long. Just a few days to figure out what assumptions we're crashing into."

"Well, now we know. They don't all like their assigned genders either, and they think motherhood is a sign of leadership potential. Which isn't the dumbest thing anyone's ever come up with, I might add."

"I think it might actually be true for the pillbugs," I said. "The plains-folk. Any of them can get pregnant if they convince other people to help out, and then those people are supposed to follow them around. It's why Cytosine is in charge, if I've followed their explanations."

"We'll go with it for now. There, that's the last glass! I understand why you worry—but I think the best way to make them accept our weird planet-based lifestyle is to make them accept *us*. As is."

I hesitated over the glassware. Should I even bring it up? But demonstrably, my own solo judgment was far from balanced. "We might have a nastier option." I told her about the antenna.

She was quiet for a while. "Even if we *could* stop it, that'd make us shitty hosts."

"Suppose the Wampanoags could've made sure the *Mayflower* was the last European ship to show up?"

"They would have needed either really excellent foresight algorithms, or an incredibly callous attitude. And this *doesn't* need to be that bad, if only because the odds of plague seem lower. If we have the chance for a *good* relationship with our neighbors, I think that beats having no relationship. And it's worth the risk of a bad one."

My insomnia had a fun time with that one. I spent half the night trying to figure out how you'd calculate that trade-off, and whether Dinar was right or just kind.

INTERLUDE 1
SCANNING THE NETWORKS

March 6, 5 p.m.: Viola St. Julien took the call in a near-whisper, trying not to wake Brice. "David, you know I'm on parental leave, right? I don't mind getting pulled in, but if this is a real emergency maybe you want to call someone who slept last night?" She cursed herself quietly, but at least her unmasked irritation illustrated the point. What the hell was her boss thinking?

On the video, he ran his hand through thinning hair. She considered turning on her own pickup by way of further illustration. If he kept pushing, it might be worth showing off her stained nursing bra.

"Viola, I'm not kidding. The fate of the world literally depends on pulling someone with negotiation chops off parental leave."

"The fate of the world doesn't depend on NASA doing anything." Exhaustion made her blunt. "Hasn't in decades."

"Maybe we can change that. Tell me, have you been on the common feed anytime in the last twenty-four hours?"

"I haven't been on the common feed in two weeks. The news of the world can take care of itself until Brice starts sleeping through the night. I've been binge-watching all the Star Trek series in order. I'm halfway through *Quest of the Surak,* and I have really strong opinions about what species you can reasonably bunk together."

"You know what? That may be just as relevant. Check your feed. I'll wait."

Ten minutes later Viola handed a yawning Brice to her husband. "Check your feed, wash her, and make me coffee while I shower. The kid and I have an appointment with some aliens."

March 7, 4 a.m.: Carol Wallach-Stevens cracked her eyelids, muzzily aware that something needed attention. These bursts of late-night consciousness felt like one of Judy's sensory enhancements: a mental radar scan, a convenient program that would run through all possible needs before dropping her back into slumber. Dori? No, reassuring baby wheeze-snores still came from the bassinet. Judy? Her wife lay still, but that didn't mean much. The scan went on to the dog (fine), the house (silent save for the usual creaking floorboards), and her own body (a little achier than usual) while she rolled over to check Judy's sleep monitor. The swift lines of beta waves showed that she was in fact awake, staring quietly into the darkness.

Carol rolled back the other way, laid her arm across Judy's chest. "Time to lock up the hamster wheel, hon."

Judy buried her forehead beneath Carol's chin. "Sorry, I didn't mean to wake you."

"Shh, it's okay. Ridiculous things are happening in our living room, but you're not going to solve anything tonight. Get some rest, and let your backbrain work on it."

Judy snuggled in, murmuring. Her breath seemed to even out, but of course now Carol couldn't check the sleep monitor again. She smelled her wife's hair and let herself drift back down. Her own brain toyed idly with the problems that fed Judy's insomnia. *I really met them. They're really here. They speak our language so well, but how do we know we're really understanding each other?* The modulation of radio waves, the loss of signal over even a few miles. The Ringers had to have been looking so hard, must have signals technology as impressive as their ship itself to reconstruct the degradation of light-years. But radio was simple and sturdy by comparison to so many more advanced technologies—one of the things that drew her to it in the first place.

I need to talk to their engineers. I need to know what they use when they're at home, what they sing to each other. She slid back into sleep, still picking over the pattern of the sweater swarm, what it meant to communicate well enough that people heard what you were really saying, and what she could do to make it happen.

March 7, 6:30 a.m.: Rhamnetin woke with the turning of the land toward its star. He wanted to understand how planet-bound life shaped the humans, but these short rotations were hard even with his own biochemistry modified to match. It was one thing to make sure the right chemicals told his nerves to sleep when the locals turned off their lights, and wake when their star paled the atmosphere. It was another to disentangle leg from vine when a lifetime of habit said the sky should still be dark. He swung around the sleeping forms of his brothers, plucking sweet fruit for breakfast, and dropped beside Glycine. He nudged his cross-brother (cross-sib?), who he knew would go right back to sleep after the ritual.

"Hsst, Glycine, I need to go out."

Glycine scrunched tighter, eyes curled in. "Ge'back in a tree."

"I'm awake. Please?"

Glycine grumbled open. "All right, I'm here. Some symbiote you are."

Rhamnetin crouched and grasped Glycine's limbtips. His manipulators tingled with the touch; the plains-person was too tired for more detailed skinsong. "How do you think we'll change the ritual when there are three of us?"

Glycine rubbed an eye against his belly. "I have no idea, but I hope one of the first things humans learn from us is how to appreciate days with a decent length. The Gift is found when we reach, trusting that we will find."

"We waited, and did not know that we were waiting."

"Together, the cycle is open to us."

"Only together can we reach again, and grasp what we find. Thank you, Glycine."

Glycine rolled up, pointedly, though he did release an encouraging if minimally semantic hum. Rhamnetin stroked his back, and let him go back to sleep. He let himself out of the ship next to the river, away from prying senses both human and Ringer.

The water rushed by, swollen from the previous day's precipitation. In the Rings, rivers were beautiful but docile. Regular floods, planned each cycle, fertilized forests and fields. They didn't rise unexpectedly. This one twisted against rock and tree, spilling over miniature precipices and breaking into white spray against the cliff. The result was beautiful and disturbing. Judy had sensors to mark the changes, he knew, but there was no one who could turn the river off at its source if things got out of control.

The humans felt the same way: superficially similar to people he knew, but unpredictable. They might be as hazardous as a miscalibrated river. It was exciting. *They're nothing but dangerous questions.*

Cytosine might fear that rushing risk, but she feared losing them even more. Rhamnetin couldn't blame her. A thousand years of anticipation lay behind this mission, the first beyond their home system with even a chance of succeeding. The Second Reach—maybe. Failure would mean a greater loss than all four Fallen Worlds put together. To arrive too late deserved mourning. To reach out, only to watch a world refuse your grasp and plummet into their gravity well . . .

And how many people had considered what would happen if they *did* succeed? There had been two Rings, two symbiotic species, since the plains-folk first touched their neighboring world. A third would change everything—the morning ritual the least of it. Cytosine doubtless imagined new scientific insights as humans explored the Rings' technology and reflected it back transformed. Anticipating more profound transformations, though, was Rhamnetin's job.

Whirlpools rolled against the island, changing its shape from moment to moment. If humans accepted symbiosis, how would that affect the way the Rings saw the universe? As the Third Ring, how would they change the way the first two saw each other?

And how could a thoughtful asker make sure those changes were the ones the Rings needed?

March 7, 10:20 a.m. (Australian Eastern Time, Zealand Artificial Island): Adrien dove into the wardrobe, dragging options onto the bed. Kay watched thon with amusement from the upper bunk. "Associate Mallory's got you in a twist."

"Associate Mallory *and* Associate Kelsey. Be at the copter pad at 11, they told me. Pack for an auction, with travel to follow if we win. And"—Adrien paused to inhale before continuing the rant—"don't stop to read the common feed until you're on your way. Afraid I'll get distracted. If they think I can't hold a thought, why are they bringing me? And what do I *pack*? I wish they'd explain themselves; I'm not just a captive audience for their cryptic memos."

By then tha'd laid out dozens of options: tuxes and velvets, prom dresses and thigh-high boots, leather suit jacket and pants. These last, far beyond an intern's salary, had been supervisory hope-gifts at the start of thos internship—would the associates appreciate seeing them in use? Or would they suggest unearned arrogance?

Kay rolled seir eyes. Sie made a gorgeously sarcastic femme, and Adrien took a moment to appreciate the effect. Sie sighed in exaggerated impatience. "First, pick a presentation for the auction, and get dressed, and pack changes for whatever you've picked. You've got about twenty-five minutes to pack before you have to leave; if you can finish dithering over presentation in five, I'll read you from the common feed while you fill your bag."

"But they said—"

"Not to stop to read it. And not to get distracted. If you stop packing, I'll stop reading."

"Done." They shook hands, and Adrien considered the leathers again. Maybe tha should save those for after Asterion won the auction. "I've been playing princess at the office all week. Normally that would be okay for an auction, but this feels really big. And there'll be other interns all over the place. Do you think I could get away with butch?"

"Mmm. *I* might get distracted, but okay. You dress, I'll read."

By the time hie'd gotten changed, Adrien knew it hadn't been any lack of trust in hes attention span. Hie tried to concentrate on the practicalities: North America in the growing warmth of spring, trade talks with stakes like nothing in history. Hie packed a larger rollbag with the most flamboyant presentations hie could construct from hes scanty wardrobe. Hie needed to communicate *I am in the service of great power and wealth* to people who wouldn't recognize any but the most blatant messages. And hie needed—this was the best opportunity hie'd get in hes life—to convince hes bosses, and their bosses, that hie was strong enough and skilled enough to serve that power at a higher level.

CHAPTER 8

By morning the whole neighborhood knew about the Ringers, and the streets broke into festival. Our little local network's coverage was almost as ragged as the Chesapeake, and no one wanted to risk the grid by piggybacking communication on the power distribution algorithms. But the bike carts circulated messages along with anchovies and cheese and pastries, and to step out onto the walk was to learn which porches were hosting concerts, who'd thrown open their kitchens, and the route and timing of the parade. Before the network crashed, we'd been searching millennia of painting and theater and song for the very best to show the Ringers. Maybe this was better. *A Doll's House,* or a Kevin Koto picture, or even the oldest oral traditions mapping ancient flood and upheaval, could surely be reproduced on a space station somewhere. But festival art, intimate and ephemeral, grew rooted.

I tied my sunset-streaked parade scarf around my waist and went outside to meet the shuttle with Carol and Dori. It settled onto the street without any consideration for gravity, like a floating magnet toy pressed down by a child's finger.

"Would your kids like to see the festival?" I asked, and so Carol and I managed to lead Cytosine away before NASA or anyone else got a hold of her.

Colorful flags twined streetlights and windmill stakes. This week's work crews were still hanging final touches. Dangling from mulberry and catalpa and holly and sycamore, bells chimed their chorus in the cool breeze. Children waved pinwheels and chased ribbon-drones down the street. Kyo strained at the leash for every smell and sound.

Carol sniffed. "I smell fried dough," she declared. "This way."

"You're more focused than Kyo," I teased. "You only track pastry."

"What better use for natural selection? Or enhancement—I could make you a sensor that picked up volatiles from deep fryers and chocolate, and a belt that vibrated in whatever direction the treat was. Ooh, caught one!" Temporarily distracted from the fried dough hunt, she pounced on a beetle-shaped puzzlebot.

"What is it?" asked Cytosine.

"See, there's a code inside. This one is visual—you need to figure out how these pieces fit together, and when you do the bot will modify itself. By the end of the day it'll combine with all the others, and if people have solved enough of them they'll perform some sort of dance, or a light show."

I watched Cytosine try to help Carol with the puzzle, worrying at the source of my unease. The obvious issue was the crashed network. Normally the neighborhood offered layers to be read: auras of discussion and commentary and history. I could dive into upcoming repairs, stories behind flags, whether trees were blooming early or late. I'd feed in my own observations and judgments, too. Without that interaction, the world felt oddly shallow. And the easy logistics of a well-run neighborhood, dependent on that feedback, could break down quickly. Would everyone stay on their current task rotations indefinitely? How would we handle resource distribution?

Beyond that, there were normally two reasons to hold an unscheduled festival. The first was after a big storm: as a celebration of resilience, a kickoff for rebuilding, and the first growth of defiance and determination out of wind-borne mud. The second cause was less common: a welcome party for an influx of refugees. Watersheds competed to take in communities whose own lands fell to rising waters, to integrate the skills needed for everyone's survival. Welcome banners from past parties hung among today's flags, in all the languages of the people who'd joined us. Nothing in the Ringers' unknown tongue, of course.

Today's festival hovered in the misty gap between possibilities. We might be welcoming eagerly awaited neighbors. Or we might be defying disaster.

Carol and Cytosine solved the bot, sliding the last piece into place despite the Ringer kids' constant poking. The beetle unfolded itself and transformed into a blue crab. It scuttled sideways, shell sparkling, and clicked its claws before running off toward whatever location its newly released program directed.

"What are Ringer celebrations like?" I asked Cytosine. I wanted a deeper answer to what home meant, if it wasn't soil and air and the mysteries of a planetary core. Carol led us onward in the quest for pastry.

"They're all different," she said. "Some are like this, just for one habitat, and others are old holidays from before the Rings came together. I like the big celebrations best, the ones that connect everybody." Diamond chittered, and she said, "Yes, Meeting Day is their favorite. And mine. We have light shows big enough to be seen across all the Rings, and pageants re-creating the moment of contact, and feasts with contributions from every habitat. You're supposed to try and eat something from everywhere, to remember how we're all bound together—but it's hard to fit it all in! We count it a triumph if your whole family manages the task together."

I laughed. "I guess food's an important way to celebrate no matter where you're from. We don't try for dishes from the whole planet, but you'll see—we usually have contributions from all the cultures in the neighborhood. Jewish and Piscataway and Salvadoran and Ethiopian . . ." I trailed off, doubting I could do justice to the full palimpsest laid down by old wars and new floods.

"How do you track them all?" Carol asked Cytosine. "A Dyson sphere sounds . . . big." I saw her point: either they'd managed to make a monoculture out of hundreds of Earths, or a feast like Cytosine described would be a tsunami of information worse than anything from the brief, blighted bloom of the World Wide Web.

"There are many mothers," said Cytosine.

At which point we found the pastry cart and the fried dough, and set about introducing her to our own delicacies. I wished we could carry out the whole negotiation through food. It wasn't just that everything seemed simpler with Diamond and Chlorophyll sticky with honey, as Dinar's jam had painted Rhamnetin a sensible visitor to our dining room. It made our systems tangible. I chatted with the cartminder (his name was Yeslin) about the wheat grown outside the city, honey from wildflowers, the balance between local sources and imported sugar and vanilla. A functional network could've sketched maps across my lenses: trade routes and carbon mitigation and labor badges glowing reassuringly green for every ingredient. If I could sample Cytosine's Meeting Day feast, surely I'd understand how they lived, how the complexity of their survival was represented in each dish.

Afterward I led us toward a little park with a good view of the parade route. We paused at porch concerts, where neighbors crowded Cytosine with welcomes and questions. They'd given us breathing room, this past day, but felt more free in their own spaces. Our arrival put the fiddle choir at our first stop off-key, but at our second the old-fashioned hip-hop group went into a splendid freestyle riff, including a passable imitation of Ringer speech mixed into their usual English and Xhosa. Cytosine bounced with the beat and warbled amusement.

We could eat together. We could dance together. We just couldn't agree on where it should be done.

The park was a popular place to watch the parade—not least because someone had unfolded trampolines beside the permanent jungle gym. Several kids and a few adults kept themselves enthusiastically occupied while they waited. Amid a cluster of non-bouncing adults, I caught sight of Rhamnetin and St. Julien, along with Carnitine. Sometime in the past day, I'd figured out how to tell them apart, though I had no idea what distinctions I was picking up. Manganese was making a tentative foray onto the smallest and lowest of the trampolines, human kids giggling as they tried to help.

"Will she be okay?" I asked as we came up. "You look like you're built for leaps, but—" But Manganese was all gangly limbs, and I couldn't help thinking her fragile.

"She'll be fine," said Carnitine. "She's been practicing with your trees."

"They're too far apart," added Rhamnetin reproachfully.

"I'm sorry," I said. "Humans still climb trees sometimes, but we're not really evolved to move between them."

"The Tarzan movies aren't realistic, then?"

"You're going to need to show us some of your stories," I said. "You've got an unfair head start. And performances, competitions—have you seen our acrobats and gymnasts? Some people can swing like Tarzan, but it's a hard skill to learn, something we do to show off. Do you have anything like that?"

"*We* stay out of trees," said Cytosine. "But plains-folk evolved from ocean-dwellers—later in our evolution than most land-based animals, I mean—and we can still swim well and deep, with enough practice."

"We race," said Rhamnetin. "And dance among levels, and toss objects from vine to ground and back. Like juggling? Between members of both rings, in teams, trying to make specific patterns. I'll show you later. And I'll show you some of our theater, too."

"What about part of the long story?" suggested Cytosine. The three adult Ringers promptly fell into a discussion about what part; even the English bits were about as comprehensible as Dinar talking with a fellow fan about the intricacies of an unfamiliar anime.

"Sounds like we'll need a movie night," St. Julien murmured. She swayed constantly as she talked, jiggling when Brice fussed. Dori, who'd been distracted by the crowd, made *eh-eh* noises and reached for the younger baby.

"That part sounds like fun," I said. "The cultural exchange—that's what everyone's wanted, whenever we imagined this."

"I don't know about that," said St. Julien thoughtfully. She stroked Brice's translucent hair. "Some people probably want to find the next chocolate, or sandalwood or silver or pepper. And some want to hide. I'd expect as many reactions as we've ever had to meeting each other." She frowned, not discussing aloud the nastier end of those reactions. Some people would see conquest as inevitable, in one direction if not the other. "Technology, culture, space to grow. Contact opens so many possibilities."

I heard the faint tat of drums. I didn't mess with my auditory pickup, given the number of people laughing and talking nearby, but when I strained I could hear the accompanying horns, irregularities of rehearsal falling swiftly into melody. When I craned my neck I saw streamer-laden bikes straining up the hill. "Here comes the parade!"

Kids scrambled from trampoline and playground, darting between taller folk already lining the street. People made way for Cytosine, giving her and her kids a good view. Carnitine and Manganese scaled a magnificent old ash tree at the park's edge, drawing nervous glances from below. They clung easily to the branches, and I couldn't help envying their view.

St. Julien leaned close, masked by cheers and the approaching band. "Whatever we get from this, it's a gift to our kids."

"And whatever we give up," I said, "they'll lose."

"That too. I want you to know, that's the first and last thing I'm thinking about. I think it's something we all have in common."

"The Ringers have a point," I said. "Bringing your kids to the negotiation table—it helps us keep track of what's important." I hesitated, not sure how to approach our disagreement over what that meant.

St. Julien didn't have any such inhibition. "The watershed collectives have done good work, helping us hang onto this planet longer than we thought possible. But we can do so much more offworld. We should've left a century ago." Her fierceness cut through chatter and the stirring rhythm of the drums. The band marched past, bright with scarves and ribbon skirts, batons twirling between instruments. A whole play of sound and motion, shaped by Earth's gravity, by the exact characteristics of our atmosphere.

"You think we're just holding off the inevitable," I said. "That's the nation-state line, isn't it? That you didn't save the world because it wasn't possible."

"That's not why we didn't do it," she said. "We know damn well how many opportunities we missed. But we still have the satellites, the probes—data collection to match all your sensors, even if we're never *authorized* to act as the data deserve. Humanity *might* make it, on our current trajectory, if we're very lucky. But we've already lost a quarter of our crop yields and killed a billion people in drought and flood and famine and heat wave, and the changes have farther to peak before they get better, even if we get everyone moving in the same direction." She caught her breath. I heard frustration in the hitch of her voice, in the bitterness of her *we*. The problem with old-style governments was how easily they dammed themselves up.

"Our sensors tell us it's starting to work," I said, as gently as I could. "And our models tell us what to aim for next. We could still screw it up, but we won't. We have what we need, and we have *who* we need."

"And suppose you succeed?" Her voice dropped, but intensified. I had sampled enough now to filter her voice from the parade; all other sound fell away. "We still need what they're offering. If humanity stays on one little planet, eventually we'll lose the gamble. An asteroid, a methane breach, hell, eventually the expansion of the sun. When we spread among the stars, that's when we'll know who we really are. Not just surviving, but growing up."

"I'm not against humanity going to the stars. But if we leave Earth behind, we won't make it out there, either. That ash tree grows high and wide with its roots in the ground. But more than that—if we don't learn first how to take care of *this* world, how to be part of the ecology here, we won't do better anywhere else. *That's* growing up."

She shook her head. "There's more to learn out there than you think."

Just then, Dinar texted me on our still-functional private channel. **Can you get back home now? Without any of our guests?**

I held up my hand to St. Julien, grateful for the interruption. I needed to think about how to articulate the slow-rolling disaster, sure as a Venusian greenhouse, that would follow from trying to survive space when we hadn't yet learned our own cradle. St. Julien's here. I don't want to leave her alone with the Ringers any more than necessary.

Better there than here. You could leave Carol with Dori to keep an eye on them, and probably safer that way. The corporate reps have shown up—and they can't wait to talk.

CHAPTER 9

"Associate Kelsey di Asterion." The rep offered their hand, and I took it as briefly as I could. Like their partner, they dressed in black plastic and iridescent neomaterials. Even if the network had been up, a sourcing scan would've shown only blinking question marks. Kelsey's hair puffed into an aura of black curls. Silver glinted from their hairline, implants in place of removable mesh. Ghostly images played around the borders of their miniskirt and up the backs of their heels.

They hadn't bothered to take one of Dinar's pins. From what little I knew of corporate culture, these types wanted you to read gender, along with dozens of other things, from hair and makeup and clothes alone. They reveled in complex social games; they might never dress comfortably a day in their lives, but they'd smirk at anyone who couldn't or wouldn't play.

Kelsey's partner, introduced as Associate Mallory di Asterion, wore a leather-and-screenwear tailcoat and raven hair to their waist. Last and most discreet, Intern Adrien di Asterion tugged surreptitiously at the flaring hem of their dusk-purple tunic before straightening into an overly self-conscious imitation of their companions. All three looked like time travelers from the gilded '80s, flush with the rise of the fourth power, who'd been introduced to modern fabrics and absolutely nothing else from the last century.

Adrien held out a lacquer box. "A token." Their alto voice was smooth beyond their apparent years. "We've brought more for our visitors, of course, but we're grateful to you—your household—for hosting these important talks."

Normally Dinar would accept any sort of guest gift, but she twisted her hands tightly and made no move to do so. I took the box instead. Closer to Adrien, my personal sensors picked up a cloud of volatiles. Some from the plastics in their clothing, others an inscrutable mixture of organics and paraorganics. Perfume. In shows, corporate reps were always using biologically implausible compounds to manipulate their opponents' reactions. I resisted the urge to hold my breath. I did shunt the readings to the household network; I could run that analysis later.

Inside the box were a bottle of wine labeled in kanji and bars of baking chocolate marked with origins in Argentina and Peru (the old nation-states, not the powerful watershed networks that ought to have approved such things). Reminders of Asterion's corporate footprint, and clearly intended for the household and not for the Chesapeake. For the first time I wondered if it had been wise to offer up our house as headquarters; it made it easier for the corporate interlopers to ignore the watershed's place in the negotiations.

"Thank you," I said. "We'll be sure to share these around the contact team." I looked around hopefully—but no Mendez, no Diawara. We were on our own.

"Where are your guests?" asked Kelsey. "We're looking forward to meeting them."

I shrugged. "Still out at the parade. I'm sure they'll be back soon. The whole neighborhood, and the whole watershed, are welcoming them."

Mallory smiled. "Then maybe this is a good time for *us* to talk, human to human. We have many common interests, and we'll need a united front to negotiate with a new power. Mx. Judy—" The old-fashioned title sat awkwardly with my given name, but of course by their standards I had no meaningful affiliation. And by mine, they'd traded family for sponsorship. "We're told you head up the local delegation?"

"I do." Even more desperately, now, I wanted the network's collective expertise backing my mesh. I'd never worked directly with corporations, aside from the observers they sent to carbon talks. They didn't participate actively in such things; they obeyed the strictures laid down by the watersheds, or acceded under pressure from our fenceline guardians, or cheated when they thought we wouldn't be able to trace their emissions. I could use a crowd with guardian experience now, or even a text from Dinar. But her channel stayed silent. Whatever they'd said to her, it tightened her mouth and pulled her shoulders in close. Could they use her freelance agreements to pressure her?

Deliberately I pulled out a chair and sat. I took a muffin, and looked up at the still-standing corporate staff. In plays, people like this were obsessed with relative height; I'd seen a satire once where they carried around stepladders to prove their status. Heroes resisted the temptation. And I wanted Dinar's crumbs on their polished fingers. "I represent the delegation for the Chesapeake Bay Watershed Network. We have reps here from every continent and the U.S. government. We're coming together to speak for the world, and listen." True, and also a dig: opening words from any environmental congress. "We'd be glad to hear your interests as well."

The two associates looked at each other and sat, though they didn't eat. Adrien leaned against the wall, arms folded casually. Mallory spoke: "The common feed says these aliens—we're calling them Ringers?—are nation-style territorialists. They argue from shared ideals, and use those ideals as an excuse to make others live as they do. I know the dandelion networks don't trust us." I flagged that in my recording, the first point where any of them admitted our existence. "But corporate strength has always come from transmuting the threat of force into softer trade. If we all eat the same food, play the same games, they'll gloss over any difference in values."

"They live in space stations," added Kelsey. "With enough trade, they'll see our interest in planets as simply a place we aren't in competition. Not that we can't compete in space, too. Why not get a few stations of our own? Factories with shields of vacuum—think of everything we could accomplish. But first we need to figure out what goods appeal to them. What they'd want from us, if they knew it was on offer."

So much nuance and threat tangled in those reasonable-sounding suggestions. My undrained mesh stretched its memory to the breaking point. Still I cued problems and questions, ready to go as soon as the network came up, while I thought about how to respond.

When it *did* come up, I stalled out. It was only a moment—a stutter of status in the corner of my vision. Recordings and questions surged with that flash before it flickered away, and I wondered too late if thousands of cued uploads from across the region had overwhelmed the launch. Redbug would know. Maybe their team could lay down safeties, titrate activity for the next reboot.

They stomped out through the living room curtains, trailed by the tech team, and I braced myself. But their anger wasn't for me. "What are *they* doing here?" demanded Redbug.

Mallory and Kelsey started to rise from their seats, but it was Dinar who said, "They're here from Asterion. It's a conglomerate that trades nanomaterials and luxury foods—"

"I know what they trade," said Redbug. "What are they doing *here*?"

"Asking to meet the Ringers," said Dinar. She tensed further. "Is there something we should know?"

"Their *nanomaterials* go in half of the old server chips," said one of the tech experts. "The same servers that just failed on reboot. Maybe these bluescreens can tell us why." She pushed up the sleeves of her sweatshirt, revealing well-muscled arms inked with river maps. "I've done guardian work, I know how to handle corps outside the fence-line."

"We're not absolutely certain *yet* that Asterion's involved," murmured Redbug, without particular force. "Just that it's corporate."

Violence between humans, tempting as it might be, would do us no good with the Ringers. And, not that it was one of my expertises, I was pretty sure the scans on corporate imports were pretty thorough. But it was Dinar who spoke first. "Associates, Intern, these are our programming team. We've been feeding them here all night."

She looked pointedly at the table. Kelsey made a moue of amusement. They picked up a muffin gracefully between thumb and forefinger, sprinkled salt from the cellar, took a pointed bite. Mallory followed suit, and handed a piece back to Adrien.

"Now you can talk to them," Dinar told the tech team.

"What, you want us to just *ask* if they sabotaged the network?" demanded the woman with the tattoos.

"We didn't," said Mallory calmly. "We heard about your connection problems on the common feed, the same as everyone else. We'd be glad to lend you some of our techies as a gesture of goodwill, if you need a hand with your servers."

"We're doing fine," said Redbug. "We don't want your tentacles on our code any more than they already are, thanks just the same." They swung back toward the living room.

"And you," said the tattooed tech expert to Dinar, "I'll bet they're glad to have one of their pet data-crunchers protecting them. If you're useful enough, maybe they'll promote you."

Dinar flinched. I pushed my chair back. "You want to say that differently, or say it outside? We're only trying to keep people from getting into fistfights in our dining room—and where the Ringers might see us being 'uncivilized.' It's not Dinar's fault we don't have the setup to problem-solve properly."

I glared until she ducked her head—though she still glowered at the Asterion team through her lashes. I couldn't entirely blame her. The thing was, even if Asterion was responsible for the malware, this crowd might not know a thing. They were diplomatic experts—hell, the way companies ran things, this might be their only work—not tech specialists. Our servers were distributed all over the watershed; the only vulnerabilities anyone could exploit at our house were social. "I don't think we've met?" I asked, to give her something else to say.

"Elegy," she said. And: "I'm sorry I lost my temper. If you learn anything from your esteemed guests, let us know." And she followed Redbug back behind the curtain.

Mallory's gaze followed, languid. "Techies are the same everywhere," she said. "Swear a hole straight through you if you catch them in the middle of a bug."

"They've got reasons to be suspicious," I said. "*Do* you know anything about the network crash?" I turned up every sense I had available, ready to catch any nuance of skin conductance or breathing pattern or hesitation that made it through their polished presentations.

"I sure as hell don't." Kelsey examined their muffin, frowning. "It's not in our interest to leave meeting hosts short on organizational resources." The frown morphed to a wry smile. "I'd offer space on our own internal network, if I didn't think it would raise your techie's paranoia even further."

"But if you want us to offer," murmured Mallory, "just ask."

Their physiological signs were consistent with worry, curiosity, and the natural stress of our accusations. With the right justification, we could shove them back behind their fenceline before they even got to meet Cytosine. Of course, even with more disturbing readings and access to a good algorithm, I couldn't have gotten the probability for any of Elegy's accusations above 70 percent. Leaving aside that Asterion might be sophisticated enough to fake neurophysiological signs, somewhere in the circuitry of those outfits. It had been worth a shot.

"Do you think someone else . . . ?" Adrien asked the associates.

"If so," said Kelsey, "they'll be off this alliance fast."

Mallory turned back to me. "We know you prefer to keep in-person meetings small. If our visitors had landed on Zealand, we'd invite every power on the planet to our ballrooms. Maybe this is better—less overwhelming for the Ringers, at least. But Asterion outbid a dozen other companies to be here, and in turn we represent all their interests—as long as they represent ours. If you find out who did this, please let us know." Teeth bared, briefly. "We wouldn't mind downsizing our consortium."

I busied myself with a muffin. Even with most of their power gone, the corporations were still playing the cannibalistic games that had almost destroyed the world. The remnant was far from harmless. Yet here they were inviting us, winningly, to share a bite. As if it were theirs to offer. As if whatever advantage they clawed out of the crashes—their doing or otherwise—wouldn't be corrosive. "If we find out who did this, *we'll* take care of it."

The Ringers would return soon. The kids would be back, Dori and Diamond and Chlorophyll and Manganese, and I didn't want any of them near these people. It might've been better to let Elegy have her way.

CHAPTER 10

"So they . . . organize merchants?" asked Rhamnetin.

"Not exactly," I said. We were walking up the long slope toward our house; at this rate I still wouldn't manage to give fair warning about Asterion before we got there. Dori slept heavy and hot against my chest. "They used to organize manufacturing. And make goods available. And convince people to want those goods. They still do, to some extent, but mostly with each other."

"Pollution," said Carol. "Climate change. That's what they manufactured—everything that brought Earth to the brink, before we pushed them back."

"You've got a perfect natural experiment here, you know," said St. Julien. Irony lilted her voice. "Everyone always blames the corporations. But we don't know whether the Ringers had anything like that, or if they found their own climate traps. How did *your* planet get to the point where you needed to leave?" This directed at Rhamnetin.

Someone had gifted the Ringers with scarves. Rhamnetin wove his, flowing silk spangled midnight blue, among his upper legs. The colored patches lower down, muted now in the sunlight, he left bare. Cytosine had hooked her scarf between two upper limbs, trailing back in the breeze like a flag. Her cross-brother snatched at it playfully, unshocked by St. Julien's question.

"I told you, it's unavoidable at a certain level of technology." The play with the scarf changed to a gentler stroke along Cytosine's back. "There comes a point where you *can* feed your people, bring families together across continents in a few hours, keep people healthy, make beauty on a vast scale—but not without blighting the branches where you've always lived. The only right thing is to take that work out into the vacuum, where you can thrive without falling."

"Can we blame the corporations now?" asked Carol.

St. Julien nodded grimly. "They'd have drowned us all, happily, without feeding or healing anyone but themselves."

Cytosine curled protectively and briefly, her reflexive roll made untenable by the hill. "How was that allowed?"

Rhamnetin answered before I could. "We've had our share of branch-rotting leaders and powers. And people who'll try to . . ." He stopped and made a series of grating screeches.

Cytosine squealed a hesitation. "Trade their francium for aluminum while it's decaying? It doesn't sound as good in English, does it?"

"I can follow, I promise," I said. "As for the corporations, eventually we *didn't* allow it. People like my parents organized to stop them, and created the first watershed networks." I didn't look at St. Julien. "Everything from refusing to buy their 'decaying francium,' to setting limits on their carbon production to get warming under control, to blocking their shipping if they went over their carbon budgets. But they couldn't bear the transformation, and eventually they barricaded themselves behind their own fencelines on a few artificial islands, scamming each other after no one else would fall for it."

"We still buy from them, sometimes." Carol wrinkled her nose. "Things we need that we haven't been able to back-engineer yet, or exchanges that someone thinks will eventually incentivize them to join us. And they're allowed out among the watersheds as long as they promise to behave. Are these ones behaving?"

"After a fashion." I started to text her, then decided to say it aloud. "Except for the network crash. Redbug is pretty sure it's corporate malware, but can't make the case that it's Asterion. They'll take advantage either way. They pretended there was no advantage for them in the crash, but they also dangled an offer of tech support."

"What do they want from *us*?" asked Rhamnetin.

"The same thing they want from most people, I suppose," I said. "They want you to buy their stuff. Maybe work for them, too, if you like toiling at the bottom of complicated hierarchies." I realized belatedly that height-as-power might not mean much to the plains-folk, working with an arboreal species. Or maybe space was height *and* power for them. It would certainly appeal to Asterion, letting them expand in directions we couldn't block. Their waste would burden us less, out there, but their ideas would be no safer.

"That seems like a small desire," said Cytosine.

"Not for them." St. Julien's pace sharpened, arms clamped around Brice. "You told me how you see your symbiosis." Her head-tilt invited me and Carol into the explanation, some conversation she'd had without us. "Not the simpler trades of non-sapients, protection for food or cleaning, but a partnership of a thousand complementary exchanges. The corporations tried to do the same thing, but they'd create needs in order to fill them. It looked symbiotic, but it was one-sided, because most of the needs weren't real. Or else they created artificial shortages of true needs, to make their goods worth more. They're parasites."

I couldn't argue with anything she said—but I was surprised to hear her say it so plainly. From the glance Carol gave me, so was she. I could rant about corporations as readily as the next person, and Asterion's sleekly rational suggestions made me shudder. But among the watersheds they were treated as a danger to be kept under control, tolerable within their fencelines, gigs like Dinar's a more-or-less acceptable compromise. St. Julien's anger seemed personal.

But then, fighting the fourth power had lifted the watersheds, and we'd been able to keep them at bay for decades. The third-power nation-states had come away weakened, drained of their ability to help people by their own choices—and sometimes by misguided attempts to rebuild on corporate models.

Rhamnetin brushed my shoulder with a hairy foot. "Is that who you have in your home?" he asked.

I sighed. "We'll let them make their pitch. But you should listen to Viola."

I didn't hurry up the hill, and no one else seemed inclined either. There were flags to exclaim over, welcome banners to translate, and another puzzlebot to solve, further evolved and more difficult than the last. Fairy goats broke from weeding a yard to nuzzle us for treats. People stopped us to ask the Ringers what they'd thought of the parade and tell them about past parades, stories of memorable costumes and exciting failures of bicycle floats.

Our yard offered another excuse to linger. The garden was a skeleton of frames interspersed with copper markers and early-sprouting chives. I made minute adjustments to the stakes that marked future vines, the trellis where peas would leap and the mounds where beans would wind around maize, cushioned by summer squash. Fig and pawpaw trees, generation-old cuttings from the neighborhood's first food forest, marked a remnant boundary with neighboring properties.

"You have very small farms," said Cytosine. "Do you feed everyone this way?"

"Oh, no." I adjusted a marker. "We have bigger community gardens that everyone takes shifts working, and we import bulk crops from further out in the county." I hesitated, then added: "Aside from making it easy to pick herbs when you need a handful, house gardens are where we test new varieties—strains that might be resilient to higher temperatures or blights or storms. These peas here, they're supposed to grow for longer into the summer, and hold up better through big rainstorms."

"It's one of the things we coordinate through the network," added Carol. "Who tries out what test crops, what makes sense to grow at the neighborhood level, and what's worth transporting in. And then distribution of the harvest—a ton of the surplus fruit came through us last year, because Dinar's incredibly efficient at canning." I wished the Ringers had come in September, in spite of the heat: our kitchen would smell of caramelizing peach, of rich jams and boiling apples and mulberries spilling from baskets, and the shouts and laughter of helpers. Last year I'd been able to do little but nurse and listen and doze amid the blanket of scents; this year I'd join in.

"You have farms, in your sphere?" I asked. Somehow I'd pictured vats of algae and matrix-grown meat, even though I'd seen the inside of their ship green and fruiting. I needed to visit again—we should spend time in their home, too.

"Of course," said Cytosine. Her kids wiggled, and she released them to scuttle through the dead nettle and clover. Dori still drooled against my chest, eyes thinned into delicate calligraphy. "Grown food tastes better than any sort of synthetic, and it's better for the air mix, too."

"Except for Perihelion 50," Rhamnetin said, then added something in their own language. "They think they're traditional, but they have strange ideas about tradition. About half their food is synthetic, pastes and patties with extremely specific nutrient balances. *Not* my favorite bit of the Meeting Day feast!"

"They bring that to feasts?" demanded Carol, laughing.

Rhamnetin made his own sounds of amusement. "It's an ancestral recipe."

"I'm not sure we're in a position to complain," I said. "Passover's in about a month. Horseradish, gefilte fish . . ."

"I *like* gefilte fish. *With* horseradish."

The door swung open. I'd almost managed to forget who was waiting for us—but here came Kelsey and Mallory and Adrien down the ramp. Dinar trailed reluctantly behind.

"We wondered if you were ever coming inside," said Kelsey. Turning to Cytosine and Rhamnetin, they added: "A pleasure to meet you, at long last."

"It's a pleasure to meet you." Rhamnetin bent his legs in a bow, or a nod.

The Ringers' customs must be in the common feed by now—why *hadn't* Asterion sent a child? There were always rumors of crèches, babies suckled by machines or by servants paid for their milk. But our inspections had never turned up more than rumor. And these people, for all they raised my hackles, didn't seem that broken.

The Asterion team joined us on the cobbled path. Kelsey's heels clicked on the irregular stones, balance impeccable.

Adrien craned their neck to look at our roof, where solar cells shifted petals toward the winter-dimmed sun. Between the blossoms, tethers strained against barely visible windmill kites. The intern frowned at our garden, forehead wrinkled as if trying to resolve some mystery.

"They grow things differently on the mainland," said Mallory gently, and Adrien twitched with a guilty "Oh!" to retrieve their palette and pose for note-taking.

Carol's elbow brushed mine. Even St. Julien edged closer. I felt grateful, but awkward. It wasn't like the corporate trio posed a personal threat to our kids, and acting like they did was an overt insult. It probably looked even nastier to the Ringers. But that's always been the problem with corporations. They rarely came at anyone with weapons. They calibrated their threats to be deniable, invisible to those whose judgments mattered. And too many people had died still trying desperately to be rational, polite, forgiving.

It wasn't just the adults who noticed my discomfort. Dori scrunched up her face and started wailing. Brice followed swiftly, infant screams heart-piercing in their purity.

"Hold on!" I called over the noise. I led everyone to the benches near the fig tree, and pulled down my shirt to let Dori suckle. It took a couple of tries to get her to latch on, but finally she quieted. St. Julien looked hesitant, but settled next to me. Her clothes weren't quite as well-designed for nursing, but she got herself unwrapped. Brice balled tiny fists and kept screaming, thrashing against her breast.

Dinar dashed back into the house, returned with a pillow. She settled it under St. Julien's elbow.

"Oh, thank god!" She tucked Brice under her arm and got her attached at last. "We've barely gotten out of the house before yesterday; I should've brought more of my kit." She glared at Mallory and Kelsey as if expecting them to object. Mostly they were looking in other directions.

"Um." Carol got a funny look on her face. "I'm sorry, it's that it's both of you."

"Yeah," I said. "Go ahead and pump. We should be able to handle this. Or you can wait and take a turn after me?"

"Nah, I'll be back in a few minutes." She scurried off, presumably to avoid staining her shirt.

Diamond and Chlorophyll picked up the trend and clambered onto their mom. She rocked back, letting them lick. The Asterion crowd were definitely losing points over their lack of babies. It made me feel less vulnerable about nursing in front of people I didn't like.

Mallory offered Rhamnetin a firm handshake. "I think we have much to share with each other, and more to gain. Bringing together the resources of two solar systems—it's a once-in-a-lifetime opportunity."

"Why didn't you bring children with you?" asked Rhamnetin.

"As *trade goods*?" asked Adrien. Cytosine's children squawked as she suddenly rolled tight. It was one of the things people said about corporations, but the intern's horrified gasp suggested that rumor as dubious as it sounded. Both associates glared; Adrien flushed and hunched their shoulders.

"Of course not," said Rhamnetin. "To *bring together,* like you said— people as well as resources. To make it easier to understand each other. I know it's not a human custom, but I also know you've learned our ways quickly." He gestured at St. Julien.

"Some people learn faster than others," she said.

Mallory and Kelsey both hesitated, sharing a glance. Kelsey said at last, "We're excited by the possibilities here. We want to get to know you, and I'm sure we all plan to negotiate in good faith. There are ways we can accede to the customs of our hosts, and our trading partners. But protecting our children isn't a point we're willing to compromise."

"Children too young to dress themselves stay inside the fenceline," agreed Mallory. "We'd be delighted to have you visit Zealand—and if you come, you'll meet our kids. But they stay home."

Cytosine uncurled a smidge. The kids wriggled and chirped, stretching their limbs. "Have you carried children yourselves?"

"Where we come from, that's a private question," said Adrien.

The others looked at them gratefully, apparently forgiving the earlier lapse.

"Of course you'd all have *that* in common," grumbled Cytosine. "I think perhaps we ought to visit your territory."

St. Julien and I glanced at each other, united for a moment by our lack of enthusiasm, and the shared realization that we couldn't exactly keep people who'd traveled more than a hundred light-years tied to the Chesapeake.

Dinar smiled at Kelsey. "Great—I can get them the advisory materials for people traveling across the fencelines." Hopefully *our* guidelines, built on a history of hostility and some narrow assumptions about who'd be using them, would be as comprehensible as the corporate brochures.

"We're looking for a construction site," said Cytosine. "Nothing too large—a communication antenna. But we don't know whether anything around here will suit our needs."

I really wished I could read Rhamnetin's body language. Had he known she was planning to bring this up? Had she brought it up with Asterion *because* he'd told me? And was she seriously considering building this thing on a corporate aisland, or just trying to scare us into cooperating? It worked—the idea of more Ringers landing out there, unencumbered by environmental restrictions and with access controlled by Asterion, was terrifying. Mallory was already nodding, brainstorming potential locations with Kelsey.

"I think we can make something work closer to your ship," I started. I didn't get further because I was distracted by a sudden flicker. Dinar straightened, looking happier than I'd seen her since Asterion arrived. A trickle of datafeed grew in the corner of my vision—though the first drop was a bolded announcement that stored data would *not* upload to the network until further notice. Maybe that would keep the queue from crashing everything all on its own.

"Hold on," I said. "We might get more input in a minute." I hoped desperately that . . . no, I could do more than hope. "Dinar, can you please ask Redbug to give the contact team priority on opening problem threads?"

"Yes!" She lifted her skirt and ran back over the damp grass.

I waited impatiently, feeling self-conscious as the others watched curiously. I tried to ignore them for the moment: I burped Dori, switched her to my other breast, rearranged my shirt. The wind picked up, and I pulled the parade scarf closer around us. Finally the network window blossomed into a welcoming set of options—slower and shallower than usual, but the threadset related to the Ringers was *there,* problems and proposed solutions restored out of the ether, and best of all some basic algorithmic processing of the solutions.

I skimmed as quickly as I could, making sure I hadn't missed anything. Then I opened a new thread:

Problem: The *Solar Flare* is broken, and they need to build an antenna to call home and request backup parts, environmental impact unknown. Backup would arrive quickly, and probably be even more eager to "save" us. I left in a marker for the conversation with Rhamnetin, promising to upload as soon as I could. **Asterion reps are here, and ready to offer a site in their aislands.**

I posted, tagging in the rest of the contact team. The advantage of the network having been down was that *everyone* would be on now. Even with activity levels strictly circumscribed, the discussion picked up swiftly.

"Okay," I told Cytosine and Rhamnetin. "I'm streaming questions from people who work on the Chesapeake's infrastructure projects. Are you up for answering a few?"

At least the idea of planning construction projects in advance didn't seem completely foreign to them (at some point, we'd have to find out how they handled project management for their own millennia-long engineering timelines), and they called the ship for issues beyond their own technical understanding. For a few minutes I could settle into the rhythm of filtering competing queries from the network, passing them on to the Ringers, passing answers back—properly representing the crowd rather than working solo.

The antenna would be big, stretching through the upper layers of atmosphere, but without moving parts once it was built and without producing much waste. The footprint at the base was less than an acre—*up* seemed to be most of the point. It was built from some variant on carbon nanotubes, the first segments automatically generated but others requiring direct intervention from the Ringers. That intervention seemed to be a safety feature, since they brought it up every time our people asked about the risk of some molecular generation process running out of control.

"We need a few more days to complete impact simulations," I told them at last. "But there's an old parking lot across the river from Bear Island that hasn't been fully remediated, that we can tentatively offer as a site." I pulled up a map, reveling in my ability to do so even as I worried over the out-of-date sensor readings that layered it with rich data.

"We can offer something more definite." Mallory smiled. "If a little farther away. After the distance you've come, that has to be a minimal consideration." They pulled up a map of their own on Adrien's palette, glossy and neatly marked, detail obviously added by a single expert or coordinated committee rather than through any sort of distributed mapping. It was also clearly built from satellite imagery rather than ground sensors. They zoomed in on a flat area at the edge of a large aisland, packed earth and scrub alternating with landing strips they'd presumably replace elsewhere. In the distance, tall buildings shone with glass and bright screens.

Questions sprang up on the thread. I leaned forward, still cradling Dori. "That looks like it's practically on the shoreline. You need to run the same impact simulations we do."

Kelsey stiffened. "We have construction impact reports filed with the Australian *and* Asian-Pacific Watershed Consortia for our entire territory."

"For this type of structure?" Which of course they didn't. They couldn't.

"Our approvals are broad enough that we shouldn't need one."

"Will the continental consortia agree with that?" asked St. Julien mildly. "NASA will support the Potomac site. If it meets watershed requirements, the U.S. has reciprocity." It was an old and practical arrangement, given that our guidelines were stricter and better-enforced than the EPA's. But I was glad she'd spoken.

"It sounds like it'll be a few days before we know about either," said Cytosine. "We'd like to work near our ship, if we can. But we'll inspect the Asterion site as well. And we will meet your children."

CHAPTER 11

The festival came together for a huge feast in the neighborhood common house. Dinar, for once, only had to contribute a couple of dishes on behalf of our household. Share-bowls of amaranth pilaf and celery root salad wouldn't normally leave her looking so strained. Raven held back from racing down the long wooden benches alongside the rest of the toddler pack, instead clinging anxiously to her side. Athëo rubbed Dinar's shoulders and frowned fiercely at the Asterion reps. For their part, they ate cheerfully, making conversation with everyone in reach whether it was returned or not.

Cytosine's crew seemed comfortable despite being accosted on all sides by our community's full store of excitement and anxiety and ordinary human curiosity. I relaxed a little, feeling that from this quarter, at least, they would be offered hospitality and no seriously panic-inducing diplomatic proposals. I couldn't entirely shake the feeling that something terrible would happen if I let them out of earshot, but I could scoot down the bench and talk with friends while I eavesdropped.

In the midst of this oasis of lower-stakes discussion—how was I holding up, what did the spaceship smell like, did I want to set up a playdate or three—Mendez dropped a hand on my shoulder.

"Good work earlier. These corporate types will drain the Ringers out from under us if we let them."

"Thanks." I stretched, feeling the worries furrowed across my spine. "I wish we could keep them out of corporate territory entirely, but I don't think it's feasible. The Ringers want to keep their choices open."

She swung her leg over the bench and sat beside me. "None of your post-crash recordings have uploaded yet. You must have some sense of these people by now—how do you think *they'll* judge Zealand?"

"I'm not honestly sure. On the plus side, our brief history of end-stage capitalism left them slightly horrified. On the minus, they seem to have deliberately accepted climate change as a reasonable price for technological and medical advances. That's horrifying on its own, and it means that they're absolutely willing to make that sort of trade-off. And they know we don't like what they're offering." I took a moment to post Mendez's question to a new thread. I should have done that earlier. Even talking the situation over with one new person reminded me that problem-solving worked better collectively. "I'm afraid that's going to carry more weight. If the corporations are more willing to accept their agenda—and they'll say they are, whatever they really plan to do—the Ringers'll work with them no matter what they think of their morals."

"Damn." She shifted position, crossing her legs, resting her chin on her elbows before straightening again. She spoke quietly. "We're all out of our depths here. Even in the biggest carbon talks, we have so much more time to plan everything, from the models we're using to how many reps are needed on-site. And the participants all have the same broad goals—or else we can make them cooperate." Her eyes flickered toward Mallory and Kelsey and Adrien. "If the corporations ally with the Ringers, those talks will lose most of their weight. All the things we're finally getting right, we could lose."

The new thread whispered in the corner of my vision, but nothing there contradicted our worries. We might have suppressed Asterion's ability to drill new oil wells, but here and now their most dangerous emission was *words*.

"We must have dealt with this before," I said. "When we pushed them back the first time, they had the best persuasive technologies on the planet."

"I wonder how much of that armory they're dredging up now." She sat up suddenly, almost knocking into my empty plate. "The Ringers pick up radio signal. We have to find out what they think of the *ads*."

"Shit. Ask Carol. She's been talking with their communications expert."

"I'll do that." She rose. "See if you can learn more about their conversations with the corporations—and make sure they understand what they're diving into. Someone's got to keep sensors on this mess."

That was going to be fun. And if I was going to go deeper into the corporate "mess," I needed to talk with my parents. I loved them, but once they got involved it'd be hard to keep them down to just *talking*. I sent a private message, and worried about what I'd invoked.

The festival wound down sporadically, as festivals do. There would be scattered porches full of music and hemp wine late into the night, and even later laughter among the team cleaning the common house.

Rhamnetin found me as I was gathering my things. Raven dozed on Athëo's shoulder, and Dori lay melted against Carol's chest. Dinar had collected our bowls and silverware. Rhamnetin raised a tentative leg. I hoped the fierceness of the gesture, like a locust about to pounce, was unintentional. "Could I—would it be all right if I stayed at your house tonight? Or in the guest rooms here? I've never slept on a planetary surface."

I chuckled at his enthusiasm even as I appreciated his interest in the whole planet thing. Maybe I could help him understand why we liked them.

Dinar nodded. "Our place, absolutely." Especially since the Asterion team were staying at the common house.

"Thank you! I'll grab my things from the shuttle."

We walked home, Rhamnetin swinging a cluster of silver tubes from his upper legs. Athëo and Carol went upstairs to transfer the kids from shoulders to beds. They came down five minutes later, grinning.

"They're still asleep!" announced Athëo triumphantly.

"Both of them!" said Carol.

"At the same time!"

"At *night*!"

My mesh confirmed this remarkable report, happy indicators of heart rate and even alpha waves dancing through the household network.

Dinar looked less happy as she glanced toward the living room, where light and voices still drifted from the repair team. "Why don't I grab some snacks, and we can all go upstairs."

Dinar and Athëo's bedroom was the other half of the attic from ours, but they'd set up the bulk of it as a sitting room, with a conversation circle of cushions and comfortable chairs, and little stone tables on which Dinar deposited bread, a selection of jams, and a bottle of pawpaw juice. No hemp wine for us these days, given that the kids could wake up any minute and half of us were nursing. I could've used it. The walls were draped with hangings dyed in muted blues and greens, plus an anomalous tapestry of a clay-walled city, a gift from a friend of Dinar's in the Nahal Alexander Network.

Rhamnetin draped legs over the back of a chair. Was he used to furniture that wasn't trees? Not that growing trees inside was necessarily a bad model for seating. I would have loved it when I was a kid. Probably still would, to be honest.

Dinar leaned against Athëo, looking exhausted.

"You don't like the Asterion reps," Rhamnetin said to Dinar. Or at least he turned so that the sound came from the one of his legs closest to her. "None of the other humans do, but you especially."

Dinar's eyes opened, dubious slits. "You're good at reading human reactions, for someone who only came to Earth a couple of days ago."

He dipped his body. "You look like in your shows, when a character is upset by someone's presence, and the upsetting person is about to do something involving explosions or lawyers. Am I wrong?"

She laughed shakily. "Not mostly. Well, maybe about the explosions. The corporate reps *are* dangerous, and I don't like them. But I don't dislike them as much as most people do, and when they're here people can see that. It doesn't make me popular. I'd rather they'd be complicated at a distance."

"Judy told me why people don't like them. Can you tell me why you like them better?" Rhamnetin scrunched lower, maybe aware that this was a particularly awkward question.

Dinar sounded exhausted, as if this were just another round in the longstanding network arguments. "We still need them. They almost broke the world, when they had power—but the corporations still make key parts of our network infrastructure. They think they need us because without those exports, they lose any justification for their continued existence. But really, that tenuous connection is their last chance to find a new justification. Every time we interact, it reminds them that there's another way. Every freelance contract keeps the window open. When we finally take over the last of the manufacturing, the opportunity to change them vanishes—and we might need to fight the dandelion revolution all over again. I'd rather take them into the future with us. But most people think of it as a purely transactional relationship, something we should drop as soon as we can, and they'd rather ignore it as much as possible."

"It's been decades," I said. Maybe it *was* just another round in the network arguments—but Rhamnetin should hear both sides. "The people who're willing to change already have—we get maybe half a dozen converts from the aislands a year. The corporations use our contracts *as* justification for keeping up their old ways. They're desperate to hold on, and that desperation doesn't improve their behavior. The last changeovers really will be a tough transition. Resource-intensive."

Like the Great Shifts before I was born. Blackouts and epidemics and communications gaps had been common, and there were times when food was limited to what people could grow locally or preserve. It was always easier to put off the final transitions of power to the watersheds, always a source of friction whenever the question came up.

Of course, we were having blackouts and communication gaps *now*. "Do *you* think they made the malware?" I asked Dinar.

"Of course they made it," she said. She sounded sad rather than angry. "The corporations have the most to gain from undermining the networks, and the most skill on hand to do it. Even other groups with reason to hurt us would outsource the work to Asterion or someone like them. Which means that even if it didn't start as a corporate idea, the corporations control it now."

"Why not say all that to Redbug?" demanded Carol. She glanced sideways at Rhamnetin.

"Because the Asterion emissaries will have at least plausible deniability. They won't know who's responsible for sure, and that matters more to corporate employees than even obvious truth. And if we *don't* kick them out, we can trace the thread back through to their bosses, and their bosses' allies, and all the social connections that might help us either convince our attackers to stop, or hold them accountable. We shouldn't give that up. But Redbug thinks social connections are just as dangerous as open network channels."

"If you can't ask questions, you can't learn," Rhamnetin said, and Dinar nodded firmly. Then, seeming to hesitate, he added slowly: "Would you come with us to Zealand? At least one or two of you? Their reactions to your society have provided useful perspective. I'd like to see the other way, too. And I'd like to see what questions *you* ask, that close up."

I glanced at the rest of the household. It was an uncomfortable idea. None of us had experience with fenceline work, let alone any sort of investigation. But I'd certainly be following Mendez's guidance—and maybe getting closer to answers about the malware. It was also a chance to see what the *Ringers* thought of Asterion, and be in the ground to counter whatever offers they made. Once considered, we didn't dare refuse.

"We won't bring our kids," said Carol. "Can Cytosine cope with that?"

"They don't eat babies," said Dinar.

"We don't know *what* they do with babies," I said. "They wouldn't bring theirs here—they've got some sort of problem with how we raise kids. And I, personally, like the way we raise our kids."

"Maybe they just don't like having them glared at," Dinar suggested.

"I'll go," I said. Carol squeezed my hand. "Mendez asked me to keep tabs on Asterion. And for better or worse, I'm the Network's face in these talks."

Athëo put his arm around Dinar. "Maybe I should go along?"

She shook her head. "You wouldn't like how they do gender." She swallowed. "Besides, they already asked me."

"Wait," demanded Athëo. His surprise was kin to my own. "They did what?"

"They're—" She stopped, tried again. "They obviously think having a freelancer here is some sort of toehold. I don't like them trying to use me, but I don't think it'll help anyone if I reject a gig now. And like I said, it's a chance to follow the social threads, to trace their hierarchy until we find the people who can be pushed to make change."

"They're paying you to go to Zealand?" Athëo frowned fiercely. "I thought your gigs were all remote."

"Apparently not."

"I'd like to have you along," said Rhamnetin. "I appreciate nuanced perspectives."

Dinar laughed at that. "I think you appreciate perspectives, period. I'll bet you keep a pantry full of them, for days when no one tells you their opinions."

Keening spilled from Rhamnetin's mouths, and laughter from his speech box. "Maybe a whole cryostorage unit. Although most of the time, people are happy to give me their opinions. Sometimes the same ones, day after day." He managed a melodramatically mournful tone.

"What's that from?" I asked. "You've learned human languages from our broadcasts—the melody too, how we change our voices to show emotion. You're really good at it."

"Thank you," he said. "Luciferin's best at languages; she put together our training modules. I think you learn the same way—lots of examples of the same thing, until your mind abstracts out the patterns? But that bit—" For a moment he dropped into the mournful voice again. "That's Eeyore, from Winnie the Pooh."

Athëo clapped his hands. "If it *is* a good morning, which I doubt." One of his regular "tasks" was reading Raven all the books he'd never had Approved as a kid.

"I like your mornings," said Rhamnetin.

"I'll bet," I said. "I suppose you don't have sunrises, in the Rings."

"Of course we do. Exeligmos 136, the habitat we're from, is a signal search hub, so we turn out toward the stars every night. The *Solar Flare* has been doing cross-system runs, though, so we only get sunsets when we're grounded, and even on the biggest habitats they're fast—on a planet they last for hours. Your days are way too short, but at least you spend a lot of time on sunrise and sunset."

"How long are your days?" asked Carol.

"Almost twice as long. We modified our rhythms for the trip, but it's still weird. I keep getting startled by how quickly I get tired, and then surprised again when I wake up."

"That's a strange thing to change about yourself," said Dinar. The household network blared with sudden signal. "Though it would be useful sometimes. Do you change your biorhythms when you have babies?"

"My turn." Carol stood and stretched. "Should I bring her in here to nurse?"

"Sure," I said. "We can dim the lights."

I took care of that while she went to collect Dori. Dinar and Athëo's lights were as comfortable as the rest of the sitting room, and narrowed to orange-gold spots as they dimmed, making it feel like twilight with lanterns scattered among the hangings. Dinar brought up an auditory feed from outside, cricket and mockingbird and wind whispering through the garden.

"You'd have to ask Carnitine and Luciferin what they did when we were little. I don't think Cytosine changed her metabolism when Diamond and Chlorophyll were born. They get all that stuff in her milk, so it would have kept them from adapting. Now they just start licking when they wake up, and Cytosine barely grunts."

"Some humans do that," said Athëo. "Sleep with their kids right there, I mean. We tried it with Raven, but she was so noisy even when she was fast asleep. At least with the monitors we can rest when the kids do."

Carol came back, and appropriated half the cushions and a corner of the couch. "Or talk with grown-ups without waking them up. That's nice too."

We indulged in that precious luxury for a few more minutes. We were going to regret all being synched to the same shift, but full coverage was likely to be a lost cause for the next few days anyway. Rhamnetin was good company, in spite of or maybe because of his bluntness. I got the impression that asking awkward questions was not so much an assigned task as a natural calling. Inhibitions lowered by fatigue and friendly discussion, I asked about the *Solar Flare,* and whether his family had formed around the ship or the other way around.

Rhamnetin spread blueberry jam on a slice of bread, and didn't respond immediately. Reluctant, or just thinking it through? I watched how delicately he manipulated the knife, trying to figure out the joints on his finger-tentacle-things. "A little of both. Even before my brothers and I hatched, our sisters wanted to crew a courier ship. They like traveling among the habitats, and it puts you first in line for opportunities like this. There's more competition now than before the tunnel drive was invented—a few centuries ago it could take months to reach the far side of the Rings, and being chosen to chase a signal meant terrible relativistic sacrifice. Now you need a skilled, stable family before even putting in for one. We all bonded with Cytosine's mating cluster over the shared interest, and we put in our ratings while they were still wrestling over dominance. We're good symbiotes—for a ship crew that means a full distribution of skills and reaction styles." He sounded shy and proud. "And then the observatories found your signal, with Cytosine still nursing her firstborn!"

"And they picked you," I said. "The competition must have been tight." I wished *I* had that kind of process behind me, supporting my involvement in all this. Or that Mendez had taken the time around getting extremely competent at negotiation to have a kid. My own parents insisted that watersheds made it much easier than earlier powers to combine childrearing with other skills, but I envied the Ringers not only making it easy but encouraging it. Then again, I'd always wanted kids—the Rings must be a rough place for people who didn't.

"Dozens of ships put in applications with the Grasping Families," said Rhamnetin. "Like I said, we're good symbiotes." He squatted. "I just hope they were looking for the right qualifications."

Maybe that uncertainty was universal. No test, no method of matching skill to task, was enough to convince those in the ground that others wouldn't have found the challenge easier.

CHAPTER 12

The trip to Zealand was set for the following week. Apparently the corporations wanted time to prepare—not that the rest of us had gotten any. The intervening days were intense. On one level, we were sparring with Viola St. Julien and the Asterion team over everything: time with the Ringers, what to show them, where to take them. I watched Dori, Raven, and Cytosine's twins work out their own understanding around the playmat; I wondered what Ringer kids' lives were like when they weren't being diplomatic props.

At the same time we were struggling with the network, or at least closely tracking the people doing the struggling. It was fine—mostly—for short-term problem-solving, gathering immediate input into immediate issues. That was good, because *everyone* was online and had opinions, and it gave me the backing I needed for negotiations. But push harder, and the cracks began to show. We'd restarted with an old version and spotty data from a more recent snapshot, and could load the full historical datasets only slowly. Every file, every line of code, plodded its way through a gauntlet of scans and filters. And the algorithms that spoke for the needs of river and tree and air, and gave weight to the values that we strove to preserve in all our problem-solving—the ones that we should have been modifying to account for a completely unprecedented situation—couldn't keep up with their usual workload. Day-to-day ecological management grew kudzu-tangled while we tried to balance archive restoration with real-time data uploads.

Our attempts at opening channels with other watershed networks were worse. Direct internetwork connection was never meant to be used frequently; now the slight differences in restoration strategy threatened our tenuous stability with every packet. We fell back on the common feed, coordination stalled, and more and more of the contact effort fell back to the Chesapeake. What should have been a planetary effort stayed far too local.

Redbug's team fretted over the integrity of the algorithms, and found subtle failures in even the apparently functional processes. They glared at the Asterion team and snapped at Dinar. They weren't the only ones, and she threw herself into hosting whoever would show up even as her online profile started to reflect spreading doubts about everyone who did gigwork. Which meant that no matter how many of them pushed for more investigative work behind the fenceline, even approval for my own proposed trip barely made it over the threshold. Decisions that should have been as easy as the shifting flight of starlings got mired in unresolved argument.

That was the bad, and there was a lot of it. But I couldn't shake the simple pleasure of getting to know a set of new, interesting people. With us all bound together by urgent tasks, it felt like my Transit Year, when I'd met Carol and stayed up until all hours talking with dozens of strangers, focused as only new-made adults can be on getting to know each other and ourselves.

There were moments—that first morning, Rhamnetin woke at dawn. He'd spent the night clinging to a nest of three chairs that he'd pulled together in the sitting room, limbs wrapped around whatever arms and legs and backs would afford it. I peeked out to check on him after a bout of nursing and captured but didn't share an image; he looked like an absurdly positioned cat, and it seemed like a strangely private thing to witness. Eyes flicked open one at a time and shut again, without reaction, limbs slithering to readjust his grip.

When I came back in the morning he was already up, stretching cautiously.

"We need to get you a cat tree," I said.

"Any sort of tree would be nice. It's okay, I knew what I was getting into. But ow."

Athëo cracked his bedroom door and joined us, yawning. "Dinar doesn't feel great; she's sleeping in." He snaffled a piece of leftover cheddar. "Hotel homo sap leaves something to be desired, doesn't it? I can build you a better perch, I bet. Or you could sleep outside in a real tree."

"Full of atmospheric turbulence and strange animals? No thank you, I'd rather misuse your furniture." Foot-hands settled gingerly on the floor. "The plains-folk would like this better, though." A pause. "I just realized something else—I still have to do the morning ritual before I can eat."

"What do you need?" I asked. I suspected that candles and bread and wine didn't enter into it.

"A plains-person, usually. But with my great authority as probably the only Ringer awake in this solar system, I'm going to rule that a human would be okay. You're our provisional third symbiote species, after all. It's just saying a few words, and holding hands. It's short."

I hesitated. We'd never talked about religion before, making up for it with extensive arguments about politics. "I hope it's not rude to ask, but is this ritual dedicated to a specific deity? Is that something you believe in?" I couldn't tell about Rhamnetin, but Athëo looked decidedly uncomfortable. If the Ringers' firm beliefs about the destiny of humanity grew from some sort of religious fanaticism, he'd never want to talk with them again.

"Maybe?" Rhamnetin padded to the window, pressed a leg against the glass to look outside. "Um. What do you think of, when you think of a tree?"

"Normally?" Right now it made me think about trying to get my guest a proper bed, but that wasn't what he meant. I imagined the old willow in the front yard, roots casting deep for water, bowing and dancing to a century of hurricanes. "The life of the world. Trees are half the Earth's lungs. We breathe in oxygen and exhale carbon dioxide, and make it in other ways too. And trees breathe in carbon dioxide and exhale oxygen. It's the most basic equation—keep it in balance, and the world survives." In reality, of course, it wasn't just trees. Beyond all the restored rainforests growing lush from their steward rivers, it was deep-rooted prairie grass, vast mats of hyper-efficient algae, vertical farms of engineered moss stuffed in all the crevasses of every city. Symbolically, though, it was always rivers and trees. "But trees are generous beyond that core need. They give us fruit to eat, shade in the summer, wood to build with, habitats for thousands of species. When we design new technology, we ask whether it's like a tree—whether it leaves the world around it better and cleaner while doing the needed work."

"That's part of it for us, too," said Rhamnetin. "And most of what the plains-folk perceive, though we've taught them more. When I think of a tree, I think of moving between the branches, and how whenever I reach out I find a new branch that takes me where I need to go. The universe is the same way. If you reach out, you'll eventually grasp the next branch. Sometimes people reach in the wrong direction, or miss their grip, or find a dead stick that cracks, but that's not the tree's fault. There's always a next branch, you just need to find it.

"That's what symbiosis is to us. When we outgrew our worlds, the plains and trees were the next branch for each other—we grasped, and swung, and found our new perch together. And there's something in the universe, a principle or a force or an awareness, that makes sure that there will always be a next branch. Not everyone agrees on what it is, but everyone respects it. You could translate it as god, or chi, or—" Here he used a couple of human words I didn't recognize. "I tend to think of it as a force. One that listens, but answers in branches, not in words."

"I'm sorry," I said. "I want to help, but I think it might be against *my* religion to participate, if your ritual's dedicated to a force that isn't our god. I'd have to ask a rabbi." I felt stupid saying it. I'd always made my own calls about what counted as kosher and what I felt comfortable doing on the Sabbath. But this was out of my depth—I didn't want to be the first person to make this decision, and end up looking like an idiot in some future iteration of Talmud.

"Do I need to believe in your force, to do this?" asked Athëo abruptly. "Or to get along with your people?"

"No, definitely not. Some people think about it entirely in terms of physics. But they still do the ritual. It's a reminder to each other, as much as respect to anything larger."

"Tell me what you want me to do." Athëo listened as Rhamnetin solemnly described the exchange, brief as our own blessings. He nodded. "That doesn't bother me." As much approval as he ever gave a ritual. "Okay, let's see if I remember this. The gift is found—"

"No, wait," said Rhamnetin. "I just realized it should go the other way. The parts aren't trees plus anyone else; the first line goes to whichever species joined the Rings first, and that's *me*. The gift is found when we reach, trusting that we will find."

Prompted, Athëo said, "We waited, and ... didn't know that we were waiting." He sounded not doubtful, as I might have expected, but thoughtful in his hesitations.

"Together," said Rhamnetin, "the cycle is open to us."

"Only together, we, um, reach out?"

"Not quite. Reach again, and grasp what we find."

"Only together we reach again," said Athëo, "and grasp what we find. Whatever that turns out to be."

"Exactly! Thank you." I read in Rhamnetin's quiet joy that this moment would go into *their* history texts, the first exchange of a simple, sacred ritual with a new species.

I basked in those little oases of cultural exchange. They couldn't help being fraught, simply from the assumptions we brought along, but they were gentle in comparison with the more overt negotiations. Rhamnetin might be an expert in asking awkward questions, but his sheer love for the questions meant he wasn't hyperfocused on his people's long-term goals. His sisters, of whichever ring, fell easily into testing our factions against each other. If they didn't like an answer from the watersheds, they'd try the same query with NASA and Asterion. I was keenly aware that they had no reason to prefer any of us, beyond who cooperated more and faster. That was almost certainly the corporate consortium, unimpeded by either bureaucracy or ethics. From the circles under St. Julien's eyes, she felt much the same.

Our trip to Zealand, when Asterion would be able to make their case on their own turf, drew closer. For decades, we'd treated with corporations from a position of strength. I needed advice from people who knew where to find weakness in a corporation that held the high ground. So Shabbat eve found me not lighting candles with my own household, but on the doorstep of the chaos from whence I'd been formed.

CHAPTER 13

I suppose I should explain about Bet H'aretz Ha Y'am. *Not* explaining my family makes it sound like I'm ashamed, like they're as viciously maladaptive as Athëo's parents. But really, it's just that once I moved out, I was never able to work back up to the Bet's overwhelming pace. In all honesty, I hadn't always been able to keep to that pace when I lived there. There are a good two dozen adults in residence at any given point, plus kids—now the second generation to grow up there. My own parents were among the founders, along with several aunts and uncles and miscellaneous nominal relations. The walls and floors and screens declaim art and activism, radical cybersecurity and midnight poetry, scientific and spiritual and familial experiments outside the bounds of whatever institutions are currently in favor. If you're not contributing to at least three of those things at once, you're probably either sick or hyperobsessed with the immersive genderbending street production of *The Maltese Falcon* in mid-century Blackout-era costume that's scheduled to kick off in less than a week. To give an example not quite at random. As I came in, I accidentally stepped on the mural-in-progress of a lantern-lit stormwater tunnel laid across half the common room. Against the concrete of the tunnel wall, period-style graffiti splashed a brilliant yellow dandelion.

"Aunt Judy don't don't don't!" shouted Talia, and I made my way carefully around the rest of the props to scoop the seven-year-old into a hug. The waves of the Bet swept up to claim me.

Two costuming decisions, three requests to stand in for as-yet-unfinished scenery, several whispered mantras to avoid hyperventilating, and a hungry toddler later, I found my dad and eema in one of the side studios. Eema was swearing at a half-finished ukulele. She swore more when she saw it was almost sundown. (Bet standard time, which meant there was still a spark of light in the west if you squinted.) But she and Dad put down their chisels and hugged me, and we went together to collect Mom from the greenhouse. We joined the rest of the Bet's Jewish contingent (only a portion of the house, despite the name) in the kitchen, where Aunt Adele lit the candles in their elaborate worked-iron holders, and sang the prayers in her gorgeous tenor with Eema providing descant. I wondered how Rhamnetin was reacting to our own ritual at home, and whether Mallory had stuck around for dinner, and whether they were looking on with the same sardonic smile they gave everything else.

After I was stuffed with parsnip soup and greenhouse salad and Dad's famous experimentally significant beetroot cookies, I finally got my parents in a corner away from the chaos. Dori wriggled in Dad's arms, warm and satisfied.

"So how are your new roly-poly friends?" he asked. "And the skittery ones?"

"Very technologically advanced. They like small babies, and Dinar's jam, and taking apart gas giants to use as construction material. You must have been following the network traffic."

"And keeping up with our own contributions," said Mom, who'd helped moderate the early conceptual design discourse for the dandelion networks. "Whenever there's been a network online to accept our ideas. But there's nothing like being there in person."

"I'm surprised you haven't shown up to meet them," I said quietly.

"We're sure you've got it under control, dear," said Eema.

"She's been fretting all week," clarified Dad. "But we're sure you've got it under control. As a matter of policy."

"I appreciate that." And I did. Everyone in the Bet is constantly in everyone else's headspace, but they mostly understood that if I'd wanted that, I would've stuck around. Not that they weren't always eager for an invitation, which I was about to grant them. "I don't have it under control. I need input."

I told them about Asterion, and my fears about the Zealand visit: what the corporations wanted from the Ringers, why they'd dangled the trip at Dinar.

"Huh. Trying to be seductive, are they?" asked Eema thoughtfully. She'd stood in the lines that forced corporations to flatten their footprints or shut down entirely, using newborn SEED code to identify sites that would have the greatest impact.

You shouldn't take from this that my parents are famous, or that there weren't crowds of other people doing the same things they did. They came of age at the end of the era of big apes, and never tried to hold on to that kind of recognition. But they were among the hundreds of thousands who acted out of billions who couldn't, or who didn't want to, or who never heard about the movements until they were well underway. The whole Bet contributed their passion and time and overwhelming intensity to changing the world, at a time when the world was ready to change. They're the people *I* know who were in the heart of the dandelion revolution and understood its tools, and who are always urging me to change more, and push harder on the changes in progress.

Dad cooed at Dori, his expression thoughtful. Mom and Eema waited for him to talk; he was the bard of the trio. "Asterion isn't like the corporations we brought down. They're what grew from the remnants after the workers dispersed, and the stocks turned back into autumn leaves, and the companies lost their cloak of personhood.

"The billionaire CEOs knew it was coming. They fantasized about the utopias and reactionary havens that they could set up when they'd lost everything else. They planned luxurious retreats with their closest employees and protectors. They asked researchers how to make those retreats stable, how to convince their guards to keep protecting them instead of taking over. The ones who succeeded—the aislands that didn't fall to plague or revolution or Fly-lord Syndrome—were the seeds of today's corporations. They're built on the whims of dead men who believed they could do anything. The main thing they all have in common is that they value hoarding wealth and flaunting it, and that their ideas weren't terrible enough to actually get them stabbed."

I stood and paced. Ideas half-formed in scraps and shinies glinted from the walls; from above descended a mobile of silver gull wings, curves riding the draft of the Bet's high ceilings. "They want to be relevant again. The Ringers could give them that. Room and resources and markets across a system of trillions, and then they come back to Earth with leverage to do whatever they feel like."

"They want to be relevant," he agreed. "And they don't want to admit that they were wrong."

I threw up my hands. (The Bet brings out my dramatic side.) "I don't even know what gender they are! They won't touch Dinar's pronoun pins, after all the trouble she went to putting them out for the Ringers!"

"You know it's none of your business if people don't tell you, dear," said Eema primly.

"They're telling me, I assume. I just can't read the language."

"You probably don't have the right pins, either," Mom said. "They use different pronouns, a dozen of them—I don't know whether 'he' and 'she' even enter into it these days. They change, you know."

"Sam changes, sometimes daily," said Dad mildly. One of the newer Bet members, who I didn't know well. "Plenty of people do."

Mom rolled her eyes. "Plenty of people don't set up a system where everyone has to change gender presentation constantly just so they can sell them five wardrobes. It's the same thing they used to do with diet pills—sell dirt to fill the hole you've made."

"I'm pretty sure they enjoy it," Dad said. "And they need to do something with their time—gender play's better than coming up with new high-carbon products. The ones who feel strongly about minimalist fashion can always emigrate to the watersheds."

All this was anthropologically fascinating, and would probably shock the Ringers in ways they'd benefit from being shocked. It also didn't address my real problems with Asterion. "I guess their genders are their business, as long as they don't mind getting 'they' by default. What I really need to know is how to hold them behind the fencelines where you put them. Where are they still vulnerable?" I hated asking. Our biggest enemies these days were heat waves and hurricanes; I didn't like the thought of hurting people. Even the people who'd raised the heat waves. "They're almost certainly behind the malware, and it's giving them room to build more influence than they have in decades. If they ally with the Ringers, maybe more influence than they've ever had. We need to push them back."

"Hold that thought," said Mom. She left, walking quickly, and Eema shrugged.

"Make sure you download the full set of corporate constraints from the last round of talks," said Dad. "In their own ground, you may be able to spot things we can't pick up from the fenceline or with the occasional site inspection. Maybe drop a few extra sensors while you're at it, especially around the proposed antenna site. If we find problems there, we can make them withdraw the offer, or at least spend more time making it right."

We talked through Asterion's likely environmental violations for a few minutes, with digressions into hair-raising stories about cleaning up the Anacostia. Then Mom came back.

"Here. Look at this, but don't fidget."

This was a pocketbot, and it did in fact look like something to fidget with. It was a miniature of the puzzlebots that grace festivals, the sort that you use to pass time on a boring monitor duty. Turquoise and indigo segments folded into geometric solids, surfaces inlaid with nail-thin slots and shallow depressions and raised patterns of bumps.

"Your Aunt Priya has been in the countermeasures corner of the anti-malware task. She worked this up on the side, as a conceptual prototype. Solve it inside the core range of a corporate network, and it should be able to insert something into their system."

I reexamined the innocent-looking bot, feeling queasy. "Something?"

"The seed for a back door. Their security protocols aren't as good as ours."

"Really? Because they sure seem to have found a way around our protocols. Unless the anti-malware team knows something that should've made people stop glaring at Dinar by now."

"Attack is easier than defense, always. You know that. We used to have more exploits in their systems, but they're mostly used up. We don't have the insights we used to—if we did, they'd never have been able to deploy this thing on us."

Seeing the look on my face, Eema said. "Judy, you don't need to carry this thing if you don't feel up for it. It's a risk—anything like this is a risk."

"Priya's sure the code is undetectable in this form," said Mom. "But Eema is right. I know this isn't your usual thing—you're a chemist, not an activist. Which is what the world's needed, lately."

I stiffened. "I'm not *a* chemist. I *practice* water chemistry. Along with child-rearing and network management and sensory enhancement and also, lately, high-level negotiation with aliens. And I'm not *scared*. I don't like using malware, even against corporations who're using it against us. They won't be better people for having their own networks break down—what the world *needs* is people who can think together clearly. Everywhere." I caught my breath and tried to slow down. I wanted to sound like a respected network contributor with moral weight, not a kid mad about overcooked green beans.

"Do you think we beat these bastards by glaring at them?" asked Mom, exasperated as if I *were* throwing a tantrum.

Dad has an irritating way of sounding talmudic and rational, no matter what we're talking about. He spoke mildly: "Everyone thinking clearly, cooperating together, would be best. But that's not what we have right now. The corporations weren't thinking cooperatively by infecting our networks. We need to stop them from doing it again, or from continuing to do it. Barring that, we at least need to redirect their resources, so we can finish fixing what they broke. If it's a matter of the watersheds cooperating to handle a crisis versus the corporations taking control, we have to choose the watersheds."

Talmudic and rational, and right. "We don't even know Asterion did it. There are dozens of corporations."

"It doesn't matter how many names they use; they've always worked together as one when their power's under threat," Mom said. "Besides, if we can get this into one of their networks, we can spread it to others. After all, *they* managed it."

I was, in fact, scared. I wasn't stupid and I didn't trust experts promising absolutes—"undetectable" was like a sensor reading with no error bars, and Bet members tended to dismiss any personal risk short of certain death. And for all that we held sway over the corporations in anything affecting the planet, their own laws still ruled everything else behind the fenceline. If Asterion caught me with that bot, they could subject me to whatever discipline suited them. Fines, usually, arbitrarily large, to be paid off in indentured labor. To ransom me, the network would need to accept responsibility for my actions—and the diplomatic penalties that would follow, potentially fatal to our tight-wired negotiations with corporations, nations, and Ringers.

The trade-offs were too steep to properly decide on my own, but I didn't dare post anything to the problem boards. That would put the network's responsibility on record, and whoever developed the corporate malware might still have thread access.

I couldn't even talk about it with my family. Whatever my penalties might be if I got caught, those for Dinar—part of the corporate hierarchy by their laws if not by ours—would be far worse if she were held responsible. And with her corporate connections, and her conviction that we could talk them into changing their minds, I wasn't convinced she wouldn't try to stop me regardless of our final decision. I couldn't tell Athëo unless I could deal with him talking to Dinar. That left Carol, who I wanted to tell very badly. But leaving her behind with the burden of knowing, and worrying about it, seemed like more unkindness than I could bear.

So I worried on my own. About the real and terrible costs if I tried to use the bot and it went badly, and about the real and desperate need to redirect the network's attackers. And about the morality of the whole thing. On a rational level, I saw Dad's point, and I knew clean hands never planted a garden. But my guts churned at the idea of cutting off another community's senses the way ours had been cut.

I worried. And I tried to decide.

CHAPTER 14

"Rhamnetin should not have asked you to come." Cytosine's limbs slicked back away from me; eyes swiveled forward. Until now, I hadn't even realized that his invitation *didn't* have her blessing.

"Why on earth not?" If she wanted so badly to work with the corporation away from network witnesses, we were doing even worse in the negotiations than I'd thought.

Cytosine had been tense all day. It was raining, brief spasms of downpour interspersed with tedious drizzle. Lightning brightened the windows and thunder rattled them three seconds later; all her tendrils twitched. Kyo, who had the same opinion of storms as our habitat-dwelling guests, yipped desperately. Every time I passed a cluster of network representatives, I heard anxious murmurs. Only the kids, snuggled on the couch with Carol, Raven giggling at every flash, seemed immune to the chaos.

"You shouldn't go anywhere you wouldn't take your children," she said. Of course. "He shouldn't have encouraged you to do it."

"They came here," I said. "We can go there. Sometimes it's worth sending adults out to take risks, even if we aren't willing to expose our children. And I do want to see Zealand—maybe I'm wrong about the risks. I won't know unless I go."

Limbs screeched together, off-key. "He's overstepping."

"I'm glad he asked. Honored." Thunder growled again, and my lenses showed the local map of shifting flood risks, currents rising against the banks of the Anacostia and Potomac. I added notes to the familiar patter of runoff prep and risk mitigation threads, while I tried to figure out how to respond. "I think he was right. You've seen the Asterion team here, and us at home. The different perspective will be good for all of us. I hope I can still get a ride with you; it'll be a longer trip if I have to take one of our flights."

Another screech. "No. If you're coming anyway, you may as well come with us. But he shouldn't have asked."

I was awake too late, first pacing with Dori, and then tossing beside Carol until 3 a.m. I missed the medications that kept my biorhythms on track before I got pregnant; even after Dori was weaned, anything that made it hard to wake up off-cycle would probably be a bad idea for a while. At least old-fashioned sertraline was still okay—I might lie in the dark with my wheels spinning, but the wheels in question were mostly logistical and ethical quandaries rather than rehashes of all my imagined worst mistakes. Right now, for example, my brain was convinced that I'd missed something in the flood data. It was not, I realized, going to let go until I checked.

I put my mesh back on and leaned against my pillow in the dark, flickering through stormwater flows. Carol murmured and rolled against me.

"Just checking some readings," I said soothingly. I stroked the fuzz of her hair, trying to convince myself that I should curl back up around my wife. That was what most people did at this time of night.

The flood was higher than historical averages, but in keeping with what I was used to. I checked Bear Island, found that we weren't anywhere near the point where the causeway from the mainland would wash out, let alone where the *Solar Flare* would have to test its submergence capabilities. Cytosine was twitchy about the storm because she wasn't used to weather, not because of any obvious danger.

But what was *in* the water . . .

I'd analyzed the first spill of organics from Bear Island, then gotten pretty seriously distracted. While I'd been busy others had run with it, mapping the exact combinations of molecules and how they differed from Terran effluvia. For five days those molecules had clustered around the island, tapering downstream, every indicator confirming that the Ringer microbes were being quickly overwhelmed by the river's immune system. The engineered bacteria that gobbled nutrients from dog shit didn't mind a dusting of Ringer shit for flavor.

But they never quite kept up with storm runoff. I checked samples farther and farther out from the island, and found the new organics in every tributary all the way down to the ocean.

We had our first alien invasives, spreading through the roots of an ecosystem barely recovering from our own depredations. And among the *Solar Flare*'s three-hundred-odd species, there must be something to eat *their* organics, breaking them down to feed the trees where Rhamnetin slept. Whatever that was had food now, if it wanted to slip out of the ship. And whatever ate that, and whatever ate it in turn. Some of those species would merge easily with the Chesapeake eco-system, finding unfilled niches or sharing them generously. But others would compete with Earth's own species, resourceful and resilient as fire ants. I started a problem thread.

The day after the rain, I found Dinar in the garden. Adrien was there too, helping dig the hairy vetch into the bed it had been warming.

"Won't your velvet get dirty?" I asked, more sharply than I'd meant to. Or more sharply than I should have, at least.

They shrugged. "It's washable."

"They wanted to talk," said Dinar. "I told them to make themselves useful, because I'm not leaving the garden to tend itself while we chat." Dinar could always make time to focus on guests when she wanted to, which she usually did.

"I'll help too," I said.

We worked quietly for a few minutes. Whatever Adrien had wanted to say, they hadn't wanted to say it to me.

"You're both coming out to Zealand," they allowed at last.

I nodded. "That's right." I narrowly resisted asking if they had a problem with that, but they could probably hear it anyway.

"Corporate culture can be hard to navigate. I can help."

"We'd certainly like to know what to expect," I said before Dinar could respond. "But we're not trying to fit in. People will know where we're from, the same as they do the Ringers."

"And I've picked a thing or two up from my gigs," said Dinar. "Enough to know where a gigworker stands if she *tries* to fit in."

"You're not just a piecework number cruncher," they assured her. "Everyone will know what you're working on."

She tossed a handful of dried stalks on the sling. "People will know I do piecework, and they'll care—though I'm sure I'll hear plenty of flattery. You think I've got something to offer, now."

"Is that how you see the people who do your gigwork?" I demanded. "Dinar spends a tiny part of her life on you, and you have the nerve to judge her for it. People take enough shit here for giving you a few hours. If you don't respect them for it either, I don't see why anyone should bother."

"Judy—" Dinar put a soil-stained hand on my shoulder. "It's okay. I don't care about their judgment. I just don't plan to try and pass as someone in that hierarchy. I do the work because it needs to be done, not to earn anyone's respect."

Adrien cocked their head. "And where do I stand on *your* ladder?"

"We don't have a ladder," I said. "Are you thinking of joining us? If you stopped following Mallory and Kelsey around, and started contributing expertise and observations to network threads, you'd earn weight and get your basics like anyone else."

They looked at the garden bed and I caught a flash of distaste, wiped away by their usual mask of aloof interest. "I'll keep my salary, thanks. And my spot on the ladder. What you people don't get is that this stuff"—they gestured at the magenta velvet clinging to their torso, spreading into a skirt that flared as they stood and twirled for us—"is fun. Because of the challenge, not in spite of it. Challenges keep life interesting, even when we don't have visitors from other worlds."

"We have fun," said Dinar. Which was in fact true, in spite of her unpersuasive tone.

"Even if you don't take it seriously, you should try dressing up while you're visiting." Adrien twirled again. "Just for fun."

CHAPTER 15

The day of our trip dawned chaotic. Raven woke early with a stuffy nose. They screamed and sobbed until Dinar got some herbal tea in them, and then merely fussed and complained about every move the adults made. Dori started crying every time her sibling did. Eventually I took her outside, where I found St. Julien coming up the steps with Brice.

"You might want to keep your distance today," I said. "Raven's got a cold again."

"That sucks," she said. "I'll bet you had a rough night."

"The germs only seem to have found her sinuses this morning. But I feel bad leaving Athëo and Carol on their own tonight with both kids."

"While you head for the southern hemisphere." She smiled. "I'll let Cytosine know when she gets here, but I may as well tell you now. When you get back, we're inviting you all to a State Department reception, formally welcoming the Ringers to the U.S." She fished in her bag, and her smile widened as she pulled out a cream-colored envelope, heavy paper and wax seal and all, with my family's names in neat calligraphy across the back. "Very formal. We'd like to have all the network ambassadors there as well."

I tried not to gape at the anachronistic object. The implications didn't escape me. "Some of your fellow agencies finally picked up the ball."

"Even Congress. We're opening diplomatic relations properly— though given the circumstances, they're keeping me as the lead."

"Congratulations." I almost found it reassuring that the state could still pull an action together. But the network's first-in-the-ground advantage was fading. "I'll be there."

I paced the porch with Dori, alone. If I were a Ringer, or St. Julien, I'd have found a way to wring a diplomatic victory from her fussiness. Instead I felt the weight of Aunt Priya's bot in my pocket, a fidget I couldn't fidget and a decision I couldn't make. Not on my own. I hadn't wanted to burden my household, and Dinar and Athëo truly couldn't bear that weight. But I worked it over in my mind, and imagined how I'd feel if Carol chose to protect my feelings over being honest.

Then again, she probably *did*. I worried too much—anxiety and depression will do that, even with meds—and it would only be sensible of her not to fuel the fire. Probably she kept dozens of minor secrets, handling things that barely irritated her so they wouldn't lose me even more hours of sleep. The bot was no minor problem, but if I *did* get caught she'd deal with the crisis as it unfolded, the situation no worse for her not having feared it in advance.

As if I'd invoked her, Carol poked her head out the door. "Are you okay?"

"I'm okay."

She came out, and shut the door behind her. "If you're okay, why are you pacing ant trails across the porch?"

I gestured at Dori, still whimpering, and Carol shook her head. "You walk differently when you're calming the baby and when the baby's calming you."

I have no resistance to being understood. I led her out to the gazebo, which for a wonder was not in use. I pulled out the bot and told her, quietly, what it did. "I don't *want* to use this thing. I might as well be carrying the Blackouts in my pocket. Or some '20s horror that shares your entire network's profiles with a corporate algorithm."

She prodded the bot gingerly. "I can't blame you for feeling that way. But shouldn't it matter that it's the other way around?"

"That's what I keep telling myself. And what Mom said. That the difference between corporate algorithms working while ours are broken, and ours working while theirs are broken, could be the future of humanity. I'm terrified to wield that kind of power without distributing the decision—but that would make the cost of failure so much worse." I stuffed the bot back into my pocket and leaned against her, rubbing Dori's back. "So you're my crowd. Sorry. I didn't want you to worry."

"You're a moron. But I love you. I don't think two people can feed a decision algorithm. Imagine you're an ancient battlefield commander, giving orders as the data rolls in."

"That's exactly what I don't want to be. I'm *not* my parents. I was born *now* for a reason. I *belong* now."

"Yeah, but maybe this is the reason. My point is, if you had to make the decision right this second, with no more angsting, what would it be?"

"Not to use it," I said immediately.

"Okay, then. There you go."

"But that doesn't make it the right decision. It just means that if you back me into a corner, I'm more likely to freeze than fight."

"Okay, let's try it a different way." Dori started crying again, and Carol eased her out of the wrap and held her against her shoulder, patting her until she at last made a surprised squeak and spit up on her mama's shirt. "In twenty years or so, you're going to have to tell Dori what you did. What do you want to say?"

When we got back to the house, we found Cytosine and Rhamnetin and Carnitine yelling at each other in the foyer. The cacophony of cellos and out-of-tune saxophones echoed through a house that seemed too small for such an orchestra. Athëo had vanished with Raven, and Dinar was watching stiffly, arms crossed, from the far side of the dining room table along with the Asterion team and a couple of unfortunate Ghats-Narmada reps.

Diamond startled me by dropping from Cytosine's belly and attempting to clamber up my leg. "Mommy baby trip!"

Cytosine stopped yelling in her own language long enough to say, "She's not going to take her baby on the trip. We talked about that."

"I thought *we* talked about that," I said. "I know you don't like it, but I still plan to go." More confidence than I had a right to, given how difficult she could make it even if I followed by plane.

"And you will," she said, and I let out a breath. Then yelled, because I'd gotten a shock from Diamond where they'd brushed my hand. "Sorry, static. I was just startled."

But the baby Ringer poked my skin again, and this time I felt it more clearly: a jangling vibration deep in my nerves. "What was that for?"

"Come talk," said Diamond.

"Oh, you don't know," said Rhamnetin. "They've never touched you before." I wasn't a hundred percent sure that was true, but they certainly hadn't touched me like *that*.

"What does it mean?" I asked. "It's not dangerous, is it?" Dori reached, cooing, for Diamond, and I shifted her farther away.

"Of course not," said Cytosine. At least she seemed distracted from whatever had angered her. Limbs dropped to touch, tip to tip, with Diamond's, and there was a moment of silent exchange. "I think I can show you."

I felt dubious, but I wanted to get back in Cytosine's good graces before what promised to be a fraught journey. I handed Dori to Carol and offered Cytosine my arm, realizing as I did so that I'd probably managed to insult her again. She scuttled over nevertheless, and tiny finger-things brushed my wrist.

What had been buzzing confusion from the toddler was, from their mom, more like textured Morse code. It felt as though Cytosine were tapping my skin, slowly, with chopsticks, then something furry, then drops of rain, all in a shifting pattern. "It's another language?"

"Almost," she said. "Skinsong is an older form of communication, from before my species learned to speak in words. It conveys basic things: emotions, companionship, hunting signals. It's hard to sing to other species, but we've learned how to share with the tree-folk, and now I think with humans. Diamond, that was good work." She touched her child, who wriggled in response.

It was fascinating—and strange to think that between the plains-folk and everyone else, that kind of communication would only be one way. Did it change how they related to Rhamnetin's people? It was its own sort of power, to share all the nuances of your reactions without being able to read other people's. Come to that, it was the plains-folk who could produce everything from their own orchestral speech to human language naturally, without the translation boxes that the tree-folk relied on.

"Your language, the one you speak to each other," I said. "Whose was it originally?"

"No one's," said Rhamnetin. "It started as a pidgin, but it's swung far from the languages we spoke before the grasp. It's grown between us over a thousand years."

"It's rooted in several languages from both worlds," said Carnitine. "It has more of our sound-sets, though, because we tree-folk had a harder time adapting to plains languages than they did to ours."

"She studies these things," said Rhamnetin, and I couldn't tell if the edge of stiffness was his or a technological artifact.

"I've been talking with Athëo," Carnitine went on. "The type of work he does, constructing language as an art, is vital in the early days of symbiosis. Our sounds were more alike when we met than we are to humans now, but where tree-folk couldn't say something easily, the plains-folk shifted to sounds we *could* say. Communication is more important than continuity."

I would have loved to spend days diving into this kind of detail. Getting to know each other, with the stakes no higher than any other chance at learning. "It *is* important. What were you arguing about, when I came in?"

"Ah, that," said Cytosine. "Rhamnetin needs to stay here, while we travel to Zealand. He's not happy about it."

"It's a funny definition of need, that's all I'm saying." The stiffness was definitely Rhamnetin's own.

"Why?" I couldn't blame him for being upset, and it seemed like an unreasonable punishment for asking me to come along. *They* needed his skill at asking the right questions. Hell, I'd been counting on it. He had a gift for cutting through bullshit and getting answers, and Zealand would have plenty of bullshit.

That, and I liked his company better than Cytosine's.

Cytosine's eyes swiveled toward me. "If corporate territory is as dangerous as you seem to think, I want him safe. Someone needs to be able to explain our situation to the Rings."

"I'm not trying to be safe," said Rhamnetin.

"You never do," she said. "Nevertheless, I've made my decision. I have to get the shuttle ready now. Liftoff in half an hour, for those who are coming—and if any of you get motion sick, you should take something for that before we leave."

"Come up to my bower," I told Rhamnetin after she left. "Carol, can you come too? I should nurse before I hand Dori over. If you can help wrestle the pump into its case . . ."

Upstairs, I put Dori to my breast, feeling a little tension slide away in the rhythm of feeding. Most of it remained, though: the jangle of conflicts barely understood. "She's punishing you for asking me along, isn't she?"

"She is," said Rhamnetin. "And it's her right; I should have asked permission. But she's being too inflexible."

"Why?"

"Because she's terrified of how we'll relate to humans when you won't even let your own children play together, and she doesn't like being party to a huge diplomatic insult. She can't get her mind around the idea that leaving your kids at home won't be taken as a slight." His limbs moved restlessly across the chairs and tables. Looking for something to climb?

"She's cutting off her nose to spite her face," said Carol. "If she even *has* a nose."

"She can smell . . ." said Rhamnetin uncertainly. It must seem a particularly strange metaphor to someone with no face at all.

I shook my head, trying to keep focus. Nursing might be great for diplomacy, but it sucked for following a train of thought. "I want to get you a profile on the Chesapeake network. It's still shaky, but you've barely seen the surface of how we make our world work, and you need to understand what we're doing here. How we're fixing the damage to the planet." I took a deep breath. "And if you're on the network, you can see my uploads from Zealand, and feed me questions to ask. *I* want your insights, even if Cytosine's willing to do without them."

Carol's eyes widened. "I bet she won't like that." She started pulling up the screens to add a new network member.

"I'll ask her later," said Rhamnetin. "*After* she gets back."

The Ringers had embedded themselves in the Chesapeake ecology, from the moment they first spilled organics into the Potomac. Technically, that gave them both the right and the obligation to see the data, and share the burden and privilege of mitigating their impact. Maybe with a view of the world from below, they'd understand at last why it mattered.

CHAPTER 16

We gathered outside, where the shuttle glimmered through the cloud-dimmed day. Dinar and I carried backpacks and duffles, a few days of outfits entirely inadequate to whatever Adrien wanted to doll us up in. But I'd draped my parade scarf around my neck, pinned not only with my usual pronouns, but with a tiny brooch celebrating my carbon negotiation work, engraved with the symbol of the watershed networks. I touched the raised lines of the dandelion puffball, reassuringly solid against my skin. Under a microscope, each seed stem would expand into the line of a river. The Potomac was in there, and the Nile, the Euphrates, the Amazon, dozens of others. The corporations might not see that subtle strength, but the brooch would still tell them, unmistakably, where I came from.

Dinar wore an older, simpler announcement of identity: her Star of David pendant, mosaicked in abalone. Raven flung their arms around her knees, and she gathered the toddler in a tight embrace. But at last those of us who were traveling—Cytosine and her handpicked crew members, me and Dinar, Mallory and Kelsey and Adrien—were inside, lifting away from the ground.

"We're going farther this time," explained Cytosine. "So we're climbing higher too."

The shuttle was sleeker inside than the *Solar Flare,* with no room for trees, but there was still something botanical about it. Vine-like grab bars snaked along walls and ceiling, twisted around instruments. Carnitine and Manganese always gripped at least one, whatever else they were doing. Glycine had grown more comfortable with planetary navigation, but I still felt nervous as I watched them chart a course over the projected globe.

"Oh, but this is easier," they said. "We'll be far above your own flight paths, and all those kites and towers that get in the way on short rolls. Going to the other side of the planet is more like flying between habitats."

"Pilots are weird," Carnitine told us. "Talking to them only breeds worry—look out the window instead."

I did, and the view was worth it. We were already high enough to see the Anacostia narrow into a slender spill off the Potomac, the greater river itself shrinking into one fractal crack among many spreading from the bay, the bay a perfect and improbable indigo bounding green and brown earth. The Chesapeake became a crack along the Atlantic. Clouds rushed around us and down, and at last we began soaring out in the long arc over the continent. The curve of the Earth glowed beneath us. I'd ridden a plane to and from the carbon negotiations; this was different. We moved so swiftly that I could see the world turn beneath me, yet I could barely feel our speed.

"It's a nice planet," said Mallory. "But I don't mind seeing it from farther away."

I responded before Cytosine could agree. "Neither do I. This kind of view makes me even more grateful for what we've got here."

That was all the focus I could spare for political sparring. I watched enraptured as we passed through the North American day: hills rich with pine, fields of winter rye and clover shading into the first patches of mixed spring planting. Thunderclouds hid the embattled line of the Mississippi, its silted channel down to the delta more forced and fragile with every storm. For me, every shifting view was a collage of triumph and failure. I saw festering wounds dealt by old powers, but also green places like tattoos printed across scar tissue. Reclaimed prairie, patches pale with drought; I called up an enhanced view just in time to glimpse bison trampling the undergrowth. Great spans of ash and chestnut grew free from pestilence, but there were aspen forests bruised by a decade of moth blight. Then we sped across the far side of the Rockies, and Glycine swore as they steered around the smoke from a vast wildfire. At its edges, the slopes lay barren. Finally, there was the long bright flash of the Colorado Network's desalinating seawall, and we were away from the continent and over the Pacific.

In a plane, slower than the world's turn, we'd have raced the sun and lost. But the shuttle was paced for the scale at which Ringers built. We ran backward through the day to catch up with the dawn, red and purple against indigo ocean, and dove into the night before. At some point it became the night after; the International Date Line gave me a headache every time I had to think about it. The shuttle cabin grew utterly dark. Glycine steered by instrumentation or some signal outside the visible spectrum, and the stars came out above the viewport a thousand miles from even the dimmest emergency lighting. The plains-folk who weren't working tilted their eyes to the sky and waved their limbs like anemone fronds, and tree-folk lifted eye-dotted legs. They spoke to each other in orchestral murmurs. Not a moment of silent awe, but a beauty they knew well enough to put words to.

The ocean lay dark below. But Zealand was one of dozens of aislands scattered outside Australia's boundary waters and along Asia's coasts, and soon we'd enter their spill of light. I took a moment to appreciate the vastness of the planet and the quiet night.

Too soon interrupted, as Adrien slipped in beside me at the viewport. They'd changed into a slick velvet catsuit, and they looked a bit catlike as they tucked themselves demurely into a free spot on the floor. They gazed up, wide-eyed. "Better view than you get from a plane, isn't it? I wonder if they'd sell us a couple of these shuttles."

"I hope so," I said mildly. "It burns cleaner than even modern jet fuels." I could see that much through the window, the air around us disturbed more by the speed of our passage than any detritus trailing behind. We'd never figured out how to run a plane entirely off cleanly charged batteries, which was why flights were normally limited to what we could afford to offset, prioritized based on urgency and the constraints of treaty.

"Once, trips like this were open to anyone," said Adrien. "Imagine having the world so interconnected again. Imagine being that connected *between* worlds."

"They were open to the limited set who could afford them. And you can only have a connected world if you have a *world*."

The intern waved away my caveats. "We'll get further in these negotiations if we focus on our shared interests. We have so much in common; it's our planet too, after all. Our species."

"And yet somehow," I said, "you could never see those commonalities when you held power. We'll pass."

They smiled slyly. "The Ringers want what we have to offer. We could convince them to want what you're offering, too." They stood and stretched, not quite too close. Their warmth radiated through the cool shuttle air with a smell that wasn't quite roses.

I edged away. "And then *we'll* want what you're offering, again? How much do you plan to charge to clean up your old messes? You saw those wildfires."

Adrien sighed, but let me reclaim my space. "I'm twenty-two years old. I've never burned coal in my life. Or committed any of the other crimes you blame on my ancestors."

"It's not exactly ancient history. My parents stood on one side of the fencelines; yours stood on the other." I regretted the words as soon as they were out of my mouth, both because I still didn't know if they'd been raised in a crèche, and because I didn't want them looking up the Bet.

They snorted, indecorous contrast to the smooth façade they'd been projecting. "My grandparents followed their CEO because they thought they'd eat better on Zealand. They were right, too. We aren't exactly born to the board."

That would've been during the Blackouts. "We've had plenty to eat for a while. And we don't much care what a neighbor's family did, as long as they do their part now."

"You care what mine did, though." They turned away, clearly thinking that made a fine last word.

"If you leave Asterion and join the Chesapeake Network—or the Tongala-Baaka, if you'd rather stay closer to home—no one will think twice about anything beyond the good you do and the expertise you bring to your problem threads. They won't care whether you were born on an aisland, and certainly not whether you're 'born to the board.' I can't believe you people are still playing those games. Holding people down because of their starting luck, and how rich their families are."

They were quiet a moment, then shook their head, still looking out the viewport. "I'd rather hustle to win than not play at all. You don't know what you're missing." They made eye contact again, having recovered their lipstick-laced grin: "You'll see."

Zealand had no illumination curfew. The southern stars squinted through bright bands of skyscrapers and the glow of midnight markets. Light spilled across the aisland and over sheer cliffs. The boundary far below, where cliff met ocean before descending to the seabed, was hidden in shadow; beyond that shadow the water reflected the city like a moon.

"We'll have a proper reception tomorrow," Kelsey said, yawning. "But for now, let's get you dinner and a place to sleep."

Two rides met us at the little airport: one to bring luggage to our hotel, the other, larger and staffed—though fortunately not piloted—by an actual human, to carry the people. I let the luggage go with only a twinge of worry; everything important was in either my mesh or my pockets. Our ride was modern and electric, though with no tags to show the source of its energy.

I'd expected from a corporate city . . . I don't know, towering smokestacks and foam-choked runoff streams. There were smokestacks, though I couldn't spot anything coming out of them. The volatile count was maybe a shade higher than at home. Walls flashed noon-bright ads, but dark strips in between reflected the telltale sheen of solar panels.

The Ringers stretched and stared. Carnitine spread limbs in all directions, trying to take it in; Cytosine and Glycine kept rocking back, curlicue spirals with their eyes raised toward the lights. Cytosine's kids chattered constantly, and I missed Dori with a chest-deep ache.

Even at this time of night, the streets were as busy as any afternoon in Washington. People strolled, argued on corners, stopped to look at particularly eye-catching advertisements, wandered in and out of stores. Carts, bright with scrolling adwork, sold snacks to eager passersby. Nothing looked much like the food at home or the basket-laden bikes that would have carried it, but the smells made my mouth water. Cinnamon and cumin, smoke, dripping meats, the earthy odor of mushrooms. The drifting tang of salt water, from the ocean far beneath the aisland's rim, might be only my imagination.

"We'll be at fancy banquets all week," said Mallory. "Do you just want to eat from carts tonight? There's a great little park a couple blocks away where we can sit."

Everyone agreed with enthusiasm. The rest of this trip might be steeped in horror, from negotiations around the banquet tables to the thing in my pocket, but at least we wouldn't face the notorious plastic tomatoes that my Nana swore had once epitomized corporate food.

The "little park" was blocks wide in either direction, benches arranged around illuminated fountains. Purple faded to pink, lit up blue, then shifted to an eerie red before gentling to purple again. I carried a kabob of deboned quail, grilled in some pungent marinade until the skin crackled, and a bread bowl full of black rice mixed with lime, sharp herbs, and flecks of chili pepper. Dinar had a plate of tiny fried gyoza in color-coded dumpling wrappers; Mallory had helped her work through which flavors were kosher, but their contents were otherwise mysterious. Cytosine, Glycine, and Carnitine had among them a dozen pastries filled with walnut and sesame paste. Carnitine held three cones full of grape-sized gelatinous spheres, balanced cautiously between pairs of pincers.

"What are *those*?" asked Cytosine. "They look like the"—here she interjected scraping violins—"that Perihelion 50 brings to Meeting Day for desserts." Those were the food pill lovers, I remembered.

"They're good," insisted Adrien. "Here, I'll show you." They leaned unselfconsciously against Carnitine's limb, wrapping their arm around her to lift one of the spheres delicately from the cone. It shimmered like a soap bubble. "You have to hold them lightly, or they pop before you get them in your mouth." They snaked the stolen snack back around, put it carefully between their lips, and closed their eyes with an expression of bliss. Then they took another and held it to one of Carnitine's mouths. She plucked the sphere, and Adrien stroked her fur as they withdrew their hand.

"That's amazing," Carnitine said. She bumped Adrien affectionately with the same limb. "It tastes like . . . just the inside part of ripe fruit?"

"But what *is* it?" I asked, intrigued in spite of myself, and a little unnerved by Adrien switching flirting targets so quickly.

Adrien looked at me from under their eyelids. "Try one."

"They're vegetarian," added Mallory.

"Are they some sort of drug?" asked Dinar, and I remembered hearing that aislands had very odd laws around intoxicants.

"Oh my god." Adrien rolled their eyes, but I'd seen the flash of a real glare. "Trust us at least that far, please?"

"I like to know where my food comes from." I could hear how stiff I sounded, but I was exhausted. With the quail and the rice I could at least pretend to know what the farms looked like, what sort of conditions the workers and animals lived in, filling in gaps with my own experience even if I was probably wrong.

Mallory put a hand on Adrien's shoulder. "They're made from olives; they come from Themiscyra. I don't know where the five-spice is from."

A bit embarrassed, I tried to take one, and managed to pop it exactly as warned. Carnitine jerked but didn't spill the rest of the cones; before I could apologize a long yellow tongue flicked out to clean her fur.

"They *are* dangerous, aren't they," said Adrien, laughing. "Try again."

This time I managed the trick, driven by the suspicion that if I failed Adrien would try to hand-feed me as well. The sphere sat on my tongue for an instant, slick and solid, then collapsed into a mouthful of rich, grassy olive oil flavored with anise and clove and the sun that burned over flooded Mediterranean shores.

CHAPTER 17

Dinar and I were too tired, when we finally got in, to explore the exotic details of our hotel room beyond confirming the presence of beds. Windows polarized against the dawn as soon as we lay down; a few hours later they cleared on a cirrus-streaked late afternoon.

"Why are the windows being mean?" muttered Dinar blearily.

I rubbed my eyes, frustrated that I couldn't take sufficient advantage of my first night in months without a crying baby. "Maybe it's time for that banquet they warned us about?"

On a normal trip I'd stay in a neighborhood guesthouse, or with a family from the host network. During my Transit Year I slept on the train, draped next to whoever I'd been talking with when I ran out of steam. The hotel seemed like something out of a historical novel, luxurious and anonymous. Velvet draped beds and windows; an old-fashioned hard screen hung from the gilt-crusted wall. Images from century-old films adorned the rest of the room, long-haired actors locked in denim-and-sequin embraces.

I rubbed my eyes again, feeling out of sync with the world. My mesh lay beside my pillow—I hadn't even removed it properly when we got in, just let it slide off. I let the familiar weight of fine, chain-linked sensors spill over my palm. Redbug had promised that it would be secure, interfacing only with our own towers around the fenceline. It shouldn't even be compatible with anything other than a dandelion network; the corporations used an entirely different format that worked with their implants. But something had crossed that gap, and we still didn't know how.

Looking at the gilded room, the effort Asterion was going to for Dinar, it occurred to me for the first time that "how" might be a human who already had access to our networks. Surely Redbug, more expert in this type of paranoia than I, must have already thought of that, must be scanning their team members for any hint of corporate seduction.

Of course they had. And found a match for their suspicions in Dinar.

I gave up on second-guessing my own equipment and set the mesh cap on my head. The cool weight lay comfortably against the fuzz of my scalp. I'd neglected to take my lenses out before I went to bed. I'd need to clean them later, but for now I waited as data trickled in, slowed by distance as well as the ongoing malware recovery. I wished for more sensors in the ground, the full team of investigators that none of the networks had organized well enough to send. Even more than the slowness, that failure of organization suggested some taint unpurged from our code. I pressed my scarf to my nose, breathing in the trace of baby-scent where I'd held Dori against it.

Dinar was still offline, fussing with her arm.

"Did you forget to take that off last night too?" I asked. "I mean, this morning?"

"Time is an illusion," she said mournfully. "And no, I can get this thing off and on in my sleep. What I can't do, apparently, is correctly hook it up to an unfamiliar energy grid in my sleep."

"I'm sorry."

"I've got enough charge to make it through the day. But please ask Carol about power conversion when you've got your messages synced."

I shot off the question, accompanied by promises of love and of solidarity in sleep deprivation. My inbox was full of queries about the trip. Some were genuinely concerned, but most were thinly veiled objections to me, Dinar, and even the Ringers going at all. What they expected us to do about the latter I had no idea. Nothing from my parents, of course, who knew more than I ever would about technological paranoia. The bot remained a lump in my pocket. Every time I thought about it, only every couple minutes or so, I felt irrationally insecure about my own equipment.

But I did get one happy message—Carol had managed to get Rhamnetin online. I ran a half-conscious hand over my mesh, feeling it shift against my skin. I had no idea where Rhamnetin's people kept the neural signals of interest and recognition and unconsidered bias that the mesh was designed to pick up. A *good* Ringer mesh would probably take either decades of research or a deep dive into their own neuroscience. But Carol had kludged together a set of chain-link bracelets around his upper limbs that did *something*.

This is like looking at the Rings, and trying to see all the connections at

once, he wrote. **Carol says no one person needs to track it all, but I don't know how you resist. What happened on your trip?**

I sent the record of our flight—and more importantly, the conversations during it—to the already-acrimonious thread on the Asterion negotiations, and pinged Rhamnetin with a pointer. Separately, I sent him and Carol my own thoughts: about Adrien's politically tinged flirting, about their irritation at my lack of interest, about Carnitine's willingness to flirt back, about trying to read every nuance of the food and the room and the buildings stretching skyward. I hesitated, glancing at Dinar, but included her and Athëo in the message. It wasn't like she, or Cytosine for that matter, wouldn't notice us pulling Rhamnetin in. And this discussion wouldn't make the situation more awkward for her than it was already.

It *was* getting more awkward, too. Several threads treated this trip as a failure not only of our negotiations, but of every place where the watersheds had bound ourselves too closely to the powers we'd supplanted.

I caught the slight jerk of Dinar's arm as it finally answered to her nerves, interface between flesh and synthetic not quite as smooth as usual. I resisted the urge to help as she got her own mesh on. She grimaced as she found the same threads I'd been poring through. "What do they think we *should* have done? It's never been realistic to treat fencelines as a perfect quarantine, or to think we're safer acting like they're some sort of black box. The root of the problem is *here;* Redbug's not going to solve it patching leaks at home."

"I know. But a lot of people think this whole situation proves the risk of keeping corporations around at all."

She glared, either at the room that illustrated Asterion's solidity or at her mesh's projection within it. "They lost any legal existence outside their own territory a long time ago. But we need the work they can do. And if we don't want them to be corporate forever, we need to keep reminding them of alternatives. You can't make people stop affiliating."

"You can't." I found the absolutists ridiculous—no power in our world had ever died away completely. Even the divine right of kings still echoed in our rhetoric, every storm a sign of failed stewardship and every successful mitigation demonstrating Nature's sovereign approval of our networked decisions. The tatters of power might be repurposed, but they never fully decomposed back into fertile soil.

But I understood why the absolutists thought the way they did. At the fourth power's peak, corporations and states had agreed on ostensibly safe levels for arsenic in drinking water. Then, having shown that the threshold was an arbitrary decision, they'd raised it; the more poison companies could release, the greater their profits. There could never, in fact, be a truly safe level.

The door chimed a chord as baroque as the walls. Dinar went to get it, and I closed the great pile of critiques to draft a new thread, ready to gather quick input.

Adrien strolled in, more confident and forceful in their home ground. "I hope you slept well. I'm here to help you get ready for tonight's party." They'd changed again, this time into a black leather jacket and pants, a gaudy necklace of blue and red blown glass, and red stilettos that made me wince with imagined stumbles. Adrien somehow didn't totter, but pushed aside the decorative curtain, unnecessarily but with ostentatious grace, to look fondly out the window. "It's good to be home—now it'll be boardrooms and ballrooms all week." They abandoned the cityscape and turned to grin back at us. "I hope you packed well."

"We brought our best outfits, if that's what you mean." I readjusted my scarf, and the pins holding it in place. "They'll be different from yours, but that's fine. We're different sorts of people."

Adrien sighed. "So we are. And you don't play games. Would you like to know the rules everyone else will be using?" They leaned back against the windowsill, arms crossed and head cocked, silhouetted by reddening light. "I'm trying to help, I promise. Even if you aren't playing the game, it's still possible to lose."

Probably even with Adrien's help; telling us the rules was almost certainly some move of their own. My head hurt.

"Are you giving this intro to the Ringers, too?" asked Dinar.

"Of course. Well, the associates are."

"You got stuck with us instead," suggested Dinar.

"Hardly 'stuck.'" That irritating grin again. "Though I'm sorry to miss their questions. What pronouns do you think you should use for me?"

The question caught me off guard. I'd been defaulting to "they" for far longer than was ever necessary with watershed members. "I'm sorry, I have no idea. And it would be rude to guess."

"Not around here." Adrien frowned. "I suppose that's why you wear those pins, and the same ones all the time. If getting it wrong is so awful, you've got to pick one set and stick with it to avoid disaster."

"Not everyone uses the same ones all the time," said Dinar. "But yes, that's why we badge: to be polite and avoid mistakes that hurt people." She shot me a look.

"So what does it mean, that you're"—Adrien squinted at my pins, exaggerating for effect—"female?"

This wasn't the conversation I'd expected, and I found myself curious how it would tie back to the night's corporate games. Curious, and apprehensive—were they preserving old prejudices here, old rules about how women could be treated?

"It means being a woman feels right to me—it matches my own idea of myself. My soul, maybe. I guess practically it means I'm comfortable with a certain balance of hormones, more estrogen and so on."

"Powers!" Adrien's eyes widened. "If I had to change my hormones every time I shifted, I wouldn't want to do it often either. I wouldn't want to walk around with my soul on my collar, either." They twined glass beads around their fingers, looking thoughtful. "Here, my hormones are my doctor's business. The shape of my body under my clothes is my lovers'. My inner self . . . if souls are real, they don't seem like something I'd want to advertise to the world—and even more so if they aren't real, if they're something you manufacture for yourself—far too dangerous to share. My true self, assuming I admit to having one, is for me alone."

It seemed like a disturbing thing to keep private—as if here, even one's closest friends might exploit any vulnerability. "What should we call you, then? Aside from your name? Is the default 'they' rude?"

"Rude, no. Wrong, I'm afraid so. Our pronouns don't reflect any inner essence, gender or otherwise. They shift with our presentations. Let me try this a different way. Do you non-game-players have chess?"

"Sure," said Dinar, who played regularly at the library, and beat me in about ten minutes every time I gave her the chance.

"Presentation is like if you could pick, at any point, whether you want to play a bishop or a knight or a rook. Even a queen, if you time it right."

Dinar opened her suitcase and began hanging clothes in the closet, giving undue attention to each shirt. "And some people are stuck being pawns?"

"It's not an exact metaphor. None of the presentations are *bad* to play, or no one would play them."

"And how do you win?" Dinar switched the position of a couple of hangers. "It doesn't seem like much fun to be a king, either."

"There's no definitive winning, or losing. That would end the game. You try to get concessions for your bosses, or your company—or tonight, your species."

"You never said what presentation you were—playing. What we *should* call you." I blushed, reminding myself that it wasn't rude.

"Tonight I'm playing holo. A lot of people will be; it's sort of a party presentation. You mix your signals, and you can use just about any strategy. Pronouns are 'e' and 'em' and 'eir,' which I know is the part you really care about. 'Tha,' 'thon,' 'thos' are the rasa pronouns, for when you haven't seen someone in a few hours and aren't sure of thos current presentation. You never use that one to an adult's face unless tha's naked or in the process of shifting."

"And what will people expect from us, openly presenting as women?" I asked, still worried that the answer would suit the aisland's twentieth-century aesthetic.

"Woman's not one of our options. Some people might treat you as rasa, like you aren't dressed at all. Tania . . . no, it's the same pronouns, but you don't act the part at all. Holo would be the most polite assumption."

Dinar finished her own clothes, and went to unpack mine. I let her; at least my presentation wouldn't be "wrinkled." "So what are all these strategies holos are expected to use? And what's 'tania'?"

Adrien laughed, apparently on more comfortable ground. "Okay, so there are three levels outside of holo and rasa, and two styles for each. I'm not going to try and explain styles; you can really only get that by watching, and level has more effect on strategy anyway. For prince and princess, your main strategy is wit. I was playing princess the first day you met me."

I vaguely remembered a flaring tunic, and nodded. I was beginning to see what Mom meant about selling wardrobes.

"Butch and femme are sexy."

"You were . . . playing . . . that earlier," I said.

"You noticed!" E shifted for a moment into eir overly seductive body language from the shuttle, then let it drop. "You can flirt with anyone playing butch or femme; don't try it with princes or princesses unless they start something first. Though that doesn't seem like your preferred strategy anyway."

I tried to decide how to respond—it hardly seemed worth explaining that I'd be perfectly happy to flirt with my sleeves rolled up at the aquaculture farm, with someone who knew and cared about my wife and co-parents and who had their own family waiting at home. And who didn't think of it as a "strategy." "Not on this trip."

"Right—I'll just think of you as sort of prince-y, then. Finally there's obre and tania—those're straight-up power plays, advantage through asserting dominance. You can try them at any company rank, but no one's going to hold back because you're an intern. Unless you're really good, you're likely to get eaten alive." E sounded like e relished the idea—but there was an edge of bitterness, too.

"How long have you been an intern?" asked Dinar.

E shook eir head. "Long enough. I'm ready to move up. It'd help if I get Asterion a good deal out of this business—want to help me out?"

Wit? Or power play? I ignored the lure. "And how should we recognize all these . . . pieces . . . when we spot them?"

"I'll point a few out till you get the hang of it."

On the elevator up (I couldn't even see where the stairs were hidden, though I charitably assumed they existed), I wished I could've seen the Ringers react to that same lesson. For the plains-folk, as far as I could tell, gender was a privilege that you won; for the tree-folk a birth assignment stricter than anything humans had ever enforced. Strange as Asterion's way seemed to me, masking private selves with viciously enthusiastic role-playing, the Ringers must be even more bewildered. And eager as Asterion was to get *our* cooperation, they'd play that much harder against (with? for?) the Ringers.

But those answers I could, and would, get from Rhamnetin. The other thing I realized on the way up—the thing we should've pushed on—was that we'd asked how you win the game, and not gotten much of an answer. What we hadn't even thought to ask was how you lose.

CHAPTER 18

By the second hour of the party, I was getting very tired of gold leaf. I hadn't quite caved and told my lenses to filter the stuff out, but it was tempting. I wanted to take in *more,* though, not less, to record all the night's nuances for later examination somewhere quieter and less glittery. To dissect the layers of energy emanating from the corporate party like my first analysis of the *Solar Flare,* and see the shadow of the broken parts.

I obviously wasn't the only one, because the domed ballroom was thick with drones: iridescent metal hummingbirds darting above the crowd. I couldn't tell if they were tied to individuals, or if they were free (or more likely, rented) to anyone hooked into Asterion's network. They didn't answer my pings, and it wouldn't have been a good idea to hook up if they did. The crowd glimmered likewise with the trappings of Adrien's game, a flock of leather and velvet and neofabric, makeup designed to enhance and obscure. In infrared they blurred into waves of human heat.

Mostly human, at least. Cytosine and Carnitine held court with Kelsey and Mallory near a buffet table. There they received the privilege of a little space free from the press of bodies. People filtered into that circle at an associate's nod, gained their audience, and made way for the next in favor. If there was any sort of line, I lacked access.

"All right," said Dinar. "What are they 'playing,' aside from gatekeeper?"

"They're doing that," Adrien agreed. "Like you did back in Washington. Can't host an extraterrestrial embassy if you let the entire planet squeeze into touching distance of the starship captain." E shook eir head. "Anyway, neither of them is playing holo, which is interesting all by itself. It's slightly gauche, since it's their party. But confident, saying they can do this huge important thing with limited tools. Associate Kelsey is playing obre; you can tell by the slick suit, and how his tiara has real rubies in exactly the way my necklace does not."

I wanted to get closer to Cytosine—and so did the clamoring contributors to my open thread. But I could already see how the associates had arranged the night, if not to completely prevent that, then at the very least to give others priority.

Leave that gravity well until later, suggested Rhamnetin. **Talk to other people outside the conversation, find out what *they* think.** New to the network he might be, but Carol had started him with appropriately high weight on all matters pertaining to Ringers. Even if the upvotes hadn't risen quickly, I'd've seen the sense.

"Associate Mallory is playing princess, which is *really* not sur usual style, but sui can pull it off like anything. My god, I wish I could afford to dress like that." I didn't share that sentiment, but agreed that sur dress was impressive: a multilayered concoction pink as a tea rose and edged in black, flaring all the way to the floor. An opalescent brooch flashed from sur collar.

"Why those choices?" I asked. I needed to understand these dynamics to have any clue what was happening.

"Hm. Associate Kelsey's playing to the room, obviously. Associate Mallory's playing to Cytosine. If you watch old movies, which apparently the Ringers do—and boy, someone's gonna have fun working out those entertainment distribution deals—princess is probably the most recognizably, um, female-ish, of the whole set. Which is what this lot respects."

"What do people wear when they're taking care of kids?" asked Dinar. None of the presentations seemed geared to that sort of practicality.

"It doesn't matter—the game is between adults. You don't play with kids too young to dress themselves."

I was beginning to understand how high a bar that was. Part of me wanted to stay on the room's edge all night, making anthropological observations and listening to Adrien's commentary. But e was already fidgeting, and I needed to work close up.

"Who else should we talk to?" I asked Adrien, despite the suspicion that I was giving em advantage by asking. Mallory and Kelsey weren't the only ones here with gatekeeping privileges. I might need to pull away later—but for now I needed the training wheels.

Going to dive in, I told the network. **Research requests, please.**

As I hoped, that standard language suppressed fussier input and focused everyone on simple queries.

Where do they want to put the antenna? What are the site characteristics?

What do they plan to charge the Ringers for the site?

What are their controversies about how to do this?

Who wants to do it a different way, or in a different place? Or disagrees with doing it at all?

As we made our way through the crowd, I felt an unfamiliar self-consciousness. It wasn't just the degree to which we stuck out, our clothes tailored to an entirely different aesthetic. It was knowing that those clothes, and our bodies in them, were all people could see of us. In the Chesapeake, or even visiting another network, anyone could look up my profile and know what I'd worked on and studied, tasks I'd accomplished, recommendations borne out. I could lay out other things I wanted them to know, as plainly as my pronoun pin. Here, how would people read me? Rasa, like Adrien had suggested? As in *tabula rasa*? I couldn't think of any claim less honest.

"Let's get some food," said Adrien. "You need props." We stopped at a side table loaded with platters, and I was thoroughly distracted from the rest of the party. Not a thing was recognizable.

I stared at the array of offerings: thin sheets colored like tiny abstract paintings, marble-sized gelatinous pyramids, silvery smoke drifting over a bowl of gold orbs. Scans suggested that it was all organic on a chemical level, but I had no idea whether the sources were animal or vegetable, if either. *No one told me I'd need a DNA sampler.* "I keep kosher."

We should have brought Kyo, Dinar texted, and I stifled a snicker. There's a rule that if a dog won't eat something, it isn't food—and therefore can't be trafe—so you can eat it. Kyo, who turns up her nose at Athëo's private stash of jellyfish chips, is not necessarily the best dog for these distinctions.

Adrien shrugged and popped one of the little paintings in eir mouth. "These taste like flowers and sugar—that should be okay?"

I weighed the discomfort of eating the things against the possibility of facing the night on an empty stomach.

"Can you ask Mallory?" suggested Dinar. "Sui was pretty familiar with the food last night. If it wouldn't be too much trouble to text sur."

Adrien sighed, but went vague for a moment while messages were passed. "Sorry. Sui doesn't know anything about feast food prep. Look, we can either spend the whole night tracking down the catering staff and wrangling their secret formulas, or we can go to the party."

The first sounded like more fun, especially for Dinar, but it wasn't actually on offer. "It's okay, I'll eat later."

"At least put something on your plate. It'll look weird otherwise."

So there I was, carting a plateful of abstract art that I shouldn't eat (but would probably have to eventually unless I decided to try fasting through complex political negotiations, or unless someone showed up with recognizable quail-on-a-stick), getting introduced to Adrien's fellow intern Kay, an offputtingly arch person who I suspected Adrien had picked for a "safe" starter conversation.

"E works for Junior Associate Kendra," said Adrien. It seemed a discreet enough way to tell us that Kay's gold-flecked white catsuit and feather cloak meant the same thing as Adrien's own outfit, but Kay obviously found the hint amusing.

"This must all be very new to you," e murmured. E sipped something brilliantly turquoise. "Is Adrien giving you a good introduction?"

"No complaints so far," I said. "It's always interesting to try something new." I tried to ignore the ironic lilt that seemed to creep into everything the interns said, but it was hard.

"Are you trying something new?" Kay asked. "Or just watching it? I suppose we do make a show."

"Our outfits mean things too," said Dinar. "We're saying what we want to say."

Kay tapped my scarf with a long finger; jewel-like blue lines wound from the points of eir nails down around eir palm and beneath flared cuffs. "I'll bite—what does this mean?"

I took a breath, trying to decide how to answer. The air was thick and floral. "Adrien said your clothes are celebratory; so is this. Parade scarves show where you come from. The silk, the dyes, are all made locally—they grow from the Chesapeake land and community, as much as the parade does. The pins are for the dandelion networks"—as e had to know—"and for my pronouns, which are she and her."

"Sharp," said Kay.

"Female isn't the same thing as playing tania," said Adrien hastily. "Network pronoun usage is pretty old-fashioned, no offense."

"So what does it mean, playing female?" asked Kay. The same question Adrien had asked, and it made me even more uncomfortable this time. There was something about the intensity of corporate presentations that made me want to show less of myself. A dangerous instinct.

"It means my pronouns are she and her," I said firmly. "We don't limit what we're allowed to do, or how we interact, by gender."

"So basically holo—" began Kay, amused and skeptical. But e broke off as a hummingbird drone darted down in front of my face. Its hovering wings blurred emerald and scarlet. Its beak was knife-sharp. I glanced up, unwillingly, at the now-revealed flock of daggers sparkling above. This one clasped an embossed square of thick paper. Adrien plucked the card, unfazed.

"Huh. Senior Associate Jace di Sanya is taking advantage of your unplugged state to be particularly stylish. Tha wants to talk with you."

"Do I want to talk with thon?" I asked, hoping that was the right version of the pronoun.

"Probably. Tha's an old ally of Associate Kelsey's. And Sanya had the second-highest bid to lead the consortium with the Ringers; Jace is still highly placed in the whole business."

"What sort of ally?" asked Dinar. "I've never seen any co-tasking from Asterion and Sanya."

Kay laughed. "Smart. They're not colleagues. Just . . . people who agree about the general state of the world."

Before I could unpack that, Adrien leaned forward and addressed the drone. "Hey, bird." The hummingbird gaped its stiletto beak, revealing the grooves of a slightly old-fashioned recorder. "Tell Senior Associate Jace we'll be right there." The vibrating wings swept back and the drone leapt into the air.

"Do we follow it?" I asked.

"It's okay, I've got the map. Catch you later, Kay."

"Have fun. I'll be in safer company, alas." E winked before sidling off.

Adrien led us through the dizzy panoply of leather and feathers and gemstones. When I shifted along the electromagnetic spectrum the variety dimmed again, but close up I could see that several had played with the Ringer custom of infrared decoration, wearing secret rainbows revealed only to the right filter. Without the focus of my own conversation, my mesh picked random speech to highlight for brief moments as we brushed past:

Extract a few extra gigawatts from the west side of the stadium—
That color, extraordinary but will it work in—Old plans for mining

asteroids but it was always more efficient to work planetside—Just want to swoon against hem when hie talks that way—Imagine if they'd come a hundred years ago—

The room's information density was exhausting. I felt hypervigilant to every outfit, unable to enjoy the sheer aesthetic exuberance. I could imagine, though, that familiarity would make it less stressful and more exhilarating. After all, when the network was up, I dealt every day with a different informational flood, and loved it as a fish loves the river.

"How do you handle it," I asked Adrien, "when someone isn't good at reading social patterns? Not everyone can pick this stuff up."

Adrien glanced back, frowning—not displeased, I thought, but surprised. "Some people use algorithmic prostheses to help them follow the game. Others are happier staying down in the techie warrens. My sib is like that. E's autistic, and hates parties even with a social algorithm installed. E designs clothing—loves figuring out how to say something with an outfit, just not in real time." Adrien sounded defensive, as if e were braced against some judgment.

"And do people here cope with that okay?" asked Dinar.

"People understand about techies," e said.

"I'd like to meet em," I said. It might not be appropriate to hide out with the catering staff during the party, but hopefully asking after someone's family was as reasonable here as at home. "Maybe looking at this stuff in non-real time would help me, too." With that in mind, I fed a request back to the network to try and map predictors in our own observations. I got an automated response that the effort was already in progress. The data, even adding files from other network folks who'd visited the aislands, were sparse; it might take hours or even days to reach a minimal accuracy threshold.

"Maybe. Sure!" I could see confidence grow in eir expression. "If you don't mind a two-hour lecture on the origin of princess style in twentieth-century Japanese subculture, yeah, you might like Brend pretty well. But here's Jace—obre tonight, and he always plays a sharp game."

Jace was short and light-skinned, black hair falling to his waist, suit tailored tight against the curve of breast and muscular arms. The style was a century old. A necklace draped below his shirt collar, glittering white against the dark fabric. I had a nasty suspicion those were diamonds. If so, they were a hell of a choice that even I could read, the symbol of corporate blood guilt in plays and movies for fifty years.

Oh my god, texted Dinar.

He looks like one of your anime villains, I said. **Do you think he watches the same shows?**

I could ask.

Don't—suppose he hasn't, and looks them up?

Then he'll know he looks like a sexy bad guy, said Dinar. **I'm pretty sure he already knows that, even if he doesn't specifically know he looks like Kaori.**

I shrugged. "On your head be it. But let's find out what he wants first."

Jace smiled as we approached—a theatrical smile, continuous and yet somehow personal to each recipient. He lifted Adrien's hand to brush it with his lips—"Delightful as always, Intern"—before taking my hand for a more businesslike shake. I'd been braced for him to repeat the kiss and was caught wrongfooted, struggling to adjust my grip to meet his strength.

"Ms. Wallach-Stevens. Ms. Naftali. A pleasure."

"It's good to meet you, too." We exchanged pleasantries, tinged with strangeness by the differences between how our respective cultures normally choreographed that social dance. Yes, we'd both come in the previous night. The shared plane ride that gathered representatives from around the aislands was dreadfully slow and crowded, he sighed—our own shuttle must be more like the old private jets. Not in its carbon footprint, I pointed out.

Speaking of carbon, I took a standoff reading of his necklace: it really was diamond. Probably antique or lab-grown. Probably. Either way, it . . . "advertised" was certainly the appropriate word . . . pride in the sort of power that ripped jewels from mountain veins.

"We don't often have network leaders out to see us," said Jace. "You really should visit more often. We have much to talk about."

"Like what?" Our usual witnesses came here to run pollution scans, not hobnob at parties.

"Expanding trade agreements, for example. You must have unfulfilled desires and needs beyond the electronic components we provide now. Especially with this new party in the mix"—he waved in Cytosine's direction—"you'll want new research and development, and no one is better placed than us to do that kind of innovative work."

"MIT and the Pan-Asian Maker Collective were hooked into the dandelion networks, last I checked." That came out harshly, but my parents would have responded even more reflexively to the old fourth power myth that new ideas came only from corporate labs.

"It doesn't mean we can't use new perspectives," said Dinar quietly.

"We have plenty," I said. "Including from the Ringers."

Jace nodded, unfazed. "Are you looking to back-engineer their work? We'd love to share whatever you find. Discounts on the products we already trade, perhaps, in exchange for the chance to explore new applications for whatever you learn. Or—I heard you're having challenges with your coordination platforms. Perhaps we can help."

Dinar stiffened, and my attention narrowed abruptly. The scintillation of gold trim and wild clothing and dagger-beaked drones dropped away. "I'm not sure what you mean."

"Aren't you?" He took a delicate nibble from a midnight-blue triangle. He set his plate onto the tray of a passing waiter, who shifted deftly to meet it without pausing their traverse of the ballroom. "I'm told you accused Asterion of spreading malware. Quite the claim, if everything's functioning smoothly."

"We *were* having trouble, and we do believe it was malware. We also believe we've got it under control." But was that the right thing to say? Pretend to strength—and therefore suggest ourselves arrogantly unwitting of any further attack—or admit to weakness, and open ourselves for another that might not have come otherwise. I could still sense the network's dragging response times, and gaps where algorithms should have aggregated input or objected to some too-cautious human judgment call. If Jace were one of those responsible, he'd know all of that regardless of what I said.

The skin around his eyes crinkled with amusement. "It's respect of a sort, you know."

"What is?" asked Dinar.

"Believing we're dangerous to you—and worth lying to." A thin smile. "I think both those things are true, of course, but it's not the common view. Least of all among the networks."

I wished *I* had somewhere to put my useless, tempting plate. "We've always known you were dangerous." And of course, I realized a moment later, I hadn't denied lying.

"If so," said Jace, "then surely it's worth negotiating a closer relationship rather than holding us at arm's length." He tilted his head, indicating Cytosine once more. "*They're* wise enough to deal with *all* of Earth's powers." When we didn't say anything—though I imagine

Dinar was trying as hard as me to think of something—he continued: "In any case, if your network issues rear themselves again, we
may be able to provide alternatives."

I tried not to stare. "Are you suggesting we switch to *corporate*
protocols?"

He shrugged elegantly. "The dandelion networks have their
strengths, to be sure, but we haven't had a major outage in decades.
There's something to be said for a product—or an institution—with
a long, stable history."

CHAPTER 19

The party swirled on. Too long, too loud, too many conversations layered with unspoken meaning—or occasionally spoken, in sideways insults and pointed passes. I wanted time to process each interaction, most particularly the one with Jace di Sanya. The more I thought about it—in whatever moments I could steal—the more convinced I was that we'd found one of those responsible for the network sabotage. The offer he'd made—from his perspective, the opportunity he'd identified—would remake the watersheds in the corporate image. It would place all our discussions in their hands, in the framework of power and priority as they understood it. It would be so absurdly transformative that, once envisioned, they would almost *have* to act on it. Realizing that it was possible, how could they not have tried to make it necessary?

It was, after all, a twisted mirror of what we'd done. The dandelion networks had been created in the wake of massive malware and malinformation epidemics, first as a way to maintain communications while preserving data, then as a way to reshape and reclaim those data as tools for justice and survival.

But as Dinar had pointed out, the corporations prized plausible deniability far above truth. Jace, high-ranked as he was, could easily have arranged to be ignorant of key details. And he had the advantage in any war of words. As a thread to trace—or as someone who could be pressured into withdrawing the threat—he left something to be desired. Especially without some threat of our own in return. Like Aunt Priya's bot.

After three hours, with no sign of the party winding down, and starting to think unhappily about which bits of culinary artwork were least likely to contain shrimp paste, I discovered the door. I hadn't been expecting one, since we were twenty-four stories up a thirty-story building. But there it was, tinted glass wreathed in gilt vines and camouflaged among a row of mirrors similarly wreathed. When I tested the handle I found myself on the mesa of a rooftop garden.

The evening was dark and warm with the smell of wet earth. When the door clicked shut behind me, the world grew gloriously quiet. Voices drifted from behind hedges—I wasn't alone out here—but the vast white conversational noise of the ballroom subsided. Crickets peeped, and some unfamiliar bird ululated softly. I smelled flowers and water, and only the faintest metal-and-smoke aura from the city below.

The roof was a maze of hedges. I set a ball-of-string program starting from the door, and while I was at it asked the network to ID the flowers growing from, around, and through the hedge. This proved easier than the food. The red and pink blossoms of the hedge itself were callistemon, practically native if you allowed the aisland as part of Australia. The rest gathered night-blooming plants from around the world: lavender lanterns of Japanese wisteria, nicotiana's pale stars, curling tentacular petals of some moonflower varietal in a dozen shades of blue. Trusting my string, I let the garden draw me out into the night.

I wandered the maze based on a strategy of avoiding other maze-goers. The paths twisted, widening occasionally into little nooks and oases. I made brief havens of those I found empty: a sand garden with a jade statue of three people, deer-footed, dancing around a marble bonfire; a koi pond spread with gold and violet water lilies. The places seemed tailored for private assignations, complement to as well as respite from the social plasma inside.

I started to release the jet-lagged stress of the evening, and began to scroll through the network's half-reconstructed maintenance threads. What options had we been considering for filtration algae? Did the new strain of seagrass starting up in the bay provide enough carbon uptake? But an unexpected sound interrupted my scan. The murmur of leaf-muted conversation had drifted in the background since I came out here—but only human languages. Now, somewhere closer to the building's edge, rose snatches of horn and cello.

As much as the hedge maze was built for private discussion, it was also built for eavesdropping. And I wanted *something* out of the night that didn't require a battle of wits. Subterfuge might not be one of my strengths, but in that moment, listening unseen sounded rather appealing.

Easier said than done, given that I was in a maze. The corporate aristocrats probably cheated with their drones, or just had maps. My unspooled string covered only a fraction of the building's footprint.

The voices faded, seemed to grow closer, faded again as I tried to find an adjoining passage. I was beginning to recognize them, though: Cytosine's chords with higher pitches shading into alto, and slightly more even tones from Carnitine that occasionally overlapped in strange descants.

Finally, I got close enough for my earrings to snatch words for our gangling translation algorithm.

*They * * comparison us,* offered the algorithm, lens-text lagging behind something Carnitine had said. *You-singular must/should be *.*

Cytosine: *There are *. Important *, where * intelligence(?) grows/ reaches.*

Carnitine: *And we negative * * to say what referent exist. Negative referent and win(?). Counterfactual Rhamnetin here, he would say it.*

Cytosine: *He needs to learn *. And to be safe.*

Carnitine: *Likelihood what this place/people(?)believe.*

To my surprise, it seemed to be just the two of them. I wouldn't have expected Mallory or Kelsey to let them out of visual range. Were their corporate minders still there, listening silently to an incomprehensible argument? Were we otherwise observed? It seemed unlikely that anything happened out here without surveillance, unless that was part of the game. I scanned, found nanocameras scattered around the nearby greenery. At home any such sensor would broadcast its presence and offer opt-outs. But even here there were areas left uncovered, presumably by design. I was in full view of one, of course, affixed to a nicotiana petal, and I flushed, suddenly self-conscious. If Cytosine found this whole business half as frustrating as I did, I should just talk to her directly.

The camera followed me as I walked, and I caught the ping of my antivirus as it tried to track my mesh. I kept going several steps before realizing that it shouldn't be able to do that.

The antivirus was designed to prevent infection between compatible, but normally separated, networks. No camera here should be able to sync with a dandelion protocol; the corporate networks were about as likely to handshake with ours as I was to carry Rhamnetin's babies.

I backed up, and the camera still tracked me physically, but nothing showed up on my mesh this time. *Fluke? Or strategy?* I moved forward again, this time keeping the cameras as sparks in my lens, watching for further infiltration attempts. Nothing. But I felt the weight of the bot in my pocket. Which *was* compatible with the corporate networks, but there was no way to tell whether the camera had noticed.

Deal with it later. Between this and my conversation with Jace, I had a nasty feeling about exactly how I'd have to do that. Slipping the bot quietly back off the aisland, unused, was looking less and less justifiable.

Mindful of whatever AI algorithms and senior associates might be tracking me, I went back to my search for Cytosine and Carnitine.

They were still talking—the translation even less comprehensible—when I finally came around a corner and found the pair looking out through a gap in the maze's edge. Carnitine was halfway up the trellised arch, holding tight to the branches vining the metal framework. Cytosine had reared to look over the ledge, which held a miniature rock garden. Beyond and below, the city stretched bright and shameless, opaquing the sky.

"I see you got away?" I tried to act as if I hadn't been sneaking.

Eyes swiveled in my direction, Cytosine's own along with the twins peering around her body. "I appreciate the way you kept the crowds from our door, in the Chesapeake. Nine billion people doesn't sound like that many, but this density is startling."

I joined them at the not-quite-window. "You've got room to spread out, back home."

"As much as we want," agreed Carnitine. "Though this is more like a habitat than anything we've seen on Earth."

"It's missing some important things," said Cytosine. "I told our hosts I needed time to think, and they sent us out here."

"Hospitable," I said. My stomach rumbled, and I glared again at my plate. "My standoff sensors are telling me squat about these things—I don't suppose you have any way of determining what's in them?"

"We've made sure we can handle all your nutrients," said Carnitine. "What were you trying to figure out?"

"Whether there's pork or shellfish. At this point, I'd settle for separating the plants and animals."

Carnitine took one of the mysterious objects with a set of pincers, nibbled it with one of her mouths. "Flesh." She tried another. "Flesh." The stained glass cracker, she reported as: "Fruit. Tasty, too." She handed it back to me, a tiny corner broken off. I nibbled gratefully, unsure whether the odd edge of umami was alien saliva or just some obscure herb.

"You can tell that easily?" I asked.

"Our mods let us eat whatever we like. But flesh still has a sort of musty aftertaste." She handed the rejected items to Diamond and Chlorophyll, who didn't seem to mind the mustiness.

"May I ask a rude question?" asked Cytosine abruptly. She added, sounding almost bashful, "Since Rhamnetin isn't here."

Even the tiny hors d'oeuvre made me feel more charitable. "I don't promise to answer. But go ahead."

"How do you make children?"

"I'm sorry?" Was she trying to get again at whether I'd carried Dori? "I already said—"

"Not you personally. Humans in general."

"We have several theories, you see." Carnitine sounded amused, as I supposed she must have been. "Your stories talk about male and female, occasionally other options. But they don't agree on what those mean, or whether one can become another, or how many are needed for reproduction. It's obvious that there are taboos. Cytosine thinks you're like us, with two—maybe three—reproductive roles that are set from birth. And Rhamnetin thinks you're like the plains-folk, dancing around each other until you work out who's going to take what role, and shifting what parts of your bodies are awake to accommodate each other. And *this* culture clearly does that, faster than even a"—she inserted a skirling note—"like Cytosine ever managed, but we haven't seen a one of their children. We're beginning to wonder if they have any."

"Of course they do," I said. "They're certainly not keeping their population stable by seducing our carbon witnesses. We've been here less than a day; give them time to show us around."

"That's what Carnitine told me," said Cytosine. "You at least brought your child to our ship, that first night."

I neglected to mention what a coincidence that had been. "Humans can be very protective of our kids around anything new or strange. People want to get a look at you first." And here I was, defending the people I was increasingly sure had sabotaged the network. But I couldn't bring myself to claim that everyone who meant well would parade their babies for Cytosine's reassurance. "That's what you really want to know, isn't it? Not how they're making children, but how they treat them. If they trust you enough to let you see beneath this"—I waved in the general direction of the party—"façade."

"Is that all it is?" asked Carnitine. "A mask? The Rings understand each other; we don't understand your truth enough to know when we've found it. Or when we haven't."

I looked back out over the city, bright enough to hide everything around it. "Neither do we, sometimes." I turned back to the Ringers. "Do you really feel that way? Like you understand yourselves and each other perfectly?"

"One of the advantages of symbiosis," said Cytosine, at the same time as her cross-sister said, "Maybe not *perfectly*."

"It must have taken you longer than a few days to get to know each other. How long before you met each other's children?"

Cytosine brushed limb-tips against Carnitine. I remembered Diamond's skinsong, and wondered what she was communicating. Aloud she said, "We shared math first, and the periodic table, so they could understand us. Then bigger ideas and stories. But of course we brought our children—how else?"

"Maybe we should have taken longer to build shared vocabulary this time, too," said Carnitine. "We followed all the human signals, but they haven't seen any of ours."

"There's too little time." Cytosine stroked her kids' backs. They snuggled against her and mewled. I felt my own protective instincts kick in, and my breasts let down. I tried to focus through the fog of jet-lagged social exhaustion.

"Time is what we need," I said. "There's safety in the disconnect you had at first. It must have taken your species some time to understand each other, to agree about how your relationship would work—" I stumbled against the rest of the sentence, more personal than I wanted to share. But maybe personal would break through Cytosine's script. I felt a burst of unexpected empathy for the way she tended to turn conversations from her own experiences to larger patterns. I wanted to do the same. "It's like my family. Carol and I knew each other for a long time before we had kids—we spent years discussing what we wanted out of life, and it was . . . there was no hurry to it. But then—" *Right, not mentioning who got pregnant.* "Then the baby was coming, and we never had found another couple to round out a full household, and we knew we couldn't do things properly with only two of us. So we went to a shadchan—a matchmaker—and asked them to help us find another couple in the same situation. And they hooked us up with Dinar and Athëo." I didn't mention how much I'd dragged my feet on talking to the shadchan. Even knowing that I didn't want to raise kids with only the two of us, adding more parents had felt dangerous.

"The four of us have a lot in common, and Dinar and Athëo are great people, and we absolutely have the potential for a really deep relationship. But we never got that relaxed part at the beginning, because they already had Raven and Dori was on her way. We didn't get to explore; we had to skip right to setting up a household and negotiating diapers and dishes. We're still scrambling to catch up. I think we'll get there, eventually—but it couldn't happen in time to meet all those pressures. And accepting that shortcoming is the only way we're getting there anyway."

I shut up at that point, embarrassed. The vulnerability was deliberate, but it hurt anyway, and I hoped Dinar and Athëo wouldn't be upset. I hoped it made sense to Cytosine and Carnitine.

"I see—a little," said Cytosine. Then: "But you still created your family when you needed to, not later."

"That's not—" And we had, of course. But we'd decided that for ourselves. And both couples had signed up with the shadchan; we hadn't just shown up on Dinar and Athëo's doorstep demanding they move into our house. That would have earned a rather stronger "fuck you" than anything we'd said to the Ringers so far. "All I'm asking is that you respect our judgment. And that you accept that not every choice means the same thing for us as it does for you."

"Of course we realize that—" began Cytosine.

Then Mallory swung around the corner in a rustle of taffeta, looking atypically out of breath. "There you are! You've been out here for a while." This was addressed to the Ringers, though sui certainly didn't seem happy to find me with them. I'd have expected Adrien to get stuck tracking wayward guests. Was our conversation such a danger to Asterion?

"I apologize," said Cytosine. "We didn't mean to be rude—at home this wouldn't have been too long a break. The limits are shorter here?"

"No, I apologize." Mallory regained some aplomb. "I just want to make sure we're providing sufficient entertainment. You're our guests of honor, after all."

Limbs gestured at the archway. "We were just appreciating a new view."

Mallory smiled. "I hope Zealand provides many of those. For everyone."

CHAPTER 20

I should've danced all night. Or talked and negotiated and networked, and made whatever other moves were necessary in this stupid, unavoidable game. But I was still exhausted, worse than from getting up every night with Dori. At least no one forces you to do complex social modeling while nursing a kid at 2 a.m. If I stuck around, I was going to respond to the next clever insinuation with something decidedly undiplomatic. So, massive faux pas or not, I went back to our room.

I was tired enough that I forgot to text Dinar first, but I wasn't completely shocked to find her there already. I *was* surprised to find her with Adrien.

E was sprawled on one of the big velvet chairs, with Dinar on the bed; they'd obviously been talking for some time. Dinar flinched when I came in, but Adrien waved cheerfully while stifling a yawn. "We were both getting tired, so we snuck out of the party."

Both fully clothed—so not that kind of seduction, at least. "If I'd known that was okay, I'd have come back hours ago."

Adrien yawned again. "Officially, we're continuing negotiations someplace more quiet. I think it's been long enough for plausible deniability, though—I'm off to negotiate with Kay about turning off the lights and going to sleep."

"That's an interesting person," Dinar said after e left.

I collapsed in the chair, still warm from Adrien's presence. "Were you actually not negotiating?"

"Hell if I know. But e was at pains to let me know that not everyone here wants to go back to the 'bad old days.'"

I leaned forward, or tried; the chair was a black hole. "Meaning some of them do?"

"E didn't say that directly. But Mallory's apparently of the party that thinks they can make the corporations fit the needs of the planet—make capitalism fit the needs of the planet."

"You'd have to bend the definition of just about every word in that sentence."

She shrugged. "I'm not saying e's right. Just that maybe they've learned *something* from their mistakes. We're stuck with the corporations in some form for the foreseeable future. Better if they're led by people who don't want to re-create anything from the 1980s except the fashions."

Better not to get ourselves involved in their internal power plays at all, I thought. It would be too easy to mold yourself to fit them, if you stayed long enough. "Wait, you said *Mallory* thinks that way. What about Kelsey? I thought they were partners?"

"E didn't say. Make of that what you will."

And Kelsey, of course, was Jace's ally. And vice versa.

I shook my head. "I'm way too tired to untangle this stuff. At least on a Dyson sphere you wouldn't have to cross the International Date Line. I think? Would you?"

"It could be the same time of day and the same season all around the solar system. Can you help me set up the power transformer for my arm? I need to wipe the sockets really thoroughly, since I didn't last night."

I pulled the transformer out of the luggage and figured out the plugs, and made sure the filters were set to keep anything from coming through *other* than power. "Wait—you didn't try to charge it last night *without* a firewall, did you?"

"Of course not. I didn't manage to plug it in properly at all, but I'm not enough of an idiot to get malware in my own damn prosthetic."

"Sorry." I busied myself finishing the setup, and didn't comment when she pointedly triple-checked my work.

She set the arm in its stand, charging lights all green, and rubbed lotion into her skin where the prosthetic sat against it all day. I could see that the spot had gotten red and irritated—between the flight and last night's confusion, she probably hadn't gone through her whole care routine in a couple of days. But it didn't seem like I should say anything.

I should have taken my mesh off properly, too. But instead, I sat up sharing my impressions with the network, and scrolling through threads, and worrying, until fatigue finally overcame rumination enough for me to sleep.

At some point I must have gotten some rest, because Adrien's knock woke me up.

"We're off to look at the site. Better scramble, not everyone wants to wait for you."

Out in the hall, Dinar looked the intern up and down. "Princess?"

"Close. Prince today; I don't want to muss up a skirt."

"Right," she said. "That's 'hoi,' 'hom,' and 'hos.' I've got everything figured out that far. Next question: Why are you trying to make us paranoid about these mysterious people who don't want us there?"

"Who, me?" Hoi batted hos eyes. "Making insinuations about people too high-ranked for me to denigrate directly? Never. But don't worry, I'm sure they'll give themselves away on site."

"Well, that's something to look forward to," I muttered. I could get dressed well enough in five minutes, but I was desperate for a leisurely breakfast and copious amounts of tea. "If you can't tell us who *doesn't* want us there, can you tell us who does? Did Kelsey and Mallory both send you to fetch us?"

Adrien led us toward the elevator. "In this case, yes. They both want you in these talks."

"Can I ask why?" I really needed that caffeine; I felt all sharp edges.

Adrien shrugged. "It's always better to talk with people than avoid them. If you're talking, you're winning."

Today's ride was big and open, able to accommodate the Ringers and a shit-ton of humans. Another intern passed around fruit and pastries, and I tried to wake up and appreciate the morning.

Zealand wasn't built for the unforgiving light of a southern day. Buildings that loomed like monumental spotlights at night seemed drab, flashing screens washed out to bare visibility. Greenery peeked somberly from rooftops, but even the trees at street level seemed too small, too immaculate. This was a habitat, as Cytosine had pointed out. And I doubted they had Cytosine's careful science of ecological niches. Nor had the aisland's designers had access to the various bio-libraries from which the watersheds still labored to restore decimated microbiomes and insect populations, all the things that made leafy canopies thrive.

I thought of the night-blooming garden, combining flowers from a dozen ecosystems. "Who founded Zealand, originally?" Asterion was a more recent merger, I vaguely recalled, the result of some alliance among former billionaire lineages.

Adrien shrugged. "One of the old information brokers." Deliberately vague, and I dropped a note to the network to try and find out.

The creation of the aislands wasn't as well-recorded as anyone would like. Not that it mattered much—they'd all been vampires of one sort or another. This one must have been more self-aware than most, to build a city that would thrive in the dark. Either that, or they'd expected the world to grow hot enough to make people nocturnal, an idea that had been weirdly popular in some corners. Maybe it was true here; Zealand at sunrise was barely busier than Zealand at 3 a.m. But then this was no hub city like DC, fed by a continent's worth of railroad. Except for a few converts and visitors, they had only the descendants of the people who'd arrived with their founder—allies and employees who'd prioritized fleeing apocalypse over creating community to stop it.

Cytosine and her kids talked quietly with the associates. Glycine was asking questions about the ride's autopilot. Carnitine and Manganese craned limbs out the window and scarfed breakfast. Humans did much the same; Dinar was among those gazing up at the pale screens and ad-camouflaged solar panels.

Rhamnetin would've gotten to the heart of the city by now, asking questions that cut through everything Adrien chose to tell or withhold. Carol would've sat with me in silent intimacy, or whispered commentary in our long-shared shorthand. Instead I felt alone and disconnected. I wished for the warmth of familiar skin, the draft of mint-scented air spilling from our foyer, the show of chickadees darting around our feeder: a world I knew how to read.

Part of home, at least, I had with me. I opened threads from the night before, starting to scan the wash of speculation and second-guessing around the conversations I'd recorded at the party. Not comforting, exactly, but connected. It was after midnight in Maryland, but I sent a non-urgent message to Carol telling her I loved her and asking after Dori. I sent a slightly more urgent ping to Rhamnetin: We're on our way to check out the proposed site—do you want to peek in on the stream?

Toward the northwest side of the aisland the towers vanished, and the buildings grew squat and functional. My mesh helpfully offered me the track and strength of the last five seasons of cyclones, and it was no surprise when we reached the fenceline and found a broad lot bounded with a ten-meter seawall. On the satellite images we'd seen at home, the paved landing pads and packed earth had looked solid. As we got out I saw regularly placed drains, caked with salt, opening into the depths below. Even here, storms would be the biggest strain on infrastructure. I imagined floods surging down labyrinths of pipe, spilling out of the cliffside like waterfalls.

Up close, it was obvious that most of the runways had fallen into disuse. Pavement was cracked, or stacked with rusted girders and other detritus from old construction. It could doubtless be cleared easily enough, but wasn't the sort of thing you wanted near runoff sites, even under ideal conditions.

Kelsey glanced at me, but then focused on Cytosine. "Back when flights between the aislands were more common, this was our secondary landing station. It's almost never used these days. We could clean it up in a few days, and it's rated for the weight of dozens of aircraft—it should work perfectly for the specs you showed us. And unlike a natural site, we can show you the blueprints for the structure beneath it, all the way down to the bedrock." Given the Ringer belief that the natural world was too complex to trust, I feared they'd find that last point particularly compelling.

Better to remind them that the fundamental complexity of a planet didn't go away because you were standing on a manmade structure. "How are your weather forecasts?" I asked. "It looks like this side of the aisland gets the brunt of storms?"

Kelsey nodded easily. "And the Chesapeake gets hurricanes. Corporate satellites keep our storms fairly predictable—Nicky?"

Another member of the Asterion staff stepped forward. From their subdued dress—by corporate standards—and focus on their palette, I guessed this was one of the fabled "techies." "Current forecasts are ninety-five percent accurate to five days out, eighty-five percent accurate to ten days. We can see cyclones forming further in advance, though of course predicting the path is challenging. Ten days out we could certainly spot any significant risk that one would hit Zealand. We catch the edges of at least one cyclone a season."

"What about fourteen days out?" asked Carnitine. "That's how long we'll need to build. It should be able to withstand winds of . . ." She made a series of humming whistles, and a discussion among the Ringers followed, ending with the conclusion that the ansible antenna could probably handle anything up through a Cat 3, but that a Cat 4 or worse might well tear the thing apart.

"We're just moving into hurricane season in the Chesapeake right now," I said. "That means less than it used to, but your odds of a catastrophic windstorm are considerably lower in the northern hemisphere than the southern for the next couple months."

"But more predictable here," said the techie. "We have better satellites."

Can NASA share satellite readings with the network during ansible construction? I sent to the network, flagging Mendez. I suspected St. Julien would be open to negotiation; she made a more comfortable ally than anyone here.

"Our models are nearly as good," I said. I laid out figures from the network crowd, and the discussion quickly turned technical.

Rhamnetin messaged me at last. **I'm up. What have you seen so far?**

I passed along the data. **I think Cytosine likes Zealand because it reminds her of a habitat. But it's out in the open Pacific and vulnerable to storms, even leaving aside the trustworthiness of the corporations. And I met someone who more or less gloated about the malware. I wouldn't let them near your hardware, if I were you.**

They might have a teeny bit more trouble undermining our equipment. It's not exactly running Windows.

I blinked. **Not doing what?**

Don't you watch your own movies?

Not as many as you have, I admitted.

Our operating systems don't work on the same principles as your computers. The hardware is half organic. The ansible is about as likely to get the flu as human malware—at least until you learn our equivalent of programming languages. But I'd rather build the antenna near people we can trust, too. Everything's compatible with physics.

I hesitated. **Do you trust us?**

There was a pause on his end—as plausibly an issue with connection speed as a deliberate hesitation. **I trust you to do what you think is right. That's how I trust most people.**

I pondered that. Even the worst of the corporate staff were probably doing the right thing, by their own standards. They'd built whole ethical systems around the moral imperative for profit, the assumption that acting selfishly would eventually bite its own tail and be the best thing possible for humanity.

Then again, *I* often failed to do what I thought was right, even when I could figure out what that was. Maybe the world would be saved, or already had been, by some intern deciding to act generously and be damned.

Or the world might be lost, because someone was too reluctant to follow through on what they believed. The right thing to do lay heavy in my pocket.

CHAPTER 21

"Do you miss Raven and Dori?" Dinar asked. I nodded. Our next stop was supposed to finally confirm that Zealanders really did have kids, and really were civilized enough to show them to outsiders.

"We could have brought them," Dinar went on. "The party was annoying, but everything's been safe enough. Hell, everyone has been a lot more sober than your average parade celebrant." Which was true: Asterion's idea of a good time seemed notably free of intoxicants. Maybe it was hard enough to keep track of their games without getting stoned.

"We could've," I said. "But I'm still glad we don't have to take care of them on our own. Even Cytosine travels with most of her family to back her up." I couldn't tell her the real reason I was glad to have Dori at home. Which made Cytosine right: when you brought your kids to every negotiation, you had to be on your best behavior. Definitely no sneaking around installing malware back doors. Kids at a negotiation were more than a prompt for mindful choices. In practice they were also hostages, even in a parent's embrace.

On this trip, I could risk myself in ways I'd never risk Dori. Dinar and I coming to Zealand alone wasn't merely rude by Cytosine's standards, but a threat—one that Rhamnetin had made her complicit in. No wonder she'd been furious. And if I were caught with the bot, the diplomatic damage wouldn't only be between the Chesapeake and Asterion. It might well convince the Ringers that they couldn't trust the watersheds at all.

I tried to look distracted by the scenery, rather than like someone wrestling a thorny moral dilemma. *Too many trade-offs to model inside my own head.*

Kelsey interrupted my reverie. "This is where my kid goes."

"You have a child?" asked Cytosine.

"Seven years old." Kelsey laughed. "Not old enough for an internship, but too big to carry around! Tha spends evenings with my household—but for us, family is a private haven. So this is where we start introducing our children to other people."

The school, or whatever it was, took up the ground floor of one of the skyscrapers. As we came in, screens showed cartoon figures at play. On one side, pink bears and green bears counted blocks in different colors. On the other side, they traded blocks with gestures of exaggerated excitement: three squares for four triangles. Whether they were celebrating the math or the trading, I couldn't tell.

Kelsey stopped at an office, came out with badges marked **visitor**. "Anyone can come here—to see thos kids, or play with other people's kids when they're starting to think about thos own, or to trade tutoring, but the office likes to know who you are. I've given them a list." Hoi (currently playing prince, according to Adrien) helped the Ringers get the lanyards attached. I examined the slick plastic. It wasn't intended to be disposable, at least; the letters were faded from years of reuse.

Kelsey knocked on a door and cracked it open. "Can we come in?"

In response, I heard a ragged chorus of, "They're here!" and a flock of kids poured into the hall. They all looked well past toddlerhood and not yet adolescent. They were dressed more plainly than Asterion's adults, though several wore boas or jewelry or gaudy belts along with their simpler jumpsuits, as if we'd caught them at the start of a dress-up game. They clustered around the Ringers, peppering them with questions. An adult clad in green velvet followed behind, laughing. "That was never going to work. Serge, say hi to your zaza."

One of the taller kids, with a shock of red hair above their pink boa, turned and waved—"Hi, Zaza! Hi, Associate Mallory!"—before getting back to the interesting visitors. Kelsey returned the greeting and smiled, looking satisfied, and Mallory waved as well.

Dinar leaned over to whisper, "Can you imagine never having people over to your house?"

Mallory either overheard, or had known Dinar for the five minutes it'd take to guess what would disturb her most. "We're no less social than you. But our ancestors recognized that one of their mistakes had been forcing career obligations into every part of life. Without that time to relax, to focus elsewhere, it was hard to know when situations at work needed changing. We're passionate about our careers, but now we also value having sacred space where it can't intrude."

Dinar's eyebrows went up. "Is having friends over *work*?"

Kelsey smiled wryly. "Playful work, but yes. We have plenty of places to meet friends, even cook for them if we want. But when I go home, I focus on my spouses and our children. Trust that it works for us. And that you won't miss much by not getting to ogle the state of my living room."

"I like the way we do it better, too," I told Dinar when Mallory had gone out of earshot. But then, we didn't have the sort of work that Kelsey and Mallory's ancestors had forced on ours a century ago, either. The things I did, from commenting on threads to analyzing water chemistry to nursing Dori, all wove together to make a complete life. "But we have our own dedicated spaces where certain kinds of work can't intrude. I wouldn't try to model runoff in synagogue."

"You wouldn't try it during the Passover seder, either. It's not just the place, it's that some things shouldn't be multitasked, and ritual is one of them."

The teacher (also in prince mode, my mesh guessed) approached us. "Do you want to see the classroom?" Hoi looked uncomfortable.

"Sure," said Dinar.

Hoi led us inside, away from the teeming kids. Over the door, bright letters spelled out "PLAY WELL WITH OTHERS." It probably wasn't meant to seem ominous. The setup wasn't particularly alien: work tables in the middle of the room and study stations around the edges, ranging from a relatively familiar science station with rock samples and a bridge-building set to an "economics" station with biographical posters and strange-looking network diagrams along with blocks like the ones in the mural. There was in fact a scattering of dress-up boxes in one corner, shiny things spilling out.

The teacher twisted hos hands together, looking around.

Trying to set hom at ease, I said, "I remember working with a bridge kit like that, when I was in school. They're fun, but tricky."

Hoi nodded. "We've been working on producing more relevant kits as well. Most of these kids have never seen an actual bridge."

"I guess they wouldn't, on an aisland."

"Drain systems, on the other hand—" Hoi pointed out what I'd mistaken for a marble racecourse, now revealed as a miniature set of pipes intended to divide a stream of water in as many directions as possible. It was a clever toy, and the first corporate product I'd encountered on Zealand that I *wanted*. Differently colored segments represented different drainage materials, each with its own material characteristics—and,

Asterion being what they were, with prices clearly marked for each. Students would be given a budget, and assigned to build within it.

Dinar texted me. **Why are we in here?**

To see how they actually raise their kids?

So why are they keeping us away from the actual kids?

I straightened. "Thanks for the tour—we should get back to our group."

Hoi folded hos arms. "You've got a problem with how we raise our children?"

I blinked. "I didn't say that." I honestly had less of a problem than I'd expected to—and a nasty part of me was upset that these people were doing well enough to pass Cytosine's test. I couldn't imagine her treating with people who really did use crèches.

"You didn't have to. You didn't have to follow our guests on their trip, either. Aliens are one thing—meeting them is the opportunity of a lifetime, for the kids as much as the rest of us. You—we know what *you* want to do with them."

"I haven't done anything with your children. I've been too busy trying to save mine from the things *you* did."

Dinar touched my wrist. **Judy. Hoi's *our* age.**

And this is literally the first time I've been in the same building as corporate kids.

Yes, but we're supposed to be the diplomatic experts.

"If you had your way," said the teacher, "they'd never learn anything about their heritage."

I should've turned and gone back out into the hall. "You're not preserving some deep spiritual tradition. Your *heritage* is that you almost broke civilization, and wounded the planet enough that we're still trying to fix what you destroyed."

"We *made* civilization."

Dinar tugged at my hand. "We're going now." **Please, this isn't the way to change the minds of random people who've never left Zealand.**

If this is what they're teaching their kids, we're never going to get anywhere with them.

And we should do something about that—later—but this argument won't manage it.

Adrien hurried over to intervene. "Cytosine's going to come in and tell a Ringer kids' story, so I wanted to make sure the classroom was ready."

"Of course," said the teacher. "We're fine."

It shouldn't have shaken me that there were people in Zealand who hated us. We held grudges against the corporations—justified, I thought, but of course they'd have their own opinions about their fall from power. It wasn't the sort of thing humans tended to be unbiased about. And still, the bitter pride coloring the teacher's voice felt like those kids drawing swastikas on my tablet: an intrusion so sharp that it sullied everything around it.

I couldn't shake the idea that the furious teacher wasn't a coincidence. Sure, maybe Kelsey's kid happened to get stuck with an asshole this year—or maybe Kelsey sent hos kid to a school where convincing kids we were the devil was a keystone of the curriculum. Certainly Kelsey hadn't seen anything wrong with using this as the demonstration class for the Ringers. Even if the presence of network reps brought out more vocal resentment, those feelings probably weren't silent the rest of the time. Kelsey would've known. Was foisting this teacher on us an unfortunate necessity, or a deliberate insult? Or just meant to shake us? It was blunter, but it left me with the same bitter taste as the conversation with Jace.

Anyway, I got myself looking calm. The teacher proved to have as good a poker face as the associates, and the kids streamed back in. And we finally got to hear a Ringer story.

Cytosine scuttled to a cushioned reading circle, and rolled back against a stack of pillows. The corporate kids, laughing and jostling, sat cross-legged around her and tried to look serious, not helped by the two plains-folk kids squirming to find spots among them or the inevitable bickering over who got to sit next to the aliens. Diamond ended up draped across Kelsey's kid's lap and into someone else's. Cytosine must have judged Asterion's parenting and found it worthy.

The teacher made a calming gesture, hands pressing down and aside as if kneading imaginary dough. The children quieted. I began recording livestream; I suspected this would be informative. How much could you learn about humans from *In My Garden* or the story of the golem?

Cytosine rocked gently. "Diamond, Chlorophyll, what story should I tell?"

Chlorophyll squealed. "Tell about Fructose!" They added something in their own language, which my algorithm translated as *stimulant*. A name? "And Fructose and lost babies!"

Their mother rocked faster, considering, then slowed again. "All right. I know that one well enough, and I think it'll make sense to humans, too."

I love this story, texted Rhamnetin.

There's a thread on folklore starting up—I pointed him at the link—**can you join for Q&A so they don't expect me to interrupt Cytosine?**

She's kind of used to that. But he posted to the thread.

Cytosine began: "In the days of the First Reach, the First Ring sent people to meet the Second skin-to-skin, on their birth world. Among the travelers from the plains was—I'll call her Caffeine; that has the right connotations, I think—who had helped program the original probes to observe the tree-folk. Her cleverness brought her many mates, and she carried triplets still nursing to the new world. Among the tribe that welcomed them was Fructose, who even before the Reach had learned how to grow the choicest fruits in the canopy around her dwelling place, so that all the children in the tribe could feed well and safely. She was brilliant from the egg, and still so young that her brothers hadn't hatched yet. Both Caffeine and Fructose had been born with lonely names, but had chosen new ones together, sharing diagrams of the molecules that had been most vital to their success.

"Some among the tree-folk were unhappy about the plains-folk's arrival. They liked their power as it was and feared change, or believed the shared technology was a poisoned gift from corrupt gods. So one day Fructose's sister came to her and said: 'I was tending our brothers' eggs when the Chief with the Lonely Name came with her brothers and stole them away. I tried to fight them off, but they were many and I was small and alone. I tried to follow them, but the biggest of her brothers held me back until the others vanished. I tried to track them, but they traveled without breaking a leaf to mark their trail.'

"Fructose knew that she had to get the eggs back, or the Chief with the Lonely Name would raise them as her own, and the Chief's band of brothers would grow even larger and more dangerous. 'I know the trees better than anyone,' Fructose said, 'and can find trails that no one else can see.' 'And I have devices that the Chief refuses to understand,' said Caffeine, 'and satellites to find where she dwells. I will come with you, and help save your brothers' eggs, and show the Chief what we can do together.'"

She went on, describing the pair's adventures in the wild orchards and cultivated jungles of the tree-folk's lost homeworld. Fructose and Caffeine reminded me of human trickster archetypes, or one of the folkloric travelers of North American fable—the network thread excitedly compared them to examples ranging from Coyote to Johnny Appleseed—but they were *scientific* tricksters. Caffeine was a hacker of sorts, programming new sensors on the fly and distracting predators with recordings of more familiar prey. Fructose was the sort of inventor whose name—for humans—was lost in unwritten prehistory: a first farmer who still knew the secrets of hunter-gatherers, and who could tell the meaning of every seed and leaf.

They were also both *mothers*—or rather, a mother and a sister who expected to raise her brothers as soon as they were hatched. I was surprised at how much I liked that, how much it made me feel an absence in our own stories. *But that's going to be me.* If we didn't screw this up completely, if we managed to come to a relationship that worked for everyone, I'd be the person who met the ship with my daughter on my chest, and shared adventures with our visitors.

Or else I'd be the villain, trying to hold back the inevitable loss of our world. I suddenly sympathized with the Chief with the Lonely Name. She did something hideously immoral to try and preserve the world she loved. Kidnapping eggs was nastier than releasing malware, but I couldn't disagree with her about the stakes. Saliva soured in my mouth. The cheerful adventurers, swinging and scuttling through the trees with triplets in tow, felt ominous as a stormfront.

They were real people, put in Rhamnetin. **They didn't do everything the stories claim, but you can read their records.**

I'd love that. I suspected, though, that the Ringers hadn't saved any memoirs from the Chief with the Lonely Name. Whoever she'd been.

CHAPTER 22

There was another party that evening, hosted by a contractor group that wanted to help prep the ansible site. It was smaller than the night before but no less overwhelming. The food was just as opaque too, and a full dinner this time. Adrien shrugged and said, "Feast food," as if that explained the whole thing. I promised myself that I'd sneak out later and get something recognizable from a cart. I was deeply grateful when, as dinner proper broke up into smaller conversations, Adrien pulled me and Dinar aside to ask if we wanted to meet Brend.

I'd seen Zealand from street level, with the school and the mouth-watering food carts. I'd taken in the breathtaking views from their parties, so high that you couldn't spot people but only the system that held them. Now, after catching a ride to yet another office building near the southern edge of the aisland, we took an elevator down, down, into the guts of the construct. As my ears popped I imagined some dim dystopia, full of dripping water and claustrophobic corridors. Instead the elevator let out onto a wide, airy room with a whole transparent wall looking out on the ocean. People scattered around couches and workstations, or lounged with palettes on benches next to the window. The water was wine-dark in the fading sunlight; a splash of pink and red still seeped from the west. Someone had piped in the distant thunder of waves crashing against the foot of the cliff. I felt muscles relax that I didn't know had been clenched. After two days in an environment utterly and blatantly shaped by human whim, I apparently needed the confirmation that nature was still there, still doing her best to collaborate with her exhausting children.

"Welcome to Morlock Central!" A person I assumed was Brend came bounding over, velvet tails streaming behind em. E looked unmistakably related to Adrien, albeit bouncy where eir sib was suave, frizzy instead of sleek.

Adrien moaned. "Brend! You can't just say that to people."

"Why not? It's what we call it. Oh." E clapped eir hands to eir mouth. "We don't eat people, I promise. It's because we're underground, and we make all the things everyone uses—" E waved in the general direction of the surface.

I laughed. "I kind of figured. Adrien, it's okay, I promise."

"It apparently used to be really dark down here, too, for the first ten years or so," Brend went on. "Because doing tech-work in basements was a tradition, or people thought it was, or something. But I think it's much nicer with a window, and if you don't like the light there are offices further in, but they're mostly empty. Adrien said you wanted to learn about clothes?"

"Yes," said Adrien, "but they probably want to sit down first."

"Oh—I'm so sorry!" E led us toward one of the booths near the window.

"It's really okay," I said again. I winced at how clearly both Adrien and Brend were used to people reacting badly to unpolished enthusiasm. For me, after trying to second-guess everyone's meanings upstairs, it was as much of a relief as the sea sound. But I couldn't say that. "Can I ask about how *you're* dressed?"

"I'm holo," said Brend. Adrien winced again, and I had no idea why this time. "I'm always holo; it's easier to keep track of. And besides, I never want to turn down an interesting piece of clothing just because it doesn't match what I'm already wearing." E opened eir palette, and as promised started a slightly overwhelming tour of eir design portfolio. E might not like those distinctions for emself, but e could explain precisely where in the corporations' complex symbol system each item fit, how e'd tailored it to some subtle shade of meaning, and the circumstances under which a person might want to mean that specific thing. E wanted to know about our clothes too, genuinely curious about everything from the original design of the dandelion pin to the way our network traced sources for materials.

Adrien wandered off to look at other people's work, but kept coming back to put in a comment or suggest a story Brend hadn't gotten to yet. It reminded me of the Bet, where cousins and aunts could go on for hours about SEED programming or regenerative agriculture or the history of pre-Columbian cities in North America. We didn't shuffle them away during parties—but then, our parties were more fun and had less specific performance requirements. Brend might like them.

The rest of the room fascinated me almost as much as the conversation. This seemed more like a neighborhood common workspace than a twentieth-century office dedicated to a single purpose. I caught glimpses of water sensor readings, architectural blueprints, and a shelf of rubber ducks labeled "Coding Support Staff." There were also a couple of stationary bikes in front of a screen, a virtual gaming table, and a scattering of fidgets ranging from squishy balls to sophisticated bots. Assuming no one here had memorized the contents of the place, it might be the perfect spot to leave my own bot. *Or the opposite: any of these people could recognize what you were planting.* And they'd have plenty of opportunity, since they kept stopping by to gawk at us.

One of the gawkers set a tray of small multicolored objects on the table, shaped like hollow hemispheres. "Jellyfish?"

"Thanks!" Brend grabbed a handful, explaining: "They're fruit-flavored. The red ones are either cherry or apple, and the yellow ones are mango, and the green are kiwi."

Adrien took a blue one more delicately. "Sorry. But they're good."

Dinar shook her head. "At least there's no mystery about what they are, this time."

"Oh, are you having trouble with feast food?" asked Brend. "I could download you a guide. Lots of techies like to know how things will taste *before* we put them in our mouths, which apparently is an extremely weird attitude."

"I do, too, but I also keep kosher." I hesitated. "I don't think you *could* download me a guide, though? We don't use the same network protocol."

"Oh, I'm sure someone around here could figure it out." Brend knelt up on the bench and called over the side of the booth, "Hey, Tiffany, are you back there?"

A voice from behind the rubber ducks called back, "Who wants to know?"

"Couple of visitors from the Chesapeake. You did some work on network translation a while back, right? Could you make the *Hitch-hiker's Guide to Feast Food* work on their system?"

Tiffany—olive-skinned and smooth-scalped, and wearing a startlingly plain denim jacket—poked their head over the ducks. "First, I did. Second, that's not how network translation works at all. You can't just send random things to random people. I would have to spend months altering the e-book format. So third, no. Print the fucking thing out." They disappeared back behind the ducks.

Adrien shot a glare, and Brend said, "Um, sorry about Tiffany. Tha gets really cranky sometimes."

"That's okay," I said. And blinked, because e'd used the pronoun that you weren't supposed to use for someone you could see unless they were naked. Which I didn't *think* Tiffany was. Maybe by corporate standards? Maybe the rules were different for tech experts?

"No offense taken," Dinar agreed, sounding as distracted as I felt. "You don't need to waste printer paper on us, though—thank you for the offer, but we're not going to be here all that long."

I tried to get back to the conversation, wondering all the while if it was even safe to feed my observations back to Redbug while we were surrounded by Asterion's tech experts. If "network translation" meant what I thought it did, Tiffany might well be able to pick up our signal. Hell, tha might be one of the people who'd created the malware, or at least laid the groundwork. And done it just as deniably as Jace; there were plenty of reasons an obsessive programmer might challenge thonself to connect the unconnectable.

On the way back to the hotel, I texted Redbug on a private channel.

How're the repairs going?

The reply came back immediately despite the time difference. Why—are you having issues?

Nothing major. And that was part of it, too. I couldn't put my finger on any specific thing that was wrong, but the feedback from the decision threads still felt slow, off-key, like something in the system was stalled. Just nervous, I guess.

The pause was noticeable this time. Let me know if you do. It's not all cleared out yet—we're keeping everything functional for now, but I'll be honest, we're still trying to find the roots of the problem. If we don't get every tendril of malware dug out, it's all going to break down again. Another wait, while I thought that through. More than that I'm not getting into while you're traveling. Watch yourself.

I felt sick, and not from my delayed dinner. *I'm really going to have to do this thing.*

CHAPTER 23

That night, I went for a walk. I told Dinar I was going out for recognizable food; that was true, as was the apologetic admission that I wanted time to think on my own. So much truth, yet still not enough.

Cities are stranger when you're alone, and more so without a decent map overlay. Someone on the network had found an old one—out-of-date in terms of what was in each building, but stable enough that I wasn't likely to lose the hotel. But I couldn't tell what lay ahead beyond my own scope of vision. Scarcely thinking about it, I responded to my uncertainty by adding senses: soles passing texture to my skin, chemical signatures dancing over my lenses, magnetic fields humming against my back. I could call up historical temperatures at the fenceline and see the number of records set each year—finally starting to go down, though still far too high. Asterion's original well-heeled refugees had fought against even that much progress. Somewhere amid the bowels of Morlock Central, there doubtless remained air-conditioned shelters packed with freeze-dried food, hoards enough to fill the old age of exiled dragons.

This vibrant street was a miracle that its creators never expected. The balmy autumn night, the breeze whispering hints from the ocean, the rapid-fire rhythm of busking drummers, the smell of roasting onions, sang of a world they'd given up on. A world they might still give up, for power or advantage or some remnant ideal of eternal growth.

I started watching the people. Out here, away from the parties, they wore everything from the most glammed-up high fashion to what was probably the corporate equivalent of pajamas, gussied up with a token feather scarf or poof of skirt. A few wore dramatic pattern-shifting makeup to mask their expressions, but most were as readable as anyone on the streets of DC. And as varied. They strolled together laughing, or rushed head down, or wandered as befuddled as me, caught up by internal conflicts totally unrelated to my own maundering. Except that whatever was obsessing them could be drastically disrupted by any break in their network. As I damn well knew from my own experience.

It was stupid to keep obsessing over whether releasing the bot was the right thing to do. I'd basically decided when Jace made his slip, and now I was trying to make myself feel better about it. At that, I was failing. Mom was right that I wasn't much of an activist. I couldn't make the hard thing easy.

So I let it be hard. I promised myself a few minutes to walk around and see Asterion's people as people, without trying to do anything else, before I hurt them. Some of these people, these real people, had been willing to do the same to the networks. It was the sort of thing that real people did.

Belatedly, I checked that my livestream was off, given that I was ostensibly done with diplomacy for the day. I bought the quail kabob I'd been craving, using a sliver of the credit built up by people like Dinar. This time I talked to the cartminder myself, the same way I would to someone selling goods at home. I asked what was in the marinade.

The cartminder laughed. "Everything! Fish sauce and soy and honey and a little five-spice and fennel, plus a couple other things. Can't share trade secrets, you know." But they gave me a free cone of pilaf along with the quail. When I asked where the quail came from they seemed bemused, but mentioned a nearby rooftop rookery that also raised pigeons (which they called squab) and some odd variety of duck.

I found a bench, tasted the quail. The crackling skin was sweet and spicy, the meat tender beneath. The pilaf was rich with saffron. I alternated bites, keeping myself from growing too accustomed to either. I watched people, trying not to imagine their lives—to focus, instead, on the fact that they *had* lives that I didn't know, wouldn't have a chance to question.

At home, it would be morning. I texted Carol. **I miss you.**

Seconds passed while relays passed the message around the world. **Miss you too. You okay over there?**

Just a little disoriented, I said. I hated not knowing if the line was secure, if our protocols could still be trusted. *You're going to do that to them.* And yeah, I was. **Tell me what's going on at home?**

Dori's being a complete fuss. She misses you too. Raven keeps asking where you are and trying to help with my knitting. But Rhamnetin is great with them, even though it weirds him out that he gets to play with kids.

He's getting deep into the network boards. He'll just show up on a random thread about wind kite design and ask questions.

I laughed. I wish I had him here to ask questions.

This is gonna sound weird, but I'm getting to really like him.

What's weird? He's likeable. I blinked. Oh. *Like* him. I . . . can kinda see that, actually. I thought about the way I wanted Carol here, and the way I wanted Rhamnetin. How they both felt like people who could get my thoughts to settle in rows. Yeah, I can definitely see that. I'm not quite sure how it would work.

I guess "are you ever attracted to people with heads" counts as an awkward question, yeah?

But maybe we should ask it? At least I was distracted. They probably have all sorts of customs around interspecies dating, unless they're entirely against it.

I'll wait till you get back, she texted.

Something to look forward to.

I thought about texting Rhamnetin, but it seemed too weird, and I was even less sure what to say than I would've been a few minutes earlier. I needed to stay focused, now, on what I was doing. I'd never been much for the part where you obsess over a relationship that hasn't started yet and might not happen at all—but in a few hours, it might be awfully convenient.

Okay. Deep breaths. Inhale. Exhale. Focus.

I'd thought deeply about the morality of using the bot, but only a little about the practicalities. I needed someplace less crowded, for a start. I found a reclamation point for the cone and the kabob skewer, licked the last of the quail grease off my fingers, and started walking again.

The rooftop gardens might be designed for assignations, but at street level Zealand had a distinct lack of quiet nooks. I wondered if I should wait. Sometime before we left, I might find the perfect spot. Or I might keep looking until we got back on the shuttle, reassuring myself that I'd never found exactly the right opportunity.

So I kept going, scanning for anything that might be scanning me. I needed to avoid both human and automated observation. Then I thought of the ansible site. It had been wide open, half-deserted—and best of all, full of networked drains. I didn't much like the idea of dropping a random object into a drain, but it wouldn't cause much of a blip on a chemical scan, it wouldn't be easy to find, and my fingerprints and DNA would get washed away. Not to mention that I had at least a vague excuse to be there. Any network observer would want to look at the site, maybe take more readings and try to find something wrong with it that hadn't come up yet. Hell, I could do that part while I was at it.

Assuming I could get there. Whichever corporate lord had founded Zealand, it hadn't been one of those obsessed with public transit. The city ran on an amalgamation of buses and smaller rides, schedule and direction unclear to anyone not on their network. As I tried to attract one, I realized that I had worse problems. The whole time we'd been here, Asterion's reps had ordered and directed the rides. I couldn't get any of the transit options to notice me. I could either walk across the aisland, or ask to see the site again tomorrow and hope to catch everyone with their backs turned.

Once you decide to do the hard thing, you shouldn't have this much trouble actually *doing* it.

"Need a hand with network translation?"

I whipped around—too fast, too surprised, too guilty-looking. Tiffany glowered over crossed arms. I tried to recover some semblance of aplomb. "I was hoping to get back out to the ansible site, look it over with fewer people around. But yeah, I can't get a ride. If you can help, I'd be grateful." Tha must have been tracking me. I'd done my best to avoid suspicious behavior—but if I'd succeeded, why was tha here?

Tiffany did something on thos palette, looking amused, and in a minute a small private ride pulled over. This one was trolley-style, with benches around the edges and grab rails and straps throughout. I hesitated over the greater ease and vulnerability of sitting, but gave in on the theory that I might still salvage something by acting innocent. Tiffany sat opposite me, still glaring—of course, earlier experience suggested that tha wasn't exactly friendly by default.

"You want to take readings, huh?" tha said.

I shrugged. "It's what we do. I didn't get much chance earlier."

Tha took a deep breath. Under the narrowed eyes and open distrust, tha was nervous.

"Show me what you've got in your pocket," tha said.

My own breath seemed to stick in my lungs. "My . . . pocket?"

"I understand that it's one of the things you value in clothing."

"No, I mean—" There was probably little point in dissembling, but still I pulled out my palette and the pack of nursing shields that I'd been carrying everywhere. I probably should have pumped before

I left, an ache that now twisted itself hard into my awareness, physical discomfort to match the social.

Tiffany hunched, clenching fists against thos armpits. "You've got something in your pocket that violates dandelion network protocols. I scrolled back through our scans, and you've had it since you got here. I've already warned Adrien, and if anything happens to me hoi'll tell more people. Let me see the blasted thing."

I could see the tremor tha held thonself so tightly around. It wasn't only Ringers who'd think me the villain of the piece. In the aislands the watersheds were the boogeyman. I might be able to intimidate Tiffany, even bluff my way out of this—if I were any good at playing the bad guy. But I was even less practiced in acting than in diplomacy. I fell back on my own anger, the reason I was doing this in the first place. "Last week the dandelion networks collapsed, and it took us days to restore them. Tell me—did you code the malware? Is that your 'translation' project?"

Tha hunched farther. "I haven't done anything to you. I just work on code compatibility issues."

"That doesn't answer my question."

Tha straightened, forcing thons hands down with visible effort. "You haven't answered mine, either. You're the one who's sneaking weaponized code around Zealand. You've come up with this, this story about what we did to you, because your stupid network protocol is unstable, and now you're trying to take revenge for what you imagined. Give me that thing, or Adrien will go to the board and *they'll* make you. And hoi'll tell the Ringers what you snuck on their shuttle, too."

The ride rolled smoothly onward—probably not toward the ansible site. I had no idea where Tiffany was taking me.

"The hell our protocols are unstable," I said. "They've worked without a major crash for decades. Suddenly they all fail at once during the most critical decision point in my lifetime? That'd be obvious bullshit even if Jace—" *Di Sanya, obre,* my mesh helpfully supplied when I stumbled on the name and last known presentation. "Di Sanya hadn't practically boasted about it at the opening reception."

Thos eyes snapped open. "What the fuck did di Sanya say to you?"

"Enough," I said. "He was very smug about how good our crash would be for the corporations."

Tiffany grimaced. "Di Sanya would be smug about anything that gave him an advantage, whether or not he was responsible. He'd gloat if you got hit with a cyclone, too."

"I got that. I also gathered that if he could control the weather, he'd start a cyclone for a few dollars' profit. Network crashes seem more feasible—especially with someone with your skills working for him."

I caught the wince, enough to tell me I wasn't completely off base. But of course I wasn't streaming, and a wince wouldn't carry much weight against the thing in my pocket. Tiffany could dance around thos responsibility all day; mine was plain. The moment passed.

"Look," Tiffany said. "You don't want an open accusation of tampering. You need the Ringers' trust, and the Chesapeake needs the trust of the other networks—they don't want an open accusation either. Someone like di Sanya would be glad to hurt you that badly, but what Adrien and I need is a lot smaller."

"And what's that?" I asked.

"For now, you give me that device in your pocket. We go back to Morlock Central and meet Adrien. I'll scan the thing—if it turns out to be a copy of *The Hitchhiker's Guide to Feast Food,* I'll apologize and owe you a major favor. If it's what it looks like, I'll document and disable it, and you and Adrien will talk about what hoi wants out of this whole business, which is probably something to support that promotion hoi's after, and a chance to move out of the intern dorms and set up a household. And we'll talk about what *I* want, which is personal."

I swallowed. I tried to think of a way out—but I *did* have the incriminating thing in my pocket, and I *didn't* want to talk about it with Jace di Sanya, or with Kelsey and Mallory. I was going to have words with Aunt Priya about not including a wipe switch on the bot.

"Fine," I said. "We'll go back. You, me, and Adrien can work this out."

The Morlock office was empty now. Lights flickered on. The grand sweep of the window showed a panoramic view of darkness, fading to city-glow above.

Tiffany stuck the bot in some sort of scanner, began running tests. I looked out the window so I wouldn't have to look anywhere else, but turned when I heard the door open. Adrien came in—with Dinar.

"What are you doing here?" It was a stupid thing to say, but I couldn't think of anything smart.

"Adrien came by the room," said Dinar. "Hoi said you were in trouble. Judy, what the hell have you gotten yourself into?"

I didn't answer, and Adrien pulled up a chair beside Tiffany. Around the room, I spotted sensors turning toward me, watching even while the humans' backs were turned. "What've you got?"

"There's only so much I can figure out without triggering the nasty little bug, but it's definitely designed to connect with our systems. I think it's meant to set up some sort of back door."

My cheeks burned. "It's defensive," I said, even though I wasn't confident in any such thing. "I told you, we know damn well where the malware came from."

"And *this* is how we're going to lay the accusation?" demanded Dinar.

"We've got evidence."

Adrien spun hos chair around. "Not nearly as much as we do. This thing violates any number of contracts, and it's right here in hard copy." Hoi leaned forward. "So let's talk about how we're going to get you out of this mess."

I noticed belatedly that Adrien had changed sometime in the last couple of hours. The leather suit had the stiffness I associated with something too new or too little used, and ornate metallic detailing around the hem and collar that reminded me somehow of Jace. "Let me guess, this is your special-occasions-only blackmail outfit?"

"After a fashion. That's certainly one of the moves available for obre—a conversation like this deserves us both playing at the highest level, don't you think?" Hoi—he—ran his hand across the leather suit, unabashed. "So let's play."

Everything really was a game to these people. I remembered what Adrien had said about the obre role: *No one's going to hold back. Unless you're really good, you're likely to get eaten alive.*

He leaned forward, intent. "There are plenty of people who'd like to see the watershed networks made irrelevant. Like you tried to do to us. But you never did manage it, and it wouldn't work against your people, either. At best you'd just become another set of old kings, casting your shadow over our work. What *my* bosses want is for the networks to treat us like a real power again. You can help."

Still too vague. "I don't shape the watersheds' attitudes. No one person does. What *action* will satisfy you?"

Adrien's hands sketched the air. "The Ringers are leaning against the Zealand site. It was a long shot to begin with, so far from their ship. And the ocean scares them."

Dinar smiled faintly. "They're not used to weather."

"Exactly. But they could use Asterion's experience in large-scale construction. So by the time everyone goes home from Zealand, you'll agree to our full involvement in the coalition building the antenna. First contact isn't something the networks get to do alone—you'll make us part of the conversation again."

It almost sounded reasonable. And yet I could follow the logical steps: their influence on the ansible site, their presence when the rest of the Ringers arrived, their weight in the negotiations over whether humanity got to stay on Earth. And between the watersheds, who'd poured so much work into keeping this world our own, and the corporations, who'd sacrificed so much of the world to keep growing, it wasn't hard to guess who'd gain the Ringers' sympathy. "It's not the conversation over the ansible that you care about. It's the power you'd gain if Earth's survival wasn't a concern."

Adrien shrugged. "Humanity can do better than one little world. Some people might even say the world is holding us back."

"Some people," I said. "Do *you* feel that way?"

He shrugged again. "I'm only an intern; how I feel doesn't matter. For now."

My fear of his blackmail was momentarily overwhelmed by fury at this dismissal. "You don't care what happens to the planet, do you, as long as you get your promotion? Don't you want power *for* something?"

Tiffany glanced away from thos scan, one hand still playing idly on the old-fashioned keypad. "You want Mx. Wallach-Stevens to play the game, you should probably explain the sides."

"I thought I had," said Adrien.

Tiffany huffed. "Some people around here just like the dances and the hustle for status. They're happy enough with the stakes low. But others have been talking about what the Ringers can disrupt. People like Jace di Sanya, they see a chance to go back to the twentieth century and start rebuilding where we left off. They believe our destiny is in the stars, even if we have to launch from the ashes of a world. Don't smirk like that, Adrien, I've heard thon say it. And what these people want to know—and so do I, frankly—is whether, when you make associate, you'll go along with Jace."

Adrien sighed. "As it happens, I think Jace di Sanya has a very poetic attitude toward business decisions. It's not my responsibility to stop him from burning things, but personally I think the problem with the corporate age was that we tried to have it here. It's obvious that our ideas were made for space. You could have mines the size of planets and skyscrapers the size of stars, and extract resources for centuries without breaking the systems you're extracting from. The networks can keep Earth—it'll be a backwater, but they can have it. We'll take the rest of the universe in trade."

"Poetic," said Tiffany sardonically.

I got up and paced. I itched to pick up one of the fidgets lying around the room, just to have something to do with my hands, but it seemed impolitic.

"You don't like us holding power anywhere," said Adrien. "You only want this world, but you don't want us to have anything else, either. You're as bad as everyone says." There was fury in his voice, slipping from its bonds and then reined back in. "It doesn't matter. You can't let the Ringers see the networks as potential saboteurs, and I'm offering an alternative. You bring us all the way into the work of interplanetary relations, starting with the ansible. And your mistake never leaves this room."

I could see Dinar's anger, the tension lining her face. The way her arm hung a little too loose, as if she weren't letting nerve signals through. She could easily guess that others outside the room were complicit, and must wonder why she'd been caught unawares.

"We haven't talked about what I get from this," said Tiffany abruptly.

"It can't wait a minute?" asked Adrien.

Tiffany ignored him. "It's simple enough. When we send our reps out to help with the antenna, Brend and I want to go along."

That startled me, but it shocked Adrien out of his act. "Brend? Why? E's a techie. E designs clothing. E doesn't want to talk to a bunch of random outsiders about communications equipment."

"You have no idea what e wants. *I* want to settle down with a household—same as you—but not until e's gotten a look at life out-side the fenceline, and decided e really wants to be here." Tha cocked thos head at me and Dinar. "You'd like that, right? A chance to argue with someone who doesn't fit so smoothly into our games? Easiest if you think of the whole thing that way—every corporate player who comes out to the Chesapeake is a potential convert, after all."

"You don't need to play these games to visit the watersheds," Dinar pointed out. "If you want to try things our way, all you need to do is ask."

"Sure. As long as we don't mind pissing off our bosses and taking whatever terms you stick us with. I'd rather set my own—and have Associate Adrien owe us a favor or two when we get back."

Judging by Adrien's grimace, he didn't like that part all that much, but he didn't argue. "What about it?" he asked me. "Do we have a deal?"

I wished I could see another way. "If you want to call it that." And we shook hands, palms tacky with sweat in the cool office.

CHAPTER 24

The algorithms should've picked up the change. I had considerable weight as a person in the ground, but when I suddenly started arguing for a larger corporate role in the antenna site, the change should've triggered not only other network members asking for new arguments and evidence (which they did), but automated flags and queries from the value-advocacy algorithms. Threads should have flooded with objections on behalf of the Anacostia and the Potomac, and every other entity that corporate interference had ever harmed. No such warnings appeared. Given the pushback I got from real people, the decision thread outputs should've taken longer to shift. But over a couple of days, the balance changed smoothly from Asterion-as-threat to Asterion-as-partner. Even more disturbingly, the usual constraints on corporate activity outside the fenceline failed to materialize. Normally we filled in agreements with a historical trail of requirements, built to counter every bit of under-the-table exploitation or pollution the corporations had tried over the last four decades. Instead, the incomplete reboots left us dependent on our own fallible memories. And, somehow, few of our attempts to reconstruct those restraints made it through the new rounds of voting.

All of which meant that when we left Zealand, our shuttle trailed by Asterion's plane, the corporate embassy came bound by fewer promises than they had in years. And Adrien, now leading the embassy as an associate—decked in real emeralds and a velvet dress whose meaning she helpfully explained while we waited for luggage to load—was clearly reveling in the power. Before we boarded our respective vehicles, she *thanked* me, laughing.

The associates were no longer the highest-ranked members of the embassy, though. That honor was reserved for Senior Associate Jace, along as a "visiting consultant." *Our destiny is in the stars, even if we have to launch from the ashes of a world.* The smugness radiating off the whole delegation was practically a renewable resource.

"I honestly think that in a generation or two, the aislands will have turned into just another culture with a bloody history," I told Carol. I could've used a day alone with my household, to talk about what happened and let them yell at me, and work out whatever we needed to work out. Hell, I needed half an hour of privacy with Redbug to talk about the remaining holes in our network. Instead we were scrambling to get ready for NASA's welcoming reception, and I'd barely had a chance to hug Athëo or the kids before going upstairs with my wife to look for something clean and reasonably formal. Unfortunately I've never been much for surplus clothing, and I'd just come back from a week of politically fraught parties. "But for now one of their major values is still exploiting as many resources as possible, and a lot of them want to go back to the twentieth century in more ways than style."

"You think they'll try something while they're out here working on the antenna," said Carol. She'd already pulled out her best dress and a string of heirloom pearls, and was nursing Dori while I finished dressing.

"Jace di Sanya all but told me e was responsible for the malware. Adrien says e's part of the faction that doesn't care what happens to Earth as long as the corporations wind up on top again. And Adrien *likes* em, just thinks e's a bit, um, romantic."

"I was worried about that bot—but I wish you'd gotten away with it. Or that we could trust our algorithms to help monitor Asterion while they're loose in the watershed."

"You too, huh?" I asked. I found a paisley sundress that was too chilly for early spring, and probably too informal, but would work okay with a shawl over my shoulders. At least our NASA hosts wouldn't be too fashion-conscious.

"Something feels off," agreed Carol. "After a while you get an instinct for what's going to emerge from a discussion thread. But these last few days, things haven't come out like I expected. The decisions around the Asterion delegation most of all."

"And without the backing of the network," I agreed, "we don't have a legitimate way to respond."

We took the Metro into the city with the rest of the household. Athëo was stiff with me, and I wished again that we'd had a couple days to decompress. Raven bounced around the train car, excited to be going to a fancy party and looking forward to seeing their "baby bug friends" after a week apart. I tried to reorient: we were back in the Chesapeake, trying to keep as much advantage as we could with the corporations treading on our heels. If others in the American government shared St. Julien's resentment of them, tonight might offer a chance at alliance.

I'd occasionally been to meetings in U.S. government buildings—mostly to coordinate on issues where they still claimed authority and wanted regular reports, even though we were actually doing all the work. It was easier to show up at the Department of Interior or Environmental Protection Agency and confirm that yes, we were meeting standards for arsenic levels in the Potomac, than to argue over who was actually responsible for the river. Those briefings took us to a wide selection of airless, windowless rooms scattered around downtown DC. But for today they'd found a more impressive setting. The Executive Office Building was an ancient gothic pile of crenellations and countless windows, stuffed full of miniature ballrooms with historically important paintings on the walls (and sometimes ceilings). I imagined it lit up at the third power's height: dozens of diplomatic shindigs running in parallel. The marble floors and winding staircases dipped smoothly in the middle, worn by generations. Something about the echoes reminded me of the Outgoing dance before I started my Transit Year—that sense of playing dress-up, not quite an adult yet.

It didn't help that they were determinedly checking U.S. identification cards at the door. I was sure I had one somewhere, but not *with* me. From the line, I wasn't alone. Eventually they found some compromise with their own requirements and let us in along with the people who definitely didn't have IDs because they came from another solar system.

I was willing to forgive a lot of nonsense, though, because the hors d'oeuvres included recognizable hummus.

In general, they'd gone out of their way to be legible—they'd given everyone badges with name and affiliation along with pronouns, labeled the food, and in several other ways acted like sensible people welcoming a crowd drawn from dozens of cultures.

Dinar murmured to the rest of us, "Oh, good, I'm not going to spend the whole night fuming about how I'd have done it."

"Was Zealand really that bad?" asked Athëo, and Dinar nodded firmly.

"I swear, their idea of a fun party is challenging everyone in the room to a duel, fashion choices and unlabeled allergens at dawn."

We wandered, trying to get a feel for the place. NASA—the whole government, really, or whatever portion had gotten involved—had set up a couple of rooms just for eating and talking, more gilded than our Zealand hotel and laden with questionable murals. (I questioned them, at least: I was pretty confident that U.S. relations with First Nations had never been so friendly and egalitarian.) Grand arched windows looked out over possibly-no-longer-functional balconies and the white-columned, red-roofed buildings beyond. The hallways had been lined with "Treasures of Earth," which is to say everything they'd been able to pry loose from the Smithsonian. Perfectly preserved trilobites and a hadrosaur skull mixed with an Apollo 11 spacesuit, an oil painting of fantastically cragged mountains, a statue of a woman with such an expression of peace on her face that it took my breath away.

But it was the side rooms—still marble-floored, but recognizably kin to the conference rooms I'd seen before—that ultimately caught my attention.

"Hey, that's from *Neko's Secret Adventure Frog!*" exclaimed Dinar. The screen at the front of the room—in my experience usually full of poorly visualized data—was playing one of the shows that had featured in the Ringers' coming-in-peace soundtrack. A display along the side, museum-style, gave cultural context for that along with several other shows from the playlist. What human country and time period they'd come from, which bits were drawn from real experience and which were made up, everything you might want to teach a bunch of aliens whose first exposure to humans had been broadcast fiction.

We perused the exhibit for a few minutes before Carol pointed out that the display might be mutual. "Rhamnetin's been busy with *something* the last couple of days."

We peeked in the next room down. My eyes were immediately drawn to the screen. It might have been a perfectly ordinary film—except that the color mix seemed off, and all the characters were Ringers. I joined the fascinated crowd. Connor Goldsmith was near the front, and waved before turning back to the display. Athëo scooped Raven up to give them a seat on his shoulders; they weren't the only kid who'd gotten themselves a view. "Bugs! Bugs! Baby bugs?"

"We'll find them soon, I promise," said Carol.

"Dimmy and Corvy!"

"Soon!"

On the screen a plains-person, with a tree-person behind them, had backed another plains-person against a wall—no, a tree, thick as a redwood. The cornered pillbug clutched some sort of device, and their body was painted in garish colors. A kid clung to their—her—back. She was declaiming a speech; on a nearby desk one of the Ringers' voiceboxes provided dubbed dialogue:

"—will not give you the hold you seek. If your passions are not returned, no artifice will replace that core with true heat."

A furry limb tapped me from behind. I squeaked, but turned smiling to see Rhamnetin. Or I thought it was Rhamnetin—I second-guessed my reflexive recognition until the familiar voice came out of his speaker. "You made it! I'm glad you're back."

"It's good to see you," I said, feeling distinctly more self-conscious than was appropriate. "This is a great idea."

He waved a limb at the screen and said something in his own language. "One of the plains' Shakespeare equivalents—always popular. This version was recorded about three hundred years ago. Having one of my people there is ahistorical, of course, but it's become traditional to include us in Pre-Reach narratives as a sort of Greek chorus telling the original characters that they should have known better."

"Shakespeare with Ringers!" Athëo clasped his hands. "Ringers as the fairies in *Midsummer Night's Dream*? Or one of the families in *Romeo and Juliet*?"

"If you're waiting for me to prove how well I understand human culture by having memorized a soliloquy, I'm going to disappoint you," said Rhamnetin. "The Warning Against False Passions, on the other hand, I've had by heart since I was knee-high."

Dinar squinted at the screen. "So they're fighting over some sort of . . . love potion?"

Rhamnetin shifted weight among his limbs. "It's a device for enhancing . . . charisma, I think is the best English word. Whatever it is about a plains-person that convinces mates to sire their children. In the story, it was created as a way to heal people who're injured while their children are young, in such a way that they lose their hold over their mates. That's one of those things that happens more often in stories than real life. But of course"—he inserted a skirling sound, presumably the pre-contact-style name of the attacker in the scene, no periodic table involved—"wants to use it to attract new mates. Inevitably they get the device, but it all goes very badly."

"Are relationships less fraught for the tree-folk?" asked Carol.

Laughter from Rhamnetin's voicebox echoed the chitter of his legs. "It's different, anyway. The fraughtness of getting picked to fertilize someone's eggs isn't much like the fraughtness of finding cross-family, or lovers."

"Are those different things?" I asked. I hoped Rhamnetin wouldn't pick up on my human blushing.

"Usually. Well, obviously cross-family and mating can't overlap, and cross-family only sometimes become lovers. And just because your genetics are a good match with someone doesn't mean you're going to get along other ways."

Dinar narrowed her eyes at me and Carol, and texted, **Are you two flirting with a guy with no head?**

My face warmed further, equal parts embarrassment at being caught out and self-consciousness that Carol and I hadn't even figured out if we were going to be lovers with our co-parents yet. **Let's say we appreciate his deeper qualities.**

Athëo, poker-faced, asked, "And do your people always pick lovers from the same species?"

"Symbiosis comes in many forms."

On the screen behind Rhamnetin, the villain of the piece had gotten hold of the device, and was engaged in some inscrutable dance with their desired mates. Around us, humans mixed with Ringers—far more of the former, but they managed to avoid crowding our guests even without a gatekeeper. Part of what made the crowd feel so friendly was the depth of their data. Watershed reps had their clothing reassuringly tagged with sources and materials, and for most you could read names, roles, and expertises. I was immersed again in the familiar waters of the network. Even knowing that there was some unreadable pollutant in the currents, it felt warm and welcoming. And I was laughing with my household, trying not to think of the pollutants I might have released through my own actions.

Sometimes we find peace in a moment because we have to. It was, of course, a brief moment.

"Dimmy! Corvy!" Raven called gleefully. The kids in question dropped from their mother's belly and scampered ahead, flinging themselves on Raven in an interspecies pile of limbs and shrieks. Dori twisted to watch her sib and eeked happily. A moment later Cytosine joined us, along with St. Julien—and Jace di Sanya. I put a protective arm around Dori.

"They missed each other," said Cytosine, limbs rippling at the kids.

"If they'd spent the last week together, they'd be trading languages by now."

I ignored the barb. "Yours are already getting pretty good at English. I don't know that Raven has the vocal chords for Ringer."

"We need to get you voiceboxes," suggested Rhamnetin. Cytosine reached out to stroke him with one of her limbs. Reassurance and reconnection, after she'd disciplined him for inviting us? Or something more complex in the one-way language of skinsong?

"Given the blueprints and materials, we could retool factories to turn them out quickly," said Jace. A network thread blinked up in my lenses; people had been tracking the Asterion delegation all night, and e'd been offering this type of deal to anyone who seemed to want something material. The thread also helpfully identified eir outfit as holo with 83 percent certainty.

"We do manufacturing as well," I said. "And with a lower carbon footprint. But yes, if that would let us start learning your language as well as you know ours, we should get our technical specialists together. We might even be able to adapt the voicebox programming into our network so we don't need separate devices."

I'd been depending on Raven's eventual exhaustion to limit our time at the party. But NASA had set up little cots in another conference room, and gotten a couple of carers in from the Chesapeake, so kids too big for slings could sack out as they reached their meltdown points. That meant my jetlag, and Dinar's, would be a bigger factor. I was reluctant to make too poor a showing since I was still ostensibly leading our delegation. It was disturbing to have failed both so profoundly and so invisibly. *Should I resign?* But I still had all the advantages of being first in the ground with the Ringers, first to greet them as they thought they should be greeted, and I knew that still carried considerable weight with Cytosine despite her annoyance over the Zealand trip.

So, with my brain convinced that I should just be waking up, I forced myself to focus on discussions of ansible construction, interstellar trade, and hundreds of years of storytelling in two solar systems. I would've particularly liked to be more awake for that last, but the conversation I most wanted to have was the one we hadn't been able to finish with Rhamnetin. The one I most needed to have was with St. Julien, sans corporate associates.

The Ringers were all in high demand, of course. So I wandered through the event rooms on my own, stroking Dori's back. Mental fuzziness transmuted to something trancelike, a meditation on the cultures interwoven here, and what fabrics the Ringers might add to that tapestry. Out in the hall, the Smithsonian displays seemed to morph into the story that made humanity.

"One week," said St. Julien. "It should have been impossible." I jumped, absurdly surprised, then had to reassure Dori.

"What should have been impossible?" I asked.

She swayed as she talked, her own child fast asleep against her chest. I fell easily into sync. "The Smithsonian collections are among the best in the world, even now. I want to bring the Ringers through all of them, give them days to understand what we are. I suppose we'll get to that, eventually. But we asked the head of each museum for the five most important items in their collection. Maybe we should have been more specific. Tried to coordinate the scientific specimens and the paintings and the souvenirs from the moon. I did my best."

"I can see it," I said. "The outlines of our truth, at least. I don't know if they can. There's so much you need to know to fill in the gaps; how could they? But it feels right to me."

"It's going to take us both time to understand each other's stories," said St. Julien. "You know what I was doing when they called me in?"

"No?"

"Binge-watching *Star Trek*. Every damn series. Perfect preparation for first contact, right? But now I'm thinking about how—some people devote their lives and careers to those shows. They write their own scripts, or collect ephemera, or analyze how the different captains reflect our changing ideals of leadership over the past century. And that's one narrow facet of understanding this beautiful, stupid species and everything we've done on this beautiful, stupid planet."

I nodded. I'd planned to say something strategic, but now I felt the same drifting intimacy we might have gotten from wine or pot. Nursing forces sobriety, but St. Julien couldn't have gotten much sleep lately either. "And they have two species, and planets' and planets' worth of space to make history. It's hard enough for humans to understand each other."

"Look here." She took my arm and pulled me along. "This is a lava rock from Hawaii. The Kanaka Maoli consider it an ancestor, so it's only on loan to the Museum of the American Indian. Every decade one rock goes home and another comes out to visit us. Maybe they'll send one out to the Rings, and it'll meet people who haven't seen a volcano in a thousand years. And that whole practice, sending and returning, is the Smithsonian's tacit acknowledgment of a history of complete lack of respect. All the ways we've colonized and killed each other, and all the pitifully inadequate ways we make up for it, and none of that is obvious if you don't already have at least a little of the background when you read 'this rock is an ancestor, it's only visiting DC.'

"Is there anything here from the Holocaust Memorial?" I asked quietly. "I haven't seen yet."

She flushed and looked down at her hands. "I thought there should be. The State Department folks were nervous about something that *just* shows our worst side."

It burned in my gut, worse now while the world around me felt like a tapestry in progress, that such an important thread would be left out. "They could have put in the display of righteous gentiles. Or the time capsule that the people buried in one of the camps. A recording of songs from the Warsaw Ghetto uprising. You think it's only a story of how horrible humans are? We should be telling them—" I caught my breath, realizing that I was about to burst into tears in the middle of an interplanetary reception. Really, I might as well be drunk.

"*I* thought so." St. Julien didn't even look taken aback. She looked like me, maybe: like someone whose failure hadn't received the attention it deserved. I wasn't being fair to her.

I took a few deep breaths, until I felt less like making an idiot of myself. "We should tell them that no matter what you do to us, we survive. And we remember who we are."

CHAPTER 25

Even with waking to nurse, I slept far more easily than usual that night. I was too exhausted to worry at my problems and too relieved to be back in my own bed, my wife curled next to me with her familiar scent like an aura of comfort. Even so, I woke with a headache. My mesh helpfully informed me that my neurophysiology was even more out of whack than usual. I double-checked the lactation safety tags on a painkiller, and then checked again before taking it.

"Everyone in the world's downstairs, aren't they?" I asked Carol.

"Have been all week."

Which meant I wouldn't be able to talk about anything serious with Dinar and Athëo until we had time to ourselves, probably not till evening. The disadvantages of using our own home as a diplomatic base occurred to me. On the other hand, the heady sweetness of French toast was starting to waft from below. Dinar did have the most delicious ways of coping with stress.

Redbug and Elegy confronted us over breakfast, ignoring the two plains-folk engaged in a deep discussion of film history with the Ghats-Narmada emissary in the dining room. I'd have vastly preferred to join them, or barring that enjoy my French toast in peace, if the two tech experts hadn't swung into the archway. Dinar finished spooning strawberry preserves onto my toast, and turned to face them.

"Letting the corporations send reps at all is one thing," said Redbug. "But going out there was supposed to keep their involvement under control. What the hell happened?"

My face felt hot. I was going to have to argue on Asterion's behalf so many times, and sound like I meant it. "Is it really so harmful, having them out here where we can keep an eye on them? Whatever they did to the network, they did it from their aislands."

Elegy glared—not at me but at Dinar. "Here they have access to hardware. And we don't know their capabilities as well as we thought we did. We keep finding malware in places we thought we'd cleaned out, areas where our network code doesn't match the documentation. It's like one of those funguses that takes over insects, grows into their nervous system or something, and kills them from the inside out."

"Cordyceps," said Redbug. "Like it's trying to take over the dandelion network's form and break it more thoroughly the second time around, in tiny little increments that we can just barely detect until it all crumbles at once. If it hadn't shut everything down so dramatically the first time, I'm not sure we'd even notice until it was too late. It might be too late already. Dinar, what the hell did you do?"

Dinar flinched and glared fiercely back. "You think I did this? What, because I take gigs?"

I got between them. I might not be able to be honest, but at least I could keep people from sticking Dinar with the blame. "It wasn't her fault. I supported it more than she did—and it was the best we could manage. We almost lost the site to Zealand."

"At least we'd keep some space between the corporations and the Chesapeake, then," said Redbug. "I saw your arguments, but I assumed the corporate shill was pushing it behind the scenes."

"*Everyone* thinks so," said Dinar. "Don't think I haven't checked my weights this morning. It's a hell of a thing, having your rep shifted by arguments that you didn't make. Our algorithms aren't supposed to let that happen; what the hell are *you* doing?"

Redbug ignored her question. "My point is, we have to assume that the more sensors we get on the antenna, the more vulnerable we'll be to whatever Asterion builds into it, or the infrastructure around it. What happens when people who care about the planet are stuck in the shallows in these negotiations? Without stable code for the networks, without being able to count on our algorithms, the whole governance structure that we use to protect our world dries up. How are we supposed to negotiate for the future of the planet without the thing that makes us a coherent entity, that lets us know what the planet *needs*?"

"I don't know," I said. Normally we'd open threads to solve this stuff—and I could see that such threads were in fact open, but they were taking an awfully long time to resolve. "What change are you recommending? Because keeping Asterion away from the antenna wouldn't actually have healed the network."

"It would've given us more time to fix it," said Elegy. "It would've been even better to hold off on building the antenna till we had this under control. If Asterion wants interstellar trade so badly, that might've been enough incentive to make them back off their network attacks."

I shook my head. "The Ringers would've just used the Zealand site. The antenna was going up one way or another, and we need it where we keep some control."

Redbug glowered. "Someone's going to drill that oil, so it should be us, huh? We might as well hand this thing over to the corporations; you've basically done it already."

"There's one thing we can do," Elegy said to them.

"I know." They made a mocking half-bow to Dinar. "Thank you for your hospitality when we needed headquarters in a hurry. Now it's time for us to move our debugging setup somewhere more stable."

Dinar smiled, eyes narrow, but I caught the sheen of tears held in check. "You do that."

Despite the programming experts clearing out, the house was still too crowded for a family conversation even if anyone could've pried Dinar from the kitchen. The constant stream of finicky, spice-rich dishes flowing into the dining room, punctuated by the rhythmic slap of dough, suggested how foolhardy that would be. It took me over an hour to notice that neither Cytosine nor Rhamnetin was among the crowd. I asked around and learned that they were already at the antenna site.

"We should go," I told Carol.

Dori enjoyed the train ride, peering out the window and at our fellow passengers with equal eagerness. Raven had slept in or we'd have brought them too, to see their friends and add an extra layer of authority to our presence. *If we pick up nothing else from the Ringers, I like that part.*

By the Potomac the bluebells had started blooming, and some early celandine. But the old parking lot was still a relative wasteland. Blackberry roots ate at the edges, and dandelions and moss cracked the expanse: a bare start at terraforming a moonscape of black tarmac.

Humans and Ringers clustered in the middle of that moonscape. We made our way out, rolling our share-bikes with Dori still in the sidecar. She giggled at every jolt, and Carol started singing, "Bump, bump, bump" until we had to leave the bikes at the crowd's edge. The witnesses spread around an empty area about thirty feet across, where Rhamnetin's brothers had cleared the rubble and were setting down a pattern of tiny black and silver cubes.

Eliza Mendez waved at us, and we joined her while I tucked Dori into my sling. "They're laying the seed foundation," she said. "We're about to see some high-level nanotechnology at work—better than anything humans have managed so far, at least."

Belatedly, I checked the ecological impact report, which the *Solar Flare*'s specialists had completed in our absence. "Oh, wow—it really does have a carbon drawdown effect. We could take advantage of that."

Eliza stuffed her hands in her pockets. "You're not the first person to pounce on that—unfortunately it's not as much as you might guess. The antenna will use about two tons of atmospheric carbon total along with other local elements and some materials they brought along. Astatine—apparently this falls under their engineering specialty—says that if you try to speed up the process, it gets harder to control where the builders grab the carbon *from*."

"That'd be a problem." I looked around the lot, made some calculations. "Crap, we'd do better by planting this place with pine trees."

"Right," said Eliza. "Plus the trees would create new habitat and mitigate erosion, not to mention that they're sturdier in the aggregate than a structure that might not make it through hurricane season."

"Every little bit helps," said Carol. "We could use this technology for emergency housing, circuit repair on solar panels, any task where we struggle to move construction footprints across the cherry tree threshold." That was the point where a process had a positive effect on the surrounding environment, fitting into its ecology as well as the sakura trees scattered around Washington. "The difference might not be dramatic, but it'd push in the right direction."

Eliza nodded. "A butterfly flaps its wings and maybe the next hurricane season has one less hurricane. It's a good point." She added the idea to a thread about Ringer tech, and Carol and I added our votes.

The foundation grew, block by block. The pattern echoed the ornate curlicues of Victorian ironwork, or a summoning circle from one of last night's movies, full of occult symbols in unknown alphabets. A scan picked up various metallic compounds, but no hint of how the thing worked. I stepped forward to take a closer look, and found myself next to Cytosine.

"Fascinating, aren't they?" she asked. "I've always loved watching builders. Do you want to touch one?"

"Yes! Are they safe?" A silly question, since the Ringers were handling them directly. Of course some humans dribble mercury between their fingers given half a chance. "Will you be offended if I hand Dori over to Carol first?"

"Of course not. Although—I could hold her, if you want." Understandably, she sounded tentative. We rubbed each other the wrong way so often—was this a peace offering, or a dominance challenge? I glanced at Carol, who shrugged, and wished I had time to check with Rhamnetin.

"Okay. But only if I can hold yours later."

Cytosine chittered laughter. "They may pinch a bit, but you're welcome to." So I'd played that right.

Tentative myself, I unwrapped Dori. Cytosine rolled back, making a lap, and nudged Diamond and Chlorophyll until they made room. Long, slender limbs cradled my child against chitinous skin. She waved her hands, grabbing the limbs that held her. Cytosine's kids stroked her hair gently.

"Hello, baby," said Chlorophyll, and Cytosine said something in her own language. One of the other plains-folk offered me a pair of cubes. I could have held half a dozen in my palm with room to spare. They felt touchscreen-slick and warm against my skin. Heat wavered off them on my scans, and I could catch hints of some internal circulation generating that heat. The network whispered through my vision, histories of our own failed attempts at molecular engineering, and all the fears and ethical arguments that had been raised around that never-reached possibility.

Cytosine had suggested harder limits than those guessed by our old philosophers, but even within those restrictions the cubes could as easily become weapons—or accidental disasters—as well-controlled tools. Across the circle of observers, Jace watched the proceedings with a thin-lipped smile, and Brend and Tiffany talked with animated hands. I thought of cordyceps mushrooms digesting caterpillars, of rivers eaten from the inside out.

"How do you make sure these are used safely?" I asked Cytosine. "Or do you? Do Ringers ever fight each other—at scale, I mean?" I thrilled at the thought that a species *could* outgrow war, and at the same time was terrified to think that they'd managed it. More than the Dyson sphere or the nanoengineering, that would set them far ahead of humanity.

Cytosine shifted and wrapped limbs around all three kids to

steady them. "We try to avoid it—wars are far more dangerous in space than on a planet. There's no margin for that kind of resource waste, and it's usually easier to find new resources than to take them from where they're protected. We're not short of land, or any of the things that go along with it. Under those circumstances, ideas and passions are the main things that drive violence. We're far from perfectly peaceful, but there are several billion observers ready to get in the way of burgeoning conflict." She shuffled again, and eyes swiveled to track the construction work. "Those observers particularly discourage molecular weaponry. It's far too dangerous; we lost two whole habitats early on to a fight over architectural design."

I shivered. "I hope you'll discourage it here, too." And of course, I realized, this must be the "peaceful" technology they'd used to dismantle their gas giants. My chill grew glacial as I considered some fanatic deciding to force our relocation by taking Earth apart for construction material.

"I think you have the imagination common to all sapients," Cytosine said. "You want to mark all the dangers before you examine the value. I promise these blocks are pre-programmed carefully; they won't do anything other than build an antenna out of atmospheric carbon."

I hefted the little cubes, feeling their weight. The black ones were so dark that I could barely see the corners; the silver swirled in a slow moiré. "I trust you on these ones. It's the technology's potential that worries me."

"All postindustrial technologies are potential extinction events in waiting. It's why we spread out."

Then the Ringers trumpeted a shout of pleasure or triumph, and stepped back outside the bounds of the summoning diagram. Tree-folk grasped limbs with plains-folk, and their speech turned rhythmic, voices offset like a campfire round. Another ritual, like Rhamnetin's morning prayer.

Within the summoning pattern, the blocks began to ripple as if someone had thrown a stone into a pond. But instead of dying away the ripples continued, and over long minutes I could see a second layer, then a third, growing upward. The antenna reached, slowly, for the stars.

Problem: Has anyone noticed that everyone's a lot madder about corporate involvement with the Ringers in the common board than on here? What gives? (*automated cleanup: thread filtered low-priority due to poor problem definition*) (*automated reweighting: problem priority reduced due to low response rate*) * Option: I don't know, express more anger on the network I guess? * Option: Ingest a sample of the common thread discussion and do a proper statistical comparison. * Option: Keep them away from the Ringers, I swear I've been saying this on every thread where it's relevant. (*automated cleanup: option filtered due to cross-thread redundancy*)

*　　*　　*

Automated alert: Mid-Atlantic sensors are showing temperatures and currents indicative of large-scale stormline formation, with the likelihood of at least one major storm reaching the North American coast within the next two weeks currently 67% (see linked dataset). The probability of at least one major storm disrupting infrastructure in our region this spring is estimated at 74–82% depending on the model used (see linked data set). * Comment: Right, well this is going to be exciting if the network crashes again. Maybe we should have *some* sort of backup besides the common network? * Comment: Didn't there used to be a *season* for these things? Maybe the Ringers have weather control that could point all the hurricanes at the aislands that caused them. (*automated cleanup: comment filtered due to topic irrelevance*)

*　　*　　*

Thread: This is an open discussion for Ringer entertainment, see attached for a streamed record of the movie room at last night's NASA shindig. Nation-states know how to throw a party; we ought to invite them more often! And whatever else you can say for them, Ringers know how to make movies. * Comment: How ridiculous am I if I develop a crush on the actor hamming it up with that love potion? Apparently I have no resistance to cheesy villains regardless of species. * Comment: How ridiculous am I if I invite a few aliens to audition for my teeny amateur theater that mostly does medieval revenge tragedies? * Comment: Can we just tell them we're staying put until our anthropologists get a few centuries with their storytelling tropes? *(automated cleanup: comment filtered due to topic irrelevance)*

CHAPTER 26

"I know damn well why you didn't tell me," said Dinar. "But I wish to hell you'd trusted me instead of acting like Redbug or Elegy or anyone else who's convinced I'm a corporate shill. If you'd asked, I could've told you how they'd play it when they caught you."

It was late, and the four of us were ensconced at last in Dinar and Athëo's sitting room. Angry as she was, she'd done all she could to foster a comfortable conversation, offering low lighting and the remains of the day's stress baking to help keep us connected. Kyo sniffed everything and then climbed into her lap, radiating mammalian contentment. But we were all tired, and Raven had capped the long day with a screaming tantrum well past their usual bedtime—for most of us, comfort was a lost cause.

"It's not that I didn't trust you—" I said. Which wasn't entirely true, but wasn't *her* fault either. "But I knew they had more hold over you, more room to punish you if you were complicit. I wanted to be the only person in range they could legitimately blame."

"They didn't give a fuck about who they could *legitimately* blame, did they?" asked Athëo. "They blamed whoever best served their interest."

I squeezed Carol's hand. "I expected them to use me as a bargaining chip with the rest of the network, instead of the other way around. Maybe that was stupid. I'll feel even stupider if it turns out you could've helped me plant the thing properly. Redbug's got me terrified that the malware is eating our networks from the inside out. We could've stemmed it at the source, and we won't get a second chance."

Dinar shook her head. "I'd have told you not to carry the damned thing around all week. I don't know if it was actually a good idea or not, I don't know if your aunt could've done what she said even with a back door, I don't know if it would've come back to bite us all later. But if you were going to drag that thing over the fenceline, you should've set it as soon as you had a moment to yourself, and not dithered until you got within range of someone's experimental sensors." She bit forcefully into a cinnamon pasty. "The aislands are full of that shit. When my gigwork isn't endless quality comparisons between rare earth batches, it's checking data sets from inventions that're supposed to improve some type of materials detection, or get a jump on other company's sensors. They like playing with code and circuitry almost as much as they like playing with fashion."

I tried to think of something to say and the pause stretched out, painful and ready to snap.

"What it is," said Athëo, words coming too quickly, like he'd forced them out, "is that I don't like having authorities decide what is safe for me to know. For future reference."

I winced. "That's not fair—I wasn't trying to be some sort of—I wasn't making a moral judgment about forbidden knowledge—look, it's not that I thought I'd be *better* at making this decision than anyone else. I wanted so badly to run it by the whole network. But even aside from the risks of spreading blame, I'd just been told the network was compromised. That any decision filtered through our algorithms might be flawed, or just feed straight into Asterion. And given how easy it was to get the worst of their lot involved in the antenna project, it seems like I was right. I took a chance to try and stop it, and I failed, but that doesn't make me a Purist father-priest."

Athëo hunched. "I know it's not rational, okay?"

"Hell, I didn't—" And I could tell we were both spiraling, Athëo from well-earned trauma running roughshod over all his mediation training, and me from the memory of a thousand top-volume Bet debates and the totally pointless tendency of my neurotransmitters to flee into dark corners under stress. In that moment knowing didn't help, and I bit down on what wanted to come next: telling Athëo and Dinar they could leave if they didn't want to co-parent with me, begging them not to, offering to leave myself, running off to my room because I was obviously making the conversation worse. I stared at my hands, trying not to cry and wondering why I'd thought I had the right to make decisions on my own.

Carol broke in. "She told *me* about the bot beforehand. I wasn't sure what the right thing was either, but I agreed that we shouldn't spread it around. If you're going to blame her for not putting it to the crowd, you'd better blame me, too. But maybe first you want to stop and decide whether *you're* about to report the whole thing to the network. Are you?"

Dinar sighed. "I see it, okay? If we tell more people, the corporations have something to hold over the network instead of just over Judy. Now we're complicit, even though we didn't have any say in the decision. Maybe the fact that you couldn't safely run this by the watershed, even if the algorithms *were* working, should've told you it was a bad idea. You needed to understand the system you were trying to infiltrate, and you *couldn't* collect the data you needed to understand it on your own. That's why we have networks in the first place."

"Thank you," I said stiffly. "I know why we have networks."

"I'm sure *your* parents told you all about it," said Athëo.

"Athëo, for fuck's sake," I said heavily.

Carol closed her eyes, and took a deep breath, exaggerated for effect. "No one say anything. Breath with me. We're taking a minute."

We all obeyed, probably because she'd said the same thing to Raven barely an hour ago. The point that we ought to be able to outmatch the toddler at basic mindfulness wasn't exactly subtle. I inhaled, trying to focus on the world outside my head. I was terrified by how badly I'd failed, running dozens of what-ifs in parallel, and still trying to readjust from the half-day time shift. And none of that was improved by lashing out at my household, who had every right to be pissed at me and were probably terrified by the whole thing. And I *wasn't* Athëo; I had a childhood's worth of experience to tell me that people could have screaming fights about things that mattered and still stick together and love each other. He *didn't*. And I could, damn it, talk honestly to my household without risking Bet levels of drama. I exhaled, and breathed in again.

One of my favorite things about the attic was the way a day's scents rose through the house, waiting here in the evening like a journal. Baking bread, cinnamon and coriander and cumin, Kyo's nervous-dog musk and Dinar's rosewater soap and the warm green scent of Ringers. I focused on those, tried to make them more important than all the unresolved hamster wheels in my stupid brain.

"Right," said Carol. "What do you all want to get out of this conversation? Actual goals, beyond simply wanting to yell. Yelling is a means, not an end."

We all looked at each other nervously. I supposed this part was my responsibility too. I tried to think it through—what I really wanted, hopes rather than fears and reflexive flinches. "I'm terrified on so many levels I can't even count them. But I want to keep you all in my life, keep this household working, and I don't ever want to have to make a choice that big without getting your input again, even if I can't talk to anyone else about it. I want to keep the network working too, and the planet. I know I can't get those things out of this conversation, but they're such big things to want that they take up all my processing power. This mess is too big, and I'm stuck as the face of it, and I'm probably going to make more mistakes, and I want you to know that I'm trying not to be a complete idiot." I shivered as I spoke, and a whispered "sorry" slipped out behind all that truth.

"We've all got worries beyond the household," said Dinar. She sounded calmer now, a claim of solidarity rather than pointing out that the excuse wasn't personal to me. "I've been having nightmares about trying to dig gardens on space stations. Right now, though, I just want everyone to treat my gigwork like one of my verbs instead of one of my nouns. It's something I do, not something I am. It's even less what I am than the other things I do."

"Do you still think we can change them?" I asked. After a week on Zealand, my own ethics fraying from the strain, it seemed like trying to filter gold from seawater—possible, but never worth the sacrifice.

"Maybe." She clasped her fingers, staring down as if answers lay hidden between them. "Yes, I still do. It's hard and it's dangerous, but even in the middle of all that mess, part of what Tiffany demanded for thonself and Brend was to see how we live. There are people in the aislands who still want a better world. Especially for those who don't spend their lives at glittering parties, we owe them the chance to learn."

"Working with the corporations is something you do because you see a need, and you aren't going to ignore it just because it's messy—like most of what you do," said Athëo, and Dinar leaned against him. Kyo yipped at the sudden shift of previously trustworthy lap, and scrabbled to the floor to gobble up crumbs from the pasty.

"What do you want?" she asked him.

"A family that trusts me enough to get me in this much trouble," he said.

"If we could swap out your parents for decent people," I said, "we'd do it in a heartbeat."

He glared, his arm still around Dinar. "I know you can't do that. My parents haven't been family for years, and I don't even want that from them anymore. The three of you, and the kids, are the family I need now. I want *you* to trust me. To share trouble, instead of keeping it to yourself."

"I get that," I said. "That kind of trust can take your breath away. I realize the Bet is functional and loving and embedded in the modern world in exactly the way your birth household never was—but they're also the sort of people who would send their kid off to sabotage a corporate network with a five-minute briefing and a promise that the bloody thing is undetectable. I love them, and I'm going to keep loving them after I get the chance to tell them exactly how their clever plan went to hell, but I have in fact developed a serious appreciation for protecting the people I love and trust—including from the Bet's cleverness."

Athëo took a minute to think about that. "They can be intense," he said at last.

"And if you head over there and tell them you'd like to get involved in radical activism, they will absolutely gift you with as much trouble as you want. I want my home life a little gentler." I felt something loosen with the admission.

"And you had that gentleness, up until a couple weeks ago?" asked Carol.

"God, yes. You're right. Ever since we turned into Alien Negotiation Central, our dining room has felt too much like the Bet's." I waved at Athëo. "There you go, that's my real, stupid motivation for keeping this to myself—trying desperately to keep the drama level down as much as possible, and scrambling back so hard that I fell off the drama cliff entirely."

He laughed—a fragile laugh, but a laugh still. "Right. Just, next time, please tell us so we can keep a rope handy."

CHAPTER 27

I was not, in fact, in any great hurry to have that conversation with my parents. If I were honest, I wanted them to come ask me what happened, so I could have the talk in my space instead of theirs. And if it took them a few days, all the more time to catch my breath.

Time was clearly something I needed. I'd been throwing myself into the role of delegation head, getting more and more stressed, putting more energy into it than I normally would even for work I loved. It might be the most important work on the planet, but I didn't do it any favors by burning out, or by disconnecting from the things I was working to preserve. I messaged Mendez and asked her to arrange oversight of the antenna for a couple days, convinced Dinar and Athëo to show up there with our kids on a regular basis, and put in for a neighborhood work shift with Carol.

For absolutely no reason at all beyond keeping the diplomatic task moving, I asked Rhamnetin to join us.

"Tell him it's a traditional human social activity," said Athëo, nearly poker-faced, as I put too much effort into the text message over pancakes. We were being careful this morning, consciously avoiding excess gentleness in a way that felt good but fragile: stoneware mended with a line of gold.

"But does he already know what kind of tradition, or do I need a detailed explanation of shared work shifts as a courtship opportunity?" I asked.

"It's a very recent tradition," Carol pointed out. "In most of the broadcasts he's probably seen, people either pay to experience temporary luxuries together, or ask each other's parents for permission to get married."

I shook my head. "I'll explain in person. Or better yet, you will. If worse comes to worst, at least he'll learn more about our species."

Rhamnetin, Carol and I are going to put in a work shift around the neighborhood today, checking drainage for the spring storm season. Want to join us? It'll be anthropologically interesting, I promise.

Fortunately, Rhamnetin was an easy recruit; we met him an hour later in the common hall. Dori had gone down for a nap, so we took Raven with us. That would give Dinar and Athëo time to rest before visiting the construction site. Raven immediately tried to climb Rhamnetin's leg.

"You can pick them up, if you want," I said. It would feel strange not to give him permission, having already offered it to Cytosine.

"Really?" At my nod, he scooped them carefully into a relatively stable seat atop one of his upper joints, holding them in place.

"More up!" demanded Raven.

"I'm afraid that's all the up I have," said Rhamnetin. "You're a solid little creature!"

"Ringer men don't get to hold kids?" I guessed.

"Not very often. And definitely not during tense negotiations."

"We'd better not negotiate anything tense this morning, then," said Carol. "Who points the flashlight and who scans for clogs is as high-stakes as this should get."

She led us toward our first site, and Rhamnetin dedicated an extra limb to holding Raven in place while he followed. "So what exactly are we doing? I thought it was storm season in the *southern* hemisphere; all this preparation has Cytosine getting nervous about the site again."

"We have storms year-round," I said. "They're just worse in season. Given what you told us about the antenna's resilience, it should be fine with anything the Atlantic's likely to throw at us in the next couple months." I pinged records. "The earliest we've ever gotten a Cat 4 is late May."

"So what we're doing now," Carol said, "is checking drainage features in the neighborhood—ditches, artificial wetlands, reservoirs, that sort of thing—and making sure none of them are blocked, the runoff filters are functional, and in general that nothing is going to flood or spill nasty stuff into the Anacostia next time it rains for three days straight."

"What I like about habitats," said Rhamnetin, "is that raining for three days straight is not a thing that happens. We don't get winds strong enough to knock down an ansible at any time of year."

With Cytosine, that would've been the start of a tense negotiation. With Rhamnetin I only said, "And what I like about planets is that when the power goes out, we don't have to worry about life support failures outside of specific medical needs."

Limbs that weren't holding our kid rose and fell in a passable imitation of a shrug. "Touché."

Normally I enjoyed this task because it involved walking around the neighborhood, looking at all the little details that marked change and stability and the health of the community. The bloom and fall of forsythia, the ever-shifting blossoms of solar panels and wind kites tugging against roofs, the seasonal games kids played in the street, the little routes worn by streams or anthills. This time, my attention was all for Rhamnetin. He moved more like a horse than a spider, if a horse had ten legs and no particular front. There was a prancing grace to him, and curiosity like the turn of a bird's head in the way he changed direction on a moment's whim. Raven clutched fistfuls of dense fur and rubbed it between her fingers.

The emotional connection had come first: wanting to know his opinion, liking the way he treated people and the way we saw each other. But now I found myself enjoying his scent, imagining fur against bare skin. It had been the same with Carol: first seeking out the conversations, longer and more often, and then discovering that I'd made a place in my head to model her body, imagining more and more detail until I wanted desperately to replace imagination with observation. With touch. It had made me shy and slow then, and did the same now.

My earpiece chimed. "First stop: the Hollingsworth barrier rain garden." We were at the low end of the neighborhood, where a cluster of repair shops and a broader road increased runoff risk. The garden was a long, narrow wetland standing between the road and the farther slope to the Anacostia's tideline. Reeds helped turn the patch of water into an effective filter; a nearby bat house along with dragonfly larvae and tadpoles kept it from becoming a haven for mosquitoes. I wanted the time with Rhamnetin, but I also wanted to show this off: the older powers had their parties and we had ours, but it was this merging, the blurred boundary between human design and natural creation, where our true power shone.

"So what we do here," said Carol, "is get readings from the sensors already in the pond, and deploy our own bot for a clearer picture of any problems—blockages, say, or too few frogs, or the wrong mix of plants."

I hoped no one noticed me flinch—if I felt guilty every time someone talked about bots, that was gonna be fun. To cover, I busied myself getting the stupid thing linked to my lenses and into the water. I inhaled the reassuring scent of water dripping through petals and leaves, soaking into earth. Finally I could see the bot's growing model: pixels filled in with increasing density until they skinned over with a clear image of the garden ecology, everything tagged with goal states and sensor readings.

"This is all going through the neighborhood network," I told Rhamnetin. "We'll share the aggregate data uphill to the Chesapeake later, but for now I'll project on my palette so you can see." Plenty of people stuck with palette readouts anyway; if you weren't used to lenses (or as into sensory enhancement as I was), it could be disconcerting to have that detailed an overlay atop your own vision.

"How are the frogs?" asked Carol anxiously.

I filtered out the other readings. "Within target numbers, but on the low side. We might want to get a closer look."

"What are they really like?" asked Rhamnetin.

I squinted at him through the haze of readings. "What, frogs?"

"They look so many different ways in your broadcasts, it's hard to tell what's original biology and what's fiction. Xenon thought they were mythical, like dragons but smaller."

I laughed, imagining the *Solar Flare*'s crew watching kids' shows mixed with nature documentaries and old ads with animated batrachian mascots. "Frogs are real. But several species went extinct earlier in the century, and we're still struggling to protect them against fungal epidemics. This lot are inoculated and gene-modded against the known strains, but there are always mutations—this stuff just won't die."

"Do they talk?" Rhamnetin asked.

"Huh? No, frogs don't talk. I mean, they make noises at each other? But they don't have language."

"I wasn't sure. I thought maybe they were like parrots, or dogs." Rhamnetin paused here. "Your dog just squeaks and barks. Dogs don't talk either, do they?"

"It's a wonder you understand us at all," said Carol, "given how weird some of our shows are."

"Our stories can be bad ways to learn about reality too," said Rhamnetin, ostentatiously sullen. "I just guessed wrong about which of your symbiote species actually have language."

"I think we always wanted someone to talk with," I admitted. "Hold on." I handed him the palette so he could keep examining the model and knelt, muddying the knees of my jeans. It was early in the season for leopard frogs, but a few adults already crouched on rocks. I moved slowly, and on my second try scooped one up before it could leap away. It was green and brown and spotted like its namesake, about as long as my palm was wide. I held it gently, trying not to abrade its satiny skin. Carol got a sample swab from the same kit that had produced the bot and checked for fungus, while Rhamnetin peered at the creature from two sides at once and Raven stretched over the hump of one of his knees to try and grab it. He pulled her back, deftly as if he'd been wrangling kids for years.

"It's very cute, even if it doesn't have enough limbs. What does it do in your ecology?"

I tried not to feel self-conscious about my limited number of legs. "A lot of things. The adults eat mosquitoes, and the tadpoles keep algae in check. They're also very sensitive, so when you have an area that isn't as thick with sensors as this one, dips in the frog population can flag toxins. Wait, do the plains-folk get on *your* case about not having enough legs? I can't even tell if they all have the same number."

Rhamnetin dipped in a full-body shrug. "They do, and we get on theirs for how short their limbs are. Adults usually have thirty-two; babies start out with twelve."

"Oh my god," said Carol. She rubbed her arms. "Adolescence is bad enough without budding extra hands all over. I'm itchy just thinking about it."

We returned the frog to its ordinary life and went on through the low-lying edges of the neighborhood. Raven squealed at gusts of wind and Rhamnetin squealed back. We nibbled on early dandelions and said hello to dogs (that did not say hello back) and checked drains and trenches and rain gardens. Everything smelled wet and ready to bloom, and talking with Rhamnetin felt easy and hard all at once. I put an arm around Carol's waist. That touch, something I could take for granted and still be grateful for, was a slim but much-needed anchor.

Say something, Carol texted.

You say something, I suggested.

No, you. All I can think of is, I'd like to put this whole political mess on hold while we learn about each others' sensory capabilities. That is the stupidest flirt.

I couldn't think of anything better. Subtle flirtation was probably useless under the circumstances. On the train together, minds glazed with sleep deprivation and the sort of intense discussions of identity that are only easy when you're nineteen, I'd rolled over onto Carol's seat, straddling the warm bulge of her lap, and kissed her. It was a strategy that worked best when you were too tired to think twice about it, and when you and your potential partner shared a body plan.

"I'm going to say something stupid," I finally told him.

"That's my calling," he said. "I approve of your efforts in the field."

"Right. Um." I tried to frame the stupidity. "I like the way you ask questions, and the way you think about our answers when they're different from Ringer answers. We both do. We like the way you perceive things that other people don't, things that might not be what you expected to find, and the way you try new things, and the risks you take to connect. And we like how many limbs you have. When I was in Zealand, I missed having you there in person to help figure things out. And, um. I don't know how your people do these things, but around here sometimes you get yourself on a work crew with someone to find out if they'd like to. Um." I felt hot and embarrassed and I hoped he noticed this time. "If they'd like to be lovers," I finished in a rush. "Later. After the crew work is done. Obviously. Not that anything about this should be obvious."

Finally I managed to shut up, and waited anxiously for him to respond. Maybe I should have texted *him,* from a safe distance, so I could hide in the crook of Carol's arm while I waited. As it was, all my ability to read his body language seemed to fly out the window; I could tell that he still had Raven firmly balanced and that was about it.

"I like you, too," said Rhamnetin, squatting a little. "How patient you are with us while we learn, and how impatient you get when we don't, and how you hold your kids, and how you let me hold them. I like how you invite people to define themselves, and never assume those definitions are obvious. And I'd like to be lovers—or try it, anyway. Something adapted and made new, like the morning ritual. But you can do this one?"

"I can do this one." I felt giddy, a little dizzy. Freed of political negotiation, for a few whirling minutes, and ready to be anxious about something more promising.

CHAPTER 28

There's a dance you do, getting household members to take over kids and pets and chores while you hole up with a new lover. It turned out to be less embarrassing with my co-parents than it had been at the Bet, but even with Athëo smirking and Dinar checking solicitously that we had everything we needed, I was painfully aware that our own family was still a bit brittle. Maybe it wasn't the best time for this, but I doubted the best time for anything was coming any time soon. I pushed my worries to the side and tried to focus. I wanted to be a generous lover rather than a distracted one, and it wasn't like I could coast on past experience.

We settled on the bed, Carol and I lounging against pillows, Rhamnetin embracing the posts of the hickory footboard.

"I'm not even sure where to start the boundaries discussion," said Carol. "Are there . . . are there things it would be *dangerous* to do? Or can we just jump right to the things it would be fun to do and the things we'd rather avoid?"

"Not like a spider that way, either," said Rhamnetin, and we both laughed. "Neither of you is going to lay a proto-egg, I'm pretty sure, and I'm not going to fertilize and shell them, so I think this is more like cross-species pleasure at home. Most of my body is erogenous under the right circumstances, except for the inside of my mouths, which I think is different from humans?"

"Oh god," I said. "You've watched all our porn, and we haven't seen any of yours. That seems like an unfair advantage."

"Or an unfair disadvantage, given how bad some of the older stuff is," said Carol. "Oh god, you've seen *hentai*."

"I have." I could hear the smirk in Rhamnetin's voice. "I can't kiss, but I can do a pretty good approximation of tentacles."

"Mmmmm." Carol, braver than me, stretched to stroke Rhamnetin's leg. He made a low-pitched chord that came out of his voicebox as a purr.

I hesitated. "And it's not gonna be a problem that none of us can do direct nerve stimulation? Because that sounds hot, but I'm not ready to invite any plains-folk into this just now."

"Skinsong can be fun—but so can other things." Rhamnetin tugged me toward the end of the bed. His leg was soft and strong, and his manipulators tickled the back of my neck. I shivered happily, and began looking for places to touch, to explore beyond the little bits of contact we'd managed in passing.

Extra limbs have definite advantages. When I wanted to kiss, I kissed Carol, and Rhamnetin turned out to be willing to use his long tongues in other ways—and to be essentially unfamiliar with vibrators, but to be pleased with them as an indicator of human inventiveness.

"I'd have thought that would be universal," I said. "Like arrowheads or electricity."

"Maybe it's a bilateral symmetry thing," said Rhamnetin. He didn't lose his ability to articulate words when he was distracted, something I'd always appreciated in humans, too. "Or maybe it's an erogenous orifices thing. Or maybe we're—mmmm—dense?"

I resisted the urge to suggest this as evidence that humans had invented other solutions the Ringers never dreamed of. But now was not, I reminded myself, any damn time for politics. Now was for focus. There was a lot to focus on.

Eventually we achieved our mutual goals, and lay pleasantly tangled amid the sheets. Carol fell into blissful languor, occasionally moving her fingers enough to remind us that she hadn't completely lost track, and appreciated our presence. Rhamnetin draped over and around us, like a marionette with strings loosed, and I stroked him idly, cheek pressed against fur. "No orgasms, huh?"

"They look like fun, but no. We only do anything like that when we're breeding, and it's no more enjoyable than the rest—more frustrating, actually, because it means everything else stops while you get the layering right on the shells."

"Have you done that?" I asked, surprised. "I didn't know you had kids in another family?"

"A friend of Carnitine's asked, a few months ago when we first picked up human signals and the *Solar Flare* made the short list. But fertilizing eggs doesn't really give you a relationship—the way we do things, Diamond and Chlorophyll and Manganese are much more my kids than whoever Corundum hatches."

I snuggled closer. "I wish you got to do more with them. You're good with kids."

"Raven is a little explorer," he said fondly, not quite addressing my statement. My thoughts slipped ahead, the moment washed over by questions about what sort of relationship this would be and how it affected the negotiations and how soon we needed to get up and go back to dealing with everything. I swam back against the current.

"So, successful experiment?" I asked.

"Definitely." And for a few more minutes the current stilled, and the waters paused in their rise.

And then I put my mesh back on, and was instantly confronted by a text from Athëo. **Judy, your parents are here. Plus your Aunt Priya?**

"Ack," I said aloud. I nudged Carol. "My folks are downstairs."

"Your mothers?" asked Rhamnetin, hitching himself up.

"Two moms, one dad, also one of my aunts." And they all un-doubtedly wanted to have a conversation that I couldn't have in front of Rhamnetin. Guilt, held at bay by the excitement and anxiety of a new lover, came pouring back. Damn it, I'd wanted to discuss this in my own space—just not this afternoon. **Tell them we're upstairs with our new boyfriend. We'll be right down.**

Athëo sent all three of us several unhelpful romantic screenshots from various movies. **And the Ringer version, for universal understanding—** followed by snippets of background music.

"What's that?" asked Rhamnetin as the tablet spilled soundtrack. He pulled something out of one of his pouches, and I got to see him reapply his blacklight coloration.

"Athëo teasing. What's *that*?"

"Bioluminescent algae. Substrate for the algae, actually, I rubbed a couple of bits off when we were rolling around."

We went downstairs, and I introduced Rhamnetin to my parents and aunt. Athëo watched with amusement.

"Glad to meet you," said Dad. "I hadn't realized interplanetary relations had advanced so quickly—congratulations!"

"Learning new things is my job," Rhamnetin said solemnly while I tried not to act like a surly pre-Transit kid embarrassed by their family.

My parents made conversation for a few minutes, awkward primarily because the usual questions you ask your kid's new lover—what are your expertises, is your household around here, how did you meet—had answers so nonstandard that in some cases they couldn't even be asked. All three of them were obviously very excited to be meeting an alien directly, and equally obviously trying (and failing) to make this normal.

Dad, thankfully past the new-lover part, fell into asking Rhamnetin about his work, and started into a nicely distracting story about the old days in the Bet—whether those days were good or bad was left as an exercise for the listener. I went outside with Mom, Eema, and Aunt Priya.

"Dead nettle's coming up," Eema commented, stooping to pick some. I took one of the tiny purple blossoms and nibbled on its spicy sharpness. I synched my mesh with the yard sensors, let my vision shimmer with air pressure and humidity.

"I got caught," I said, trying to keep my voice level. "There was no damn undetectable. I got blackmailed with the whole network at stake, and sent home with a train of corporate specialists doing their best to take over the antenna. They want to be relevant again, and half of them want to burn Earth to break the arguments against their power, and I gave them a path. *We* gave them a path."

"I'm sorry," said Aunt Priya. "There's always a risk with these things, but . . ."

"None of you talked me through the risks. There was no decision tree. If we ran water treatment this way, the Chesapeake would still be full of garbage." Mom started to say something and I held up my hand. "I don't want to argue about it, especially not with Rhamnetin inside. But I'm an adult now, and a parent, and if you ever want me in a Bet plan again I need better input. Not just you trying to *advertise* the fucking thing. I need you to actually tell me what's involved and talk through what happens if your plan goes off the rails. And I should've asked, and if it was water treatment I would've known the right questions. And it wasn't, and I didn't, and *you did.*"

"And you don't want to argue," said Mom. "I don't blame you. You're right."

I ducked my head, surprised. I fiddled with the tie-down on the peach tree netting, which didn't actually need it, and she helped.

"What *are* the risks from the antenna?" asked Eema. "Do we need to do something?"

I sighed. "No one on Earth has the expertise to 'do something' about it; please don't try. As for the risks, even without Asterion, more Ringers means more pressure for humans to leave the planet. Some of them want to force us. One ship is a chance for interesting conversation, but the Rings as a whole are a more technologically ept civilization with several times our numbers, convinced they know what's best for us. It scares the hell out of me."

Mom and Priya nodded, and Eema started tapping notes into her palette.

"With Asterion officially advising the construction," I went on, "the corporations get more influence, more opportunity to sabotage anything they want to sabotage, or keep up the sabotage they already have in progress. Redbug's team is furious—and at least some of the 'burn the world and give us the power' corporate types are pushing us to stop trusting the dandelion networks and use *their* code instead."

"That would require a lot of mistrust," said Aunt Priya.

"Or a lot of inconvenient crashes during a crisis," I said. "It was bad enough when the Ringers first arrived; if the network crashes again people will need something they can use to make quick decisions, even if it's a flawed tool."

"I don't like having Asterion here," said Mom. "I really am sorry for giving them a lever; we didn't expect anything like that."

"Dinar says she would've warned us, if she'd known."

Mom shrugged. "Hindsight. And I can't blame you for not telling someone who does gigwork."

I bristled. "Dinar isn't her gigwork—she's my co-parent. I didn't want to make her complicit, and I couldn't get the network input I needed to make a better decision. And neither could you."

"There must be something we can do," Eema said to Mom. "Slow the construction down, distract Asterion with a crisis somewhere else . . ."

"First, there are enough corporate types to handle any number of crises," I said. "Second, completely aside from the ethics of attacking the corporations again, the biggest thing we need now is more hands fixing the dandelion network code. You worked on the first-gen version; you may be able to ID the leaks in the algorithms beyond 'something feels off.' If you can put your back into stabilizing it, you close the cracks Asterion needs to get in."

"They'd still have the antenna," she said.

"Which the Ringers could still move to Zealand, giving Asterion full control," I said, exasperated. "Fundamentally, there's no good way to keep them from building it unless our whole species refuses them a site. And that's not happening."

Eema sat cross-legged under the fig tree; Mom rolled her eyes and took the bench. Priya sat beside her, and I joined Eema. The new clover bent easily under my weight. Everything smelled green and dry, no hint of petrichor to herald the coming storms. I checked the weather threads; buoys still showed those storms growing in strength—nothing like a true summer hurricane, but hard on the crops for all our efforts. A blink, and I watched mirror readings for the ocean beyond Zealand, switched the breeze and birdsong around me for a momentary burst of crashing waves and the wind from a Cat 4 cyclone. It had a 40 percent chance of hitting Zealand directly, 80 percent chance of crashing into one of the aislands as a Cat 3 or higher in the next week or so. I shunted the information to everyone else's mesh. "This is what got us the antenna in the first place. If things go badly here, the Ringers could decide it's worth the risk to move back to the Pacific after all."

"Hmm." Aunt Priya tapped at her palette again. "Got some ideas."

"Maybe give the negotiation team room to work instead?" I suggested.

"I won't get in your way," she promised, and that was apparently the best I was going to get.

CHAPTER 29

The stormline map was now the first thing that came up whenever I logged in. The North Atlantic, still too warm too early in the year, goaded wind into frenzied twists. As summer hit, the line of spirals would grow stronger and less sporadic, but for now three tiny galaxies fell into ragged marching order. "Since Adam woke we've named the things we made," said a poet on the common network, and so we did for these in their turn: Afia, Braulio, Chloe. A possible fourth member of the cluster was still a minor depression and an argument about whether it would be respectful to include a Ringer-style name in the mix.

Afia would make landfall south of the Chesapeake within the week. Braulio broke for the Gulf, so at least no one would get two in a row. But the Lower Mississippi was vulnerable, hotter and more weather-worn than the Chesapeake, and even early hurricanes there tended to hit hard. The common threads filled with requests for advice and backup calculations, as the southern watershed looked for resources to shore up its crumbling protective infrastructures.

We spent the intervening days working through the drainage checks and taking almost-leisurely breaks in between. Experimental results continued to be positive. I did my best to keep tabs on the negotiations and the antenna, but it felt so good to have space. It didn't stop me from worrying—about the growth of the antenna, about Asterion's influence on the Ringers and on the dandelion network, about the plans of excitable folk at the Bet—but at least the change made it more obvious when my wheels were treading the same ground. And the experiments *were* a good distraction. I could worry about where they were going later.

Rhamnetin spent one night on the *Solar Flare*, came back irritable, and spent the next night at our place. He was spending more time with us than around his own people, and I couldn't tell whether it was because they disapproved, or because they wanted him to get something political from our relationship, or what. I wasn't even sure whether their role in this whole thing was more like my parents, or my co-parents, or my wife. Ringer families didn't map closely to any of the familiar human models.

Storm prep was a spot of clarity, a problem that fell squarely in my expertise. And I could share that now with Rhamnetin, showing him in real time how we managed the complexities of our ecosystem. We projected runoff diagrams and weather maps across the dining room table, talked him through how storms had changed over the past century, even looked at models for the coming centuries. The most pessimistic showed seasonal predictability and strength leveling off sometime in the early twenty-second century; the more promising (the ones that assumed at least one major improvement in carbon drawdown) showed a drop toward baseline norms within the next fifty years.

"Glacial restoration," said Dinar, looking over our shoulders. Carol had been explaining why a *full* return to those baseline norms wasn't about to happen. "There are movies about aliens coming to Earth to steal our water. Could you steal some of it, let it freeze in the vacuum, and just . . . put it back once temperatures drop enough to keep it frozen?"

Rhamnetin blinked several eyes, slowly and deliberately. "Water's one of the easiest resources to find in open orbit. Why would you go to another solar system to steal it?"

"Because it makes a more interesting story," said Dinar. "I know you wouldn't steal our water, but would it be convenient for you to borrow it?"

Rhamnetin scratched out a rough diagram on his palette, labeled in his native language and thus hard to follow. "I'd have to ask Carnitine, but I'm pretty sure that with the amount of energy it would take to move that much mass off-planet, you could freeze it right here. The waste heat would counter the effects nicely."

"Not to mention the effect of abruptly removing that much weight from tectonic plates, even if all you wanted to do was lower sea level," said Carol. "No climate mitigation strategies that you can imagine accompanied by maniacal laughter, please."

"Slow and steady," I said. "We just need to get through a few more rough years; Raven and Dori will see the real improvements."

Rhamnetin put down the palette and stroked my shoulders; another limb came around to trace the model curves on the table. "It's a beautiful planet, and I do see that you might be able to handle the risks. But if you came out to the Rings, or made your own, you could have bearable temperatures and survivable weather all the time, starting now. Why *not* do that?"

On the floor behind us, Dori struggled toward crawling. She wasn't quite there yet, but she'd managed to push herself up on all fours and was rocking valiantly. Raven held a favorite doll a few feet away, making encouraging noises; Kyo kept darting in to sniff anxiously at Dori's legs, yipping. Two months ago, I'd had such a clear idea of what their lives would look like—not the specifics of their expertises and families, but the kind of world they'd live in, the beauties and sacrifices they'd have as options.

I tried to explain—Rhamnetin, I thought, was trying to listen. "Earth, given half a chance, makes a place for life. The planet has seen six mass extinctions, counting this one; something has kept going through all of them. Making sure human civilization survives is the real challenge, and we're figuring that out. But most of the system inputs are non-human and always were—we just need to make our own inputs harmonize with the rest. I don't see how that can be harder than creating an entire functional ecosystem from scratch."

"But there are so many more variables," said Rhamnetin. "On a habitat, you *can* control everything, and if something doesn't work you can check all the variables and figure out where the problem is."

"And if the problem is some bacterium, or a combination of hundreds of them, that turns out to be vital for fertility? One you forgot to bring with you?"

"That's what genetic archives are for," said Rhamnetin. "We've made this work. The Rings have been going for centuries, by any of our counts."

"And life on Earth has persisted for billions," I said. "I trust the planet's expertise. And I value everything here, not just the species most immediately necessary for human health. I want my children to inherit *all* of it, every damn thing we can preserve. They've got a right to that bounty, even if it comes with floods and heat warnings."

"I wish you could see it," said Rhamnetin. "Life is rich on the Rings. And safe. And if you're after occasional danger, there are thrills to be found on a ship."

There were so many things that went beyond our models and decision threads and system diagrams. I remembered reading an old paper, a classic of mitigation strategy that framed everything in terms of "ecological services" and the monetary value of forests.

How queasy it had made me feel, like calculating the exact value of my time awake with the kids. In the aislands they still thought that way: everything had a price, and anything could be sold away if someone offered enough in exchange. For the watersheds—for me— some complexities could never be broken down for trade. "A few of us probably *will* want that simplicity. Some humans will go with you, or start building something in this solar system. That's all fine with me as long as they don't block the stars or mess with our orbital mechanics. Or take apart our gas giants: St. Julien can tell you about the life NASA's found on the moons out there, and those bacteria deserve a chance too. But for me—Earth is *our* symbiosis. We've screwed it up, badly, but we're trying to fix it now, and we won't do right by any new relationship if we leave it behind."

I was thinking about that—the planet as symbiote, the things I wanted for my children—when we went out to Bear Island for a last check before Afia hit. Her leading winds were already stirring the waves in Long Bay and Pamlico Sound, and when she arrived she'd have enough strength to break trees and flood lowlands. Everyone from the Hudson down through the Carolina Collective was reeling in kites and checking seawall sensors and unfurling the stormmills that would top up batteries for recovery efforts. In the neighborhood, people tied down recycling bins and garden stakes, checked shutters, set up candles and oil lamps and flashlights that were rarely needed these days. Dinar holed up in the kitchen, wreathed by the scent of oatmeal cookies and lemon cake.

I'd managed to avoid the construction site for the past few days, but now I was back on duty. As we approached, I could see the incomplete antenna: a black lacework outline against the graying sky, a flock of starlings frozen in the shape of a tower. Around it, a scattering of prefab sheds presumably housed workspace for the humans helping out. Dori, who'd been fussing about the sling, oohed and waved her hands.

"It's really stable?" I asked Rhamnetin. "We're expecting eighty-mile-an-hour winds, maybe worse."

"Astatine says so. He can try and explain how it works; I just know how to set the things down."

But it was Brend who came bounding over first, followed at a more sedate pace by Tiffany. Brend was dressed in one of eir own outfits, but had acceded to our conventions as far as a custom badge with the holo pronouns. Tiffany wore a plain denim dress. Tiffany also looked like tha might recall, more clearly than Brend, that thos last major interaction with us had been a blackmail attempt. Or, maybe (I speculated, prodded by my own easily surfaced guilt) like tha'd found it discomfiting to work up close with those affected by the malware.

Brend was hard to resent, though; e seemed so pleased to see us. "Figures we'd come halfway around the world during cyclone season and get a baby hurricane, doesn't it? Adrien's been staying in one of the DC hotels with Kelsey and Mallory, but tha's gonna join our storm-huddle in the *Solar Flare* doing anthropology. Xenology. I can figure out what all their body mods mean, and Adrien can play politics."

"That sounds like fun." I was suddenly tempted to take advantage of Afia the same way—but we'd need everyone home to keep the household running. Besides, we could do xenology with Rhamnetin. "How're things coming with the antenna?"

"Tiffany's helping adapt the design to a planetary surface; I'm just taking notes on fashion."

Tiffany looked annoyed at the attention, but grudgingly allowed: "They need atmospheric wind models. We've got those on hand. They're easy enough to mod for Ringer structures. We're ahead of schedule." Thos glower dared us to say anything.

"We've got a lot to learn about materials engineering," said Carol. "That thing's sturdier than it looks."

Tiffany nodded. "They're used to much stronger force vectors than you get from most storms, but unpredictability is tough. You can see solar winds and asteroids coming a long way off—or at least they can. Mx. St. Julien and the NASA team were excited."

Up close, the antenna looked even stranger: spiderweb-thin and spiderweb-strong as we'd never managed with our own attempts at nanotube construction. It shimmered in the moisture-laden air, up past the limits of even enhanced vision. I thought of starlings again, spiraling through the edge of atmosphere, chased past the limits of our ecology. Homing pigeons might be a better comparison, carrying word of our existence back to the stars. To ten trillion people who would change everything.

"Will you come out to the ship?" Rhamnetin asked. "I'm a little nervous about *our* preparations."

We made our way down the causeway onto Bear Island. Sycamores and chestnuts spread over the path, casting pale shadows across the budding tangle of honeysuckle and grape and wild rosebushes. Rhamnetin swung from branch to branch, scrambling down to wait for us when he got too far ahead. I spotted an orb weaver spider hanging in a freshly woven web, and called him over. He raised a knee to examine the elegant tiger stripes more closely. "See? Fewer legs, I told you."

The shifting surface of the *Solar Flare* had sloughed off encroaching moss and bird droppings, though a few wet leaves clung to its sides. Our initial encampment was now expanded into a cluster of prefab buildings paralleling those around the antenna: embassies from the various powers paying court to the Ringers, plus a cultural exchange center now plastered with artwork.

"Oh, beautiful, that's Cobalt's work," said Rhamnetin. One of the screens showed an installation by an apparently well-known Ringer artist. A section of forest, trunks thicker and more gnarled than anything on the ship, lay shadowed in dusk, every surface coated in luminescent colors. They flickered like fireflies, then blazed into psychedelic glory. Gradually the colors began to resolve, until I could nearly make out meaningful shapes, phantasms slipping from tree to tree. The background chaos faded, and the phantasms became clearly visible: silhouetted Ringers of both species meeting and touching and parting again, stylized interactions that I suspected were as recognizable as a kiss or a pirouette. The figures dissolved into fireflies, and the cycle began again.

"She makes beautiful places." I turned at Cytosine's voice, and Dori squealed happily and wriggled at her. "We got to visit this one during a delivery to Syzygy 32."

"It must be even more intense in person," I said.

"Her family helps with the perspectives," said Rhamnetin, "so it works from above, too." He dragged a foot across the screen, turning the image until we were looking down from the branches above as figures wove among the leaves.

"Judy please please," called Chlorophyll, and Diamond took up the cry. "Judy, Judy, Judy!"

"I told them you wanted to hold them," explained Cytosine.

"I do." Dori was still wiggling anxiously, squeals taking on a distressed tinge. Trading off with the Ringers would distract her almost as well as what she really wanted, which was to be back on the ground trying to crawl—not ideal this close to the cliff. "We'd better take one each; I've only got two arms."

I loosened Dori's sling and handed her to Rhamnetin, only realizing afterward that I'd probably scandalized Cytosine just as she'd honored me with what had to indicate serious approval of my judgment. Screw it, she could cope with men's ability to carry babies without dropping them.

Diamond scrambled down from their mother's belly, and made a valiant effort at my pants leg. I helped them up, and slender limbs latched onto sling and shirt. I put my arms around them. Their carapace was grooved and covered in small bumps, like the shell of a tortoise if a tortoise shell were jointed, warm where the shell would have been cool. Their limbs clung wherever they touched. I'd expected them to be prickly, but they weren't. Instead, each point of contact buzzed with skinsong: sine waves of silken softness and tickling vibration, once a sharp pinch as they pressed their infant excitement into my nerves. "Gentle."

Chlorophyll tugged on Carol's skirt, and Carol scooped them up, cautiously, like an unfamiliar cat. They curled limbs around her arm, and she hummed at them.

Rhamnetin, apparently unwilling to press scandal too far, handed Dori to Cytosine, who sang something in her own language. Dori listened intently, wide-eyed. Athëo had already started to pick up vocabulary as he worked on the translation algorithm; I still had trouble getting my brain to treat their speech as words rather than melody. It occurred to me that Dori and Raven might learn Ringer, rather than Yiddish or Spanish or Athëo's favored Quenya, as their second language.

"I'm glad that you and Rhamnetin have connected," Cytosine told us. "We need stronger links, for our people to truly understand each other."

Is that what we're calling it? I suppressed a giggle. "Yes, we do. It sounds like some of the human reps are riding out the storm on the *Solar Flare;* we'd be glad to have Rhamnetin stay at our place—along with anyone else who wants to join."

"He's welcome to," said Cytosine. "I have to admit, these atmospheric phenomena make me nervous. I don't know if the ship is safer, but at least I know the excess water won't get in."

"Our house is two hundred years old," I said. "The basement may leak occasionally, but it'll hold up."

"That's about the age of the *Solar Flare*," Cytosine told us. "In your years. We're its fourth crew."

For some reason—probably because Earth had never kept even the most workhorse spaceship in service for more than a few decades—I'd assumed the *Solar Flare* was relatively new. "It's odd, thinking about someone building your ship at the same time humans were nailing the frame for our house." And a little disturbing, more visceral than the abstract knowledge that they'd strung habitats together long before humans harnessed electricity. They'd used up their worlds while the Roman Empire stood strong.

Cytosine rocked forward, still cradling Dori, to brush limbs along Diamond's back. Limb-tips paused on my arm, and I felt the pulse of Cytosine's skinsong, subtler and more complex than her child's. I leaned into it, just a little, appreciating the touch—a level of connection instinctive for both of us even when the higher-level stuff eluded understanding.

"I don't know how to interpret that yet—but it feels like people playing drums without the sound, the way it passes through my body."

"Something like that." She gestured at the image of Cobalt's installation. "Even if you can't see through the trees, you can still sense each others' actions. People are around you, and you're a part of something."

As Rhamnetin had asked, I looked around the ship, giving what input I could about its stormworthiness. Truth be told, there was little I could do with construction I didn't remotely understand. But I could run the same scans I had at the beginning, and confirm that I didn't spot any leaks. The damaged patch hadn't grown.

Something had changed, though, among the crew. Friendly people had grown friendlier, and even the standoffish ones were more welcoming. Ytterbium, Cytosine's mate who'd built the pseudo-radio, got into a geekfest with Carol over signal frequencies; Carol promised to come back later and show off the sweater swarm.

It was all much more pleasant than having Cytosine irritated with us, and not all that far off from how my parents had treated Rhamnetin. I couldn't help wondering what it meant: what expectations the Ringers had for their brother's new lovers, and what sort of relationship we should be building with them.

Eventually we extricated ourselves. Brend and Tiffany and Adrien, along with St. Julien and her husband and Eliza Mendez, were setting up camp among the ship's trees, laying out picnic blankets and staking spots for sleeping bags. I felt a twinge of envy, but I wanted to be home with my own family, and with Rhamnetin. And with windows. I wanted to look out at the storm from a place of relative safety, and love the wildness of my world.

CHAPTER 30

Everything that we could bring inside was inside. Everything that we could tie down was tied down. The light had grown dim and yellow, and rain stuttered the leaves; trees bowed to the wind, not yet at any risk of breaking. The air was awake with petrichor and ozone. Oatmeal cookies and lemon cake, supplemented by a batch of lavender scones, made a warm hearth of the kitchen table. Scattered among the platters lay projections of the storm track, readings from the roof sensors, and the neighborhood's best predictions for wind, rain, and hail.

Dori, released at last from our protective wraps, rocked on all fours on the floor. She lifted one hand, another, scooted her knee back and forth. A few days ago she'd have given up with a wail; now she thinned her lips and kept trying. Her expression, adult in its seriousness, sparked a pang of fearful delight in my chest. I'd loved her for her whole life, and before that as well as one can love someone before they enter into the world. But at that moment I first felt her as a separate entity moving inexorably toward adulthood. She wanted something beyond the survival instincts she'd been granted at birth, beyond my power to give her—but not beyond her own power.

I curled in a cushioned chair, watching her, leaning against one of Rhamnetin's legs where he draped over the back. Carol perched on the arm, her embrace warm across my shoulders. Dinar, taking a break between bouts of baking, perched on Athëo's lap while they alternated bites from a cookie.

"This is surreal," Rhamnetin said. "We can swing as soon as we hatch, and the plains-folk only take a few days to lift themselves, even if they can't go far. Spending so many months sessile, and then having to learn two separate ways to move yourself around, sounds terrifying."

Carol wrinkled her nose. "Kids who can wander away and grab books off the shelves at two days old also sound terrifying."

"But they don't—you've seen Cytosine's pair. They've got strong instincts to stay with their mother. And we tend to cling to our sisters, but with all your brothers scrambling around, you want to be able to grab tight when someone knocks into you. Will Dori start running away from you?" He stretched anxiously in her direction. She reached for him—and scuttled forward. She froze with a shocked smile on her face, and swiveled her head to check everyone's reactions.

"Baby, you did it!" I told her, and Carol and Athëo applauded enthusiastically. Dinar offered her a congratulatory bit of scone. She crawled a few more inches to get it, and set up an excited cry of "Mam-amamamama!" while we all babbled our parental glee and I made sure to save the record. Raven flung themselves onto their sister for a clumsy hug.

"You lied!" exclaimed Rhamnetin. "She runs toward you!" He held out limbs, and we all spent a few minutes encouraging her to crawl in our various directions. She giggled madly, loving the game. Rain picked up, spattering the windows like the distant drumming I'd felt through Cytosine's skinsong. *People are around you, and you're part of something.* I felt safe—and quietly, watching myself like I watched Dori, surprised by the feeling. The storm wrapped us in a cozy domestic space where no outside demand could touch us. Even the network was relatively quiet, a steady stream of reports on prepa-rations completed, water levels and patterns of flow compared to pre-dictions.

It was a loud enough coziness that no one heard the knock on the door. But we'd never locked it often to begin with, and had gotten entirely out of the habit since the Ringers arrived. The first I noticed Aunt Priya was when Kyo started barking furiously at her umbrella.

"What are you doing here?" I asked. "I mean, you're welcome, but this is a hell of a time to be out. Is everything okay?"

She shook the umbrella at Kyo, methodically spattering him with droplets, and he shook the water back at her. She put down the um-brella, picked up the dog, and caught sight of Dori. "When did she start crawling?"

"Five minutes ago, it's amazing. *What are you doing here?*"

She sat at the table and took a scone, nibbling as methodically as she'd shaken the umbrella. I waited impatiently: it was never useful to rush Aunt Priya, just tempting. Amid the chaos of the Bet, she did everything thoughtfully, one step at a time—I was never sure how she managed it, but she was a major reason that anything there got com-pleted from start to finish, with an actual middle in between. And a major reason why I knew how to be quiet and listen. So now, with effort, I did.

"The network troubleshooting team is disturbed by the tenacity of this malware. I am, too." She didn't look at Rhamnetin, but also didn't mention what she'd done about that feeling. "Having Asterion here is a risk, but I think it's more social than technical sabotage. Whatever vulnerability they found originally, they didn't need to be on-site to exploit it."

"It *is* a social risk," I said. "Being here lets them take advantage of whatever did to the dandelion networks. I know Jace di Sanya wants to convince people that the dandelion protocols are inherently unstable and that we should switch to corporate systems. And to convince the Ringers to treat the watersheds as an obstacle rather than an ally."

"I don't know how they're doing on those things," Aunt Priya said. "But they've managed to convince the troubleshooting team that they're building something into the antenna to worsen the sabotage. And I think they're giving that impression deliberately."

"Could they actually use the antenna that way?" asked Rhamnetin. "There's no direct interface—they're calculating interactions and passing them to Astatine, who uses the results to shape construction."

"I don't think they could," said Aunt Priya. "But every time the troubleshooting team gets near the Asterion folks, which is frequently, because they're trying to figure out what they're doing, someone acts suspiciously smug about the completion of the antenna. And Elegy got into a late-night discussion with Tiffany di Asterion that involved enough drinking that she trusts what tha said, and supposedly tha let something slip. I don't believe it. I think this whole thing is social engineering."

"Tiffany's more than capable," I said. "But engineering them to do . . . what?"

Now Aunt Priya did examine Rhamnetin before she spoke. "Try to sabotage the antenna, under cover of the storm. They asked me to help. I told them I thought it was a terrible idea and doomed to failure, but I wished them luck. And then I came here. Because I'm eighty percent sure it's a trap—make that eighty-five, with what you say Jace is doing. If a Chesapeake team tries to take down the antenna, why would the Ringers keep working with us?"

Dori, no longer the focus of grown-up attention, began crying. I scooped her against my chest, swayed side to side, rubbed her back.

"What do Redbug and Elegy think they'll get out of this? Even if the antenna comes down, it'll just get rebuilt." I glanced at Rhamnetin to check this prediction. "You're not going to . . . run out of material or anything, are you?" God help me, that would still be tempting. Even caring for Rhamnetin, knowing what it would cost him and his family, I couldn't simply dismiss the allure of keeping Earth safely isolated.

"I don't think so," said Rhamnetin, though he didn't sound very sure. He trusted us enough to *sound* unsure. "Most things that would break the antenna wouldn't break the builder seeds themselves. Dropping them in the ocean, maybe? We have extras; I don't know how many."

Aunt Priya frowned. "I think they'd be almost as happy if it were rebuilt elsewhere—even in corporate territory, rather than in ostensible collaboration with the watersheds. They think it's less dangerous to our networks, and right now that's the only danger they care about."

"But if Tiffany's been baiting them," said Dinar, "it'll never get that far. Asterion will 'catch' the attempt as soon as it's underway, and make themselves out as heroes."

"I need to tell the rest of the crew," said Rhamnetin.

I paused in my pacing. "Is that necessary? All we have to do is let the troubleshooting team know that we know—that we'll warn the Ringers if they don't back off. They won't try if they know they'll be stopped."

"Oh, good," said Dinar. "Then they can hate me even more than they already do."

I hugged her, reaching around Dori. "It's just, if the Ringers find out about this attempt, Asterion gets exactly what they want. Present company excepted, but Rhamnetin, you can't tell me that Cytosine wouldn't hold it against all of us. Redbug and Elegy will figure out who stopped them, either way."

"Right." Dinar sighed. "Yeah, go ahead and try to talk them out of it. But maybe let's try argument, before we give them an ultimatum. It's more likely to work long-term."

"I tried that," Aunt Priya pointed out.

"And you came to us through the storm because you thought we could help." I came up short. "Why didn't you text me?"

She shrugged. "Maybe I'm old-fashioned, but there's no communication as secure as meeting in person."

"Right. Well, hopefully we don't need that much security to talk the team out of being idiots." I opened a shared channel to Redbug and Elegy, projected it on the table, and sent: **I found out what you're planning. It's not going to work, and I can tell you why. We need to talk.**

I hoped that would get their attention. But minutes stretched with no response. Dinar went back to the kitchen, continuing her work with unhappy determination. Athëo looked out the window. The unmistakable rattle of hail joined the cacophony of wind and rain. It was no night to be out, but that was far from the stupidest part of what I feared the tech team was doing. I pinged them again.

"Are they ignoring us?" asked Carol. "Or are they not getting the message?"

"I'm sorry," said Rhamnetin. "I need to call the *Solar Flare*. I'll argue your case afterward, but they need to know."

I had nothing to offer against that. "They do. Go ahead."

Rhamnetin fiddled with his voicebox. Then he fiddled some more. After a minute, Carol asked, "Well? What do they say?"

"They don't say anything. I'm not getting through. Ytterbium was worried about this. Our comms—they're shielded against all sorts of radiation, the hazards you expect in the vacuum, but they're not re-silient to serious atmospheric disturbance. It's not an issue, at home."

Dinar came out of the kitchen, sighed, nodded. I shared an ex-change with my co-parents, all eyes: the sort of communication that requires high bandwidth and people you know well. That was new, I realized. Somewhere in the last few days, we'd crossed some thresh-old of comprehension—not yet where I was with my wife, but for the first time I could imagine getting there.

"Let's try our own people on the ship first," said Carol. I sent a private text to Eliza Mendez, and for good measure opened a prob-lem thread, priority-flagged: **Solar Flare comms are out and I need to reach them right away. Anyone in the ground there?** I dropped a similar message onto the common feed, though normally it'd get less notice there amid the storm-related chatter. This time, I'd err on the side of involving the crowd.

"Okay," I said a minute later. "I can see perfectly well why Red-bug and Elegy would ignore me, but not Eliza. And I can see other network threads flowing smoothly. I shouldn't be shouting into the ether—what the fuck is going on?"

Just for the hell of it, I posted an unrelated message to one of the sensor tracking threads, and got an immediate response. Carol reported no issues pinging her textile exchange feed. But when either of us posted off-topic, asking for help passing a message to the *Solar Flare,* our words sat in unread isolation.

"Am I being paranoid?" I said at last.

"No," said Aunt Priya. "Something's keeping us from getting through. I'm not reaching anyone either, even with encrypted messages."

If it was malware—and I didn't see any other obvious explanation—that meant the corporate team didn't want us interfering with whatever mistake they'd provoked from the troubleshooting team. "But they can't have infested the Ringer communication channels, right? They couldn't count on those being out?"

"They could have gambled," said Rhamnetin. "Ytterbium wasn't exactly silent about the risk. Or they might not have expected me to be here. Or they might have thought it was okay, as long as Cytosine learned about the sabotage attempt. Even if I can talk her down . . ."

"You can't promise that she'll forgive us, yeah. Though she was unusually friendly, this morning." I hesitated. "Any idea what that was about?"

Rhamnetin shuffled his legs. "She's pleased that we've become lovers. It's not entirely reasonable, but you know some of our stories now—we're like Caffeine and Fructose."

I tried not to show how much that worried me. Relationships were hard enough without having them stand in for the connection between two entire species. I wanted to work out these nascent connections—not just between me and Carol and Rhamnetin, but between our households—as ourselves, not as archetypes.

"So if things go wrong," asked Carol, "will she be more forgiving, because she likes what we're doing? Or less, because we're not following the script?"

"Redbug could be the Chief with the Lonely Name?" suggested Dinar wryly.

"Maybe?" said Rhamnetin. "Caffeine and Fructose were always great advocates for symbiosis, and no one in the Chesapeake has been that . . . heroic . . . yet in her view. It could go either way."

I shared another high-bandwidth exchange of glances with my household. We could keep trying to reach people by text, and we'd have it on record that we'd tried. But it wouldn't keep Redbug and

Elegy out of Jace's trap, and it wouldn't meet anyone's standards for heroism. "Right. I hope you all understand that going out in the middle of a hurricane is a terrible idea. How many of us need to do it?"

CHAPTER 31

The trains had shut down, and the Ringer shuttles were all back at their ship. The ride system, on the other hand, would still accept emergency overrides. Whoever was screwing around with the network hadn't thought of that. Yet another data point that the malware came from someone not embedded in the life of the watersheds. I sent out the override, made up some nonsense excuse for the records, and a few minutes later darted through stinging rain to take a grateful seat in the van. Carol joined me—with her sewing kit this time—along with Athëo and Aunt Priya and Rhamnetin.

"You will reach your destination in forty-three minutes," the ride told us. I grimaced as it went on, "Travel times may vary due to weather-based transit suspensions."

"Never heard that one before," said Carol.

"That's because you've never gone out in the middle of a hurricane before," Athëo pointed out. "There've been a dozen threads over the years arguing about the trade-offs between letting people get where they need to go, and the accident risk with variable wind speed and surface friction on the roads."

"So if we pull over because it's slippery, we can blame the folks on those threads?" I asked.

"And if we don't roll into a ditch you can blame the threads for that, too."

The rain drummed overclocked asynchrony on every side. At home the clatter against window and roof had felt reassuring, reminding me that we were inside and safe. Here the sound defined the limits of our safety with uncompromising accuracy. We were surrounded by the storm.

If I was nervous, knowing how foolhardy we were being, Rhamnetin must have been terrified. Four of his legs plastered against the window, eyes pressed to the glass. "Hey Rhamnetin, what sort of stupid things do Ringers do when you're scared?"

Free legs turned toward the sound of my voice. He might not only be pressed against the side out of worry, I realized—the ride wasn't meant for quite so many people of quite so many shapes. "When we're not thinking, we scuttle up trees in the middle of conversations. Plains-folk will roll up tight and sting if you get too close. When we *are* thinking, probably the same shit humans pull. The people we're going after, they're scared, aren't they?"

"Terrified," said Aunt Priya. Her lips quirked. "I don't know whether they're thinking or not thinking. Maybe both."

The ride pulled through driving rain. Streets recognizable on the map seemed strange to unaided vision. We swerved, and I could sense how we steered into the wind to stay as level as we did. I pulled telemetry into my lenses, knowing it wouldn't be the most reassuring data in the world and there wasn't much I could do if it showed something wrong. But it was a cooler, deeper sort of worry than letting my monkey-brain listen unthinkingly to the rain and wind.

Carol started singing:

"It's a damn tough life full of toil and strife we sailors
    undergo
And we don't give a damn when the gale is done how hard
    the winds did blow . . ."

Athëo and I came in on the harmony, him pushing the low end of his range into baritone on a song that deserved it:

"But we're homeward bound from the Arctic round on a
    good ship tall and free,
And we won't give a damn when we drink our rum with
    our loves in old Maui,
Rolling down to old Maui, my child, rolling down to old
    Maui,
And we're homeward bound from the Arctic round rolling
    down to old Maui . . ."

I'd sung it often enough—it was a good working song, a good rhythm for planting or baking or pacing the floor with a baby. But this was the first time I'd sung it as the original had been sung, in a vehicle in high wind, the hazards and comforts wound through our voices the same ones that wound through our lives. Rhamnetin, who of course knew more of long travels than any of us, came in on the second chorus. I smiled to imagine salt-stained sailors from a rougher age staring at this new singer, as far from their experience as Arctic cold was from mine.

While I was thinking about icebergs and asteroids, we slowed and pulled to the side of the road.

"We can't be there already," said Priya doubtfully.

Telemetry flickered in my lenses. "No. I think this is one of those weather-based transit suspensions." Rain shifted abruptly to the clamor of hail. Aunt Priya hunched and clapped her hands over her ears. Rhamnetin flinched and I squeaked as he flung a limb around me. A furry python of nervous alien squeezed my chest. "Urk. Careful, Rhamnetin, I'm not a tree." Realizing how that probably sounded to him, I added, "I mean, metaphorically, yes, totally a branch you can grab. But I bruise more easily."

"Sorry." He loosened his grip, but didn't let go. Soft whistles and chirps emerged from his mouths. I stroked his fur. He wasn't so different from Terran mammals that way; his hair stood on end when he was scared.

"It'll be okay," I told him.

At last the hail tapered off. Aunt Priya opened the ride door to squawks of protest, and a moment later dove back inside, drenched, with a handful of hailstones. "They're for luck," she explained (to everyone except me, who was used to it). "Have one."

The ride started up again, going far too slowly, and I examined the hailstones. They weren't the prototypical "golf-ball-sized" ones, at least, more in the pea to marble range. I popped one in my mouth, letting the high-atmosphere cold ease some of the tightness from my muscles. I tried not to think about how far ahead Redbug's team must be, whether they'd gotten stuck too or been luckier than us.

"You're just going to eat them?" asked Rhamnetin incredulously. "I guess . . . it has to be H_2O, right? It can't really be anything else, here."

"Not outside a lab," promised Aunt Priya.

I failed in my not-thinking. "Do you know when the tech team left for the antenna site? How long did it take you to get to our place?"

"Over an hour," she said. "But I don't know if they were going straight there. I think they still had some prep left, because they wanted my help. Unless they had collaborators going separately, or had already done some advance work." She paused. "I hate this. We need these corporate douchebags out of our network, and instead they're forcing us to work against our own people. They've barely been in the watershed a week."

We stopped twice more, pushing our travel time well over an hour. Wind and rain and hail would almost have become background noise, except for the times we should've "suspended" and didn't. The ride shook and swerved, and after a terrifying second slammed to a hard stop scant inches from a tree that hadn't lain across the road a moment earlier. It backed up and flashed a detour search while I gripped Carol and Rhamnetin with bruising irrationality and tried to stop shaking.

"You have reached your destination." It was good that the ride said so, because it wasn't obvious. We handed around ponchos—Rhamnetin plain out of luck—checked the covers on our bags, and emerged into the soaking downpour.

The poncho gave scant protection: rain flung itself into my face and sleeves and neck. We stood in a swift sheet of water rushing over the broken blacktop. My toes felt like hailstones; my eyes stung like open cuts.

"Great Reach," said Rhamnetin, "I'm not grown for this. I can't see anything."

"Neither can the rest of us." I had to shout to be heard. "So how are *they* getting any work done?"

"A team was bracing the prefabs earlier," said Carol.

Thankfully my earlier recordings of the site were still buffered on my mesh. I called them up, projected a rough map over the curtain of rain, and squinted at it through aching eyes. "This way!"

We picked our way carefully across the lot. I cursed Redbug and Elegy, and Jace or Adrien or whoever's brilliant idea it had been to provoke this idiocy. Our people should have known better, but persuasion had always been the corporations' most dangerous art. Their fine-wrought messages had tempted the world to the brink of ruin; how hard could it be, up close and in person, to convince a couple tech experts to make a fatal mistake?

"Found it," said Athëo, rubbing his wrist. "Ow." But there, blessedly, was the rain-slick corrugated wall of one of the prefabs. I wasn't sure which one and didn't care. We felt our way around until we found the door—and found it locked.

"Does that mean they're inside?" I asked. I was shivering, desperate for even a moment's shelter. Whoever had sealed the door had kept the lock off the network. I crouched to peer more closely at the thing: a plain silver keypad with thick loops binding the door to the wall. Not part of the original design, but that didn't tell me anything; all the prefabs had come from local storage.

"We could knock," suggested Athëo. I tried it—even saboteurs wouldn't leave people outside in this weather, right?—but there was no response.

"Aunt Priya, can you get through?" I asked.

"Hold up," said Carol. "Help shield my bag, please?" I held the poncho skirt over her sewing kit while she fished around inside.

"This isn't any sort of serious lock," she went on. "The place is crawling with people most of the time, and who expects thieves in the middle of a hurricane? You'd have to be running your decision algorithms backwards and inside out. Bolt cutters, there we go!"

I backed off, shivering in the driving rain even a foot from the prefab, and let my beautiful, brilliant wife have her way with the lock. She swore more creatively than she usually allowed herself in front of the kids, as she tried and failed several times to get the blades around the cord. At last she managed it, and came up with new obscenities as she levered the cutter against the metal.

"I don't know those words," said Rhamnetin.

"Context is everything," said Carol. Then: "Got it!"

The lock dropped off, and when we tried to slip inside the door wrenched open, banging hard against the outer wall so we had to drag it closed against the brute force of the gale. Only then could we look around—and confirm that we had not, in fact, found the tech team.

"Why *aren't* they in here?" asked Aunt Priya. "I'm pretty confident these are the readouts from the Asterion sensors."

They were the simplest of visual readouts—a few rollup screens glued to consoles. The Asterion people would get most of what they needed through their implants; these were just to share insight—or misinformation—with anyone from other networks who might want to see what they were doing. A couple boxes of electronic miscellany, the sort left over after basically any sort of computer setup, lay half-shoved into a half-built cabinet.

"How much could you do, here?" I asked. Inside and able to see again, I found that the hard rain had been full of leaves and mud. I tried without success to brush myself off, but everything was too wet.

"Not much," said Aunt Priya. "But more than from one of the watershed setups. I might be able to tell if they're modding the sensor input. Or what the tech team is up to, if it's affecting Asterion's readings." She tossed her poncho over an unused hookup and bent to examine the screens.

For the hell of it I tried pinging Redbug and Elegy again. Still no response. "I hope to hell they're actually here. No, delete that. I hope to hell they're not actually here, and we can be mad about wasting our time."

"No, they're here," said Priya. "I can see their work."

Athëo peered over her shoulder. "What are they doing? Those readouts don't look like normal wind vectors, even in the middle of a storm. What the heck is putting pressure on the antenna that way? Or . . . is this the misinformation you were worried about?"

Aunt Priya shook her head. "It's way too obvious for that. I think they're using bots."

"What kind of idiotic—" I stopped, realized I couldn't very well say, with Rhamnetin here, that Asterion had someone on-site who'd already proven able to detect our most subtle bot-based sabotage efforts. And of course the tech team didn't know, because I hadn't told them. "Doing what?"

"At a guess, nothing with the software. I think they're just . . . hitting the antenna. Or drilling, or cutting—whatever they've got makerbots on hand for—Rhamnetin, would direct force break the thing? I know you said it's resilient to high winds, but how is it with localized impacts?"

"I'm not sure. Show me?" Rhamnetin rubbed his legs against each other, for all the world like a cat washing itself or rubbing against a scratching post, clearing more water from more eyes. Two limbs rose to examine the display. "We design for a certain amount of debris impact. But this looks like a lot, hitting the same places over and over. That could do serious damage. Delay the construction, maybe even get the builders to collapse the antenna. It's a safety feature, if they find enough variables that don't match what they were expecting. I've only ever seen it happen once—a ship crashed into a habitat extension while it was under construction, and the whole thing went to cubes." He shuffled, nervous. "Can't we do something?"

"Are the bots remote-controlled?" asked Carol. "Or are they on autopilot? This isn't great weather for remote signals, but we're pretty close, and probably so is Elegy."

"Makerbots are usually set up for remote control," I said. "Are they encrypted? Maybe we could reach them."

Carol looked in her bag—she had the contents memorized, I was pretty sure, so that was more fidgeting while she thought than searching for anything specific. "Maybe. If we can pick up their IDs. That should tell us whether someone else is controlling them too. If they're smart, though, they'll have the bots on a hyperlocal network."

Athëo plopped onto the floor, cross-legged, and began sorting through the electronics crate. "Oh, hey, puzzlebot."

I grimaced, not appreciating the jab, even if it was well meant. "Those things are everywhere. Is it one of ours, or theirs?"

"Ours, and no, what I meant is, we could use it. Look at this little bug; it's sturdy and low to the ground. Stick a couple of sensors on the front, and we could send it out to where we think the tech team's bots are. If we can calibrate that way, we'll be able to target them much better."

We got to work. Between us we found a couple of miniature cameras and a basic tactile translator, along with a miniature manipulator arm, and got the puzzlebot into a form that would hug as close to any surface as possible—sort of a scorpion-centipede thing with the manipulator as its tail. Meanwhile, Aunt Priya and Carol scanned for the tech team's bots.

"Got them!" Carol finally announced. "Okay, there's a mini-network set up, but it's compatible—I think it's split off the site's network of Things. It's on Chesapeake security protocols."

"Don't access it yet!" exclaimed Priya. A minute later: "Oh, fuck you. Hold on. Okay, I think it's safe now. That was *not* a nice thing to do on your own network."

I could only follow about half of what they were doing, and can probably report it even less well now. But while they were trying to hack the tech team's bots around whatever booby traps they'd set up, Athëo and I finished our makeshift sensor-carrying puzzlebot, cracked the door, and sent it out into the cold. The metal centipede scuttled away from the prefab, clinging to broken blacktop. It disappeared into the storm, crawling toward the antenna, and we went back inside to watch its transmissions. Earlier, I'd had some vague idea that Rhamnetin might climb the antenna and pull bots off like giant ticks—but I doubted he could do any such thing in this wind. The bot, smaller and sturdier and rather more expendable, was a better idea.

"Right, I've found one." Priya pulled up the telemetry for the makerbot on her palette, and the rest of us crowded round. My own bot's vision lay over half my field of view, but at the moment all it was doing was crawling through the lot. Its camera blinked away droplets, revealing a few scant inches of ground. Against my back, the tactile translator gave me claws clinging to asphalt and mud, the slow press forward through wind and rain.

"This one's got a drill," Carol said, peering over Aunt Priya's shoulder. "If we pull the drill out from the antenna surface, and make it release the anchor grips—right, there it goes. Whee!"

"Whee?" I asked.

"Whoosh? It blew away, is my point."

"How many more are there?" asked Rhamnetin.

"The problem is that we're not entirely sure," said Aunt Priya. "I think a couple dozen."

"Shouldn't the network tell you how many Things it's got?" I asked.

"Normally, yes. But it's treating them as a swarm—it wants to read as one Thing with a variable number of modules. We have to isolate them one at a time. We'll know we've got them all when we stop reading the swarm."

I did that sometimes with sensors, and it made sense. Swarming was resilient, especially if you cared more about the overall project than about the fate of individual objects.

Right now, though, I didn't have a swarm, just one bot to supplement Aunt Priya's piecemeal hacking. It sped up, protected by the antenna's rain shadow. "Could you reprogram some of the makerbots to attack the others, instead of just tossing them away? That might be more efficient."

"Or it might turn into a coding tug-of-war with the tech team." Carol shook her head. "This is the only way to know for sure we've got 'em—it may not be elegant, but it works and you only have to do it once per bot. There goes another one!"

It worked. It was also, once we took care of a certain critical mass of the swarm, noticeable. The door banged open, and Elegy barged in.

Unlike us, she'd had the sense to bring proper goggles, surfaces treated to keep them from fogging, and she glared at us with clear eyes. Her arms were bare, and her river tattoos gleamed with real stormwater. "What the fuck, Priya?"

Aunt Priya ignored the glare. "I told you this was a bad idea. I told you it was a trap. I'm trying to get you out of it."

"You told us the Ringers were going to catch us. So you told a goddamn Ringer?"

"I'm trying to get you out of it too," said Rhamnetin. "I don't actually like attracting Cytosine's attention to things that are going to make her mad, and I don't believe this action reflects the way the dandelion networks think. Does it?"

"Given that you didn't run it by the network," I said. "Which is *supposed to* be how we think." But even as I spoke, I remembered the silence in response to my own posts. Quietly I handed off the sensory input from the bot to Athëo so I could focus on my so-called diplomatic expertise. "*Did* you post to the network? I couldn't text you, and I couldn't get to you through the problem threads—that's why we're here in person. I just wanted to talk, but it wouldn't let me. Whatever you're trying here, it's not going to fix the damage the malware is already doing."

"But it'll keep Asterion from doing even worse—yes, I still think so. Maybe it'll distract them from playing with our protocol long enough to root out the actual problem." She brushed water from her arms, claiming space. "And no, we didn't post this particular plan where Asterion could look at it. We did try to post a description of the symptoms on the network. And it looked to us like it went up, but it didn't actually get to where anyone could see it. We need to stop this thing, now."

"Yeah, but this isn't the way to do it." I tried to think. Backed into corners, people need alternatives. Ways to feel like they're moving forward. "We could turn this around. Stop trying to sabotage things ourselves, and show the Ringers evidence that Asterion is sabotaging the networks. The patterns are getting more obvious; it should be enough to convince them. We can use that against Asterion in the talks, force them to call off their viruses if they want to stay involved."

Rhamnetin closed in behind me, a breath of humid air against my neck and a firm voice backing me up. "We want to work with humans who know how to cooperate. You've got the best infrastructure for cooperation on the planet, and they're trying to break it. That matters to us. It'll matter to Cytosine."

Elegy's eyebrows rose. "Depend on the Ringers to keep us safe? I thought you knew better. If we want to protect Earth, we can't afford to answer to anyone outside the watersheds."

"But we will," I said. "You've made sure of that."

Carol frowned, and a moment later sent a text: **She only came here to figure out what we're doing; she's cut off our signal to the makerbots. That's why we've got to talk. Convince her. Somehow.** Athëo was ignoring us—had our own bot reached the antenna? Could we use it to finish plucking off the swarm bots? Or at this point, could we say we'd done our best, get credit for trying even if we didn't succeed? What if we let the antenna fall?

I pushed the temptation firmly down, imagining Rhamnetin's disappointment. We'd find another way to keep Earth safe. A stable way, that came from mutual respect with the Ringers rather than an extension of our old wars.

"Suppose this works?" I asked Elegy. "What happens then?"

"We get Asterion back behind their fenceline. The Ringers can rebuild here without them, if they have the resources, or take their chances on the aislands if they really want to. And we get some breathing room to work, and to rebuild."

"Suppose it doesn't?" I asked. It was a strange conversation. *I* was talking because I needed Elegy to listen. But Elegy was talking to buy herself time for the work she was carrying out in parallel. She didn't need to listen. The only thing we had in common was the need to keep talking. "You have to plan for failure, too. And you have two failures modes here: you can't stop the antenna, or you can't keep your involvement quiet. Either way your whole plan collapses—what then?"

"Taking down the antenna . . ." She shrugged. "If that doesn't work, we're no worse off than we were before. Secrecy"—she looked pointedly at Rhamnetin—"is no longer an option. So we'll have to explain ourselves. You obviously get along pretty well with this fellow. I may not like what Cytosine is doing, but I respect how she does it. She takes her goals seriously enough to follow through, whatever she needs to do. She's more like us, and maybe that means she'll see how seriously we take Asterion's threat, and start taking it seriously too."

"She might," said Rhamnetin, "if you weren't trying to undermine her. I wish you'd come to her directly. Call off your bots now, and that *might* still work."

"I'd rather the fait accompli. Argue from a place of strength, and all that. What the hell?" This last seemed unrelated to what she'd been saying. I tried not to look at Athëo as she examined the room with narrowed eyes. "Not one of ours. *You've* been busy talking . . ." I

tried to get between her and Athëo, but she did something—Judo?—
and I was on the floor discovering that yes, I did remember how to
fall without twisting anything, but Elegy had grabbed Athëo's mesh.
He rubbed his scalp, glaring, and I gulped air in sympathy with what
I knew was a headache-inducing backlash.

"Whatever you've got out there," said Elegy, "it'll have to get by
on its own."

"Are we hitting each other to solve problems now?" I asked. "Such
a mature species."

"Sometimes hitting things is the best way to make them better."

"Yes, but this isn't—" I stopped. Rhamnetin was jittering, trying
to get attention. "What's going on?"

"We warned you you'd get caught," Rhamnetin told Elegy. "My
comms just started working, and Cytosine wants to know what the
hell is going on and why the fuck she had to learn about it from Jace
di Sanya. That's a poetic translation."

CHAPTER 32

In case you ever have a choice in the matter, inside a prefab workshop in the middle of a hurricane, with hail starting up outside, is a shitty place to have an argument. I wanted to find someplace, any place, quiet. I wanted to curl up on myself like a frightened plains-person. Instead I dug nails into palms, breathed as slowly as I could, and tried not to scream. I thought Elegy might be doing the same, and that didn't help.

"If we run off now," I said, "we let Jace and the corporate team tell the story of what happened here. By the time the storm's over, we'll be completely screwed. We need to talk with Cytosine *now*."

I wasn't a hundred percent sure that my conviction was anything more than anxiety talking, the flip side of my desire to hide in a box. But Carol and Athëo and Aunt Priya didn't argue, and maybe more importantly neither did Rhamnetin.

"It's the middle of a storm that they're all terrified to go out in," said Elegy. "They're not going to complain if we hole up until the wind calms down."

"Probably not," I said. "But Asterion will milk the extra time for all it's worth."

"I don't want to go back out in that atmosphere either," said Rhamnetin, and I realized that he'd been digging out from under his own fear. "But Judy's right. I know Cytosine—she's furious, and whatever she comes to think over the next couple of hours, she's likely to stay convinced."

There were a few more go-rounds, but I think Elegy knew there was no real alternative. Whoever was hiding out in the other pre-fabs could still duck out, and probably would no matter what I said, but Rhamnetin's witness and our records all showed Elegy here. She could try to defend herself personally, or she could hope the rest of us managed it.

That left the question of getting to Bear Island. Athëo retrieved his mesh and reported that there'd be a window of relative calm in seventeen minutes—twenty-three minutes long, more than enough time to get to the landing site under normal circumstances. If Cytosine wanted proof of how much we cared about this, we'd drip it all over her floor.

It was a long fucking seventeen minutes.

"Now," said Athëo, and we went out into what would've been a perfectly respectable rainstorm any day. We could see a few feet ahead, and open umbrellas without losing them, but it was impossible to stay dry.

The path was a mess of mud, the river beside it a white torrent. Readings told me it was five feet above its normal level and considerably faster, but the readings were sparse; the sensors had all climbed out of the rapids and clung to crannies in the banks like artificial barnacles, trying to minimize post-storm replacement needs. The final records would be all right, but if there was a surge we might not spot it in real time.

And that was a problem when we got to the causeway. It was barely five feet above the river's normal level, and a sheet of mud and sticks rushed shallow but slippery where there should've been solid ground.

"I'm not going over that," said Elegy. "A branch could come along, you could slip on the mud—I'm not *drowning* myself for this. Cytosine can fucking wait."

"*She's* got no problem waiting." But Rhamnetin stuck a tentative toe onto the causeway. "How dangerous is it, really?"

"Dangerous," said Athëo. "Judy, we've got kids at home."

Carol ducked under my umbrella and put an arm around me. She squeezed my shoulders tightly. "We do. And they need us to convince Cytosine that the watersheds are worth working with, or they might not have a planet when they grow up. One way or another. But we don't all have to go."

I heard it in her voice: one of the two of us needed to stay safe for Dori. And I was the one with the diplomatic cachet. I was the one with some modicum of diplomatic expertise. And Carol wasn't quite willing to admit, aloud, that it should be me.

We had thirteen minutes left in the window, plus or minus thirty seconds. I pulled my wife close and kissed her, trying to taste and feel and not fear for a precious few seconds. She smelled like rain and mint balm. Then I handed her my umbrella, held out my arms, and hugged Athëo and Aunt Priya.

"You all go back to the prefabs," I said. "You should be able to ride out the storm there, and once Rhamnetin and I get to the ship, we'll stay there until it's safe."

"I should go with you," said Priya. "I know more about the tech aspects of this than anyone else here. Except Elegy, of course." Who wasn't likely to be persuaded. And we still couldn't count on texting.

I forced my voice steady. "And your sense of balance is . . . ?"

"Not great on the best of days. But still."

"You won't convince Cytosine of anything if you fall in the river. Rhamnetin?"

He edged closer, listening.

"There are a few low branches across the path. If you take the high road can you sort of dangle down, and steady me if I slip?"

He lifted two limbs' worth of eyes to peer down the path. "I think so. Most places, anyway."

"Great. You go ahead of me, then."

I checked my pack, made sure the straps were tight and not likely to get in my way. I took a deep breath, and another. At least this wasn't the sort of thing that made me anxious. It was just terrifying.

Of course a nasty argument, where the fate of the watersheds and the planet might hang on my ability to say the right thing, was waiting on the other side. It didn't feel real, but was exactly the sort of thing to make me *extremely* anxious anyway. I kept breathing, tried to focus only on mud and rocks and sticks and keeping track of where Rhamnetin hung in the branches.

Mud squelched. I moved slowly, and still stumbled when I hit one of the roots that straddled the path. We lost a couple of these old trees every storm, came out later to plant far more saplings than we needed. Most would wash away before they could grab tight to the earth. Now I was the unsteady sapling, an East African plains ape picking her way over unsteady ground, my only real advantage over those distant ancestors a friendly grip waiting above. In the corner of my eye, Rhamnetin swung across a gap. I caught whistles and chords over the sound of the wind. I would have to ask later whether that was prayer or complaint. Would have to make sure there was a later to ask.

About a third of the way through, the river had cut a gully across the causeway. Water rushed through the low point, brimming with detritus. I couldn't tell how deep it went, but fording it was almost certainly a bad idea. I might have jumped across, given stable earth on both sides—but there was only slick, messy ground sloping into the hungry river. "Rhamnetin?"

He lowered himself gingerly from the overgrowth, clinging with several limbs and letting three more hang down like furry vines studded with eyes and mouths and pincers instead of leaves. (So, in fact, not much like vines at all.) I grabbed on, testing to be sure I couldn't pull him down, and tried to figure out how to steady myself for a jump. Instead, he wrapped a limb around me as if I were a branch myself, and lifted me over the gully. I stumbled on the landing, startled, but he kept hold of my waist until I'd caught my balance.

"There you go, Fay," he said. "Oof, you weigh almost as much as I do."

"The weight's all in my head. Fay?"

"Fay Wray? King Kong climbing buildings? Never mind. I know your movies better than you do."

"I think I've seen a different version." I wished he didn't have to let go. The moment of shared balance passed, and we pushed on. Seven minutes. We wouldn't make the ship in that time, but we needed to at least reach the island.

I moved faster, eyes wide for any hint of safe footing. I was wet enough to almost imagine my discomfort an ordinary state. If I could just believe I'd always been soaked to the skin, always had mud caking my pants against my legs, leaves plastered to my arms and face, it couldn't distract or distress me. I slipped, grabbed for whatever was nearby, found Rhamnetin again. I murmured the Shma—if I fell, that was supposed to be the last thing I said, right? No, focus on the walking, not the falling. I turned the gain on my soles up all the way, and it still wasn't enough. The signal stuttered through sensors never designed for this much moisture. I clung to Rhamnetin while I pulled my shoes off entirely. Now I could feel the packed earth beneath mud and roots and stones, whether they moved or stood still. Wood and rock scratched my feet, and the rush of brown water stung my skin, but that's what bacteriophage cream was for.

Three minutes left, plus or minus thirty seconds, and I thought we were almost there. The sound of the river changed, echoing a nearby shore, and curtains of rain misted a higher canopy ahead.

"Judy!" I jerked my head up, almost losing my balance, and sodden spider legs snatched me into the air. Something slammed against my thigh, and Rhamnetin swung me higher. My stomach cringed with vertigo, a sickening hint of the plunge barely avoided. A tree lay across the path where I'd been. It shifted, settling, and I belatedly processed the close-thunder crack of its breaking.

"Hold on," called Rhamnetin. "Baby grips, don't ball up."

"Can't," I called back shakily, "only got two hands," but I wrapped my arms tight around one limb, my legs around another, the opposite of what my monkey brain wanted. My muscles strained and my guts lurched, and Rhamnetin swung us over the broken oak and down its trunk to safe, muddy ground.

"Oh god." Everything ached when I let go. I wanted to lie down, and I wanted to puke, and through the lash of adrenaline I tried to remember how to avoid either. My head swam, and I found myself on hands and knees, throat burning with the remains of the scone I'd eaten only a couple hours earlier.

"Judy? Judy, please! Please be okay! What did I do? Did I break something?"

I waved him off, lifted my head to get rainwater in my mouth, spit out terror along with acid. "I'm fine," I said at last. "Just fear and vertigo. You don't get motion sick, do you? You couldn't, swinging around like that." I tried to figure out how someone with ten mouths would even throw up, and started giggling. "Sorry, more—more mal-adaptive fear reactions. Give me—give me a second."

"Okay. I think I strained a couple of legs."

"You and me both. Ow. We'd better get going, though, the storm is about to get worse."

The rain closed in, bringing visibility down to almost nothing, and the wind slammed against us. But the path was clear enough, as long as we moved slowly and remembered that runoff would always edge us toward the cliff. It was better than the causeway, and I could brace myself when Rhamnetin had to boost me over fallen branches. I was limping, slowed by strained muscles and a nasty bruise where the tree had grazed me, by the time we stumbled into the clearing and onto the scaled hull of the *Solar Flare*.

"Will they let us in?" I shouted. The ship felt like metal, like the rain should drum against it, but instead it seemed to slow as it approached and roll off gently. Hail wasn't much different from micro-meteorites, I supposed.

"I've got signal here," said Rhamnetin. "Someone will come."

He steadied me up the slope, a scramble made bearable only by the promise of its end. I wished for more legs and hands. But light glowed fuzzily ahead of us, and we stumbled through the door into the Ringers' tame forest, watered only by hydroponics. Moss cushioned my feet, and warm air soothed my aches. Plains-folk and tree-folk surrounded us, exclaiming over our state, Rhamnetin's injuries as apparent to them as my bruises. Towels, or something close enough to serve, draped over us. Mine was sized for plains-folk, and I didn't mind at all. I huddled, trying to decide whether it was safe to remove my soaked clothing. It wasn't like the Ringers wore much, but I needed all the dignity I could get.

"Take that off," Rhamnetin told me as I picked at my sleeve. "We'll find you something else later."

"I know you're more used to this kind of nonsense," said Phenylalanine, attempting a cursory medical examination, "but it can't be good for you."

"Not really." I looked around, didn't see Cytosine, and said fuck it and stripped off my shirt and jeans and bra. I dried my mesh and my scalp and put the mesh back on. I got only the same thin trickle of signal I'd had outside. I texted Carol, just in case it might get through.

I heard Cytosine before I saw her, a cacophony of untranslated Ringer. I wished for Athëo's translation skills, but not enough to want him here sharing my danger. I stood, tried to make the towel into a dignified wrap rather than a pile of absorbent fabric. Tried to keep it around me without crossing my arms, to keep my body language open and honest. Or maybe I should play up my drowned-kitten state—no. What I needed was to stop second-guessing myself. Pick a course of action, and act.

Loud enough to cut through the furious string section, I called, "We tried to stop the sabotage. I think we succeeded. You should know that Asterion pushed the tech team into it in the first place."

"The hell we did." I hadn't heard Adrien over Cytosine's anger, but here sui (I recognized the outfit) came beside her. St. Julien trailed behind, jiggling Brice.

"My god," she said, unguarded. "You look like someone gave the cat a bath. What happened?"

"These people"—I jerked my head at Adrien—"convinced some of our tech team that the corporations were routing malware through the antenna. The team came to my aunt for help, she came to me, we went out in the damn storm to stop them from sabotaging your construction. Asterion caught the tech team, exactly like they planned in the first place, and reported them to you in order to drive a wedge between us. They set them up."

Adrien cocked sur head. "Faced with all this supposed villainy on our part, why didn't your techies bring everything to your crowd and poll opinions about whether we were actually doing anything? The networks don't suffer people haring off on high-risk missions on their own recognizance—or so you boast. Every decision goes through every possible expert until you know it's right."

Sui knew that was bullshit, and knew I couldn't say anything without admitting that this was our second harebrained sabotage attempt in as many weeks. But there was no mockery in sur voice or stance, just the semblance of disbelief worn as perfectly as sur leathers.

"Not everyone follows the rules," I said instead. "As you all damned well know. Your malware—which is real, even if it's not going through the antenna—is keeping us from talking properly on the network." Which was the first time that we'd formally laid that accusation in front of Cytosine. I hoped it stuck. "I can't even count the number of messages I've sent today that never arrived."

"In the middle of a hurricane," said St. Julien quietly. I glared at her, but it wasn't in her interest for the watersheds to weigh heavily in the negotiations either. She wanted off-planet. She was as sure of Brice's best future as I was of Dori's and Raven's.

"They're *designed* for disaster response," I said. "We spun up our core code to hold things together during the cluster storms of '47. Don't tell me I can't get eyes on a thread about corporate sabotage because of a fucking Cat 1 hurricane."

"This is nonsense," said Adrien evenly. "She's trying to distract you from what the watersheds just tried to do. They want us all stranded on Earth."

I pulled my towel-thing tighter around me. Arguing with Adrien wouldn't solve anything; it was Cytosine I needed to convince. She'd gone quiet, eyestalks flicking between us, waiting.

I turned to her, trying to focus my communication so she could understand, even through our unfamiliar body language. Even through my shivering, only partly from cold, and the shudder of breath in my throat that threatened to shatter my words. "Cytosine, I appeal to you. Asterion—maybe just Jace's group, I don't pretend to understand internal corporate dynamics—has undermined our networks in an attempt to co-opt these negotiations. All the tools we've developed to help us cooperate, they're doing everything they can to wreck. Unless you refuse to work with them, they'll continue to undermine us—and you'll be stuck trying to form a symbiosis with people who'll subvert any decision they don't like. They think every-thing is a game, and cheating part of the rules."

Cytosine's gaze turned on Rhamnetin. "Explain this *eccentricity*." I stumbled over the venom in that last word until I caught up with the Ringer metaphor: an eccentric orbit, unstable and about to crash.

Rhamnetin might not like Cytosine's anger, but he was used to it. "It's like Judy said. Her mother's sister traveled through the storm to warn us. She's an expert in the code underlying the networks, and she believed Asterion had *misled* the rogue group about the risks of the antenna." Here he added something in his own language—a bet-ter term? "We couldn't message the rogues either, so we rode out to stop them. I saw Judy and Priya and Carol and Athëo take great risks to save our antenna, and watched Elegy attack them. And then you called. I could only get one human over the causeway to the ship, so Judy traveled with me and the others went back. She risked her life to make it here. She's been courageous, and we'd be wrong to hold the rogues' actions against her."

"I hold nothing against her. But the watersheds are another mat-ter. They want to keep humanity on Earth. They wouldn't object at all if the antenna failed."

"I *did*," I said. "I worry about Earth's future, but I didn't think it was right, and I risked myself to protect your way home. My whole household shared those risks, and Aunt Priya shared them. Others would too, if we'd been able to reach them. The watersheds care about means, not just ends. If we don't do things the right way, it poisons any outcome." Something I should have remembered on Zealand, before it proved itself true.

"But you still want to keep humanity earthbound," said St. Julien. "The sabotage could have forced that outcome."

I turned on her. "We're not arguing about our goals! We're argu-ing about what we *did*. The watersheds aren't trying to screw anyone over—the corporations are, and it sounds like you plan to help them." I winced as I said it. Losing my temper with St. Julien wasn't going to get me anywhere. Losing my temper would push Cytosine to stay angry, our similarities keeping her from taking anything I said seri-ously. Rhamnetin stroked my shoulder.

"Enough accusations," said Cytosine. "I can't trust anything you say, only what we know happened. I won't put you out in this atmo-sphere; you can wait with the others."

CHAPTER 33

My presence made the slumber party more awkward, but there was little choice; there was no other place on the ship even remotely suitable for humans to rest. Rhamnetin and his conspecifics slept in the trees, and I still wasn't sure what was comfortable for the plains-folk. I should've invited some of them to stay over. Rhamnetin had been so friendly, so willing to put himself forward, that it had been easy to get to know him to the exclusion of the others. But I could depend only so much on his mediation, and I should've tried to get to know his family as he'd gotten to know mine—to figure out how we fit together. Now Cytosine had separated us, either because she wanted us apart or simply because she wanted to yell at him more.

St. Julien gave me blankets and a nightgown and a couple of NASA "ration bars." I wolfed one down before I even tried talking to her; Dinar's scones seemed days ago. The ration bar was better than you'd expect from the name: granola and honey and dried fruit, backed by the earthy undertones of some sort of mushroom flour. St. Julien watched, and offered an inadequately apologetic shrug, and I realized there was no useful conversation to have with her. It wasn't as if she was going to say, on the ship where Ringers might hear, "I like you, but I'll do anything to restore power to my nation and get us into space."

Tempting, to tell the Ringers to take the remnant governments, the corporate boards and their eager employees, and bring them to the Rings to do what they would. Leave Earth to those who believed as I did. The watersheds could join in our own time, once we truly understood ecosystem management—not what made a world minimally functional, but what made it beautiful and wild, a worthy dance partner to a species grown worthy in return.

Then we'd get to the Rings, and find the old fight waiting for us: their habitats full of our most toxic hierarchies, welded in place by Jace's darkest marketing arts. Getting there first had power of its own. We might have to run ahead, just to keep up. And then we'd lose everything Earth still had to teach us.

I wondered if St. Julien read as much in my unfocused gaze as I did in her shrug.

I settled into the blankets, let the others get back to friendly conversation. I listened for some hint of the outside world, but the ship cushioned itself against the storm. Other sounds filled the air, disconnected: the whisper of ventilation, the hum of engines, the chitters of insectlikes and birdlikes, the music of Ringer conversation in other rooms. Unable to think of a reason I shouldn't sleep, I slept—and only realized when I woke about two hours later exactly how tired I must have been. Now in the dark, lights reduced to some level that didn't match Earth's familiar moonlight and starlight, my brain had recovered enough to churn over everything I should be worrying about. My breasts ached, swollen with milk.

A pillbug curled beside me in the dark.

"Cytosine?" I asked. But no babies curled against their belly, and I thought they were smaller, limbs subtly different in shape.

"Glycine. You really can't tell us apart, can you?"

"Not in the dark. What's going on?"

"Cytosine says you violated our welcome and tried to break the antenna, and Carnitine and Luciferin say the same. Rhamnetin insists it was Asterion, but Cytosine is convinced you and he are playing out some sort of Pre-Reach hormonal drama. What happened?"

I rubbed my eyes. "Exactly what I told Cytosine, damn it. I thought she *liked* us being romantic with Rhamnetin. What's a hormonal drama?"

"You know. Artificial pheromones to warp his reactions."

"What? No!" I lowered my voice. "If anyone knows how to do that, it's the corporations, and I'm pretty sure that's only in stories."

Glycine rocked slowly, limbs weaving like fronds. "We're all frightened. The idea of being stranded on a dying planet is bad enough, without being reminded how dangerous a living planet can be."

"Earth's *not* dying. But I don't want you stranded, either. The watersheds don't. It might be convenient politically, and I know that's all Cytosine perceives right now." And again my hypocrisy cut into my thoughts: I'd let myself forget everything but practicality, and it had worked out very badly. Maybe I'd poisoned the Ringers' trust somehow, even without letting them find out about the puzzlebot. Or maybe they just understood how fear pared people down to gut responses and ruthless decisions.

But with Glycine, I thought, we might have a chance. They'd been willing to learn from us, to admit we had something to offer. If they could accept our tools of self-definition, maybe they could accept our openness on a larger scale. "We know what it's like to almost lose your home. Because Earth *was* dying, because of how much work we've put into preserving a living world for our great-great-grandchildren. We want you to be where you want to be, because you deserve the thing we want for ourselves. We want to share what we've learned, without assuming we know what's best for each other. But the watersheds need you—" I tried to put it in their terms. "We need you to imagine new kinds of symbiosis, beyond the ones you already know. Maybe even new possibilities for your own people."

Glycine unrolled, and I thought they were going to say something else. Then, abruptly, they scurried off. I waited, holding still in the dim light, trying to spot whatever had startled them, hoping they'd come back. But nothing showed. Eventually I lay back down.

Long hours later, the ship's forest brightened. Diurnal things woke, skittering and flying among the leaves. Magenta blossoms unfurled and dropped bright pendulums that twirled in the artificial breeze. The other humans woke and stretched, eyeing me as they discussed logistics.

My mesh, when I pulled it into place, churned with messages. The storm was over, and there was no sign of the blackouts that had plagued us yesterday.

Mendez alone headed directly for me. "Everything's working now. I'd swear all the weirdness last night was the weather, if it weren't so obviously targeted."

"And if the whole thing weren't such a wild anomaly," I agreed. "Asterion will say we're making patterns out of noise."

"So what happened last night?"

I blanched at the thought of explaining it again. "Maybe I can upload my records now." I could; I did. The critiques would be worse than anything I'd gotten at the beginning of this mess, and more deserved.

I texted my household and received assurances of survival and further demands for explanation. I could check in alive, at least, and tell them that we were comfortable if bruised. Then, testing my fears as if dropping a sensor into a pond: Athēo, if you're up for triaging my

inbox, I could honestly use the break. I let the message sit in my vision, unsent, while I wavered. He'd asked to share my troubles, and sworn he wouldn't compound them. Maybe I could try it. I bit my lip, let the text flow out before I could change my mind.

Mendez interrupted my private anxieties, frowning. "Check the common feed. We're not the only network that's a mess."

The wider news was starting to trickle into the Chesapeake. I tried not to look at Adrien, but it was hard. There were minor disasters all over, new and ongoing and imminent. Nothing that should be overwhelming—these were the sorts of storms, droughts, fires, and outbreaks that the dandelion networks rode out every day. But the Lower Mississippi, prepping for Hurricane Braulio, had stumbled over their usual flood projections. For decades now they'd been moving populations slowly, not just retreating from the rising sea but getting ready for the inevitable moment when the Mississippi would tire of its old route and shift permanently to the Atchafalaya. It grew likelier every storm, and the projected impacts only a little less dire: there were people and places that couldn't or wouldn't be moved in advance, that would suffer when forced. They'd run the simulations for moving the river deliberately a thousand times, and never quite hit the balance that would make that seem like a good idea.

Sometime yesterday, about the point when we'd been dueling the tech team's bots on the antenna, a rogue group had placed explosives at key points in the aging Army Corps of Engineers levies, and let the river go where it had long wanted to go. The common feed was mercifully free of images, but a few had been virus-scanned and shared with other networks: bodies and broken homes where no one had been expecting a flood. In New Orleans, people stared blankly at the slowing trickle where the great waters had been. In the common feed and across networks, the Lower Mississippi unleashed a flood of threads: some begging for help replacing now-irrelevant storm preparations and resources overwhelmed by the flood, others demanding justice under the shared guidelines of the watersheds.

"This has to count as unapproved geoengineering, right?" asked Mendez. Her usual confidence faltered; this was even further beyond her expertises than mine.

"*I* think so. But it's not like atmospheric seeding; you'd have a hard time making the case that it was meant to impact anyone outside the one network." And even if it was, they had no idea who did it.

Except, whoever set the bombs, we knew who was behind them.

Redbug and Elegy had been convinced that a stupid sabotage was necessary, then cut off from the crowd that might have suggested better options. It was the same in the Lower Mississippi: an even more horrific sabotage unsupported by the numbers—unless some people had seen different numbers, different threads, different arguments. Networks made untrustworthy, turned against themselves, right as we most needed to work in concert. If I met Jace di Sanya face-to-face again today, I was sure I'd find him smirking.

And what would happen if I tried to post *this* problem to the network?

"We need to get home," I told Mendez. "We need in-person meetings, as many as we can manage. People need to know."

The Ringers were only too eager to let us go. I wanted to bring Rhamnetin home with us, but couldn't find him, and everyone I asked explained with bland equanimity that he wasn't available. "Asleep." "Healing." Or no explanation at all. And no response to my texts. It would've been easy enough for Cytosine to confiscate his makeshift mesh, and no one here would even be shocked.

"Tell your network," said Cytosine, "that we're turning on the antenna. The signal's weak, but it's out."

I felt a lurch in my stomach, equal parts relief and fear. My breasts pulsed painfully in sympathetic echo. "I thought you had days of construction to go."

She stroked Diamond and Chlorophyll methodically, as if reassuring herself. "Taller and stronger would've been better. But *now* is best. The signal is out, and none of your people can stop it. Maybe our backup will have better luck than we have."

Mendez and I left the island alone and watched the antenna pulse light into the mist, silent against the roar of the swollen Potomac, as we flagged down a ride to the train.

CHAPTER 34

The Chesapeake watershed covers 64,000 square miles, five major rivers, and close to 25 million humans. It has no capital but the ocean, no center but the bay. Which means there's no grand building where everyone can conveniently gather to make decisions during a crisis. It's not supposed to be necessary—no capital, no center, and no court or congress but the network itself.

When we trusted that infrastructure, everyone was happy to send representatives who fit in our dining room. Now the neighborhood commons overflowed, a thousand-year flood of people needing their opinions heard, even the best moderators overwhelmed by conflicting efforts to organize and prioritize the shouted messages. Mendez and I had gone straight there from Bear Island, and I regretted it already. My breasts had moved from dull ache to stinging pain, and I felt hot and fog-brained. I sat in a corner and tried to listen.

"—supposed to wait for input—"

"—why didn't we learn sooner—"

"—demonstrated that we can't use decision infrastructure to discuss restoration strategies for the decision infrastructure—" That was Redbug, shouting along with everyone else.

"—anything so urgent it can't wait for real repairs—"

"You fucking idiot!" That was close, and I looked up and blinked at Dinar, trying to clear the blur of my thoughts. Why was she here? "What the hell have you done to yourself?"

"Is she okay?"

"Carol!" My wife jiggled a crying Dori—I made grabby hands, and then my arms were full of squirming baby. I scrabbled at my shirt, and got her latched on. I whimpered through clenched teeth, but it still felt so good to have someplace for the milk to *go*.

"Oh my god," said Dinar. "Athëo, can you please do your whistle?"

Athëo bent to examine me, then cupped hands around his lips and gave a piercing whistle that cut through all the shouting. Suddenly the whole room was staring at us.

"Hey," yelled Dinar. "We need a lactation-safe anti-inflammatory over here, and a dose of bacteriophage. You can go back to arguing now." The volume rose again, but someone ducked into the healer's closet and Dinar pressed capsules into my hand.

"You didn't bring a pump with you," said Carol. She put her arms around me and I leaned against her. My wife, warm and solid at my back. Muscles began to untangle. "I thought you'd hand-express, at least."

"I didn't think of it," I said. "Probably because I was distracted by how badly we fucked up."

"Probably because you're feverish," said Dinar.

"Cytosine won't let Rhamnetin off the ship. Grounded, like some kid who misbehaved. I couldn't even talk with him." I hoped my recordings were making events clear to everyone—I certainly wasn't up to articulating it. "Do plains-folk get mastitis, do you think?"

"Let's go home," suggested Carol. "The network can figure things out without our input for a few hours."

I honestly couldn't tell you whether they put me on an electric cart, or called a ride, or whether I walked the five blocks leaning against Carol. I remember seeing the detritus of the storm, the fallen branches and shingles and ordinary stuff of recovery, and wondering whether we still had the capacity to organize cleanup. Everything seemed overwhelming, little problems inextricable from the big ones.

My parents were at our house, and I remember telling them anxiously that *they* needed to be at the commons, because they knew how to manually organize problem-solving. I don't know if that happened, because then I was in my bed, and Carol took Dori, and I slept.

When I woke, I felt cooler—no less overwhelmed, when I stopped to consider our situation, but at least more rationally so. I prodded my breasts. They remained tender, but no longer pulsed pain across the rest of the world. Unready to face too much of that world, I put on my mesh but stayed away from my messages. I let in only the most basic maintenance threads. That, and my own natural senses, seemed more than enough.

Downstairs, I found Dori crawling circles between Carol and Raven and Athëo. Athëo got up and hugged me. "Dinar's sleeping. The network's a mess."

"I believe it." I swallowed. "Did you clean out my messages? I'm terrified to check."

He squeezed my hand. Surprised, but strangely reassured by the hint that he knew how hard this was for me, I squeezed back. "I did a little," he said. "It's pretty bad, but not just you. On the open threads it seems like weights have crashed for everyone involved in contact at any level, and everyone in malware recovery. None of the usual fail-safes against panic are working. Asterion's completely screwed us over, and no one knows what to do."

Carol hunched over herself. "I don't like this. It feels like we were just getting things fixed, and suddenly they're falling apart. Is it always like that?"

"Is what always like that?" asked Athëo.

"It's like—Passover starts tomorrow night."

"Yeah?" Between storm and Ringers, I'd barely noticed the impending holiday. At the moment it felt like yet one more thing, the rituals of preparation and feast something else to fit in, somehow, among the other stresses.

"Jews go to Egypt, we do pretty well, they get scared and enslave us." Carol gripped one wrist, miming a manacle. "Again and again, the same thing happens. We're managing fine, pharaohs or fascists come along to try and kill us. We stop them, a generation or two later they show up again, or someone else does. Good times end. Only now when the bad times come, the whole planet's at risk—we can't simply ride out the falls, not anymore."

I shivered. "Is that really what's going on? It's only been a couple of weeks."

"Something's going to have to change," said Athëo. "Everything is going to have to change, I don't see how we can avoid it. Maybe we could've threaded the needle of making those mostly good changes, but—"

"But the corporations think this is their chance to make better times for themselves," I said. "I don't know, what could we have done to change *them,* before this happened? To get them to a point where what seemed good for them was good for the planet, whether or not it was good for the watersheds?"

"People were talking at the commons," said Carol. "You were right about what Jace wanted. The corporate team's been talking to people, offering chances to try out *their* network. Just as a workaround, of course, until we figure out what's wrong with ours."

"Has anyone tried it?" I asked.

"Whatever's going on with the networks hasn't kept people from blaming them for the malware, so no one's been seriously tempted. But a couple of people gave it a go with clean meshes, as a test. They said it doesn't much feel like a dandelion protocol, but the aggregation works pretty quickly and they were able to get through test decisions without anything really stupid rolling out. Or at least not as stupid as what we're getting already. I'm worried. People may hate them, but they'll do what they need to keep basic stewardship processes rolling."

"Holy shit." Athëo stood abruptly. Raven toddled over and clutched his leg; he picked her up and leaned his cheek against her head.

"Dada mad?"

"Not at you, baby. It's okay." He made a visible effort to look okay. "I just thought, what if that's what the malware does, long-term? Not break the networks, even if that was the first obvious effect. But now our decision processes have gone from not working to working strangely. Redbug was talking about cordyceps—it doesn't only kill insects, it turns them into puppets. What if they're turning our protocol into theirs, like the builder bots turn carbon into the Ringers' antenna?"

"Hell," said Carol. "But then why push us to use a network we *know* is theirs?"

"It's a decoy," I suggested. "They make us think they're trying something obvious, so we can feel smug when we don't fall into the trap. Then we get our system working again, and it doesn't quite feel right, but that makes sense with a reinstall—and we're so relieved that we stopped them from breaking it, plus the world's changed so much that everything feels different anyway, so probably we're just imagining things." I stood and paced, scooped up Dori and buried my nose in her sparse hair and familiar scent. "We've got to—what? What do we do about this?"

"Even if we could post about it," said Athëo, "our weights have gone to shit."

"And to get attention on the common network, we'd need something more solid than rumors of catastrophe," I said. "Aunt Priya might have suggestions. She needs to know. Hell, so does the tech team. They screwed up with the antenna, but they've been working the network fixes for weeks now—they can tell us if we're completely off track. God, I hope we're completely off track."

Dori squirmed, bored by my anxious embrace, and I set her back down to explore the strange world of the dining room. I texted my parents, begging for help with Passover cleaning. **Bring Aunt Priya, too.**

And sent up a prayer that no one would decide they were too busy getting chametz out of the Bet to come over. Would it be too obvious if I asked the tech team for help with chores? "Carol, why don't you ask Redbug and Elegy if they want to come to our seder?"

"I'll do it. All who are hungry come and eat, even assholes."

Meanwhile, the cleaning really did need doing, and it was a good way to get my mind off our real troubles. I texted Rhamnetin sporadically, got no response, checked his records and found that he never came back online after the storm. Cytosine must have taken his palette and mesh. Maybe he was grounded, or confined to quarters, or whatever his cross-sister-slash-first-mother had the authority to do to him under Ringer law and custom. I should have thought to invite *them* before going home. I should have thought of a lot of things, but fevers are inconvenient that way.

Shut up, brain. I swept, occasionally relocating the kids away from the pile of dust and dog hair. Athëo and Carol moved the oven, groused about the floor underneath, made bad jokes about when goyim clean under the stove ("I'll tell you when I find out," Athëo said, the same as he had last year, even while he helped mop.) I discovered that we hadn't actually washed the tablecloth since Chanukah, and picked off candlewax before throwing it in the wash. Beeswax clung under my fingernails like garden dirt. Carol rounded up bread and crackers, informed Athëo that it all belonged to him, and he formally took possession. Dinar wandered downstairs and began chopping apples. Athëo lay down on the couch, announcing that being responsible for so much bread was hard work. Slowly the rhythms seeped into me. Here was one thing that would continue, in some form, for as long as humanity continued.

That night I paced the Chesapeake threads: useless habit, given my current expertise ratings, even if the algorithms had been doing their jobs. But I still wanted that kinesthetic sense of the watershed as a whole. It felt like a hike or a prayer, but deeper: knowing in my brain and belly and bones the rivers flowing silty with stormwater, every particle that washed from land into ocean, the health of the air that filled our lungs and the seagrass that held the bay in place. I wanted to work *with* the planet, to understand everything she told me. My mesh picked up on those desires, or my trend toward holistic processing, and shifted from text and numbers to graphics and textures, impressionist topography that felt more detailed than the details.

And amid that whole coherent system, the glaring discontinuity of the ansible, spilling waste signal from a center that we couldn't even detect. Close by, though, the *Solar Flare* was already putting out roots, chemical and energetic, thin threads of new connection.

Carol slept beside me. I shook her shoulder gently. "Carol, wake up."

She stretched an arm over her nose, Kyo-like. "Mmm-unh."

"We need to invite the Ringers to Passover. We need to show them."

"C'n we do it in the morning?"

"Yes, but how? They're not talking to us."

Carol blinked, bleary-eyed. "Are they really not taking messages?"

"Not from anyone in the network. Unless Cytosine calms down tomorrow, we can't get to them through any official channel."

She closed her eyes again. "Ask Adrien, and they'll hear about it. Those people can't *not* talk about a party, right?"

"They can not-talk about anything if it benefits them. And I don't want to end up with Adrien but no Rhamnetin."

"Okay, okay. Put a message in a basket in the river? It's thematic."

"We'd notice. They wouldn't. As far as I know they haven't dropped a single sensor."

Carol was quiet for a long time, and I thought she'd fallen back asleep. I probably should try as well; it wasn't like I was getting anywhere awake.

"What *are* they picking up?" she asked at last. "They're not sitting out there holding their noses and closing their eyes. They have to be reading *something* about their environment."

"They're normally zooming around in space, so—radiation, collision risks, gravity. And our communication signals—everything we send out into space instead of hiding it in cables. Old-fashioned cell networks, broadcasts . . ."

Carol pushed herself up abruptly. "Radio!"

I caught my breath, then held it as Dori fussed in her sleep. She quieted, and it was safe to talk again. "Radio. That, we can do."

Carol lay back down. "In the morning." But she was smirking, and I couldn't blame her. Now we just had to hope the right people were listening, and that whoever was listening cared enough to hear.

CHAPTER 35

Our first thought was to slip something in alongside the NPR legacy transmission. But I couldn't find a contact there, and I didn't care to mess with the station or have that many listeners.

"We can use the sweater swarm," said Carol, "but we'll have to go out to Bear Island. It's a weak signal." Dinar, now completely swamped in the kitchen, told us we could go as long as we were back well before sunset, and as long as we took both kids. Raven, once tempted away from the crumbs of broken meringues, was happy for the adventure.

"Baby bug?" they wanted to know.

"Maybe," I said. "It depends how mom bug feels."

"Sad mom bug?"

"Angry mom bug, I think." Their face scrunched, forehead wrinkling in preface to a wail, and I hastened to add, "Not at you, kiddo."

Then again, maybe Raven was right. Cytosine had thought we were finally following her script—or more charitably, finally moving toward the outcomes that would make her once-in-a-dozen-lifetimes mission successful—and then, from her perspective even more than ours, everything had gone wrong. It was the sort of thing that blurred the boundary between sadness and anger, regardless of species.

The sweater swarm, you should understand, was more alliterative than literal. Dinar wanted it wearable most of the year, so the yarn twisted sensor-compatible smartthread with one of those new materials that kept air moving near the skin with tiny cilia; the weave was light and the design sleeveless. In artistic commentary on the value of retro nostalgia, each sweater was knitted with the bright, pixelated image of some holiday item: a menorah, a dreidl, bright yellow latkes. I didn't have to speculate about whether this commentary had been intentional, because Carol had been very amused with herself.

The swarm also included an extremely functional, and similarly old-fashioned, set of radio transmitter/receivers. (Carol called them, unironically, "Vingean.") Normally they were meant for entertainingly anachronistic communication between sweater-wearers, but it would be easy to up the gain and send a message to other nearby pickups.

"We're not trying to be subtle, I hope?" she asked. We certainly weren't keeping a low profile on the train, two moms wearing sweater-vests emblazoned with images from the wrong holiday, Raven bouncing in their seat and pressing their face against the window, Dori crying because I wouldn't put her down to crawl in the crowded car.

"I hope not," I said, though the idea of sending a private message to Rhamnetin was appealing. It also wasn't practical. "The problem is getting noticed and acknowledged in the first place."

"Just checking."

I thought we'd have to call a ride for the last leg, but for a wonder there were two bikes with sidecars available—which Raven loved and Dori hated, but we were able to get as far as the causeway to Bear Island under our own power. There, unfortunately, we discovered that we were not going to get farther under anyone's power. The Potomac surged in Afia's wake. The path lay under a foot of rushing water, along with a beaver's toolbox worth of branches and brush.

Carol scooped Raven up, forestalling their fascination with the current. "I'm pretty sure we're in range, if I turn the gain all the way up."

"It'll have to do."

The sweaters came to life in my lenses: signal reaching out into the void. The frequency where the Ringers had first contacted us sat quiet now, tuned to dead air.

I'd thought about that contact, staring ceiling-ward in the night. When the Ringers arrived they knew our languages, enough to have picked up the most frequent ones, and to pick the right one for their landing site. But they hadn't chosen to simply say, "We come in peace." Instead, they showed they understood culture as well as vocabulary. We couldn't do that with the Ringers' own stories, not yet. But we could tell them that we'd been listening too.

I didn't have a full crowd backing me this time, but I did have my family. So we began with our own well-loved songs and soundtracks. The climactic, high-energy vocals of the final episode of a years-long anime, the diplomatic feast that ended a war. Samples of a symphony gifted from one watershed to another. Songs about bridges and celebration and peace.

There was no response.

"They have to be listening, right?" I asked.

"I can't imagine Ytterbium *not* monitoring the airwaves. Should we go live?"

"Go ahead." Dori squawked as we shifted from music to the open mike. I hoped that was a good omen. Certainly it was the best greeting we could send Cytosine.

There was no pickup to lean into, aside from my own clothing; I spoke to the open air. "This is Judy Wallach-Stevens. I'm speaking for my household today, not for the Chesapeake. Tonight is a holiday for us, a night when we feast and tell stories in honor of freedom, and of making a better world—a better universe for everyone. We invite you to join us. Everyone is welcome. It's a holiday for asking questions, and for eating food that means something."

"Some of the food is good," put in Carol, "and some of it is very traditional."

"Yummy," said Raven helpfully.

I made a face at them both. "We say, 'All who are hungry come and eat.' We hope you will. We miss you."

We were packing up when the channel opened again, a quiet trickle of music. Flutes and violins, slow and gentle. I didn't recognize it.

"Well, fuck," I said. "Now would be a really good time to have more ears."

"No, wait," said Carol. "I think I know this one . . . damn it. I'll send it to Dinar; I swear it's something we watched together."

It was a slower ID than the first time. But the two of them were able to work it out: it was from an anime version of *Romeo and Juliet*—a version with a happy ending, which was promising. "There's a lot of repetition in the soundtrack, but I think this is a bit from the middle, when they're separated and trying to plan how they'll get back together. And they're urging each other to be patient, not jostle each other's families while they work things out."

I put Dori back into the sidecar, and dragged the bike out from the mud. "Right. Message received."

The rest of the day was a blur of preparation and guests. My parents arrived and fussed over me endlessly, then finally relieved the pressure by fussing over Dori's crawling. Aunt Priya, they swore, would get there before sunset. Carol's parents were celebrating with her sibling's household this year, and my sisters were working on forest restoration in the Amazon watershed, but Dinar's dads showed up and fell neatly into chopping apples. There was lamb to marinate, and nut roast to mix, and a batch of eggs to devil with fresh parsley from the garden.

Elegy showed up alone at about the point we were getting Raven to bed. She glowered from the doorway. "You don't really want me here." I hadn't—aside from whether I liked her, I'd hoped for Priya to show up first.

"Religious obligation," I said. "Come on in."

She came in, glowering at the now-clean dining room. She picked an olive, deliberately, from the tray of nibbles intended to tide us over until the feast—accepting hospitality in its most minimal available form. "Redbug thought the invitation was an excuse to argue again, and the rest of the team doesn't want anything to do with you lot either. What's this really about?"

Athëo was upstairs with Raven; I'd have to handle it. "What do you think Asterion is up to? With the malware, I mean."

This didn't improve her mood. "Sabotage, so they can take over the negotiations. It's working."

I resisted pointing out how much of that was her team's fault. "What's the end state?"

"Maybe the network breaking down again. Maybe just shitty message transmission, algorithms spitting out nonsense, whatever it takes to make it impossible to use."

"Suppose it starts working smoothly again—but it works the wrong way?" I leaned forward. "Would we catch that? The algorithms are supposed to reflect our values, and shift as we teach them what those values are, and make sure we take those values into account even when decisions get stressful. But we trust them. Athëo got the idea last night, and we couldn't let go—would we be able to tell if the network settled down shaped by corporate values instead of our own? Or would we just think, sometimes bad decisions happen?"

Elegy whistled quietly. "We *didn't* think of that." Wryly: "And you don't consider it just as paranoid as what you accused *us* of?"

"That's what I'm trying to figure out. It's why I asked you—I *know* we disagree on all sorts of things, but I'm pretty sure our basic values are the same. We can't discuss this through a compromised network, but we can do it here. Thread on this horrible idea until we work out whether it makes sense, without any algorithms to facilitate or get in the way. I'd like more experts in the room, but this is what we've got."

"Yeah. Okay." Elegy leaned back, eyes closed like you do when you need to track your own thoughts more closely. I suspected she was still glaring behind her lids. "Part of why we believed them, about the antenna, was that we couldn't find code in situ that would break the network permanently. Everything we found was short-term, scripts that would run for a while and then erase themselves. Shit, that could work. Incremental shifts, every one leaving the temperature just a little higher. You wouldn't need much more than we've found already."

"I wanted to be wrong."

When Elegy opened her eyes, her glare had dissipated. Worry replaced it, a gentler expression. "I'm glad you told me. I'll stay for your holiday; I need to compost this a few hours before I tell the others and we dive back into the code. I don't want to rush in half-cocked again."

CHAPTER 36

Aunt Priya arrived scant minutes before sunset—long enough to get the shortest possible version of our fears directly from Athëo, and to make some justified but tactless remarks to Elegy. But as we lit the candles, all our guests were human. The whole second table, stretching into the hallway, sat empty. We'd done everything we could.

"We thank you for protecting us and enabling us to reach this season." My favorite prayer, at every holiday, but this time I shivered at the thought of seasons to come.

We took turns with the prayers and readings, passing them around the table. Carol was next: "All that you touch, you change. All that you change, changes you." A more recent addition from the Bet's interfaith seder, and the part that convinced Athëo this particular ritual was worth joining. And even more appropriate now than any year I could remember. I couldn't say it was more comforting than the traditional words, but then it wasn't meant to be.

Dinar lifted the seder plate with its crowd of symbolic foods, explained them all—ritual to the rest of us, new to Elegy. She proved she knew something of the holiday by asking questions: Was the egg ever eaten, why did we draw patterns on the orange? In a couple of years Raven would be old enough to ask the formal, required questions as the youngest child. Tonight it might in fact be Elegy. It should've been someone else. Most of the *Solar Flare* crew I'd hoped for on an abstract, diplomatic level, but I wanted Rhamnetin fiercely and couldn't imagine how we'd fix this without him.

We were past the first cup of wine, joking about the bread of affliction (for the record, Dinar's home-baked matzoh is really good), when there was a knock on the door. Carol and I both jumped up, and Dori, awake again and crawling under the table, made a beeline for the foyer.

"Elijah's early," Dad announced, deadpan, and I opened the door and flung my arms around Rhamnetin's nearest leg.

"You made it!" said Carol. "We were so worried, are you okay?"

Fuzzy limbs crept around my back. "I'm okay. Probably in even more trouble than I was, though—both of us." That's when I noticed the plains-person behind him, eyes twitching nervously. "Glycine helped me sneak out."

"You're both welcome."

They came in, and there was shuffling while we set a couple of chairs together for Rhamnetin to drape over, and extended one of the cushy chairs with an ottoman for Glycine. Glycine, I saw, still had their pronoun badge from their first visit.

"Why on this night do we recline on pillows?" deadpanned Dinar, and Carol and I snickered.

"Sorry," I said between giggles. "It's just—this is a very old ritual, and some parts have changed more than others. There are four specific questions you're supposed to ask, and there's one about leaning on cushions, which most people don't actually do these days. So here you are to lean on cushions for us!"

"There's our symbiosis," suggested Carol.

"Bringing more meaning to our rituals is a real part of symbiosis," said Glycine. I listened, hoping to understand. The deepest exchange I'd ever had with them was that one odd conversation the night of the storm. I felt a rush of connection, glad that the things we could offer had mattered to them. Whether or not the relationship between our family and Rhamnetin's followed either culture's scripts, Glycine's presence seemed to open up the promise that there *would* be a relationship.

"So what's all this about?" asked Rhamnetin. "There wasn't much bandwidth in your invitation." He paused at our expressions. "Is that one of the questions?"

"Not one of the four," said Carol, "though you're definitely taking care of those tonight. It's what the distracted child asks, though, in one of the stories."

"And then what happens?" asked Rhamnetin.

"Then we tell the story," said Dinar. "Passover is a holiday about freedom from slavery, but also from the things that hold us back from our full selves, and from oppression that keeps any human— any sapient—from being free."

And then we told stories: the traditional ones and the ones that interrupted the traditional ones, and stories that grew from questions about other stories. This would clearly be one of the years we ran past midnight, but even before the feast there were olives and cheese and deviled eggs, and Raven was asleep upstairs with a full belly, and Dori curled against my chest, and candlelight flickered over so much of my family all in one place, and the windows lay open to the spring breeze. Mint drifted into the dining room from the foyer. The moment was itself and it was years of moments spiraling, becoming something new each time we sang these songs and asked these questions.

"The wandering sounds hard," said Glycine.

"We've done too much of it," I said. Explanations came more easily tonight. "It's good to live in a time when we *have* a home we can love. Someplace we can afford to grow attached to. To be forced to leave a place you love—as a people, we know exile far too well." And the lesson of history was that it always happened, eventually. A paradox: you could always do something to hold off the bad times, but you could never hold them off forever. Maybe this time? Long enough, at least, to get the world to a point where it could survive the badness?

"We're not trying to exile you," said Rhamnetin.

"*You* aren't." Glycine said it before I could. "But many of us believe you have to drag people out of a burning building, whether they love the building or not. The question is whether Earth is burning."

"It's burning," Athëo said, and shrugged under half a dozen glares. "Well, it's true. But we're getting the fire under control. It's a matter of whether you trust us to know the resilience of our own home, whether you treat us as adults who can calculate our own risk rather than kids who don't know any better."

"What do *you* need?" I asked. "To be free, I mean? What choices do you have to be able to make for yourselves? Is that part of being free for you, or of being home?" And a question I couldn't quite get off my tongue: Did they in fact think of themselves as free? Did they value freedom, and were there things they valued more?

Was that one of the things they argued about?

"That's a hard question," said Rhamnetin.

"High praise, coming from you," I said.

"High praise coming from anyone. I don't think you have a single word"—Rhamnetin said something in his own language, a rising and falling chord—"but it means questions where the answers help people see all the branches around them. Map questions, maybe? Like the posts that start a new thread on the network. Those are what we need to be free together. I'm not sure what it means to be free as a single person—I don't know if that's a meaningful concept.

We make our decisions together, like you do, even if we don't use the same methods."

"It looks to me like Cytosine makes the decisions," said Carol.

"Cytosine's terrified of how much we're carrying," said Glycine. "But she's always been a little high-handed. You have people like that too." Eyes swiveled to Elegy.

"Mm," said Elegy, and I suspected under other circumstances that would have been, "Because other people make stupid decisions."

"Deciding together doesn't mean deciding the same thing for everyone," I pointed out. "Different watersheds use different conservation methods, and make different trade-offs. We have different ideas about what's absolutely necessary for a good life. Some places have foods they aren't willing to part with, or celebrations that are a bit wasteful."

"Most neighborhoods squish their carbon budget into ridiculous shapes to get one good yearly fireworks display," Mom put in.

"I wish you could see our fireworks," said Glycine. "They're spectacular, big enough to watch from dozens of habitats at once."

Dinar laughed. "Beautiful explosions must be a universal art form."

Rhamnetin shrugged, bobbing on his chairs. "Fire is the first step toward technology. Who wouldn't make art with it?"

"And now," said Dinar in her moving-on-with-the-ritual voice, "we drink the second cup of wine."

We drank the wine, and washed each others' hands—and other grasping appendages—in a bowl of rosewater, and began at last to bring out the feast. I thought about putting Dori in the downstairs bassinet so I wouldn't have to eat around her, but I didn't want to wake her up. So Carol served slices of lamb onto my plate, and a piece of nut roast, and mushrooms and spiced broccoli and quinoa pilaf and both kinds of charoset, and I was glad nursing gave me the appetite to eat so much.

"Freedom is complicated," said Athëo after a few bites, "but in the exodus story Moses makes it sound very simple. There's forty years of wandering in the desert ahead, but all he says up front is 'let my people go.'"

"We've used that language other times, too," said Aunt Priya. "That same demand, with wars or laws or fenceline fights to back it up when we don't have a plague-bearing deity behind us."

"What I'm saying," persisted Athëo, "is it may not be that particular demand, but it needs to be that clear. We need to articulate what we want in a simple way that everyone can understand, that no one can deny."

"Pharaoh doesn't actually listen to Moses," pointed out Aunt Priya. "Neither does anyone else, not without some sort of force to put a point on it. Is that what we need, now?"

Everyone looked at Elegy, who'd obviously thought so. She didn't answer, of course, and I just said, "I hope not. Not with the Ringers, at least."

"Cytosine *can* listen to reason," said Rhamnetin. "I swear you'll get to see her do it one of these cycles."

Maybe the knock on the door shouldn't have surprised me, this time.

"You think?" Glycine asked Rhamnetin, and I looked at Dori and figured it was my job to answer.

It was, sure enough, Cytosine. By herself except for her own kids, which was interesting.

"Please come in," I said. I resisted pointing out that she was late. "We're so glad you could make it."

Her eyes shifted as she tried to look behind me. (Not too difficult, since as previously mentioned the second table stuck into the entry hall.) "Rhamnetin, I expected this from you. Glycine . . ."

Glycine didn't move from the table. "I give way to you in many things, but your anger shouldn't shape everything we do on this world. And keeping Rhamnetin inside when you couldn't even name his transgression, just because you were mad at his cross-lovers—it's a failure to reach out, and not one you'd be happy with later."

"I don't need you to be my voice on the next branch."

"Please come in," I said again. If the argument moved into the house, she'd be a step further from leaving, and from forcing Rhamnetin and Glycine to leave with her. "This is one of our most sacred holidays, and we have a religious obligation to feed everyone who shows up."

"They've been talking about it all night," said Rhamnetin. "It's a holiday about escaping to better places and asking questions. You'll like it. There's more, isn't there, after we're done eating?"

"We go late with these things," I agreed, laughing at his eagerness.

Athëo stood abruptly. "Raven's crying."

"Baby please?" piped up one of Cytosine's kids. I had no idea when they slept; maybe they were as bad with schedules as Dori.

"We'll see," I said. For the third time, hoping there was some magic to it, "Please come in. Join us, and we'll talk."

She crossed the threshold, and I breathed relief. And stopped, as she said, "Elegy the technical expert. I recognize you. You tried to destroy the antenna."

I hadn't told her Elegy's name—she must have learned it from one of the Asterion team. They'd have footage from the prefab where we'd sheltered, of course.

"I did," said Elegy. "Judy thinks we were wrong about how Asterion was using the antenna, and if that's true I apologize. I thought I was protecting my own home—and if I was, I'd do it again."

"That's a half-assed apology," said Dinar quietly. I couldn't imagine she'd forgiven Elegy for calling her a corporate shill.

"No," said Elegy firmly. "It's a contingent one."

Carol went around to the head of the table and leaned down to hug Dinar around her shoulders. Dinar took a long, shuddering breath, and let it out. "I'm sorry, Elegy. I shouldn't have snapped." More generally, to the table: "We invited all of you, and you're all welcome. Cytosine, please join us, and we'll tell you the story you missed. We can always get back to our old arguments tomorrow." Without waiting, she segued into a summary of the exodus story while putting together another heaping plate of food, and Cytosine was no more capable of overcoming her social momentum than most humans.

Eema texted me: **I'll bet your co-parent is a star at moderating meetings.**

Athëo came back with Raven, who was rubbing their eyes but chanting, "Baby bug, baby bug, baby bug!" They squealed when they spotted the objects of their determination, and the two Ringer kids scrambled to the floor calling their name in return. Dori woke up and yelled until I gave up and put her down too. Kids are never good at linking their biorhythms to planetary cycles, and at this point it seemed like a lost cause. And it kept Cytosine here—it might even remind her why she thought we were worth working with in the first place.

"When your species met for the first time, what did you do?" I asked. "Did you demand changes from each other right away? Or did you take time to learn and talk and play first—to earn trust and understand where you were starting from?"

"We were very confused, mostly," said Rhamnetin. "We'd never seen anything like them. But we knew they were people, and we recognized their tools as tools, like ours but better."

"We wanted to tell them everything," said Cytosine. "But we were afraid we'd be mistaken for something supernatural, or that we'd hurt them. You have examples of that in your history, just as we do—isolated populations sharing plagues when they meet, accidentally even if not deliberately. We didn't want to bring that bloody history to a new world."

"There was time for learning and talking," said Glycine, "but there was also careful negotiation. We came to symbiosis slowly, and with very patient guidance from the tree-folk. We're a competitive species, but their sisters must tend their brothers so carefully, and it's not exactly like parenting. They knew how we could use our head start to lift them up instead of exploiting the advantage, and they explained it until we understood."

"I think all species must be capable of both ways of thinking," said Carol. "You need competition *and* cooperation to survive."

"Different species find different balances," said Rhamnetin. "You can argue about how much that balance is shaped by what comes 'naturally' and what's learned, and whether it's possible to untangle those. And of course, I'm naturally a diurnal fruit-chaser who's used to a *much longer day,* did I mention that your planet turns too fast, and here I am up late into the night with my system artificially shifted, because I like talking to people and eating eggs more than I like living on a sensible schedule."

Athëo nodded. "Humans might fall more on the side of competition. We kill, and we pollute, and we stick each other in horrible little boxes based on biology and pseudobiology and the raw ugly desire to force obedience. We've fallen so deep into those urges that we can't tell whether they're natural or not—but it doesn't matter, because we're also learning how to climb out. And one of the biggest things we've learned is to never tell other people what they have to be. Even when it seems like the answer should be obvious, we ask, and we keep asking."

"Are you sure you're not Jewish?" I asked.

"Like that," said Athëo. "And yes, I'm sure. Cytosine, that's the kind of relationship we want with the Ringers. The kind where we ask, and respect each other's answers. Where we know that the answers will lead to more questions, but won't ever lead to force even when we don't like them."

This time, I ducked my head and kept quiet. I hadn't always been great at those things, even when I wanted to be. I felt a surge of gratitude toward Athëo. Our kids would have what he'd lacked: someone to speak and live those truths *because* he knew what it was like to live without. *I* had that now, and maybe eventually I'd learn something from it.

Cytosine wasn't great at this stuff yet, either. "It's not a matter of disliking the answers. It's a matter of what's right. You don't respect Asterion, or let them do whatever they want, because you think their answers are dangerous and wrong."

"Okay, yes, we do keep people from destroying the planet," said Carol. "I dare you to tell me what harm we're doing by staying here and saving it, instead of meekly accepting the exact relationship that you planned for us. Humans who want to go with you can go— though I'd warn you against ingesting corporate philosophies, or letting them spread. Space stations don't have *less* need for conservation than a planet."

Cytosine's eyes went rigid. "At least Asterion doesn't believe in perpetual motion machines!"

"They don't what?" Aunt Priya, and several other people, stared at her.

Cytosine's eyestalks relaxed marginally as she tried to articulate what had infuriated her. "When they need more resources, they're willing to go to the places where those resources *are*. They don't constrain themselves to a closed system and expect that to work forever. On one world, pulling in a fraction of your sun's energy, your civilization's limits will only get tighter and tighter. There's no fitting yourself in a shrinking hole."

I tried to hold back knee-jerk frustration myself, to understand the trap she'd imagined. "It's not that we need to limit ourselves to Earth forever—or even that everyone needs to stay here now. But we have no intention of abandoning our world while we're still learning with it."

"And corporations do believe in perpetual growth," added Aunt Priya. "It's what makes them so dangerous. No matter how far you expand, there are limits you can't escape."

Athëo leaned forward, intent. "Let's stop focusing on the flaws in each other's systems, just for a moment. Can you imagine what we could share with each other, without demanding the sacrifice of all that came before? Without preconceptions about what shape we have to fit into? This is such an opportunity. There's art and music and all our different ways of thinking about the universe. You know things about using resources efficiently and building stable structures that we have no clue about, and the things we've discovered in repairing our world could transform your habitats."

"He's right," said Rhamnetin. "I've seen it. There's room for a connection here, but we need to be open to it taking unexpected forms. Humans aren't exactly like either of the first two rings—if they were, imagine how little we'd gain."

Raven toddled over, waving a ragged copy of *Bonnie Bumblebee's New Dance*. "Bug book!"

"Not now, sweetie," I said reluctantly. "I'm having a grown-up conversation."

"I'll get it," said Dinar. "You all keep talking—divide and conquer, right?" I watched her settle in the side chair with three kids trying to fit in her lap. She ended up with Diamond and Raven each leaning against one of her shoulders and Chlorophyll half-draped on her lap, one eye poking over the book to see the pictures. I felt again that surge of connection.

"They'll figure it out," I said, "if we give them the time."

Glycine's eyes shifted between the table and Dinar, and Rhamnetin shuffled. Cytosine said, "They're exactly why we can't abandon you to your chosen limits. In your story, some of the Israelites must have been reluctant to leave the place they knew—would leaving them behind have been right for their children?"

"They were slaves!" said Carol.

Cytosine ignored the distinction. "One of my ancestors wanted to stay on her homeworld. She wrote about it, she argued publicly for cycles. But when enough habitats were ready to fit everyone, the plains-folk brought her anyway, and I'm grateful beyond expression that they did. I wouldn't exist otherwise."

"None of us would exist without a thousand ancestral decisions, good and bad and ugly," I said. "That's doesn't make every one of them right." But I felt sick, imagining how hard it would be to convince Cytosine with that as her family story. I imagined her ancestor's grief.

"You approve of your ancestor's enslavers," said Elegy, "because they made your life more convenient. Fuck you."

Cytosine's eyes swiveled to Elegy. "Do you really want to have this fight at a holiday feast? You tried to strand my crew on this world. That makes you a slaver by your own definition. The last time the Rings used forced labor was almost a thousand years ago, when one last holdout subculture discovered what a bad idea it is to make unwilling workers build a habitat. Your own story says that there are places it's impossible to be free—ours says there are places where it's impossible to keep slaves."

"Huh." I had to think about that. "I wonder if the corporations would have more trouble exploiting their own labor, or if they'd be able to talk people into it. Maybe I'm cynical, but I lean toward the latter. Adrien swears sui'd rather get exploited and 'play the game' than do without it." Nor had life in space stopped the Ringers from carrying on with all sorts of fucked-up hierarchies. It might be a mix. There were real places in human history where new technologies, new societal forms, had made freedom easier to achieve—and others where those things had created new chances for authoritarian control. I wondered what kinds of nastiness their habitats really did forestall and what kinds they just called by nicer names. Maybe we could help them find what they'd missed.

We wound down to gentler topics, sang songs, and finished the ceremony at last. "Next year in Jerusalem," we said, and that part had never meant much to me, born to a culture that considered all places sacred—but now I thought about that one sacred place as practice for loving the whole planet, for learning to share without letting go.

We passed around meringues and preserved figs and a tray of chocolate toffee matzoh. All the kids but Dori fell asleep on the couch with Kyo, a puppy pile of multi-limbed stalk-eyed plains scuttlers curled around a long-legged, flat-faced plains ape and a domesticated wolf.

Ultimately all the Ringers stayed the night. Cytosine, at the ragged end of her forcibly extended biorhythm, slept on the carpet next to the kids, rolled up tight with limbs flattened against her skin. Dinar dozed in a chair, and the Bet crowd and Elegy returned to their homes. The rest of us stayed up doing dishes and cracking jokes that probably made equally little sense to all three species. We deposited Glycine in the guest room, and Rhamnetin sacked out at the foot of Carol's and my bed and we made our own puppy pile for the remainder of the night. Once when Dori cried, no diaper alarm evident, I woke to see his leg stretched to the bassinet, stroking her back until she quieted.

"Come back to the ship," Cytosine said the next morning. Dinar was, remarkably, up and making matzoh brie, a great contribution to interplanetary diplomacy if ever there was one. "I'll . . . consider how to treat with the watershed networks as a whole; for now I'm inviting you as a family. It will give us more time to talk."

"Thank you," I said. It wasn't what we'd wanted, but it was a break-through nevertheless. I tried not to think about how much it placed on our shoulders, and what it would mean if we couldn't ultimately convince her to keep the watersheds in the negotiations. I posted an update and request for suggestions to the network. I let out a breath when it appeared to post, but copied the request to the common thread all the same.

"Our own backup is arriving today," Cytosine went on, and my thoughts froze again. I hadn't expected a response to their SOS so soon. I hadn't processed that a trip by interstellar tunnel wouldn't take much longer than traveling to Zealand.

"That was quick," said Rhamnetin.

"*Elliptical Orbit* was waiting by the transit point. No one would authorize them to come through until they heard from us, but they were ready to mount a rescue mission as soon as they heard there was any possibility of success."

There was only one thing to say, even as I scrambled to warn the watersheds. "We'll be honored to meet them."

CHAPTER 37

All six of us went back in the shuttle with Cytosine and Glycine and Rhamnetin. If we were all the hands the network could have in the ground, we'd be there, though our current weighting meant we were hardly the network's ideal. They were welcome to send other ambassadors and try to get them inside—hell, we'd argue for it as well as we could.

Below us, the land lay mottled by storm. Fallen trees, scattered leaves, debris of all sorts: the familiar and smooth-worn corners of our resilience. For the Ringers, though, planetary hazards were a thing out of legend. They exclaimed over the view as if it had been scorched by a dragon.

The *Solar Flare* was clean now, dirt and plastered leaves swept away. From above it shimmered, fractal folds shifting beside the rush of the swollen Potomac.

Carnitine met us outside, followed by a good handful of the rest of the crew. "You're late—they're in orbit already!"

Rhamnetin sounded bemused. "Sodium does everything in a tearing hurry."

"She competed with us for this mission," said Cytosine. Eyes and limbs waved toward us. "Perhaps she thinks it'll be hers now."

"The problem," said Carnitine, "is that there are no other good landing sites on the island. We could take down the antenna and send them to that site, or direct them farther away still—but what she wants is to mate the ships."

"I'll bet she does," said Cytosine.

"Let me guess," I said, feeling my way through. "That's as fraught as the real thing?" But Cytosine was a nursing mother, and presumably so was this other competitor for the honor of contacting Earth . . . "There's no risk to the kids, is there?"

A trace of amusement crept into Cytosine's voice. "We're not barbarians. But you aren't completely off base; a few centuries ago there might have been. Risk to the mission, on the other hand . . . Judy, what's the nearest place they could land, other than the antenna lot?"

I thought of a couple options. "You'd need to ask someone with the authority to speak for the Chesapeake."

Rhamnetin snickered, and even I could recognize Cytosine's equivalent of a glare. But I hoped her anger would give way before her desire to keep control of the situation.

"I actually think—" said Carnitine. "That is, they've been waiting by the transit point for any hint of trouble, like I said earlier. They have plenty of resources loaded, but they didn't prep for the specific repairs that we need."

"Meaning we go back mated to them," said Cytosine. "Or we wait for a more patient rescuer."

"Sodium's tendency to prioritize dominance wrestling over optimized solutions is exactly why she *didn't* get the mission," said Ytterbium.

"Invite them down in our name," I suggested. "Tell them we're glad they're here to support you."

"You'd need to speak for the network to do that, wouldn't you?"

"They'll back us," I said, hoping it was true. Even now my lenses filled with argument: back Cytosine and bring her around to supporting us again, or take a chance with this new leader who might like us better than she did. I ticked a vote on the former, and added: **This newcomer's status games remind anyone of Asterion?** "But you'd have to acknowledge that we represent more than ourselves."

"Very well. As long as none of my people object." That surprised me: Had others on the ship argued against us? Until now, everyone had made it sound like Cytosine's decision ruled alone. But it would've been easy enough to misread. Even now it was hard to read whether she really thought anyone would object, or was leaning on formality, or was just spreading the responsibility around. "Carnitine, you send the message to her cross-sisters; that will make it even more obvious that this isn't about relative status between first mothers."

We waited on the cliff. We'd captured no recordings of the *Solar Flare* landing, and had no idea what to expect. A cloud grew slowly, glinting silver. I might have missed it if I hadn't been primed to watch for something, and then I couldn't have missed it. The shimmering mass dropped slowly, weightless, and shaped itself to settle atop the *Solar Flare* like stacked blocks. It was smaller, and brighter, and despite the perfect fit obviously of a different make. Bands of etched silver delineated its curves, and it was domed rather than spired. Jointed extensions unfolded like spider legs to grasp the larger ship beneath.

"Let's go back in," said Cytosine.

Inside, the crew of the *Solar Flare* mingled with human guests from both Asterion and the United States. Walls I hadn't known were movable had withdrawn to make room for the crowd. Even with the extra space we jostled each other; Rhamnetin swung Raven up so they could get a better view. He earned stares for that, and I was glad he'd grown comfortable enough to need no one's permission but Raven's. Someone's limb brushed my hand with a momentary jolt of skinsong. Before I could decide whether the contact had been deliberate I found myself pinned by Jace's narrowed eyes. (*Probably tania,* an algorithm reported.)

"What are *they* doing here?" she asked.

"They brought their children," said Glycine.

"What they did to us—what they did to you—"

"Was done by others, not by this household," said Rhamnetin firmly. "This is not your ship; Cytosine decides who's welcome." It was well played—with a threat to her power hovering above, he made us a bulwark for Cytosine rather than another threat.

On the other side of the room, Viola St. Julien frowned at us as well, looking more worried than angry. Her spouse, suit rumpled, put his arm around her and said something soothing to Brice. Adrien hadn't noticed me yet; I followed eir anxious glance and found Brend and Tiffany perched in a sort of hammock slung from a tree, chatting with Astatine above the press of the crowd. Kelsey and Mallory were deep in conversation with Phenylalanine. *Everyone* was here to greet the newcomers.

In one of the walls, a hatch unfurled. A tree-person came through, followed by one of Cytosine's people. Like their ship, they wore bands of metal: the tree-person around the spaces between mouth-and-pincer sets, the plains-person in a rainbow of colors at the base of each limb. The plains-person—presumably Sodium—carried a child a little larger than Cytosine's twins, and the tree-person had one of the pet lizard-things clinging to one knee-shoulder. It spotted Luciferin's pet and yipped excitedly before being hushed.

The crowd parted for Carnitine to step forward. "Carbon-14, you're welcome to the *Solar Flare*—and to Earth. Sodium, we welcome you and Bronze as well. Thank you for being so ready to come to our aid."

"We've been waiting anxiously since you went through the portal," said Sodium. One of the translation boxes produced English a split second behind her native speech—however eager they'd been for the contact assignment, they hadn't prepared as thoroughly as the *Solar Flare*. "These opportunities are so rare, and so many things can go wrong. We're glad we were in a position to meet your need."

Introductions followed Ringer custom: children first, their care-givers second, and others third. It was an advantage for us, and for NASA. The Asterion team's discomfort was readable only in a slight stiffening, then too-casual relaxation as they made their bows.

It was Cytosine, who only a couple of days ago had rejected our embassy, who'd very carefully ensured that we'd be here for this meeting, kids in tow, in a situation where she could be pushed into accepting us again as watershed reps. Had the seder really changed her mind so thoroughly, even more than she'd admitted to us, or was something else in play?

Or maybe I was thinking about her too politically. She *was* political—had to be, to handle this mission—but normally if a lov-er's family had been partial to us, it would've been no surprise at all.

Introductions done, people began to disperse, and we had more breathing space. Adrien had taken advantage of their late introduc-tion to draw Carbon-14 into immediate conversation; her lizard-thing had clambered onto eir shoulder, which had to be some sort of sign of approval. Raven tugged Athëo toward their usual playmates, and I joined Viola St. Julien and Sodium.

The plains-person rocked back in a Fibonacci spiral and tilted her eyes. "Does your polity really insist that humans remain on a single planet? Everyone at home is worried about you."

That seemed intrusive, but I could imagine it. "We don't want humans to abandon Earth—and we believe that our species will do better in space when we've learned better how to cooperate with our own ecosystem. But we're eager to learn from you, and to share our own wisdom." Rhamnetin had followed, and slipped a limb around to embrace me and stroke Dori's hair. It was as much a diplomatic move as an offer of reassurance, and I appreciated it on both counts.

"Some of us are more eager to see the Rings," said St. Julien. In her eyes I read a flicker of guilt. "And more eager to start building a fu-ture offworld. But we'll still need to negotiate treaty terms. The U.S. has always been happy to ally with other polities, but we've worked hard to retain our sovereignty."

These caveats Sodium seemed more comfortable with. "You'll be interested to see how the habitats interact, then. There's always tension between local governance and the things that must be decided by the Rings as a whole."

"In some ways," put in Carol, "your system sounds more like what the dandelion networks do. So much has to be coordinated if we want to stabilize the planetary ecology, but every watershed is unique in the specific solutions it uses. And most practical decisions come down to the local level."

"It *will* be an interesting comparison," said Sodium.

Sometimes you sense a change only belatedly. Air pressure drops, clouds darken, petrichor rises from the garden, but you're caught up in distractions: then the first raindrops shock your neck and you realize the tempest.

The ship's gravity strengthened for a second, making me stumble. I sensed the change: the deepening pulse of machinery at the edge of hearing, electromagnetic auras that brightened my lenses and stirred the hair on my arms. More disturbing still were the plummeting bars of my network connection. "Rhamnetin, what's going on?"

His grip tightened and he stretched to grasp the vines that drooped around us. For a dizzy moment I thought of how he'd steadied me as he clung to swaying trees. "We're taking off. Sodium, did Cytosine give you permission?"

Sodium's limbs made a protective cage around Bronze. "I asked; she approved. We came to bring the *Solar Flare* back to the Rings for repairs, and that's what we're doing. Why are you surprised?"

"Because no one told *us*!" I said. "No one told our network. No one asked *our* permission. What the everloving fuck?"

Across the room Dinar grabbed Raven, who shrieked and flailed even as Dinar and Athëo made a beeline for us.

"Bring us back now," said Carol. Her voice had gone to bare steel. She moved closer to me, to Dori. "You want to be welcome in any watershed on the planet again, you bring us back right now."

"It's a mated starship, not a—" Sodium dipped her eyes, the rhythm of a bouncing ball, and said something that her box didn't translate. "Cytosine invited you."

"To the *ship*," I said.

Cytosine scurried over, limbs waving anxiously. Athëo stepped between us before our tempers could flare further. Very gently, he said, "Let's discuss this before the ship goes further."

"Come with me," said Cytosine, "please." She sounded more uncomfortable than I was used to, though that was hard to trust given that all her human intonation was consciously shaped. Then again, she'd never bothered dissembling her reactions.

"Is there any way to hold the ship in place while we talk?" he pressed. "At least stay near Earth?"

"The *Solar Flare* could do it," said Rhamnetin. "We're designed to change direction quickly, to turn wherever our cargo's needed. *Elliptical Orbit* is a slingshot carrier that drops into danger and pulls out fast. When it's released for return, it doesn't brake well."

"Please," repeated Cytosine.

We followed reluctantly, pressed close. Dinar clutched Raven's hand.

St. Julien interrupted us on our way out of the room. Ignoring everyone else, she told Cytosine, "I'm not leaving without seeing Earth from space. You promised."

"Every Reach in the Rings," said Cytosine, exasperated. "Fine. Come along."

St. Julien seemed to notice our moods for the first time. "You knew where we were going. Right?"

"No," said Dinar shortly, and St. Julien flinched. She must have suspected, and said nothing.

The *Solar Flare* had previously shown no hint of an outside view, but the room we now entered had miraculously bloomed either a window or a screen so clear and high-resolution that my head swam with vertigo. I stumbled over moss. Rhamnetin caught me and I steadied myself against him, wrapping my other arm around Dori. Raven squealed and ran forward to look. None of the Ringers seemed alarmed, so I resisted the temptation to call them back. St. Julien joined them only a little more sedately. Her hand rose to touch the invisible surface. I moved forward, dizziness fading, drawn by the view from above framed in golden leaves. Without thinking, I turned so Dori could see too.

Below us was Earth as I'd only seen her in images. We were pulling away all too rapidly, but I could pick out the Atlantic coast of North America, the indigo dendrites of the Potomac and the Hudson, the shredded spiral of Afia diffused over New England. My breath caught in my throat, and awe washed over anger. I suspect it felt that way for all of us, seeing our world like a prayer.

Well, all of us humans. The Ringers don't think much of planets.

"You would have said no," explained Cytosine. Our argument seemed suddenly incongruous, but she went on. "You persuaded me that we should keep the watersheds in the negotiations. We'd already invited the Asterion and NASA contingents to send emissaries. Even if you agreed to come, you'd have left your children behind. It would have been a disaster."

"I tell the humans that you're capable of listening to reason," Rhamnetin said to her. "I tell *you* that *they're* capable. But does anyone listen to me? My lovers aren't eggs to be stolen!"

"This isn't anything like egg-theft!" Cytosine was indignant.

"It shouldn't be! But you've taken their first trip to the Rings and turned it into an insult."

I tore myself from the view, and back to everything it meant. "Rhamnetin is right. How can you respect us enough to negotiate, but deny our input and consent? Do you really want to negotiate—or are you planning to force something else on us once we get to the Rings? How can we trust you now?" I turned on St. Julien and her spouse. "Can *you* trust them now? What will they do, when NASA's plans don't perfectly align with theirs?"

"A sister can make decisions for her new-hatched brothers, because she knows what they need to survive," said Cytosine.

Athëo glared, ticked off points. "We aren't 'new-hatched.' We aren't your little brothers, or your children. And we recognize colonial exploitation, no matter how it's dressed up." He took a deep breath, visibly trying to center himself. "This is an injustice by all our laws. If you want to be better than that, if you really want to negotiate, you need to start treating us as people worth listening to."

St. Julien wouldn't look at us, but said: "He's right. You're bigger than humanity and more powerful, and we can't force you to treat us as equals." She turned around. "So it's up to you to decide: Are you going to act like symbiotes, or parasites? Are you going to risk this mission going badly because you gave us the chance to screw up? Or are you going to risk it going badly because you convinced us that there was no hope of real cooperation—because you started a war that Earth can't win, but that the Rings can't come out of with your morals intact?"

Cytosine's eyes, and all her limbs, focused antenna-like on St. Julien. Then they dropped away, and she left without a word.

I blinked. "Well said," I told St. Julien. "Thank you."

"Holy shit!" She leaned against her spouse, who was watching her with admiration. "Holy shit!" She made a show of collapsing against her spouse, who was watching her with admiration. "If I never do anything else in my life, I've made a speech about human dignity to an alien leader. That's gotta count for something, right?"

"If she realizes you're treating her like one of those hyper-advanced *Star Trek* species that have forgotten what it means to 'be human,' none of us will ever hear the end of it," said Rhamnetin.

"Crap, has she seen *Quest of the Surak*?" asked St. Julien.

"I hope not. You have an abundance of broadcasts, and she particularly likes telenovelas."

Whatever decision Cytosine was going to reach, she hadn't made it yet, and there was nothing more for us to do just then. So we turned back to the window-screen, and watched Earth shrink to a pinprick.

CHAPTER 38

It *was* a short trip. As short as the shuttle flight to Zealand—Rhamnetin explained that they could only use the tunnel drive a certain distance from nearby gravity wells, so most of the trip was spent getting to that distance. The movement between star systems took almost no time at all.

It was the longest I'd been on the *Solar Flare* without either a specific goal or being too exhausted to think. I watched the foliage shift around our explorations, blooming interfaces and screens for Rhamnetin, and I started to get a sense of how it was its own sort of network. We used root systems and mycelial networks as models; the Ringers seemed to use them directly for sharing information and input. Was that one reason they valued simplified ecologies? Maybe we could learn from their work and grow our own networks amid complexity.

Brend and Tiffany came in to the window-screen room a few minutes before the shift. Tiffany gripped thos lover's hand; Brend looked scared but excited. Tiffany spoke as if daring us to object: "We heard there was a view in here."

"Everyone else hobnobbing?" I asked sharply.

Dinar put a hand on my arm. "It's a little overwhelming out there, I bet."

Brend shrugged. "I let Adrien take care of the social dance. I'm just here to figure out how the Ringers signal their steps."

"I thought your expertise was clothing design," I said.

"My expertise is social signaling. Though textiles are pretty amazing too, in terms of texture and material qualities. The Ringers have their own signs: pockets and sashes and that bioluminescent moss. They don't worry about temperature control, did you notice: everything they wear is either for carrying stuff or pure symbolism. Which I guess is what happens when you've had climate control for that many generations, plus they've amped up their internal temperature control the same way they adapt their day/night cycles. If we could get that tech, imagine how much more flexible our fashion design could be."

"Not to mention our ability to cope with summer temperatures," said Tiffany, "though you'd still need cooling for computers."

Brend went on before I could consider how fascinating that idea was: "The *Elliptical Orbit* crew uses a different symbol set—I think they're from a different culture. Maybe a different habitat? Astatine said some of those get pretty strange. Though who knows what Ringers think is strange."

I interrupted. "Jace di Sanya. Why is she *here*? You said you didn't want her faction along for the ride."

"We lost, what do you think?" asked Tiffany. "Adrien doesn't care much as long as e gets ahead, and Jace is the only Sanya here, and she outranks our whole delegation. She sure outranks the techies."

"She wants to burn the planet," I said. "She's going to find allies on the Rings."

"I heard a lot of people in Zealand complain about the fenceline restrictions," said Dinar. "But people like her are *why* those rules are necessary. Are those vicious games really the best input the corporations have to offer?"

Cytosine skittered in with Glycine and Luciferin behind, forestalling what might have been a productive conversation. I hoped they'd heard us. "It's time," she said. "I thought you'd want to see."

"And you wanted to get away from Sodium's wrestling?" asked Rhamnetin.

"That too."

Thanks to Dinar's anime I anticipated a spectral hole in space, a circle of rainbows, stars going to streaks—a drama of transition to make clear how thoroughly we'd broken Newtonian measurement. But we barely needed to steady ourselves: one moment Earth was a distant marble shining in the distant flare of the sun; the next moment a new sun bloomed before us, and we spun to watch it gleam off a patchwork of jewels and wirework scattering into starlight.

"This is the natural view," said Cytosine. "We can enhance it, if you like."

"Not yet." I moved closer to the screen. It felt unreal, like I might click away a layer and see how the special effects were done. I wasn't ready for extra data. "Let me just look."

The sun lay behind us now, its aura creeping around the edges of the screen. Before us the jewels grew slowly into a sky full of moons.

White moons and green, etched blue with rivers and lakes. Moons round and oblong, and spiderweb moons bright with metal. At the equator, a dense ring of habitats captured the power of their star. But above and below they sketched the outlines of the full sphere, promising room for trillions more Ringers, whoever built in that name in generations to come.

Dori twisted against my chest, staring, solemn as if she understood the magnitude of what she was looking at.

"How far out are we?" asked St. Julien.

"About a hundred million miles from the sun," said Glycine. "Almost halfway between the Rings and the First Ring's original planetary orbit. We'll dock in about six hours."

I thought about those distances, and tried to process what I was seeing. The closest "moons" looked about the same size as our own did from Earth, but we were half an orbit away. Those were oceans out there, not lakes, each ready to swallow Earth whole. I filed estimates along with my recordings: emotions held together by math, and math that might preserve some hint of the place's Olympian immensity. Or maybe a different myth would suit: a world tree, pendulous planets swinging from every twig. Filing data made the hope of reporting back—the promise of return to the Chesapeake, sudden light years away—feel real.

We had to decide how to pursue that hope. We could stamp our feet and yell about kidnapping, and demand immediate passage back to Earth. Safe, with our children safe alongside. But St. Julien, Jace, Adrien—none of them were likely to head home on the first available transport. They'd been ready for this trip, prepped for whatever negotiations awaited. Our own status was ambiguous and our preparation nonexistent, but we were all the watersheds had in the ground. We couldn't afford to waste the opportunity.

I looked at Carol, then at Dinar and Athëo. Carol was easiest to read. A shift in body language, a nod—and we were agreed. Not as happy as we'd been to stick around the *Solar Flare* with Dori for first contact, but some things were worth the risk, and this was still one of them.

Dinar's eyes shifted between the view and the corporate tech experts, then to Raven. She took a deep breath, touched Athëo's wrist. They looked at us, and something shifted as quick and subtle and huge as the trip between stars. We were one unit, maybe for the first time, a single network passing data eye to eye and finger to finger, deciding together. My heart sped, and I felt the shiver of tension across my arms, and I couldn't say whether it was excitement or fear.

Rhamnetin stroked my back. I was falling in love with him, but we didn't have that connection—not yet, maybe not ever. Could I ever learn him that well, without common physiology or instincts to back my desire? We could be lovers and friends, but what would it mean to become more? And what about the rest of his household? I liked Glycine, and thought we might have something to build on there. Some of the others I barely knew, and Cytosine . . . sometimes she seemed too much like me, sometimes too strange and discomfiting to understand. She reminded me of my parents, all grand gestures and idealistic drama. Building family was terrifying enough with humans.

Cytosine reared up to the screen, let her kids waggle their limbs against it. They chattered in the Ringer language.

"Bug house," said Raven happily, and then shocked me by making a noise that . . . didn't sound exactly like their Ringer friends' language, but sure sounded closer than anything I'd heard outside Athëo's half-coded translation algorithm. Maybe I was underestimating the power of sheer monkey curiosity to overcome barriers. Space has a way of making things feel distant.

Cytosine's eyes swiveled, and she said something else, and Raven said something else. "Your child has a talent for languages."

Athëo smiled wonderingly at Raven. "They come by it honestly."

We watched the view for a while, but even awe-inspiring vistas can only hold monkey attention for so long, and as my initial fury and fear ebbed I found more mundane things to worry about.

"Oh crap," I said. "How many *diapers* do we have?" This set off a few minutes of scrambling as we inventoried accoutrements for dealing with various inconvenient bodily fluids, discovered that the Ringers hadn't really processed either our regular changes of clothing or strong social expectation of wearing same, freaked out about being several light-years from the nearest hormonal implant refills, and decided that Kyo had enough on-call caregivers that we didn't need to worry about whether he'd get fed. Eventually Dori set to wailing; I checked the monitor and began unwrapping her. "I'm gonna need some of that laundry now. And something to pack out into. Look, more historic diaper changes—first one in this solar system. Oh no."

"What's wrong?" asked Carol.

"Chargers. Things to plug chargers into." My mesh would last a week if I didn't overuse it, but after that I wouldn't be able to record, or text anyone, or use any senses beyond the biological. "Oh god, *Dinar*."

"Yeah." Dinar sounded grim. Maybe she'd just thought of it too. "I don't have my arm charger with me—I was expecting to be back home this evening, you know—and it's a lot finickier than mesh."

"I can probably explain the current requirements for our mesh, at least," said Carol. "Electricity's electricity, there are only so many variations on how you can use it. Your arm, though . . ."

"Unless you can explain my whole nervous system to one of their tech experts, I doubt it. The charger is set to keep the same level of stimulation going through the nerves that it gets from my shoulder. Without matching that pattern, it turns into a cute lump of protoflesh that twitches all over the place. No thank you." Her expression tightened, tiny wrinkles shading her eyes. "What if one of us gets sick? What if one of the kids breaks a bone or gets an infected scratch? I'm sure Phenylalanine knows Ringer physiology backward and forward, but there's no one in this solar system who can do anything for humans beyond first aid."

"Look," said Cytosine. "If it were up to me, we'd have spent longer planning this. But Sodium has the propulsion. And the momentum, literal and otherwise."

"You said she does disaster response." I glared. "Does she know that people need to pack things?"

"She knows that in a real emergency, they do without. Which this isn't, but I suspect—I know—it feels like one to most of the Rings. This is the first time we've found a new species before it was too late, and it's easy to treat 'not too late' like a deadline." She picked up a squirming Diamond, put them back down when Raven tugged at their limbs. "You were right. Not trusting you to understand the importance of this trip—that was counterproductive. It was wrong."

"*Thank* you." I successfully resisted telling her all the reasons she'd been wrong, again, now that she'd admitted it. This wasn't the time for a rant. "So what can we do differently from here?"

She rocked back, tail curling into her belly. "Once the *Solar Flare*'s fixed, I'll bring you back. If you want. I think you should stay, but it's up to you."

"Could we just go back for a day or two?" asked Carol. "Pack a few things, consult with the network, and return better prepared?"

"Maybe? The triangulator blew because something about the

jump to your system pushed the ship's limits, and we still don't know exactly what it was. If it happens again, we'd have to call for another rescue—I'd probably lose our ship over doing the same stupid thing twice, and whoever came to get us might have their own ideas about who from Earth to bring into the talks. I'll take you home, if you ask—but I can't guarantee the ride back again."

"You'd risk your ship?" I asked.

She didn't speak, and it was Rhamnetin who said, "It's the right thing to do."

"We'll stay," I said, "for now. But thank you for giving us the option."

So we'd finally gained Cytosine's respect for our choices—just as we were about to meet billions who might feel no such thing.

The other human guests wandered into the viewing room, trailing members of both crews. Things got crowded, though we were able to keep space open for the kids to play. Brend stayed near them, unsurprisingly; e liked crowds about as well as Aunt Priya. E pulled out an intricate little cross-stitch, threaded gold and copper and carbon, and began working on it as babies frolicked around em. I watched Jace cozying up to Sodium, Adrien and Kelsey and Mallory working the room, St. Julien and her spouse playing Terran ambassadors for all they were worth. I watched the screen.

This time, trying not to think too hard about my battery life, I felt ready to add extra scans to my sensory input. I studied the spectrum of the light (sun a little younger than ours, same basic type, I'm not an astrophysics expert), read the greenery (probably chlorophyll-based photosynthesis, same as ours, supported by the kid's name), took standoff readings on the habitat atmospheres (oxygen a touch higher than Earth's, inert gas balance a little different but basically harmless, greenhouse gases concentrated in hotspots that Rhamnetin told me were reclamation plants). The mix varied, he explained, based on aesthetics and which original planet they drew their numbers from. The habitats varied in temperature, most of them livable, a couple teasing the high end of what humans could tolerate, at least one shockingly cold. Seasonal variation, maybe, or someone trying to preserve an old polar ecology. Everything here was centuries-old compromise, a mix of what people had thought worth salvaging from two lost worlds.

They say German has a long word for everything, but among the dandelion networks, plains-ache is the yearning for an evolutionary ecology you've never lived in yourself, the body's bone-deep knowledge of things that would make it not healthiest but happiest, that would feel right and quiet the anxiety-monkey behind your civilized forebrain. Walking for hours till you can feel it from spine to sole, a picnic with people you've known your whole life, a fresh-picked berry, a midday nap—a tiny taste of what your brain thinks it's good for. Sometimes those things are actively bad for us, like waiting for the big ape to yell about the latest emergency, but even that can feel like a surge of *home* as overwhelming as the smell of baking bread. What did Ringers ache for? How much of it was left, here among these compromise-design worldlets? How well did their reshaped metabolisms ease those instinctive desires?

Or had they learned to feed the ache with their forested ships? Maybe their artificial worlds fit them as well as a dandelion network, designed for long-term comfort rather than immediate reward. You could go pretty far from your home ecology and still be okay, if you understood what lay at your core.

CHAPTER 39

"Well, that's not ideal," Rhamnetin said.

"What's not?" several of us asked at once. We'd been holding position at what was probably, objectively speaking, an extremely large distance from the equatorial ring; habitats filled the viewscreen. The time supposedly allotted for our trip was long since up, Raven was sacked out on a moss-covered mound, the pack-out bag was swelling with diapers, and I was already sick of what passed for sanitary facilities on the *Solar Flare*. Not everything, it turns out, works better when integrated with plant life.

"We're going to Pulsar 18."

"That's a problem?" I asked.

"Pulsar 18 is the *Elliptical Orbit*'s home port. Exeligmos 175 is ours, and was supposed to get the honor of hosting you since we were leading the mission—but apparently once Sodium's ship got picked as backup, the Grasping Families started arguing over whether it was fair for the same habitat to get all the honors when the original decision had only been between ships. Both habitats put in to compete all over again, and the arguments stretched out, so they've both been preparing welcome feasts. Cytosine and Sodium have so many pheromones in the air that *I* can smell them. And now we've finally got a decision: we're going to Pulsar 18." We were beginning to move again, swinging to center on a habitat like an emerald-and-lapis crescent moon.

"So what does that mean for us?" asked Dinar.

"For a start, it means the *Solar Flare* will have to queue up for a compatible repair dock, instead of working with our own damn mechanic. It also means we're facing more people who sympathize with Sodium, and fewer people inclined to listen when we tell them things they weren't expecting—and a different balance of power in the Grasping Families. I don't know what stories people have been telling while we were gone, so I couldn't predict exactly how the balance has changed, except that they did pick the *Elliptical Orbit* as backup. Even though they lost out in the first competition because of how, um, abrupt they can be."

Pulsar 18 grew on the screen. I could see now that it wasn't a crescent but a loop, the second half a skeletal framework of some darker material rather than full-on ecology. The material shimmered faintly even at this distance, probably with the same self-renewing surface that protected the *Solar Flare*. It must have been turning slowly, because the blue-green half slid toward us and out of the sunlight.

"Curling mother, that design's called," said Rhamnetin. "It's an old setup; it used to spin for false gravity, but now it's only to produce the diurnal cycle. Three of the oldest habitats are full racing loops that never upgraded, but they're pretty much historical parks these days. You can adapt to live on them, but it's not exactly comfortable." I could make out pseudo-continents now, one on either side of the mid-arc ocean, coasts lined with gulfs and curving peninsulas. I wondered if they had tides—easy enough with artificial gravity, if they wanted them.

"Is that a city?" asked Carol. I followed her direction, and saw flashes of silver, a patch of colors beyond leaf and water, along the coast.

"Yes, that's where we're going. Forest-on-the-Lake is their mother city; it's one of the biggest in the Rings."

First Pulsar 18, then Forest-on-the-Lake, expanded to fill our view. Everyone gathered to watch, except for the first mothers and Glycine and whoever on the *Elliptical Orbit* was doing their share of navigation. We weren't the only incoming traffic. Some of the other ships were only distant glints; others were close enough to see: mountainous asteroids and pyramids, little darting ovoids, ships shaped like pillbugs or spiders or trees or other species, fantastical or just unfamiliar. Except for the ones modeled after flying creatures, none of them looked particularly aerodynamic, but I supposed they didn't need to. A flock of ovoids looped, trailing colored smoke.

"Is that functional, or are they showing off?" I asked.

"They're welcoming you with beautiful things. Like your parade scarves."

"That's another thing I wish I'd brought," I said. I hadn't been expecting a celebration today—well, at this point it was yesterday, but when I got dressed.

"That, I can probably make," said Carol. "And tunics, if we can get some fabric."

Athëo tugged gently on Rhamnetin's leg. "Can I ask you an awkward question?"

Limbs dipped; knees tilted to point eyes in Athëo's direction. "That's my job."

Athëo lowered his voice. "How much of Cytosine suddenly getting more cooperative is because of Sodium? Is it going to last?"

Rhamnetin swayed, thinking. "Not all of it. She really was impressed by your stories at the seder, and I think by St. Julien's speech as well. But—all species have this at least a little, humans too—you're different in different spaces, right? There are people who bring out your stubbornness, or your quiet, or your flexibility. And you change like we do—your body shapes your mind differently when you find your adult balance of hormones and transmitters and so on."

"No matter how many times it happens, yeah," said Athëo.

"Exactly!" He crouched lower. "When you met Cytosine, she had a settled dynamic with all the plains-folk around her. But in some ways her species is more like Asterion than like the watersheds. They have this constant dance of pheromones and skinsong, even when they're not negotiating a mating dynamic. When there's another nursing mother around from her own species, Cytosine knows under her skin that she doesn't have to be in charge of the universe. When she's the only one in an entire solar system, which hopefully will never happen again, she kind of worries that she is." He pulled himself up. "If you ask me, that kind of biological roller coaster looks like more fun to watch than to do, but then they think we're weirdly stuck in our ways. It's part of how we complement each other. Plains-folk constantly shift how they interact with the universe; tree-folk keep everything connected and stable."

"That seems like a particularly strange distinction, looking at you and Cytosine," I admitted.

He sounded amused. "Breeding role and hormonal balance aren't everything, it turns out. Maybe teaching us that is part of *your* niche."

And maybe when she had less riding on her shoulders, so to speak, Cytosine would be more willing to listen to us, to compromise. I'd met and judged her unimaginably far from home, carrying the hopes of trillions—and while I was carrying too much weight as well. Possibly I should take that into account.

We dropped close enough that it was no longer possible to tell that we were flying over a habitat rather than a planet. The horizon felt subtly off; that was all. A little of the wonder crept back: *No human has ever come here before. No one has ever seen this the way we see it.* We sped across water, green-blue in the sunlight. Scarlet flashed under the surface, gone before I could tell what it was. We slowed, colors resolving to trees grander than redwoods, crystal towers and arches draped with greenery rising among them—or growing from them, maybe. Some looked more like abstract sculpture than buildings, impossible at that scale under normal gravity. Something leapt in the water, bright as a rainbow.

The shore was more like the Gulf Coast than the open beaches of the Atlantic, though more orderly, especially at this moment. I thought of the Lower Mississippi, struggling with their catastrophically unplanned shift amid whatever chaos we'd left behind. Here, greenery dripped tendrils and elaborately rooted knees into placid water; Ringers crowded wide boardwalks like a second sea. But a landing pad had been cleared, broad and ready to receive us. I once again found myself in a starship on the ground. Raven woke, crying.

INTERLUDE 3
ARRIVAL

Silver clung to a tech support vine near the edge of the landing area, checking his drones for the tenth time. Good imagery could answer dozens of questions in a moment.

"We *have* pictures of humans, you know." His cross-brother called some up on a spare screen, as if they might learn something in the scant seconds before they met their new symbiotes in person. "From the broadcasts, and from the contact ship."

"But this will be the first glimpse of them in the Rings. We'll need to see where they fit the environment, what needs adaptation—"

"All of you, be still." His cross-sister Mercury's firm tones cut through the discussion. "It doesn't matter what habitat we're on. You all know what you're doing. You've been red-teaming this data since we picked up the first signals. The only way you can make a difference now is by having your eyes synchronized and your limbs steady."

Silver drew in oxygen, fastidiously straightened the embroidered bands that held his equipment. Mercury was right. They had this.

Excitement spilled into his cross-sister's voice. "Here they are!"

The two first mothers led the way—side by side, neither giving precedence to the other—and their cross-sisters. That must have been an interesting trip. They scrabbled down and to the side; the *Elliptical Orbit* lead started to speak, trying to get the crowd's attention, but gave up. Everyone was waiting for the aliens.

A cool breeze spilled from the hatch. Silver inhaled again and tasted strange volatiles, musky esters, something wet and unfamiliar: breath from another world. Behind it came the humans. Until this moment, some part of him had considered them a carefully animated special effect, drawn from the thousand stories anticipating this moment. Now they were real: uncoordinated with each other or their shipmates, babies crying rather than posing proudly for the drones. There were two human mothers—no, three. One grasped the limb of a child just old enough to move on their own.

"Mercury, hsst!" Silver's cross-sister was frozen, watching, and he had to nudge her to join the mothers welcoming the newcomers. One of the tree-folk men scrambled from the ship to translate; Silver waited anxiously for the moment when questions would be permitted. Several families had been chosen, and there'd be a rush. He eyed the competition, sizing up their equipment and what he knew of their styles and wits.

Asking the right questions would matter. There were only a few billion humans, a single planet's worth, organized into their own family units with their own interests and primitive fears. They'd want to live near each other. Only a few habitats would receive them at first, setting the pattern for this newest form of symbiosis. Pulsar 18 had swung ahead by getting them to land here; everyone else would have to scramble to catch up.

CHAPTER 40

As the door opened, it occurred to me that the Ringers could have miscalculated a thousand things. There could be subtle poisons in the air, or pollen that would throw us all into anaphylactic shock. My throat tickled. It was almost certainly psychosomatic, but my first direct view of the habitat was overlain by the reassuring glow of every standoff reading my mesh could manage. There were no obvious flags. Even so I pressed Dori against my chest as though she might breathe safety from my skin. She squawked and twisted to gape instead.

Nothing killed us. Ringers clung to trees and perched on mounds, fidgeted with sensors and cameras, pressed toward the ships. The scent of wet greenery filled my lungs, salty as the bay and fertile as a greenhouse, and the now-familiar musty aroma of tree-folk. There was something not-quite-floral in the air—though whether it came from the equivalent of real flowers or perfume or something stranger I had no idea. My sensors laid out molecular structures, ran them through the decades-old analyses that sifted safe substances from long-term carcinogens from immediate hazards. I marked a couple of don't-breathe-this-for-too-many-years issues, reminded myself that my grandparents had inhaled worse every day, and tried to focus on the people.

Once more I was grateful for the good sense of Ringer diplomatic tradition. Introducing kids first not only gave us an advantage over the Asterion team, it gave me a chance to get my fears under control before I had to demonstrate creativity and tact. As long as I wasn't required to reproduce names—and as long as my batteries held out—I'd be fine. So far no one had the sort of voicebox Sodium used, but Rhamnetin joined us to translate rapid-fire, glossing the adult dignitaries with roles like "host" and "witness" and "hearth-minder." I wondered how our names were getting through. If I'd thought about it earlier, I'd've tried to come up with Ringer-style names, more suitable for the chemistry of first contact.

The first wave rolled back. "Questioners now," said Rhamnetin quietly, "but this bunch have a different role from mine—a combination of journalism and scientific research. There were nine families approved when we left, but either some of them got pulled or they're still catching up to the location change."

One of the plains-folk scurried forward. She, at least, had a voice-box. "This is Silver, and I'm Mercury. We're glad to have you on the Rings at last, and my family wishes to make them as welcoming as possible. Our research helped ensure the safety of our air and water for you, and later we'll carry out further tests. Symbiosis often requires measurement; that is what we do."

"Thank you for making the habitat safe," I said. Then, hesitantly: "How much did you need to change?"

Limbs waved like grass. "Minor things. Adjusting the levels of trace elements, genomic shifts in a couple of plants. Nothing incompatible with our own needs."

I hesitated. Their "minor things" were hospitality—and respect for our natures—on a biological level beyond anything humans were capable of. Beyond the threats the Ringers presented, they offered untold opportunities. What might come from matching the Ringers' offerings to the watersheds' desires? Could the technologies that removed trace toxins from a habitat scale to heal a planet? Could humanity reengineer our own metabolisms to become more hospitable to oak and cicada and salmon? We had so much to learn here, even if it wasn't what the Ringers thought we should learn.

But we couldn't let that disconnect slide. The Ringers needed to know where we stood. "You must have heard by now that most of us don't intend to leave Earth behind. We've spent the last fifty years keeping it livable after our own industrial mistakes. The technologies you've used to adjust your habitat atmosphere could help us—and some of the things we've learned, working on a whole planet, could be useful to you. I know your technology is in some cases literal light-years ahead of ours, but I've also heard Cytosine claim things were impossible that we've done." I felt compelled to add, "It's not my area, though. If we'd been able to plan this trip, we'd have brought an atmospheric chemistry expert." We'd have brought a whole constellation of experts, and the hardware to run a small network between us. But I bit back further complaints; I'd said what was necessary.

Mercury rolled back. "Do you really object to symbiosis?"

"Not at all. We object to forced symbiosis. We welcome a relationship based on input from everyone, and on accepting that everyone has the right to refuse it. Symbiosis, like friendship or love or co-parenting, needs to be equal."

Athëo texted me: **You know you're talking to someone who finds co-parents through hormonal domination, right?**

Fuck. Well, they need to know we think differently. "Like sisterhood, I think you'd say. Cytosine told me first thing that you wanted us as sisters. Where I come from we choose our equal relationships too, and that's what we want with you."

Mercury's eyes darted among us. "The humans who came here—are you all one family?"

"The six of us are one family," said Athëo. "The St. Juliens are another. I don't know how to describe the Asterion delegation."

Those delegations were surrounded by their own sets of questioners—were we assigned, or would they pass us around? There were more questioners than huddled sets of humans, waiting impatiently a few yards away.

"Be reasonable, Mercury," said one of the waiting tree-folk (or so Rhamnetin translated). "When the plains came to the second ring, we didn't drop on you with questions right away. We asked them over a sun-hearth. How are these people supposed to understand us, watching everything from a landing pad?"

"If you hadn't dragged them here at the last minute," said Mercury, "we'd have hearths of our own to offer."

"I didn't have a reach in the negotiations, and they'll still like us better when they've been welcomed properly. On behalf of all the habitats, whichever hearth we feed them from."

"Dinna!" declared Raven. Then, in case we'd missed the point, "Dinna bees!"

"I don't know if they have beans, sweetie," said Dinar, "but I'm sure they have something tasty for dinner."

"We do," said Rhamnetin, "and some of it's a lot like beans. Let's go see?"

Against all reason, I'd expected a big room with tables of food, like the common house or Asterion's overwhelming ballrooms—or maybe, given their emphasis on small family units, more like our dining room. So it took me a while to realize, as the newcomer led us from the dock into the forest, that in a land of perfectly controlled weather and temperature, rooms were optional.

There was a time when human cities were made of cold stone and concrete, fortresses against nature. The first time people imported squirrels to New York, trying to reconnect with a sliver of nature, the little rodents died for want of food and shelter. It was only when trees were planted that the creatures could flourish. People gasped and fed them roasted peanuts by hand in the cold early-industrial winters. Now we lined our streets with trees and roofed our buildings with gardens. But the Ringer city, designed from soil to sky, went beyond tree-lined streets to something more like street-lined trees. Perfect climbing trees, tall as skyscrapers. Ramps twined them, machinery grew from their not-quite-bark, shelters glowed in their high branches. And everywhere Ringers and their pets swung, rolled, and scuttled—and peered at us from between the leaves.

A young plains-person—bigger than the twins and smaller than any of the adult crew I'd met—approached carrying a bowl of clear liquid. Water, from my scans. They spoke carefully; I got the impression they'd memorized a little English. "Here is water, the same everywhere."

"Thank you," I said, and glanced at Rhamnetin.

"Eat and drink," he said. "It's safe. And . . . it would be good if you did the morning ritual with them, after."

"I can do that," said Athëo.

Another contact, another bit of history. I made sure I was recording, and knelt to take the bowl. I scanned it again, nervously, found nothing dangerous. *We've been eating on the ship for hours, and had them in our house for weeks—if their bacteria could hurt us, we'd know.* I sipped, admitting my immersion in a new world, making myself part of their ecology.

With my wet lips I kissed Dori's forehead, admitting that I couldn't keep her isolated either. Athëo took on the formal words, telling the Ringers yet again that we'd been waiting for them, that we'd grasp what we found.

Other youths crowded around, offering slivers of fruit with the sweet bite of oranges, meat in a dark herbal sauce, a salad of leaves puffed like aloe. Watching Rhamnetin, I gathered that you were meant to take a bite at a time, licking fingers (or pincers, or whatever), no plates or silverware necessary. I kept an eye out for anything bread-like, worrying about the Pesach rules even as I gave up on asking whether the meat came from something with a backbone.

In a break between servers, a grown tree-person asked, "When will the rest of your people arrive?"

The state and corporate powers were somewhere among the trees as well, giving their own answers. "When they choose to. We're glad to work together, but we're keeping our homeworld."

Our interlocutor danced back, and their translator crackled. "I'm glad we rescued you. You can stay, and survive with us."

"We're pretty good at survival, thank you."

Rhamnetin nudged my side—and Carol's, Athëo's, and Dinar's with other limbs—and said, "We need to move on. So many people want to talk with you."

There was no one center of feasting. There were groves, trees, platforms, and a long hierarchy of people who'd competed for the chance to meet us, who might tell their children where they'd stood in the order of people who first spoke to humanity. At every stop there were crowds of youth eager to press new dishes on us, exchange a word or two, and claim their own moment in history. There were too many questions that took for granted humanity's mass movement to the Rings, too many assumptions that might morph to demands. And, frankly, too many people convinced that we saw them as saviors.

Ringers were enough like us to react badly to contradiction—or to gloss it over entirely. The dandelion protocols had been designed to help us get past that hardwired resistance to being wrong, and they helped only in part. The Ringers, advanced in other directions, had no such thing. They saw the universe no more clearly than we, and it was going to get us all in trouble.

"Who's actually in charge here?" I asked Rhamnetin eventually. I was embarrassed even as I asked it—looking for a big pillbug in place of a big ape—but I wanted some excuse to be done for a few hours. To find a bunk or a treehouse or whatever they'd set aside for us (and of course there'd be no bassinets for light-years any more than decent mattresses), and to put Dori down and get Raven the nap she desperately needed. Maybe Ringer kids were evolved to spend hours as diplomatic props; ours were about to melt down, and so was I. "Is anyone?"

"Take me to your leader?" suggested Rhamnetin. "You'll meet formally with the Grasping Families tomorrow; they're not all here yet and the dynamics are finicky."

"All right," Dinar broke in, "then who do we *have* to talk with now?"

"Probably more people than is practical. Are you full?"

"Very," said Dinar, to nods all around.

"Then people can wait. I think they've set up your nest; let's go find it."

St. Julien and the Asterion team would probably keep chatting up our hosts until all hours, but if I kept going I wasn't going to make a good impression on anybody. We'd been walking so far, but now Rhamnetin called a ride—automated, like ours, but with the same antigrav technology that powered their shuttles. It was smaller than the shuttle, a clear bubble with cushioned platforms inside, and trundled close to the ground. Assured that it was safe, I let Dori crawl around inside, and watched the dappled sunshine through the trees. It was light still, and I remembered that their days were a few hours longer than ours. I didn't even try and calculate the potential jet lag; better at this point to sleep when I was tired. They'd brought us here; they could cope.

More structures appeared growing alongside the trees. I held off on calling them buildings. Scans suggested metal and living wood mixed with some sort of plastic, which if you were breaking up planets for parts I supposed you'd have plenty of resources for. Maybe they'd managed stronger bioplastics than ours—hell, they must have made massive improvements in materials science or the habitats would never hold together. Either that or they were cheating via gravity manipulation . . . I wandered down rabbit holes of speculation, trying to record questions for every expertise humanity had to offer. If they'd *asked* first, we could have sent so many more people, better qualified than me and with kids of their own. We could have divided all these awkward conversations among the whole crowd.

We came at last to a flock of platforms and ramps swooping around one of the lower world-trees. Happily, someone had realized that our kids weren't great with drops, and found us a room-like area with walls (open to the breeze and sounds of the habitat beyond and the leaves above, but hard to fall out of). Unhappily, no one had noticed that we liked some modicum of privacy. St. Julien and her spouse were already there—and so was Adrien. The rest of the Asterion team was still out and about, but there was plenty of space to hold them.

"I do not want to sleep in a room with Jace di Sanya," I told Carol, in what I hoped was sotto voce. I didn't want to share a room with Adrien or St. Julien, either, but I did have about one neuron's worth of diplomacy left in me.

"You all wait here, and I'll see what I can do." Rhamnetin swung up and was gone.

Adrien sauntered over. If e was tired, it didn't show. "Enjoying the party?"

"Sure," I said. I busied myself unwrapping Dori, and let her down. She began to explore, and I kept an eye out for choking hazards and attempts to climb anyone/anything unfortunate. "How many times have you been asked about your kids so far?"

E shrugged. "Cytosine keeps reassuring people that we do have them, and that we have our own ways of showing respect. Then Brend jumps in and starts asking about their body mods. Bringing em along was an *excellent* idea." E ran a gold-painted fingernail along the wall—smooth and eggshell-blue, dotted with maroon and scarlet. "I think they build these the same way they made the antenna. I've *got* to talk to their construction companies. Maybe start by trading for a ship, then set up an outpost here . . . the opportunities are endless."

"So why are you here," I asked, "instead of out at the party?"

E wrinkled eir nose. "Someone's got to scout out our home base. Jace would probably like a heads-up that she's bunking with you, too. You may recall that we *don't* normally take our work home. The Ringers make no distinction; it takes getting used to."

"It does," I admitted. I felt a momentary pang of sympathy, in spite of everything, for the corporate team being forced to sleep with their pronouns on. I hoped Rhamnetin would be able to find them a separate closet or something, and make everyone happy.

I returned to the corner Dinar had staked out. She and Athëo had done their best with the cushions. Carol, keeping close to Dori, texted:
Anything we should worry about her putting in her mouth?

I shook my head. **Microplastics are an issue long-term, but it'll be okay for today. Why am I exhausted?**

Probably because you got kidnapped to a different fucking star system and then had to be polite to a billion people who think "kidnapping" is pronounced "rescuing"? Either that or PMS.

Not just me, huh?

She gave up on staying at Dori's heels and plopped down beside me. I leaned against her, allowing myself human warmth and human smells. I closed my eyes, switching sensor feedback to auditory, a quiet burble telling me the shape and content of the world around me. "Got to make a vital signs bracelet for Dori, now that she's mobile."

"Yes, but I'm watching her, it's fine."

Raven climbed into Athëo's lap, and his gentle tenor joined the wash of the sensory stream and the whickers and whistles from the canopy above. I loved his lullabies, souvenirs from all the languages he'd learned or built. This was one of the Quenya songs, unless it was Finnish—probably Quenya, if he needed comfort as much as I did. I meant to wait up for Rhamnetin, but I must have dozed.

I woke to screams, and I processed all at once that I was on the Rings, that the scream was Carol's, and that others were shouting: St. Julien and Adrien along with Dinar and Athëo, and then Raven's ear-piercing shriek. Then everything else was blotted out by Dori's wail, frightened rather than hungry or tired, and only then I saw her in the grasp of a strange tree-person. They'd obviously meant to flee, but were stymied by the difficulty of holding her—not a natural like Rhamnetin, I thought dizzily even as I flung myself after them. Someone grabbed me; I struggled against a tangle of furry limbs.

"Put her down!" I probably yelled other things too; that one's all I remember.

Carol dropped, rolled, grabbed one of the kidnapper's limbs and pulled. They were hard to trip, but it didn't make their job any easier. Raven struggled in Dinar's arms, calling for their sib. And Dori kept screaming. Whoever had me wouldn't let go. I twisted, sank my teeth into fur, scratched behind me, tried to kick. None of it made a difference.

Athëo stepped forward, looking calm enough that my first reaction was fury. He pulled something from his bag, but I couldn't see what.

"Why are you doing this?" he demanded, and Ringer words came pouring from his hands: his palette, with the half-built translation program.

The Ringer holding Dori jerked in startlement, but didn't respond. All my instincts said it didn't matter, that this was time to fight rather than talk, but I had enough hold of my reactions to realize that any answer would be a clue to their motivations. A clue to stopping them, or finding them if they got away. I was overcome with the vertiginous awareness of exactly how big the haystack would be if they did. They could hide my child on any of a thousand worldlets, and I'd never be able to find her . . . I tried to breathe, to think.

At home I'd have known the keywords to alert the whole local network, to bring out emergency responders and surround myself with protective neighbors. Here, though . . . Rhamnetin hadn't ever regained his mesh and palette. They must be on the ship somewhere, and maybe someone was near them. I sent a stream of high-urgency messages with every override I could think of, trying to trigger the heuristics that would set off attention-grabbing alarms. And to my family: **Radio! Use the radio!**

Why were they doing this? I breathed slowly as I could, forcing my muscles looser against the stranger's grip. Did they think they were rescuing Dori from a dying world? Or taking away our diplomatic standing by proving we couldn't protect our children? I remembered the story of Caffeine and Fructose—Fructose hadn't kept her brothers perfectly safe, but all the tale's disgust was for the Chief with the Lonely Name. Did these people identify somehow with that chief, and want humans away from their balanced status quo? Or did they think *we,* with our fettered eagerness for symbiosis, were as unfit as the Chief for child-rearing?

"Athëo, tell them my name is, um, Dopamine."

He twisted to look at me. "How? I don't think we have human neurotransmitters in the program yet."

I remembered Caffeine and Fructose scratching amino acid molecules in dirt. We didn't have that kind of time. "Never mind Dopamine. Call up a diagram of water on your palette; tell them that's me. Me and the kids." Hydrogen and two oxygen atoms, inseparable without disaster.

Adrien was attempting to sneak around behind the tree-person who held Dori. It was a noble try, doomed by radial symmetry: legs shifted to track em. Something launched past the Ringer, too swiftly for them to grab. My two limited eyes flicked without conscious thought to follow the flash of a corporate hummingbird drone, and followed its path back to Tiffany hunched over in a corner, looking utterly oblivious.

Athëo held up the palette and pointed at me, at Dori and Raven. The Ringer hesitated, lowered limbs that had been reaching toward the branches. Dori continued screaming, and I tried to keep my thoughts in order, to come up with more diplomacy-by-chemistry.

And then our backup swarmed in: Cytosine and Carnitine and, thank god, Rhamnetin and his brothers.

This did not, unfortunately, cause the two strange Ringers to let go of either me or Dori. Cytosine reared, displaying her own children clinging to her belly. Rolling on her back would have been shock or fear; this, I assumed, was threat. "How dare you steal our guests' eggs?"

Rhamnetin translated her words, and then the response: "He says:

these aliens have sworn they won't join the Rings. They want to tie us to worlds again. They're a danger to their own eggs and ours." Exactly what I'd been afraid of.

Cytosine: "They just got here. Do you honestly believe stealing their children is going to persuade them?"

"The flexibility of the plains is a great strength. But this is no time to try and change the stubbornly lonely-minded. Their eggs need protection."

"She's not an *egg*," I yelled, and the Ringers ignored me. "She's my *child*!"

"How do you plan to protect them?" Carnitine demanded. "They can't lick your cross-sister's bellies, and this one's not even old enough to swallow fruit! You'd be starving eggs, not protecting them."

"My family knows how to nourish eggs." Rhamnetin put into that translation all the scorn and fury he could convey. "We'd share them with more cooperative humans, of course."

"Who?" I demanded. I twisted in the grip that still held me, glaring at Adrien, at the only group of humans who'd come to the Rings without a child to hold.

Adrien flung up eir hands. "We didn't! I swear it—you know we don't even think kids should travel in the first place. We would never risk them like this!"

"The corporations wouldn't?" asked Carol. "Or you, personally? Can you swear Jace isn't behind this?"

"Jace has kids." But e didn't swear.

"Return her child," Cytosine said. "You've made enough trouble that the Grasping Families will have to pick up the question, and I'm sure that's all you really wanted."

If they were human, the strangers would have been thinking about the likelihood that more help was coming: whether they could still get away safely, and how to back off without losing their reputations entirely. I didn't know what these people were thinking, or how the worlds' worth of people surrounding us would react. But finally the limbs unwound from my waist, and the stranger in front of us lowered Dori into Carol's arms. I scrambled to them, unthinking, wrapped my arms around them both, buried my face in Dori's hair.

At home, reconciliation experts would have joined us now, and begun the process of understanding what happened and what everyone needed. I'd have been able to check the kidnappers on the network, and see their identities confirmed and their contributions suspended until Athëo's colleagues determined where they might still contribute. Here . . . I felt suspended myself, adrift with no comprehension of what would happen.

Athëo's expertise might not entirely apply, but practice and presumably a more manageable adrenaline crash still let him ask, "Rhamnetin, what now?"

I felt friendlier limbs warm against my back, and fur brushing my neck. "Now the egg-thieves will leave your nest, and remain in the habitat until the Grasping Families hear their explanations. They'll want yours, too. Cytosine is right that this was a ploy to make them decide immediately whether humanity should be forced to join us—and to argue that you can't be trusted otherwise. It could work."

"Wait," I said. "*They* tried to kidnap Dori, so *we* can't be trusted? The hell?"

The one who'd been holding Dori answered in Ringer, and Rhamnetin translated: "If you were trustworthy, we wouldn't have done it."

CHAPTER 41

Our attackers left at last. St. Julien assured us that NASA would object to this treatment in the most strenuous terms; she clutched Brice tightly enough that I could appreciate the truth behind her diplomatic noises. Adrien also made a racket, mostly demanding to know whether Asterion would still be penalized for not bringing their own kids. Cytosine stationed Astatine and Ytterbium on opposite sides of the platform, as if more kidnappers might show up any minute. Maybe it was true; I had no idea how to judge.

With all an infant's focus on the moment, Dori wanted to crawl again, and neither of us was willing to do anything but follow exhausted at her heels. At last Rhamnetin picked her up (despite Cytosine's startled objection) and spun her slowly to look at the trees. She squealed, and I sat in the shelter of his legs. "Weren't you going to find us more private quarters?"

"I was trying. I'm sorry. Even if I'd found something, this would add . . . so many political complications, no one would want to carry them."

"What, are we too untrustworthy now?" Carol glared up at him.

Cytosine came over, limbs rippling toward Dori as if she worried Rhamnetin would drop her. "Not that—though some people would hate to take a side before the Grasping Families drop their judgment. Others would love to take that leap, of course. But for you to change where you're sleeping now, you'd be saying that whoever you went to could protect your child better than anyone else in the Rings. They'd be saying the same, and insulting everyone else. You haven't had time to make a proper comparison of the question—the sort we used to decide who'd greet you—so if you chose a protector anyway, it would suggest that you didn't have the discernment to compare. As Rhamnetin said, the politics get complicated."

Raven had fallen asleep at last on Dinar's lap, but Athëo joined us. "Can you at least explain the politics of what already happened? It sounded like . . . if someone took kids away from their partner after a divorce, then claimed it was because the partner was abusive."

Cytosine's eyestalks pivoted toward Rhamnetin and he hunkered down, considering. "Something like that. But it's more formal, even if not exactly . . . modern. Before the plains-folk came to the second ring, egg-theft was common. That covers both actual eggs and children who've hatched; it's called egg-theft because stealing male eggs during their long incubation was the easiest and most common form. It was a way to start feuds, or end them. By stealing eggs, you claim to be better able to raise the children, to have more right to them—but you also create family. Even if the eggs are restored later, the work of bringing a male egg to term, and the physiological influence of the hormones themselves, makes the children your brothers as well as theirs."

"But no one's done that for a thousand years?" asked Carol.

"Of course they have. But the . . . let me see if I can get this right. You accused Asterion of attacking you with malware."

We nodded, and Adrien, leaning arms-crossed against the rail, glared pointedly elsewhere. A smile played on Tiffany's lips, but tha didn't say anything.

"Suppose instead of malware, they'd challenged you to a duel, with swords."

I tried to picture that. But Adrien grinned and straightened. E twirled an imaginary sword and made an en garde salute. It would suit em better than us—and anyone who'd ever seen a historical drama would know what it meant.

"It would be weird. But they wouldn't simply be attacking us— they'd be accusing us." I wished, for a moment, that we did have something like that—some way we could've called the corporations out from the start, and made gut-clear how seriously we took their attack. But I didn't like the Ringer version at all, and I could see all too clearly how it followed from the place children held in diplomacy.

"Exactly," Rhamnetin said. "Now imagine that duels aren't weird, only rare—something that happens every few years, and attracts everyone's attention when it does. The last big egg-theft case was, I think . . ."

"About seven years ago," said Carnitine. "One of the leading ecologist families of Perihelion 50 led a raid on the Grasping Family of Perihelion 9, and got away with all their unhatched eggs. It came up before the full Families, and they found that Perihelion 9 had been altering sensors and records to hide growing problems with their air quality. The habitat got new representation in the Families, and new ecologists too—and the eggs stayed with the people who caught the problem."

I felt nauseated, my stomach hollower than it had been already. Not just an accusation, but an accusation of ecological mismanagement—that people were used to believing. The whole story was framed against us.

"But you interfered," said Athëo. "That's allowed? We're glad you did; I'm just trying to understand."

There was a pause—an awkward one, I realized as it lengthened. At last Rhamnetin said, "By protecting you, we argue that staying on Earth isn't inherently dangerous for your children. Cytosine is betting on my judgment."

"You said we had the right to stay," I told her.

"I said you were right that we needed to treat you as equals, if we want you as symbiotes. You convinced me, and I'm acting on that conviction. But standing in front of the Grasping Families and saying it's safe for you to stay on Earth—they'll be able to tell I don't believe it."

"So tell them what you do believe," I said. "That it's better for us, better for our children, if we're allowed to make our own damn choices."

She considered a moment. "That," she said, "I can do."

It was a long night, literally and emotionally. I couldn't sleep. Somewhere in that time the habitat turned away from the sun, and something like moonlight glinted cool through the branches. Rhamnetin told us that solar collectors, mining drones, and asteroid detectors orbited out beyond the habitats. Jace returned, smirking, and pointedly ignored us.

Sunlight came swift and sudden. Warm mist fogged the air, softening the light. I blinked against it. "Oh, no."

"What?" asked Carol nervously.

"The nearest tea is light-years away. And trying alien stimulants sounds like a terrible idea."

"Fuck. Wait, isn't Caffeine a legendary trickster figure?"

"It's a poetic translation," I said sourly.

Unfamiliar limbs poked over the rail. I yelped, "Rhamnetin!"

Rhamnetin sprang to his feet, then relaxed. "No, it's okay, I know these guys. Come in!"

Carol poked me. "The nearest adrenaline, fortunately, is right here."

A pair of Ringers, one of each type, scrambled over the wall.

"My colleagues," explained Rhamnetin. "Sucrose and Aluminum—questioners like me. Cytosine, can you go find out where and when we're supposed to meet the Families?"

"I can do that from here." I'd have caught the eye-roll even if Cytosine's eyes were as limited as mine in their rolling capacity. "Speaking of politics. I'd rather make sure someone keeps your branch steady while you're swinging."

Rhamnetin's limbs straightened. "I thought you were going to trust me."

"Your judgment about how to handle the humans, yes. Your judgment about what needs questioning when we talk to the Families, not as much. You're my cross-brother—it's my responsibility to make sure you don't go flying off with no handholds." They were both keeping to English when they didn't have to, but I wasn't sure why Cytosine wanted us to hear this. Maybe she just wanted us to understand the nuances of their relationship, and to build a stronger, less adversarial connection with her cross-brother's lovers.

"Cytosine . . ." Rhamnetin lowered his center again—trying to look less threatening? Or less threatened? "You've never liked spending time with my colleagues. You're used to *my* questions; they'll ask different ones."

Limbs rippled, a field of nervous grass. "I need to hear everything I can before I testify."

"All right. Are you going to grab me when you don't like the direction I'm swinging, or find out what we can reach together?"

She didn't answer, at least not in any way I could see. Still, Sucrose and Aluminum seemed to accept her non-response. I tried to read as much as I could from them, practice for the more fraught confrontations to come. Aluminum was plains—and judging from the colored metal bands ringing their limbs, a local. Or maybe not: unlike the versions we'd seen earlier, these bands were inscribed with intricate script, dozens of elven rings carrying unknown messages. Sucrose was tree-folk, wearing moss and pouches like Rhamnetin did. They were taller than him, fur shaggier and with a white patch running down one limb. At the patch's center, raw black flesh covered the spot where a mouth should have been. A scar from an accident? I knew from Rhamnetin that not everyone responded well to their regenerative medicine. In any species disability must be a window on society's flaws, maybe even an impetus to do something about them. I hadn't talked with Rhamnetin about how his bad eye affected his life. He had a dozen others, but Ringers might well build tools, interfaces, art, with the assumption that everyone could see 365 degrees of their full spectrum. What changes had they made to live with two species' limits—and how far had they thought through doing that again?

Well, I had questioners here; I could ask. "How much would you have to adapt for us to live with you? We have fewer arms and legs, we only see in one direction; there are probably dozens of ways your habitats won't work for us. And the reverse is true on Earth."

Sucrose tapped the side of our platform. "This is one adaptation—a place to bring the plains up into the branches. We meet, and we share what we've found with our separate strengths—when it's not obvious how our differences are an advantage, we talk and study until we figure it out. If we can't figure it out, we engineer new abilities to fill the gaps." Before I could ask another question, they went on: "Rhamnetin says you've claimed to make a whole planet livable long-term, without giving up your technology. What adaptations does *that* require?"

"Millions," I admitted. "But the main one is learning to be symbiotic with the world—not only with the species that have adapted to live with us, the dogs and cats and goats and squirrels, but the ones whose role isn't obvious to the untrained observer. So we train our observers, and share everything we perceive, and work together so we can understand the worth of our full ecosystem—and make ourselves part of it."

"And sometimes we do engineer solutions," added Dinar. In her lap, Raven rubbed their eyes and squinted into alien sunlight. "We're part of the whole system. Making a crop more nutritious and easier to access, or an insect less likely to spread plagues—that can be part of our ecological niche without taming the whole thing."

St. Julien joined us, slipping in with Brice at her breast. "I'm going to talk about this later, I'm sure—but there's a symbiosis between space travel and planetary life, too. NASA has always done both. We learn things from research in a different environment, or just from surviving the vacuum, that we bring back to Earth to make *it* livable." I nodded cautiously, but she went on: "However, we can't keep Earth at the center of everything—humanity's done too much damage there. The U.S. doesn't want to give it up entirely, but we need to spread out. Once we get out to the stars, we stop being so vulnerable.

And with less pressure from us, Earth can recover, or evolve in a different direction."

"Earth is part of us," I said. I hoped I sounded passionate, rather than exhausted and frustrated. "And we're part of it. Without our world we'll be—cloned thylacines in cages. We'll survive, maybe, but we won't be what we should be. And we won't have learned Earth's lessons; we'll repeat the same mistakes over and over."

"Is that what you think we're doing?" asked Aluminum, rather sharply.

I should have phrased it differently—the problem was that yes, I did suspect they'd lost something. I just wasn't in any position to say what it was. "Maybe it's different for you," I said weakly.

Sucrose shifted their grips. "Your third faction thinks differently."

Adrien looked at Jace and Kelsey and Mallory, then nodded and leaned back, arms crossed. "We do. Humanity's progressed a long way away beyond anything that could be considered natural, and that progress has been good for us—we live longer, we're richer, we eat better and live more comfortably than anything natural. But now we've slowed down. We've stopped innovating. We got scared. We outgrew our planet a century ago, and instead of finding a new environment that could handle our growth, we tried to fit ourselves somewhere too small. We need to grow again—and we're ready to stand on our own."

"Or at least," said Jace, "the corporate conglomerates are ready. With the help of friends and allies, of course." They bowed in the Ringers' direction. Smooth, in control, and to all appearances well-rested. And probably responsible for last night's attack in the first place, but I doubted we'd get anywhere by responding to philosophy with an accusation. Even though the things they were willing to do belied their claim of maturity.

Rhamnetin touched my shoulder. "I didn't bring my cousin questioners here to get a preview of the arguments we'd lay for the Families."

"Here we've been questioning them when we should've been questioning you," said Sucrose. "What *should* we talk to them about?"

"Plumbing."

"Plumbing?" I said stupidly. If their composting toilets weren't at least the equal of ours, they wouldn't have millennia-old space stations. Then again, they'd dumped sewage into the Chesapeake—and they had plenty of space to dump in. "You want us to scan your water quality?"

"We have extensive control over our air and water. You know that, because we made sure we could breathe on Earth, and that you could breathe here. But we work with relatively simple systems, and there are errors—" I didn't pick up on anyone's body language, but someone must have objected. "There are, even if no one likes to discuss them. Eclipse 2 has given up producing a dozen fruits because of blights, and no one can trace the problem. This habitat right here is constantly overcoming filtration problems through raw force, and so are a dozen others. The Chesapeake Network claims to handle those problems with planetary-complexity systems, and that's beyond our ability. Let's take advantage of what they do that we don't." He tapped my shoulder. "I invited these colleagues in particular because if they ask how your science could be useful to us, they know enough to understand the answers."

I was grateful to Rhamnetin, but he'd underestimated how quickly we'd be able to communicate. It was a token of Ringer cultural faith that chemistry was a universal language—thus their names—but they'd clearly forgotten how long it must have taken to work out that language between them. On the one hand, humans weren't hunter-gatherers anymore; on the other hand we already had our own traditions of how to draw molecules, complicated by a century of argument about how quantum theory should change the original models. The Ringers had a millennium of complication from using stylized diagrams not only for actual chemistry, but for names and, it turned out, their equivalent of an alphabet. (Athëo said it was more like a hybrid syllabary/hieroglyph system, and as excited as that made him, it did not help me figure out whether the Ringers' water filtration problems were because of oversimplified reef equivalents, or whether they just needed better-engineered algae.)

By the time messengers came to "invite" us to meet the Grasping Families, we were all frustrated. I was sure Rhamnetin was right—our experience working to revive a destabilized planet could make a real difference here—but I doubted I'd convinced his colleagues. And equally, I was sure that a thousand years maintaining artificial biospheres bore lessons we could apply to our own efforts—but only if we were permitted to keep those efforts going. And only if they were convinced that our goal was worth supporting.

CHAPTER 42

For this gathering, deeper within the city-continent, we were herded onto a set of open-topped floating platforms. Ours included my family, Rhamnetin and Carnitine and Cytosine, and somehow Tiffany and Brend. I wondered if they wanted to talk to us privately, but they huddled in a corner. Either they needed a break from their own group, or they'd been ordered to talk to us about something and were working up the nerve. Or else they'd been told to listen in, as if we had new secrets to mutter on the way. Rhamnetin had meant well, but the conversation with his colleagues had wrung me out even before starting to argue for the entire future of my entire species.

The barges flew more slowly than the shuttles, but made up for it in comfort. The breeze cooled my face, reminding me of spring cleanup shifts on an Anacostia sun-boat. I watched broad leaves and bright petals, small animals clinging to branches and flitting between, and tried not to think too hard about our destination. Instead I played at distinguishing species, slots in their constrained ecosystem. Here: human-sized leaves with five jagged tongues dangling tiny purple flowers, branches corrugated like mountain ranges and mottled with lichen. Nets full of mysterious goods slung from the branches; platforms decked the bark between them. There: a smaller tree with waving fronds like grass or soft pine needles. Practically a bush in this setting, but the least of them would have shaded our roof at home. I knew, of course, that the photosynthetic organisms on the Rings could be only marginally similar to earthly plants. But sunlight's a good source of energy, and all my bio expertise focused on water filtration, so: leaves. Flowers. Fucking bark, even if you could probably never graft it onto an apple tree. (Or maybe you could. You can graft almost anything onto an apple tree.)

The barges swept between massive trunks. Above us the alien sun made a sky more jaundiced than our own, but full even in daylight: bright slivers and ovals calicoed with the shadows of distant geography. They were larger near the horizon, probably close enough to threaten earthquakes if the Ringers didn't hold gravity back by main force.

In a crisis, we still look for the big ape. So I'd imagined the Grasping Families as some prototypical council up on a dais, shadowed spider and pillbug figures gazing down in judgment while I argued humanity's case with a crick in my neck. I hadn't done the math. If every habitat sent one family half the size of Rhamnetin's, that would be one hell of a dais. They'd need mesh to chat with councilors on the far side of the row. Instead we left the gargantuan forest and landed in a valley of mossy terraces. Jewel-toned flowers dotted the green; water fountained from translucent sculptures and splashed rivulets on the ground. Among the sculptures waited hundreds of Ringers, clustered into families or factions.

"How does this actually work?" I asked.

Rhamnetin fidgeted, and it was Cytosine who answered: "No one is sure. Normally there are smaller committees for specific issues, but this affects *everything*. The usual judiciaries for egg-theft have claimed relevance, but so has Resource Distribution, and Exploration, and Habitat Placement, and at that point Requirements Conflict gets involved. Probably they'll let whoever has an opinion state it, but use a redundancy rule. We're not really set up for this."

"Oddly," I admitted, "that's how we felt when you showed up." Would they do better than we'd managed?

"What's a redundancy rule?" asked Dinar trepidatiously. She rubbed the empty nub of her shoulder.

"It means no one can make a point that someone else has already made. Including repeating yourself."

"Arguments only, then," I said, not entirely comfortable with the idea. A couple of watersheds had tried that, years ago, before realizing that it just devolved into arguments over what constituted an objectively persuasive argument. "No weight on the number of people who agree with them." I wondered how much nuance was permitted, the sort of tweaks we used to shape starting suggestions into effective action. "They need a dandelion network."

Brend eyed the crowd through eir lashes. "This is a lot of people. If they're not all allowed to talk, that's *good*." The other barge landed nearby. Adrien got out, stretched ostentatiously, waved at eir sib. The rest of the Asterion and NASA teams followed.

Raven tugged at Diamond. "Baby down! Play!"

Dori twisted against my chest and screeched, reaching for her sib.

"Can we let the kids play?" I asked. "Or is putting them down a horrible faux pas? Dori's still excited about crawling; if I try to keep her wrapped up through however-many speeches, she's going to scream." Which would do nothing for our case.

Cytosine considered. "As long as they stay near us. Pick them up when you're talking."

"Right." And I'd be speaking far too much. I was the nominal face for the network, but I'd left my weight at ebb and I had no access to the voices I should be representing. There was no overlap between the power recognized here and the power that backed me—and the dandelion networks had never been designed for high-stakes decision-making by lone individuals.

Or by families. The Rings *wanted* every group personified by a family, and it seemed abruptly obvious how they'd pushed mine into that role for Earth. Yet another thing they'd failed to respect in bringing us here. St. Julien and the Asterion team would have no such compunctions about taking up the script they'd been offered. I swallowed, trying to bank the sourness of fear and anger into manageable passion.

A plains-person, with a child little bigger than Cytosine's twins, approached the Asterion team and began arguing with Adrien and Jace. I couldn't make out the words.

"That's Phosphorus," said Cytosine. "Not a good sign."

"Why not?" asked Carol.

"She's the one who sent her cross-brothers to steal Dori. Didn't they say?"

"They were kidnapping our kid! Why would they?"

"Because it's rude not to." Rhamnetin shuffled sideways, so he stood between her and Raven.

"Ruder than kidnapping?" I demanded.

He raised a leg, trying to get a better look. "Egg-theft isn't rude, if you've got reason. Not saying what family you represent, though, if the eggs are guarded . . . it would be like challenging someone to a duel without telling them how they insulted your honor."

Cytosine added: "They were going to tell the whole Rings about it anyway, so it's not like they were hiding their identities. It's a sign of contempt, not to introduce themselves directly to you."

"Ah. Good."

A young tree-person scurried up and handed me a small box with a strap. "Thank you," I said automatically, and the box echoed me in chords and whistles. "You're welcome," their box told me, and they continued to pass out the translators. I saw others doing the same. I remembered some of the history of AI translation on Earth, and the limits of the program we'd come up with so far, and hoped Rhamnetin would catch if they screwed up badly.

"Who goes first?" I asked him.

"No idea. With all those interests, it's going to get pretty smelly."

Raven squatted on the ground with the twins, doing something complicated with flowers, and I let Dori down to join them. I tried not to think about how the last time they'd held a hearing like this, the original parents had lost their children along with their case. I had no idea what I'd do if they tried to enforce that with Dori and Raven. Start a war, maybe.

The argument between Phosphorus and Adrien and Jace, whatever it had been, ended. Adrien relaxed, a satisfied smile on his lips as he gazed around the valley. Jace looked pleased too.

Phosphorus spoke, and some hidden system amplified her voice. Separately, my new box murmured translation. "The gift is found when we reach, trusting that we will find. We say that every morning, and it's true, even when the finding takes a thousand orbits. Three times now worlds have slipped from our grasp before we even knew they existed, but we've finally found the next branch."

A tree-person joined her—("Pepsin, her cross-sister, you didn't meet her yesterday," Rhamnetin explained)—with a child clinging to her limbs. She picked up the thread: "We cannot let humanity slip. Just as the plains had an obligation to the trees when they found us, we are obliged to ensure in turn that humans survive their world and join us in symbiosis."

Phosphorus took over again. "But many of them are frightened of change, and insist on clinging alone to a rotting branch. They will let their children fall, and it would be immoral of us to allow such neglect."

"Frightened of change, hell," I said, and realized too late that *my* words had been amplified. Across the valley, eyes and limbs turned in my direction, and I only had one chance to make my point, regardless of how badly I made it. "We've *been* changing our world. We welcome your help, but we won't reject our—" How could I say this best? My heart pounded and my gut churned. *I'm going to puke in front of the alien custody court, oh god. Please let me say the right thing.*

I took a deep breath, and went ahead and said the wrong thing.

"We bless the creator of the universe, all its branches, and thank Them for enabling us to reach this place and this season." Definitely the wrong thing; if there were seasons here, the Ringers themselves bore sole responsibility. But it helped. I caught my breath as I imagined myself lighting candles instead of speechifying to several hundred worlds' leaders. "Like you, we don't all understand that creator the same way, or even agree about whether there is one, but we've learned to understand our obligations regardless. You wouldn't give up your symbiosis with each other to join with us, and we feel the same way about Earth. And it shouldn't be necessary. Unless we create artificial constraints, cooperation isn't zero-sum."

"Maladaptive biological metaphors," said Phosphorus. "Species are symbiotic, not planets. Planets are complex, and brittle, and humans are at the same snapping point we once were. Their claims echo those made by the most misguided of our ancestors. If someone is falling, you catch them. If someone tries to swing out over an abyss with children clinging to them, you catch their children."

Adrien and Jace looked at each other, and Adrien stepped forward. "Humans do not speak with one voice. I am here for Asterion and the larger corporate consortium. A hundred years ago we ruled Earth—and we strove for a future in the stars. All that you offer, we hoped to do for ourselves, but the networks stole that. They wanted to limit humanity's potential, just as they do now." The lies were tight, quietly furious. I bit my lip, holding back my kneejerk response; I didn't want to lose my temper and another chance to say something that mattered. "Ironically, we've spent the past decades living in our own artificial environments, the only place they'd give us to follow our own ways. We would rather join your habitats here, with unlimited room for growth and a safe place for our own children, than stay on the storm-tossed artificial islands that imprison us now."

"But you're here childless," someone said. I couldn't tell who: one of the mass of Grasping Families dotting the hillsides.

"Because we won't take them through network territory. Will you hold us back for that?"

Among humans, I'd be able to read the room. Here . . . well, after a few weeks with the *Solar Flare*'s family, I could a little. Tree-folk steadying themselves on siblings and cross-siblings. Plains-folk curling around their children in fear or maybe sympathy, or tapping neighbors to say something in the privacy of skinsong. There was no consensus here, not yet, but these people were used to a shared, stable understanding of the universe. They'd try to find a new one as quickly as possible.

Cytosine poked me, a flash of child-smooth chitin in her own jolt of skinsong, and scooped up Diamond and Chlorophyll. I grabbed Dori, bouncing to keep *her* from squawking at the whole crowd.

Cytosine reared up, the twins plainly displayed. Even I could tell that the usual harmonies of her language were pitched for the crowd, lower and slower. My box translated: "My family is the only one here that has lived among humans, on the world that is precious to them. We are the reach of the Rings—how dare you presume to judge how they care for their children, and their willingness to grasp what we offer, when *you* met them for the first time in the act of egg-theft? You've never had a single conversation with a human, and you have no right to make accusations against them.

"I came to Earth anticipating, like you, that humans would act like grateful tree-folk in a period drama. But the real history of the First Reach is one of teaching and learning, patience and curiosity. Symbiosis does not evolve in a day or an orbit—and is not gained through force or theft. And—this we should know already—it does not look like what either side had before. Many of you want to bring a new species into symbiosis without altering your current comforts. Humans are not our mates or our little brothers. They think in new ways, and will—if we take the time to do this right—fill new niches. We owe them that time, and the same effort at understanding that we gave each other."

I listened, impressed by her willingness to change her mind, and to share that change. I was ashamed of how long it had taken me to reach out to her. I'd talked with Rhamnetin, who was easy to talk to, and avoided the challenge she presented. Something she and I had in common, and I suspected there was more to be found.

Phosphorus spoke up. "We've failed twice by leaving species too long on burning worlds. For the humans who understand the urgency of leaving theirs, we can take all the time we need to learn their ways. But we can't waste time placating those who refuse to leave!"

Cytosine swiveled her eyes toward my family. "My cross-brother, the questioner of the *Solar Flare,* believes the watersheds may be right about keeping their world habitable. I share your fears that he, and they, may be wrong. But there is no saving people without respect. What kind of symbiosis will we have, if we assume from the start that humans know nothing we can learn from? Suppose we'd dismissed as madness every divergence between what we see from the plain and the view from the treetops? We must not let this sense of urgency misshape our next thousand orbits."

It was a powerful speech, but I could still sense the crowd's uncertainty. Then Rhamnetin asked an awkward question. "We *are* the only people from the Rings to spend more than a day in the company of humans. There've been shifting branches everywhere today, and pheromones all over the place, but I'd have sworn at the welcome feast that people were ready to learn and to argue. So who gave Phosphorus's family such a bad impression of humanity, so swiftly, that egg-theft seemed like the only option?"

"We did!" The voice that rang over the valley was human, and *wasn't* pitched for any great speech. Brend clapped eir hands over eir mouth, startled as I'd been by the projection. E huddled against eir knees, Tiffany hovering the way you do when someone needs comfort but isn't ready to be touched. Adrien stared in open horror.

Jace, though, sounded merely dry. "Do you expect to keep a place in any company, making absurd accusations against your own employers? Gentlefolk, please forgive em; our technical staff don't handle crowds well."

Brend, talking into the crook of eir arm, was still easy to hear. "You explain. You said you would, if I asked. This isn't right."

Tiffany got to thos feet, stretched, shot Jace a look that was difficult to interpret before settling into thos usual glower. "Yes, I promised. Very well, I have a confession for you all: Sanya and Asterion have been trying to undermine the networks' negotiations with the Rings. We saw a gamble that could pull us out of irrelevance and we took it. I thought it was a good idea at first—everything Jace says about what happened a hundred years ago is true. And I don't think much of what the networks do to preserve the planet. But convincing people to kidnap kids is a hell of a way to market ourselves. If that's the best our associates can bring to the table, maybe the networks are right about our worth."

It wasn't hard to read the room now—kids scooped up, an orchestra's worth of people talking at once, limbs grasping limbs. Tiffany approached me—this time, the overwhelmed speaker system didn't mike thos words. "I'm afraid I have to ask you for sanctuary. Jace di Sanya doesn't have the authority to fire us, and Adrien won't fire eir sib, but there's no question what'll happen when we get home. The best we can hope for is some awful scut work at the sea line for the rest of our lives."

I stared, still trying to catch up. "The malware," I managed.

"I made it, I'll fix it."

"Just like that?" Dinar gaped at thon.

"Well, I'm not the only one who worked on it, and probably not 'just like that.' But I don't invoke anything I can't banish. Don't you dare look smug—neither of us is looking forward to living in sackcloth and gender pins forever."

"I wasn't going to, and you don't have to," I said. "But thank you. And of course we'll give you sanctuary; welcome to the Chesapeake."

"Thank Brend, e's the ethical one." Tiffany's scowl cracked into a fond, if rueful, smile. "And where e goes, I go."

The rustling confusion of the crowd subsided as a Family representative spoke: "This is exciting for the factions involved, but doesn't change the question. We've learned that humans believe strongly enough in their principles to attack each other over them. We've learned that they can cooperate with Ringers who share those principles. Isn't that promising rather than disturbing? Cooperation is the foundation of symbiosis."

"Symbiosis depends on honesty, not subterfuge," said Cytosine. "The watersheds claim that when the corporations roam unconstrained beyond their limited territory, they do grave harm. Asterion claims that the watersheds deprived them of everything. We've been to that territory, and Asterion's people lack only political power. They travel where they please so long as they promise to avoid doing damage. They've broken that promise twice now. They tried to hide their actions, which means they knew they were wrong. Habitats can be destroyed by such deceptions. I want a quick and easy symbiosis as much as anyone—but it's hard enough to form family. I think we've forgotten how much harder it is to bind species together."

The Families were not persuaded. Dozens of other people spoke up. The urge to repeat points that didn't get desired responses the first time turned out to be universal, and so there was additional chord-filled shouting whenever someone succumbed to temptation. St. Julien did her best to play the sensible middle point between watersheds (whose opinions most Ringers found disturbingly wrongheaded) and corporations (whose tactics most Ringers found disturbingly wrong-headed), and was largely ignored. Human kids, not used to being waved around as status signals, demanded to be let down, picked up, and allowed to nap at points inconvenient to the discourse.

Finally they called a break. Young Ringers of both species brought around trays of fruit and seedcakes and something strange and vaguely eggy. The fruit I was confident I could eat this week, and I did, accepting the moment of sweetness. Better yet, someone turned off the pickup. I lay back on the ground and let Dori climb Mount Saint Eema, grateful for a few minutes when I didn't have to resist the siren call of saying important things badly. She tried to lean on my neck, and I moved her back to my chest. She tried again, and I moved her again. She rolled off onto the moss.

"I'm impressed they got all their reps together for this meeting so quickly," I told Rhamnetin. "It's exactly the sort of thing that gives us trouble, when we need input from multiple watersheds in a hurry. But I get the impression that they don't have a set way to make this kind of decision."

"It's not really what the Families are for. My colleagues and I, we're good at getting them to think of complications, but we've never been able to teach them how to *handle* those complications."

"It's supposed to be a consensus process," said Cytosine. "Or at least a clear plurality. That's easy enough when it's the type of question they've dealt with since the first habitats, but hard when the boundaries between opinions aren't fully formed. Harder still when we can't agree on the urgency of a decision. Normally egg-theft cases are fast; if they're too convoluted to decide quickly, it speaks ill of the thief. But with a new species . . . it's harder to claim that all the confusion comes from Phosphorus being wrong."

Athëo knelt behind Dinar to rub her shoulders. She winced; even aside from the stress of the situation, her spine must be out of whack from going around without her prosthetic. "Do they have mediators here?" he asked.

"For arguments between individuals or families, yes," said Cytosine. "For this scale—as Rhamnetin says, we're better at raising complications than resolving them."

I sighed. "If we had the means for a network . . ." I eyed Tiffany speculatively—but even if tha knew dandelion networks well enough to set them up instead of just break them, there was nothing to program with. It wasn't like you could go into one of the Ringers' vine-screens and start coding in SEED.

Tiffany caught my glance. "Give me twelve months, a team of Asterion's best coders, and a magic wand to convince them your foundational assumptions make sense, and I'll get you a network."

I sat back with a sigh. "How can they want a symbiotic relationship with us, but not believe we have anything to contribute?"

Rhamnetin sounded wry. "It's perfectly possible for people to think you have something to contribute, and still be convinced that you're utterly unqualified to make decisions on your own."

"They won't like it if one of the things we contribute is gender equality, will they?"

"*I'd* like it," said Rhamnetin. I stroked his leg, wondering when moss-scented fur had become a comfort.

"Your genders don't work anything like ours," Cytosine said. "I've figured out that much, even if you won't explain the details. But I'm pretty sure your siblings are all born at more or less the same time. Rhamnetin may be my cross-brother, but in your terms he's more like my sister's child."

"And we give parents some right to shape their kids' lives," I said. On the grass, Raven was pointing to body parts and naming them—"Nose! Eye! Knee!"—and laughing hysterically every time Diamond came up with a match. Dori was climbing on Chlorophyll, or possibly being climbed on. "But when they hit adulthood, they'll be our equals. As far as I can tell, Rhamnetin is a grown man."

"I hope so," said Carol. "Rhamnetin, please tell me you're not secretly an adolescent? I kind of assumed . . ."

"I promise I'm old enough to breed and have lovers," Rhamnetin assured us. "But there's a level of adulthood that never gets acknowledged, for men of my species."

"And you," I went on to Cytosine. "I know you have a lot of, um, power dynamics involved in having kids, but I'm pretty sure it wouldn't hurt for you to acknowledge Glycine as nonbinary, if that's how they want to be treated."

Cytosine tapped her belly, a quick staccato. "If my mates don't support my status, I will literally stop lactating."

I blinked. "I have to admit, that's a new one on me. But there's probably still room for equity and respect. There usually is. Maybe we can help you find it."

Athëo flopped back and looked at us upside down. "Have you heard the good news about hormone therapy?"

I poked him. "It's literally in their Shakespeare."

I worried, though. The Ringers' matriarchy—a literal rule of mothers—carried uncomfortable echoes of the gender-based tyranny that had pervaded all of Earth's previous powers. The remnants of those powers had mostly grown beyond it, as we had—the corporations thought even admitting one's true gender in public was a step too close. But patriarchy was an unquiet ghost. People like Athëo's parents would be all too happy to latch onto the Ringers' essentialism as justification for their own. No matter how well things went today, we'd need to guard against that.

I thought again about the dandelion networks. Encoded in algorithms and input interfaces, their root was a set of ideas: that everyone brought worthwhile perception and insight to the decisions that shaped society, that our technologies embodied our values, that they should be consciously designed to do so. And, also, that resilient systems could thrive and grow between cracks, in the face of all opposition. That was hard to remember, when they'd cracked through the concrete and turned it to meadows before I was born.

"When Asterion's malware crashed the network," I said to Athëo, "we kludged our input face-to-face. And again when everyone got together after Afia. We must have done similar things during the Blackouts, right? Probably even better, because we had to do it every day. One of the first things the watersheds did was plan more resilient power grids. Did you study any of those methods, when you were learning mediation?"

"Yes, a little. But even at the beginning, when we didn't have the algorithms in place, people would use AI. Hook up a computer to a solar cell, program it to provide input for a specific value-set—have one that would advocate for the river, and one that would put in arguments about within-neighborhood interdependence, and so on."

"Oh—" Sometimes, a casual phrase can invoke a childhood memory, something you haven't dredged up in years. "You can do that with people, too. Dad used to make a game of it—'What does the river say?' It has to be what they used for those meetings before they had AI advocates in place."

"Harder for humans to keep their own views out of it, in the moment."

Tiffany glanced up, said, "Skip lunch, and your code will be hungry too. Everyone knows that." Which was the most sensible thing I'd heard anyone from the aislands say. Algorithms were inherently biased—it was why you had to design deliberately for the biases that mattered to you.

The break was ending. Carol squeezed my hand, and I stood up and said to the crowd, "Do you want to see how humans make these decisions?"

CHAPTER 43

Terror is a different flavor from pure anxiety, both harder and easier to handle because it's grounded in reality. I'd been terrified plenty of times that month, of everything from saying the wrong thing to falling into the Potomac in the middle of a hurricane, and anxious most of the rest of the time. But for an utter mash of reasonable and unreasonable fears, I can only suggest trying to help several hundred alien dignitaries half-ass a values-based crowdwork session while trying not to think too hard about what they're using it for.

Did I mention that this involved trying to elicit clear value statements from the people who'd just tried to kidnap my child?

We started by giving some examples of *our* values: the things our algorithms normally input to balance the human tendency to fixate on short-term goals and immediately salient stimuli. Rhamnetin, and several of his colleagues, turned out to be particularly good at coming up with arguments from statements like *The complexity of natural systems has value even when we don't yet know what all the moving parts do* and *All people are owed equity in shaping the systems they've consented to.* Cytosine didn't do too badly either. Then we tried some basic ecological exercises, getting people to speak for the ocean we'd landed beside and the forest we'd slept in. Athëo walked them through a basic conflict resolution between the two. Nutrient runoff was an issue they were familiar with, a source of friction here as at home, and it was fascinating to hear how much of that conflict remained even with vastly advanced technologies for reclaiming and reusing nutrients. They still struggled over the right balance of resources, and what species they most wanted to support in each ecosystem.

But sitting down with Phosphorus, who'd despised me without ever meeting me, was so much harder. On Earth, people like her had never given in—only died and made way for those more willing to listen, or been stripped of the power to make reality out of their bigotries. Part of me—a big part, really—wanted those solutions here, *now.* But this couldn't wait generations, and the dandelion revolution wasn't happening in the Rings this afternoon. I could only hope that fresh-sown hatred could be more easily weeded out.

I put Dori deliberately to my breast, grateful when she latched on. Carol took her hand, letting Dori's little fingers grasp her own. From a Ringer perspective, it was the most pointed thing we could have done. "All right. I've heard your arguments, and to me they sound more like fears than values. You don't trust us to know our planet, you don't trust us to keep our kids safe. But what's—" I took a steadying breath. "What are you trying to preserve, or build? Separate your goal from the means you use to reach it. I'm trying very hard to make that separation."

Phosphorus curled and uncurled, her kid wriggling in response. She hadn't contributed much to the earlier exercises, treating them as another symptom of our irrationality. Her body language now was like nothing I'd encountered on the *Solar Flare*. Dismissal? Inattention? Even at Cytosine's worst, she'd thought us worth speaking with. If Phosphorus allowed us even that minimum of respect, she'd have to concede that we'd deserved it earlier.

"When a mother swings out over an abyss," she repeated at last, "you catch them, or their children if they won't reach for you. You don't *wait* to see if their absurd risk succeeds."

"That's fear speaking," I said again. "You're afraid that we're wrong. You're afraid of the complexity of planets. But risk aversion isn't a strong enough value to live on." I stopped, realizing that there was only so far I could explain without worse insult.

"We *value* catching people who fall. We value having been caught ourselves—our ancestors were saved, and thus we were."

"Cytosine said something about that," said Carol. "That one of her ancestors wanted to stay behind on your homeworld. How do you know that if their choices had been respected, they wouldn't have thrived?"

"Rivers dried in their beds and storms flooded cities with salt. Earthquakes spread from mines and wells; fires turned oxygen to searing poison. They could barely breathe, and still they clung to what they knew."

I wanted to say it was the corporations who'd given us our forest fires and megastorms—that her family was helping them birth new monsters. But I held my tongue; I wasn't trying to win an argument. I was trying to change it. "So you value a safe home for your descendants. You value clean air, stable ground, safety from storm and drought."

"That's right. And we have those things in our habitats. Your children should have them too."

I nodded, hoping the movement made sense to her. "That's two things: the value and the means to achieve it. I'm trying to tell you that we share the value. Our ancestors either didn't share it, or didn't act on it, but we do. And we do *because* we've developed technology for not only identifying our values, but for consistently acting on them.

"We've put fifty years into that technology, using it to undo the damage to our world and make it right for our children. You've put a thousand years into making your habitats right for your children. But no matter the ecological damage, it's easier to sow fertile seeds in an inhabitable planet than in raw vacuum. What were your habitats like at the beginning? Was it perfectly safe, living in space for the first time? Did you escape from risk?"

A shiver ran across the sections of her armored skin. "There were disasters. But they were nothing to the risks on-world, and we've overcome them. You wouldn't face the same dangers—we've scouted the way for you."

"We all try to give gifts to the future," said Carol. "It doesn't mean they'll use them the way we envision, or even in ways we'd approve of. You have to give gifts lightly—that's one of my values. I'm going to tell you something."

"You've been telling us things already," said Phosphorus, I thought a bit sharply.

"Something new. We haven't talked about it yet, because we didn't want you to think that our genders work exactly like either plains-folk or tree-folk. Humans are kind of like your species, in that our genders aren't set at birth. But it's not completely uncertain, either. Parents can guess, and be right most of the time. Some choose to guess, and some don't.

"My parents guessed. They gave me a male name, instead of one that could fit anyone, and when I realized they'd been wrong I had to change it. But it was okay, because the name was a gift given lightly. Because my parents loved what I was more than they loved their guess about what I'd be, they picked backup names in case I needed them, including one that fit my true self. And so I was still able to have that gift from them, and the relationship that goes with it, because they were willing to let me use it in a way they didn't expect."

I leaned against her, loving her for her courage, and Dori's fist tightened against my skin in response. "You know, there aren't many firsts left for people like us, but I think you just won 'first coming out in another solar system.'"

"I hope posterity appreciates it." She gave Phosphorus a piercing look. "Telling you this is a gift, given lightly. We can use your gifts in ways you don't expect, too—if you can cope with us using different means to achieve our shared values. Your technologies for making habitats livable could help save Earth. The structures you use to keep people connected across a solar system could help us maintain shared values across the watershed networks. Symbiosis with Ringers could give us both new tools, new ways to survive in a cold universe. You want to grab people who're swinging over abysses; we want to string nets over the drop. And neither of us wants our children to fall."

"Planets are too complex to control," said Phosphorus. "Our technologies work in constrained systems where we understand all the parts."

"You don't know that," I said. "You haven't actually tested it. And the idea that just because you create a complex system you know everything that it does—you have to know that isn't true, or your so-called constrained systems would have fallen apart long before this."

Phosphorus hemmed and hawed. She wouldn't admit that we did share values or that there was more than one way to act on those values, but her arguments grew less confident. Eventually she made noises about talking to her family, and left us sitting alone. St. Julien, also freed from whatever conversation she'd been in, came over to join us.

"I've always wondered if network governance was really that different from congressional debates." She patted Brice against her shoulder; the baby seemed torn between looking at the strange world around them and whatever digestive uncertainty they were presently experiencing. "Turns out it really is. If we tried to force our senators to be this blunt about how their goals and policies connect . . . I don't know. Either everything would come to a standstill, or we'd get fewer stupid laws."

"Your senators are human," I said. "Sapient, even. I think they'd get smarter outputs. We have."

"Hm." Brice spit up, and St. Julien smiled fondly at them before gazing over their shoulder. "I still want this for my kids. Room to grow as a species, and more than one place to try more than one solution."

"I've been looking at how they live here," I said. "The habitats have amazing ecologies, and they seem like exciting places to grow up. But I can't help thinking about what they've lost—species and marvels and history and prehistory they'll never discover because they left their worlds behind. Can we have both? Let the people who want to leave Earth come here, or explore new systems, without giving up our monuments and rainforests and all the dinosaurs we haven't uncovered yet?" I glanced at the Asterion team. "And without giving our worst mistakes room to take root and grow alongside the best of what we've learned?"

"I think we could," said St. Julien. She switched Brice to her other shoulder. "But I do think you're right that we should be mindful about it. We need to think consciously about what values to bring along. I'd like to see you run one of these workshops for us in the States. We've been going along the last few decades trying to preserve what we were; maybe it's time to pick a direction before we take our next steps."

"Assuming these people don't decide to kidnap the whole species en masse," said Carol.

"Assuming that, yes." St. Julien jerked her chin in the direction Phosphorus had gone. "How did talking with the kidnappers turn out?"

"So-so," I admitted. "I think we got through, but I don't think we got through enough."

"I was looking for something dramatic," said Carol. "Something that would make them see that they don't know everything about us."

"I think you managed that," I told her. I let Dori back down, stood and paced. The ease with which she crawled on alien ground, the similarity of her play to Diamond's and Chlorophyll's, seemed like a sign that connection was possible. But as soon as we went from kids to mothers we found places to disagree.

Of course, that was true with human parents, too. We argued with Athëo and Dinar, and sometimes our perspectives seemed as different as if we came from different species, but we worked through it and came out as family. And the working through had been *okay*—more than okay, had helped us all learn things from each other that we'd never learned from our childhood families. I thought about that, and about what it took to build that kind of relationship.

And then—because I wasn't only a child of the Bet anymore, because I'd learned from my wife and co-parents and children, because I was starting to learn from Rhamnetin and Cytosine and *their* siblings and cross-siblings and mates and offspring—I sat with my conclusions, feeling them quietly until I could speak something I was sure of. Something for which, I found, I did have the courage.

"We need both," I told Carol. "Ways to show that we aren't what they expect, and ways to show that we have enough in common to solve problems together. Athëo! Dinar!" Our co-parents looked up as I waved urgently. They stood, got their conversation to some sensible stopping point while I bounced anxiously, trying to hold onto that core of courage and certainty.

"Excuse us, please," I told St. Julien, and she rolled her eyes and wandered off to find her own spouse.

"What's going on?" asked Dinar, and I started explaining what I'd thought of. Excitement, embarrassment, and fear made my words tumble over each other, but Carol caught the thread and helped me get it across. And Dinar and Athëo, who somewhere in the past weeks had finally become people I could communicate with in all my anxiety-addled glory, got it too. I'd become someone who could communicate with them, who could listen to their input without deciding that the original idea had been a mistake in the first place.

That freshly discovered comfort made this new idea—for all I was sure of it—even more terrifying.

Gathering the *Solar Flare* crew took time, but eventually they joined us in a dip in the moss. Cytosine let the twins down to play with our kids. That was appropriate: this was family business, not diplomacy, and the kids' interactions mattered at least as much to its success as our own.

"Go ahead," said Athëo. "This was your idea first."

That "first"—the acknowledgment that he and Carol and Dinar shared the idea now—gave me the strength to speak.

"The stories your people tell about symbiosis," I said. "They're all about people forging personal connections across sides and species, learning how to share strengths and compensate for weaknesses. They're about families. And our people tell stories about finding new ways to come together to overcome long odds: crowds and teams, and families that we make in whatever shapes work for us."

I was going to get tangled in this speech if I wasn't careful; I took a deep breath and forged on. "We've been getting along pretty well with Rhamnetin since we first met you. Cytosine, we've crossed wires and swords a few times, but I think we're figuring each other out. And we're still getting to know the rest of you. But I think all our species need someone to learn how we can mesh our stories along with our cultures and our different ways of living, and show them by example.

"So we were wondering if you might like to join our family."

"What would that look like?" asked Cytosine after a moment. She didn't sound entirely shocked, at least. Or completely opposed.

"We'd have to figure that out as we went," said Dinar. "When you're creating new ways of doing family—or when you don't think everyone has to do it the same way—that's usually how it works."

"We wouldn't all just answer to you," I warned her. "We're more democratic. If that would be an issue for your nursing, we'll need to figure out something else."

"I'm not *mating* with you." She sounded reassuringly exasperated. "You don't smell like anything sensible to begin with."

"She'll forget sometimes," said Rhamnetin, "even if she agrees to it. Especially when there are fewer plains-folk mothers around to keep her pheromones in check."

"We can manage that," said Dinar. "We manage with each other, after all."

"Where would we *live?*" asked Rhamnetin.

That, we'd discussed. "Can we spend time in both systems? We don't even have to all be in the same place all the time—I doubt we're up for raising Dori and Raven aboard ship on any kind of extended basis—but the goal is to show people how we can make both lifestyles work. It would give you more experience with how scary a planet is and isn't, and give us the chance to learn more about how you make your habitats work. And together we'd figure out what each system has to learn from the other."

"It would get people's attention," said Rhamnetin thoughtfully.

"They'd tell stories about us," said Cytosine. "And it would prove that we really do trust you with children."

"Especially if we went into orbit when your atmosphere throws tantrums?" suggested Carnitine.

"We'll think about it," I said. At the height of summer, a vacation on a starship might not sound like such a bad idea. It would give our kids more chances to see the moon, even when the nights were sweltering. Though we might have to show the Ringers a lot of data, to convince them that the unbearable nights were growing fewer every year.

Humans would have huddled in a corner, checking in with brothers and sisters and co-parents, or sent private texts. The Ringers . . . made rings. Plains-folk reached for tree-folk, who reached limbs to other plains-folk, an intimate network of skinsong and quiet consultation. At last they broke apart.

And it mattered, I suspected, that it was Rhamnetin they chose to give their answer: "Let's try it."

CHAPTER 44

I was honestly alarmed by how quickly our proposal (in both senses of the word) captured the imagination of the Families. Some seized on it merely as evidence that we could be reasoned with; others seemed to interpret it in a way that felt dangerously close to manifest destiny. Reach, and the next branch will be there, never mind that the branch might continue to make choices of its own. I suppose thinking about branches making choices was a very watershed-ish perspective—one of those we'd have to share. In any case, when someone opined, "Of course, a family as distinguished as Cytosine's, however they expand, can be trusted with children," no one argued, and the generalization to the rest of humanity seemed to flow naturally.

Almost.

"Are you really going to accept everything the networks want to do," demanded Jace, "simply because they've added a couple of your people to their household?"

Phosphorus's eyestalks scanned the crowd. "You are, aren't you? You won't admit that nothing has changed—this is only their way of getting around the argument."

"It's a better way of carrying across the argument," another representative said, and the valley murmured agreement.

"These humans will pull you into the abyss behind them," said Phosphorus. "This gathering has lost its meaning; anyone who recognizes farce can come with us." She turned and stalked through the crowd, accompanied by mates and cross-sibs, a dozen or so Family representatives—and Jace and Adrien. Adrien twisted back toward Brend, anger and helplessness mingled on eir face, before following eir allies.

"Adrien never agreed with Jace before," said Brend unhappily into eir knees. "E wanted to get us back in the greater game, not break the networks entirely."

"E likes eir promotion," said Tiffany.

"I'm sorry." Adrien's compromise seemed the perfect illustration of the flaws in the corporate system, the forced choices between principle and work. But this was exactly the wrong time to raise that argument; I felt our obligation for the tech experts' sacrifice. "What do you need?"

"Besides a ride back to Earth?" asked Tiffany. "Unless . . . Brend, maybe you could design status signals for courting plains-folk? Does that sound like more fun?"

"It's all smells." But eir chin emerged from behind hunched knees. "I've never tried perfumes. Maybe some of our florals would complement their pheromones. And they're doing interesting things with body mods."

"Will you come back to Earth long enough to fix malware?" I tried.

"Oh. Yeah, that, sure." Tiffany sighed. "And we're gonna need a flat, and food, and all the shit you assholes give away for free."

"We'll need that too." Cytosine brushed a limb over my arm, a flash of fur and silk that I took for comfort. "And we need to register you as members of my family. But we should return to Earth before Phosphorus's faction hires their own ship. I know you don't like dominance wrestling, but it matters here. We need to show that we can do what we promised, and we need to share what's happened with Earth before they do."

I felt dizzy. "We're heading back right now? With who? Do we need to give Asterion a ride?" I sure didn't want to spend twelve hours on a spaceship with them, but return tickets are a civil right even if you're only taking the train a few miles, let alone between solar systems.

Her skinsong sharpened, velcro hooks against my nerves. "There are other ships."

We started after her. Athëo tried to scoop up Raven, but they started crying. "Baby play!" They flailed and shrieked, exactly the sort of tantrum you don't want to handle in an open-topped antigrav barge.

Cytosine scurried back and hesitantly reached for the toddler. They wailed harder, trying to tug the twins from her chest. In a moment *they* were going to start, and then Dori.

Rhamnetin bent close. "Raven, do you want a ride?"

Sniffles subsided. "Up ride?"

"Up ride," Rhamnetin confirmed.

"Are you really going to—" Carnitine started, and Dinar said, "Yes, he is. Frequently."

Raven settled sunnily atop Rhamnetin's legs, and we headed for the barge.

"Is the *Solar Flare* ready?" Carol asked.

"Repaired, yes," said Glycine. "Free for travel is another question. The *Elliptical Orbit* should have pulled claws from our back yesterday, but I haven't gotten the notification."

"Local docks are overwhelmed, if you hadn't noticed," said Ytterbium. "They might be sitting there because there's nowhere else to go."

"Or they might be sitting there to keep us pinned."

The barge lifted off, skimming the valley where Families still milled. The weather remained perfect, warm and cloudless. I'd need to find out how they scheduled rain, or whatever it was they did to irrigate their ecology. A whole independent set of technologies and strategies and policies, solutions that we'd never thought of or never achieved. I wanted to be done worrying about whether we'd be allowed to apply those solutions on Earth, and start the everyday labor of doing it. The mundane parts of saving the world, not these dramatics and confrontations, were the work my generation had been promised. I wanted even better promises for Dori and Raven.

Cytosine would've preferred to head directly for the ship, but Tiffany and Brend and the St. Juliens had overnight bags back at the tree, and Dinar had reluctantly left her prosthetic there rather than carting it around all day. I braced against the likelihood of crossing paths with the Asterion team. Tiffany and Brend squabbled over the urgency of retrieving their bags, and I guessed they were afraid of the same thing. But the platform was silent; we collected everything without trouble.

I'd say I shouldn't have relaxed—but I'm not very good at relaxing at the best of times, and I didn't actually do it then, either. What I did do was stop worrying about specific confrontations, and start taking inventory on our dwindling supply of clean diapers. The kidnapping attempt had distracted me from figuring out alien laundry, but there had to be facilities on the ship, right? Even if the Ringers weren't big on human-style clothes.

I was obsessing over this question when we got to our dock, and found the *Elliptical Orbit* still draped firmly over the *Solar Flare*. Around the joined ships, we had company. A few enterprising questioners had shown up with cameras and questions—and found people to talk to. From Jace and Adrien's angry gestures, they were making the most of their audience. Ringer allies stood behind them, along with Kelsey. Mallory stood uncomfortably a little ways off, and I recalled that Kelsey was Jace's partisan. I recognized Sodium, and assumed one of the others must be Phosphorus. The whole crowd of discontents from the gathering, in fact.

They weren't likely to let us go without an argument. And if what Cytosine said was true, all they needed to do was delay us while their allies elsewhere headed for Earth. Whatever contradictory plans we brought home after that, trailing behind them, might sway Earth but would hold little weight here. Fail to win the Ringers' dominance games, and the ground we'd gained with the Families would be thoroughly lost.

"I don't suppose we can go around?" I asked.

"Oh, please," begged Brend.

"Avoiding them would not look good," said Cytosine.

"And besides," Glycine added, "we can't just dump the *Orbit* in the sea. We need to confront the others to look strong, but more than that, we need to convince Sodium to back off and let us fly."

I tried to think of the right thing to say, the right person to focus on. But all I could see was the chaos of our opponents' anger. Instead, following a thread of instinct, I reached out. Carol patted Dori's sling-wrapped spine, then grasped my hand. On the other side, Cytosine rolled on her back and met my reach with one of her own limbs, skinsong vibrating. Carol took Dinar's hand, and Rhamnetin stretched a leg to brush Dinar's shoulder, and we stood in a network of touch, facing the people between ourselves and the ship and waiting for them to notice. Even Brend and Tiffany, not quite willing to join hands with us, stood close in unambiguous solidarity.

Gradually, the people we were staring at quieted. They looked at us, but didn't form up in turn. They were still clustered in factions, allies of convenience with disconnected goals, and camera-wielders there to get it all on record.

And now I had a network behind me. "Sodium," I said. "Phosphorus." They were the ones we needed to move. The others just needed to see us unafraid. "On Earth, my family protected the antenna, even knowing your arrival would bring danger. Are you going to block *our* way home?" Sodium didn't move, didn't respond. Her child chittered quietly.

"*We'll* block you," said a plains-person who had to be Phosphorus. "For the Rings' sake, and for your children's. Look at you, letting a male hold them."

Rhamnetin deliberately stretched a free limb to stroke Dori's back. "Humans question the way things are done. We think that's valuable. And the full questioners' guild stands with us. We need what humans have to offer more than we need them to act the way we expected. If you want to keep *our* feedback, you need to listen to theirs."

"You want symbiosis without change," said Athëo. "But change is the one thing neither of our species can avoid, no matter how this goes. What do you want that you can *have*?"

They wanted conquest, I thought, instead of change they couldn't control. But if the Ringers had any advantage over us, it was that they'd gone longer without that kind of violence, and most of the Families seemed eager to avoid its resurgence. If we were lucky, they'd keep it from Phosphorus's reach. Now she, too, needed a chance to go in a different direction—one she could bear to take. "'Planets can't be sustained' is an article of conviction. But we can turn it into something testable. We can set thresholds of atmospheric carbon and temperature and storm intensity, and tell you our goals. Together, we can agree on what it would look like if we were going in the wrong direction. The methods we demonstrated for ecological management could extend to decisions about whether it's safe to stay on-world, too. Hard data may not be as dramatic as rhetoric, but sometimes it's the best way to resolve an argument—if everyone is willing to look."

There was a long pause. Sodium shifted her many legs, and Phosphorus twisted an eye to track her. It was Phosphorus who spoke. "You expect us to go along with whatever 'thresholds' you come up with, and trust your data."

"We'd love to get some of your sensors in our streams. And we can negotiate the thresholds—if you're willing to agree that there *are* thresholds where it's reasonable to let those who choose stay on Earth."

Another pause, longer. At last she said: "We'll talk on the trip. Before I agree to anything, I want to see this horror for myself."

Jace glared at Phosphorus, but didn't try to argue. I wasn't sure what they could say that they hadn't said already.

"Sodium!" Cytosine's voice thrummed beside me. "That's more of us who want to get off this habitat, and you're still clawing up my ship. Lift off, and find another berth."

Sodium reared—then turned and clambered up the linked ships. Her family scrambled after, disappearing into hatches in the *Orbit*. A minute later it began to peel away, first from the *Solar Flare* and then from any acknowledgment of gravity. I let out a breath, and shifted my sweating grips with Carol and Cytosine.

"Grab your things," Cytosine said. "We've got work to do."

Suddenly, Brend pulled away from our group and ran toward Adrien. E stopped a few feet away like e'd hit the grand window of Morlock Central. "Are you just going to ignore me? I thought you were better than this."

Adrien glared: no playful shield, only someone furious with eir sib. "I thought you had my back. What else is there to say?"

"There's more ways to have someone's back than doing whatever they want." Brend turned away, fingernails digging into shoulders and eyes swollen red, and followed us into the ship.

At the midpoint of the trip, we all gathered by the viewscreen. The *Solar Flare* cast its tunnel into the vacuum between the snowflake cathedral of the unfinished Dyson sphere and the Ringers' sun. Reality blinked, and the familiar spectrum of Sol and the still-distant blue dot of Earth appeared in vision grown suddenly blurry.

Unimpressed, Phosphorus's kid careened against my knee before chasing after Raven. Rhamnetin steadied me. "Have you considered a more robust design than bipedalism?"

"There are worse things than needing to lean on people."

We watched for a minute. Watched planets, it turned out, do not get obviously closer—though my lenses assured me of minute changes in brightness and visual radius. We were still moving. "I think the threshold discussion is going well. Between loads of laundry, I mean."

"I think so too. But you realize you're going to have to run through half of it again, after Phosphorus gets to feel your atmosphere moving in person. Data is important, but you think about it differently when you've touched what you're measuring."

"That's inevitable. It makes a difference to me, too, having visited *your* home." Our home too, now—both homes, shared. That would take getting used to.

In a few hours, we'd be close enough to connect with the Chesapeake network. Close enough to see the dendrite twigs of rivers spreading from the bay, and probably the shredded storms still flowing northward. Close enough to learn what fears had spun out from our departure, and how the still-cracked networks were handling the malware-caused messes, and what new crises were straining our decision threads.

From the records spilling over my mesh's memory, I began organizing what we'd share with the network: a report of tentative triumph. Phosphorus was not yet a solid ally, but growing more inclined to argue over methane releases, and less inclined to force humanity into mass exile. Rhamnetin was full of plans to bring questioners to study on Earth, and I had the opening post ready for a thread gathering the most important queries for Ringer experts. Maybe people used to creating entire watersheds from scratch would be able to help us adapt to the Mississippi's changes—and our adaptations could help them work with complexity when their own creations spun away from their grasp.

And of course we had Tiffany and Brend, bringing both confessions and solutions. The networks would be made stable again—and we'd start working on better backups for the next time *our* creations didn't act like we expected.

Humanity's future, and Earth's, seemed more promising than they had since the day Cytosine first threatened to rescue us—even if they also seemed more dangerous. That part was inevitable: whatever happened to our species in company, it wouldn't look like our future alone.

The blue dot grew, misty outlines of cloud and shore resolving to familiar patterns, and I spotted the white mirror of the moon, dry seas reflecting the sun back at the ocean. Carol joined us by the screen, cuddling a Dori finally worn out from the chase.

Together, surrounded by family grown larger and more complex, we held her up to see the way home.

EPILOGUE
6 MONTHS LATER

Tiffany (di Asterion, or di Chesapeake, or di Nada, if anyone here cared) grimaced at the projection on the table.

Brend, still doodling in eir notebook, asked, "What's wrong?"

"Nothing. In shocking news, it's harder to fix things than it is to break them. Especially if you've lost your documentation. I need to go out and stare at trees."

"How does that help? *Does* that help?"

Tiffany stretched and glared around their network-provided quarters—the whole top floor of a house twice as old as Zealand, in a neighborhood full of network techies (sorry, tech *experts,* don't you know you're more than your work) who knew exactly what tha'd done and were not only eager to discuss the details but *critique* them. "Around here, you can't troubleshoot code without going outside and seeing how it's fucked up the data layers on every goddamn bush."

Brend flinched. "You hate it here."

Tiffany cursed thonself, silently for once, and went to pull Brend up. "I'm sorry, it's just the change making me grumpy. And having to undo a knot I tied myself. And the way everyone here is so . . ." Tha tried to put it into words. "Open. Serious. About everything."

"Naked."

"Yeah, that. They want us to go around naked, too." Tiffany had never been any good at presentation—was naked thonself by most civilized standards—but was discovering how many layers of protection tha'd worn at home that were simply meaningless here.

Outside, the early evening air finally held a bite of autumn. Summer had been worse, not because it got any hotter than Zealand, but because you couldn't just stay under the surface or hang out on spray balconies, and also because every time someone complained in Fahrenheit it sounded like they'd moved to the surface of the sun. Tiffany tried to appreciate the breeze and the scent of dying leaves, reminders that the Chesapeake was heading for the best part of the year while Zealand was tilting toward the worst.

Brend, at least, was enjoying emself. E ignored the trees, and the fastidious details of their augmented tagging, in favor of the people. There were plenty of them out, this time of year and this time of day, and of all three species. People walking dogs and the weird skittery ferret things that Ringers were fond of, shouting questions at neighbors, chasing balls and drones. If Tiffany could only relax, Brend would happily dive into writing subversive reports about how the networks covertly signaled status using material origin tags, and differently subversive reports about how Ringers might build on their existing gender markers to expand their presentation options.

Brend put a hesitant hand on Tiffany's wrist. "You're ruminating again. And not looking at the trees."

Tha shook thonself. "Sorry. I'll try to stop looping. Okay, let's try this . . ." Tha pulled up the repair thread, where the wounded network was finally proving itself up to the task of tracking its own modification, and dropped a message: I've pushed another round of fixes to the carbon uptake tag function. As a reminder, in the error condition these tags were underweighted and did not properly link to all relevant threads. I'm putting in a test reading of a blight affecting the—checking tags that none of the actual locals would've needed—elms on Longfellow Street between 38th and 41st; this reading is incorrect and should retract along with all propagated impacts in 24 hours (which is also a test of the retraction function).

Tiffany watched the imaginary blight spread down the block, watched the thread report back on all the little ways it affected the Chesapeake's carbon balance, watched the algorithm spawn automatic responses and hook up with a weird Ringer feedback model that wasn't even part of the original propagation chain, let out a triumphant "Ha!" as the pings to human-in-the-loop checkers *worked* this time. Which was the part tha hadn't fully understood, back in Morlock Central, and therefore hadn't been able to figure out how tha'd broken it for weeks running.

Sure enough, one of the neighborhood's on-call sensor nerds poked their head out from an old apartment building, spotted Tiffany and Brend, and called: "I'm guessing the trees don't actually have chicken pox, yeah?"

"Should've inoculated them while you had the chance," said Tiffany deadpan.

The in-the-loop human came out anyway, flipping on wristband sensors as they approached the supposedly ill elm. "Best check to be safe. Anyone want an ecological management demo?" That last was loud enough to attract a couple of tree-folk who did, in fact, want a demo. Tiffany stepped back to give them room, and watched as they ran cheerfully through their protocols. After they were done, they turned back to thon. "Thank you, by the way."

"Why?" asked Tiffany, annoyed. "I broke it." Tha tried to remind people of that as much as possible; if you were the boogeyman you might as well get some mileage out of it.

"And now you're working to fix it. Isn't that what we're all doing, as a species?" The sensor nerd waved, and left before Tiffany could comment on the dubious wisdom of this philosophical statement.

"You were a curmudgeon at home, too, you know," said Brend. "You don't need to feel weirder about it here. I know who you are, and I know how you *act*. It's okay."

"It's not," said Tiffany. Tha hunched uncomfortably, and admitted what had been going through thos head. "I'm holding you back."

"You're not." Brend reached out to grip thos hand, but kept watching the world around them. "I'm learning this place in my own way, and you're learning it in yours. And I can tell you're enjoying the challenge even though you're also mad that you set it up. And if we don't like what we learn here—once you're done with your cleanup, we've got a whole universe to go be ourselves in."

Tiffany gripped back. "We do, don't we? I've got a few more weeks of work to go, but then—yeah, let's give the rest of the galaxy a try."

There were Ringers everywhere you turned on Earth these days, but it had still taken Viola St. Julien months to get the right people in the room. Months of feeling people out, not simply to secure agreement on immediate action, but to find kindred souls who sensed the logic behind those actions. Beyond this room, this meeting, they could play out the art of the possible, could build towers from the sordid little compromises that were the life and limitation of nation-states. But the heart of the work needed passion and ideals powerful enough to carry their goal over all those barriers. Otherwise the long game would play out like one of those cartoons where someone offers up a glorious idea, all golden gears and shining wheels, and passes it through grant applications and committees until it turns into a kid's broken-down wagon.

So this would be a test—hopefully the first of many—of Viola's vision for adapting network-style value algorithms to something new. Of using them to excavate the beliefs that had lifted people into space in the first place, and polish and strengthen those beliefs until they could bring humanity to the stars. The people in the room today would create the seed for that algorithm.

That seed, so far, started with Viola, still backed by NASA along with the State Department and a faction of NOAA, and given interstellar authority by Brice's babbling presence. She'd found sympathetic ears in the vestiges of JAXA and ISRO, in a frustrated circle of spaceflight enthusiasts from the Niger Delta network, and in a small group that ostensibly still represented the UN Committee on the Peaceful Uses of Outer Space.

And, finally, she'd found the representatives from Perihelion 50. The Peris were obsessive about a future in space by *Ringer* standards; their questioners were the sort of people you had to drag away from their desks to eat reluctant lunches. They'd actually managed to invent food pills. They'd be called transhumanists if they were human, and their lifespans averaged out at normal for their species via a combination of bio experiments that turned out spectacularly well and those that ended spectacularly badly. They were thoroughly alien and utterly familiar, delightfully argumentative guests at interspecies movie marathons as long as you didn't let them bring the snacks.

Adenine, one of their plains-folk questioners, had hitched a ride to Earth despite not being part of a breeding family. Out of all the people here, Viola was most certain of them. They had no attachment to the way things were done now, nothing to hold them back from building something different.

She wouldn't, until today, have listed any of the others as the *least* trustworthy of the group. That was before—after months of planning to get exactly the right people in the room where everything was going to start—the State rep had arrived early and brought a guest.

"Sunil—" She was not going to ask *what the hell,* that was not going to put this meeting on better footing.

"I know, I know." Sunil Anagnos held up his hands. "But you really do want to talk with Ezrin. Sui has things we need, if we're serious about starting the first human colony in the Rings."

Viola eyed the corporate rep in sur silver-and-black dress and rocket-ship earrings, and thought about how much she regretted her last decision to play nice with company types. "We're going to need people from everywhere, long-term. But we haven't discussed this."

Ignoring the obvious lack of welcome, Ezrin offered a curtsey, which was weird but had the advantage that, unlike a handshake, it didn't take two. "Ezrin di Lunestra. And before you say anything, we stayed out of Asterion's conglomerate after the auction. Didn't trust them to handle this right. No one else is affiliated with us now, either—I'm only here for Lunestra Enterprises."

"And that should matter to us because . . . ?"

"Because we'll offer you what we offered at the auction in the first place. Experience and honest dealing, and the promise that we want this for the same reason our ancestral companies did."

Viola frowned and shifted Brice from one hip to the other. "Your ancestral companies."

"Asteroid mining. Private launch vehicles. Lunar hotels. We barely got started before the networks cut off our power and the nations cut off our funding, but for us, the money was a way to follow our dreams, not the other way around. That hasn't changed. We've played games with the rest of the aislands, but we never stopped our research or our storytelling, and we never stopped dreaming either. We'd like to be part of what you're building here, and to combine the work we've managed to scrape together in the last fifty years with what the nation-state space agencies have done on your own."

Viola considered. They were leaning heavily on Ringer tech for this plan, out of necessity—but that did nothing for the psychological and biological challenges of making a human city work on a Ringer habitat. If Lunestra had relevant results, it might make a difference. On the other hand, if Lunestra had cunning plans, they could scuttle everything.

While she was considering, the door to the conference room swung open and Adenine scurried in. The Ringer, familiar enough with corporate fashion from—well, mostly from interplanetary movie nights—rolled back in alarm. "Viola," they sang out, "what the hell?"

Ezrin looked at Viola's friend, taking in the carapace embossed with circuitry, the points of color around their sensory bumps and along their limbs that represented even more sophisticated implants, the way their eyestalks swiveled to examine sur in return. Sui raised sur hand, split fingers two and two with the thumb jutting out on its own, and offered a hopeful, "Live long and prosper?"

And Viola thought about what it would be like to build a city with people who—whatever other differences might separate them—had been telling stories about the stars for generations, holding tight to isolated hopes as societies fought and argued, waxed and waned around them. With people who'd each preserved a sliver of those early dreams, and could bring them together to resurrect the whole.

"All right," she said. Warnings and protections could come later, another barrier to be overcome by their shared vision. She knew what she valued. "Let's give it a try."

Algorithms and crowdsourced threading were all very well for mass-scale problem-solving and management. For organizing a household, though—even a big one—everything still came down to a weekly meeting. Over the summer we'd held it half the time on the *Solar Flare,* sprawled on the moss or perched in branches; this week we were back at what I still thought of as home, around the now-expanded dining room table.

"Canning's basically done, storing still in progress," said Dinar, and the task list, projected on the half-cleared table and slightly distorted by a stack of ball jars and a couple slices of hazelnut cake, updated itself accordingly. The house still smelled of peach and fig from the last round of preserving, scents that would linger until overwhelmed by baking apples and chestnuts. She frowned and continued: "Add 'Divide storage between basement and *Solar Flare*' to task sequence."

"Some of that should go in with the trade samples," suggested Xenon, and the list updated again. Homemade jams weren't going to be a major trade item, obviously, but given the relative populations of the two solar systems, not much from Earth was going beyond the sample stage for a while.

"Some of that needs to go in *me,*" said Rhamnetin, who'd been threatening to invade Earth to steal our stone fruit all month. I poked his nearest limb, winning another battle in the Great Plum War.

"Is everyone staying here all week," I asked, "or do you need to be back on the Rings for anything?"

"I think . . ." said Cytosine, prodding at the calendar. We were still working on a mesh that would read plains-folk neural signals properly, but for now we were faking much of the interface with skinsong signals. "No, you and I and Astatine are supposed to go down to the Atchafalaya and evaluate the updated split."

"Oh shit, that's *this* week?" I asked. "I thought it was next week."

"Your inbox," said Athëo, and I banged my head gently against the calendar and put clearing my messages on his task list again. I checked it myself and, sure enough, they'd gotten some weird readings and wanted us early. I was tagged into way too many things these days, but at least my expertise ratings were recovering nicely.

After much kludged discussion, re-weighted by hand every time Tiffany thought it had been warped by thos work, the Lower Mississippi had accepted the offer of Ringer construction tech to reallocate the river's flow between old and new beds. It was a more nuanced solution than anything we'd been capable of, a compromise between the needs of existing communities and the river's own inevitable transmutation. Long-term, they'd shift both river and people to the new bed on a less catastrophic schedule, with Ringer nano-construction letting them adjust the flow in ways that were manageable and even reversible.

The same technology clung to the side of our house now, creating extra rooms for the crew of the *Solar Flare,* suited to their needs. The best part, from my perspective, was the convenient bridge between their aerie and my and Carol's bedroom.

"If we take a shuttle on Thursday—Diamond, stop that!" Cytosine pulled the kid back from where they'd been using their own skinsong to color in random calendar squares.

Raven ran over to tug on Diamond's eyestalk, which always looked uncomfortable but didn't seem to bother them. "Diamond, bad bug!" And then in considerably better Ringer than I could manage without Athëo's synthesizer: "Come *play!*"

I leaned back from the scheduling discussion for a moment to watch Raven and Diamond and Chlorophyll return to an inexplicable-to-adults game with blocks and three species' worth of dolls. Dori ignored them, focused on cruising hand-to-hand between the dining room's varied chairs and perching frames, an expression of fierce concentration on her face. She wasn't quite ready yet to let go and become fully bipedal, but it would be any day now.

We were all learning that way. It wasn't romance, precisely, for most of the family, but it *was* that absolute desire to make our next steps as good as they could possibly be, and discover what we were capable of together. A different, equally valuable sort of love.

I turned back to the questionable sensor readings. I'd been given special access to the live flow, and I tuned into that next, transforming the data from both familiar human technology and Ringer mycelial sensors into tactile readouts along my back. I'd been using skinsong as inspiration to make those readouts more detailed and intuitive, and for a moment I immersed myself in the power and life and health of the river. I swam in the pH of the water, the bacteria levels, the speed of the current, the health and species balance of fish and crabs.

"Okay," I said at last. "I can spot what's bothering them. I *think* it's just predictable changes from the last round of storms, within the tolerances Astatine laid out. But yeah, we should go down in person and make sure the nano-construction's not breaking anything."

We probably *would* break something, at some point, and the thought still kept me awake some nights. It would be almost impossible to share as much as we were sharing, learn as much as we were learning, without a few massive screwups. But we *were* sharing, and we *were* learning. And so far, Earth was doing better for it. We were going to give this the best try we could and—I promised the kids silently, watching them share and learn and find their way beyond anything the adults had figured out—we were going to make it work.

ACKNOWLEDGMENTS
OF SEVERAL SORTS

A couple of days before the 2018 election, I panicked. I called up equally anxious friends and—on occupied Piscataway land, in Holli Mintzer's vintage clothing store, a couple of blocks from the eventual site of Judy's frog pond—Malka Older and I attempted to attract people to a phone bank by reading hopeful science fiction. Our attendance was sparse, but the event did give Malka an early introduction to *A Half-Built Garden,* and touch off several years of her asking when the diaperpunk novel would be ready.

It was not going to be ready for a while. This book has run late again and again, delayed by fascism and climate change and pandemic, which for some reason make it challenging to maintain a consistent writing schedule. So my first thanks are to Carl Engle-Laird for his patience, and for excellent editing through delays of his own. Thanks as well to my agent, Cameron McClure, who dealt empathetically with my deadline woes and maintained her excitement about this book throughout. I'd also like to thank Liana Krissoff, Carl's answer to my increasingly anxious requests for a neopronoun-wrangling rock star capable of copyediting this thing. Any remaining screwups are my own.

Thank you to my household/spaceship, the ragtag bunch of misfits who've kept writing possible at all through these past years: my wife and loyal alpha reader, Sarah; intrepid reporter/remote-schooling supervisor Jamie Anfenson-Comeau; search guru and anime consultant Shelby Anfenson-Comeau; baker who would like to cater a no-notice first-contact reception Nora Temkin; enthusiastic guide to local terrain Lemur Rowlands; voice of reason and righteous fury Noor Pervez; and ambassadors to the future Cordelia and Miriam.

The problem of the Mississippi and the Atchafalaya is well-described in John McPhee's *The Control of Nature.* The metaphor of the cherry tree comes from William McDonough and Michael Braungart's *Cradle to Cradle: Remaking the Way We Make Things.* The starlings come from Adrienne Maree Brown's *Emergent Strategy: Shaping*

Change, Changing Worlds, and of course the Passover reading on the divinity of change is from Octavia Butler's *Parable of the Sower.*

The weather and coastlines of 2083 are—roughly—based on optimistic scenarios involving a steep drop in carbon emissions over the next few years, which models will probably be at least somewhat outdated by the time this comes out. Judy's tools are descended from current work on sensory substitution and portable sensors. The dandelion networks grew from many happy hours enmeshed with the DC citizen science and crowdsourcing community. Most of the foundational technology exists except for the neural interface and the algorithms that treat human values as features rather than bugs: someone get on that, please.

Thanks are due for useful conversations and ideas to Henry Farrell, Kevin Kuhn, Marissa Lingen, Malka Older, Ada Palmer, Denice Shaw, Ruth and Lila Wejksnora-Garrot, and Jo Walton, and doubtless many others whose names I've neglected to record properly to my mesh. Special thanks to Ruth for being the only person to successfully send beta reading feedback, one more than I could reasonably expect given that I shared the manuscript around for comment in early March 2020. My Patreon patrons have provided ongoing feedback, patience, and support, as well as early appreciation of Rhamnetin's confusion about frogs.

Finally, thank you to all who are in the ground getting your hands dirty with the art, science, organization, and disciplined hope that we need in order to build a future worth having. Next year in a better world!